To Lynne
Thank you for
book!
wishes
x
4/12

The Streets Fall Silent

Jenni Thornley

Published in 2012 by FeedARead.com Publishing – Arts Council funded

First Edition

A CIP catalogue record for this title is available from the British Library.

Chapter one

Sunday 2nd to Tuesday 4th August 2015

'Her heart's going like a train Doctor; I don't think she'll last much longer,' Sister Johnson said, concern toning her voice as she monitored Mrs Joan Kerr's vital signs on the LED screen above her bed in the Norleigh Hospital. Joan was the twelfth elderly person to have been admitted with symptoms deteriorating unaccountably this week alone. Sister Johnson dabbed perspiration from her fevered brow with another paper towel and added it to the growing pile in the waste paper basket. The air conditioning strained overhead but still the room felt stifling.

Milton Kerr, Joan's husband, sat in the restfully decorated forget-me-not blue Emergency Room waiting room and flicked blindly thorough the July 2013 edition of *Gardener's World* magazine. His long gnarled fingers flipped the pages lightly; the liver spots on the back of his hand were darkened by the hot summer's tan. His gaunt sunken features showed none of the turmoil of emotion going on below the still surface. He and Joan had been married for fifty five out of the fifty six years he had known her. Only when Joan had been in hospital, giving birth of their two daughters Hayley and Bridget had they been apart during that time.

'Have a drink, Dad,' said Hayley, holding a small upturned pyramid cup of cool water for him. He took it automatically, without being aware of its presence, or that of his daughter.

Joan had collapsed less than an hour earlier, suffering from a tight pain in her chest although as far as he knew, she had never had any heart trouble before. Dr Bragg was concerned by this for, despite showing bodily symptoms of having had a heart attack, the equipment disagreed. In the ER, machines beeped frantically, lights flashed threateningly and staff raced frenetically all in an effort to save a life.

Hayley stared at the door to the ER watching the activity of the nurses, hoping her mother would come out alive. 'She's always been so strong,' she said to herself, brushing her damp fringe of dark hair from her oval face before lifting her tortoiseshell rimmed Tommy Hilfiger glasses to wipe a tear from her eye. Milton had telephoned her at her office to tell her Joan had been rushed to hospital. Hayley had dropped the involved legal case she was working on to be with not only her mother but her best friend and mentor. Joan had been her stalwart champion, overcoming Milton's prejudice, supporting Hayley in completing her law degree and other legal qualifications to become one of Norleigh's top barristers, running her own private practice with two assisting clerks.

As he heard the ER door opening Milton raised his rheumy eyes from staring at the pages of gladioli and greenfly spray. Dr Bragg removed his face mask with a reluctance which telegraphed what he was about to say. 'I'm so sorry Mr Kerr, but there was nothing we could do; she faded so quickly, we couldn't do anything to save her. I really am truly sorry.'

Joan was dead.

'Oh no!' whispered Hayley.

'What am I going to do without her?' asked a stunned and distraught Milton mournfully as he and Hayley clung together sobbing uncontrollably in each others' arms.

~*~

Bruce Salmon had blacked out and collapsed at his greengrocery business at around the same time Joan had suffered chest pains. It took the ambulance slightly longer to get to him, but he was treated with the same care and dedication by the nurses and doctors as Joan once he arrived at the ER of Norleigh Hospital.

Leanne, Bruce's daughter in law, working for her boss Tony Ridgeway at Ridgeway's Building Supplies Ltd on Western Street, was given permission reluctantly to visit him. She parked her Mini Metro a bit precariously and definitely illegally on the path outside the Out Patient's clinic and sprinted as fast as her bulk would allow to the ER waiting room.

'Mr Salmon shows signs of having had a stroke Mrs Salmon,' explained Dr Dixon softly once she'd found the right waiting room and asked what had happened. 'Please take a seat and I'll get you a drink of water,' he added solicitously while she tried to catch her breath - he didn't want another patient on his hands. Leanne plumped into a chair and waved a chubby hand in front of her face frowning at the other side of the room where Hayley and Milton comforted each other.

Just as the doctor was about to return to the ER a grubby young man in dirty jeans and sweaty T shirt flung through the waiting-room doors. 'What's happened to granddad!' he demanded of the man in the white coat.

'Oh Charlie!' exclaimed Leanne, bouncing to her feet and wobbling across to him. 'The doctor says he's had a stroke,' she wailed loudly in her despair. A louder howl rose from Hayley in the opposite corner.

Charlie gave her a quick glance then put a comforting arm around his mother. 'But he's as fit as a flea. How can he have had a stroke?' Charlie asked, disbelieving. 'He was fine this morning when I dropped off the carrots. He didn't say anything about feeling ill, or any pains or anything like that,' he pointed out, frowning in frustration.

'I'll bet he's been lifting boxes of apples or sacks of spuds,' said Leanne, sniffing before blowing her nose on an already saturated tissue. 'They say you're not supposed to do too much exercise in this heat wave.'

'I shifted the heavy things this morning like I always do before I go to work,' protested Charlie, knowing Bruce had a bout of sciatica at the moment; his granddad might be stubborn, but he wasn't stupid. This news improved Leanne's spirits and she reappeared from Charlie's shoulder wiping her nose on her sleeve instead of her useless tissue. Charlie grabbed a new one for her from a complimentary box on the coffee table. He sat next to her as she gently hiccupped soft sniffs, relieved her son was with her. The overhead strip lights hummed electrically as he watched Milton and Hayley leave the waiting room, there being no reason for them to stay any longer.

Time past slowly as he looked around the hot stuffy room. Various people sat sadly in the rows of blue padded benches anxiously looking towards the doors, biting fingernails, staring into space, or vainly trying to read magazines.

Charlie watched the ceiling fan rotate rhythmically, remembering his conversation with Bruce that morning. Bruce would be seventy in two months and while the rest of the family wanted to throw a surprise party, Charlie knew his granddad wouldn't like that, so he was arranging for them both to go for a quiet fishing trip on the Tweed. He'd sorted out a bed and breakfast in Innerleithen and found out how to get permits. A tear slowly cleared a white streak down his grimy cheek at the thought that Bruce might not be able to make it.

Dr Dixon emerged from the ER and much as his colleague had done a few minutes earlier, withdrew his mask in a way which did not bode well for the family. 'I'm sorry, but Mr Salmon didn't respond to treatment. I'm afraid we've lost him,' he explained frowning.

Leanne laughed as if Dr Dixon had told her the funniest joke she'd ever heard, then promptly burst into tears and sank to the floor. Charlie, whose face had gone completely white, tapped his mother on her shoulder and tried to raise her. She simply wailed and pushed him away from her. The doctor and a couple of ER nurses helped raise the hysterical Leanne onto a chair while Charlie brought her another beaker of water.

'Bruce … Dad … Dad,' she moaned. 'What are we going to do without you?'

'Who's going to look after the shop?' asked Charlie practically, too distracted by his mother's grief to feel the affects of his own.

~*~

Dr Andrew Bragg and Dr Graham Dixon sat in the staff room at Norleigh Hospital at the end of their first shift later in the afternoon. Neither spoke, each held a glass of barley water with rapidly melting ice cubes as the ceiling fan whistled overhead on maximum. They'd been dealing with the usual cases brought to accident and emergency wards; the uncontrolled nose bleeds, the child who'd swallowed a Lego fireman, the drunks, the failed suicides, but this was something new.

'I just can't understand why all of a sudden we're getting so many older people with undiagnosed terminal health problems,' said Andrew staring blankly at a cup ring on the low oak-stained table in front of him. Graham didn't respond. 'It can't just be the heat. It was hotter than this last year and we didn't have half … no … a quarter of the people we've had this last week, and they didn't all die.'

'People just don't listen to the advice they're given … or think it applies to someone else, not them,' said Graham.

'Drink lots of fluids, wear a hat, don't do unnecessary exercise, keep off the beer … it's not that difficult,' agreed Andrew.

‘It’s not as if this is the first time we’ve had a heat wave recently … this is what … the fourth or fifth in the last ten years. People should be able to cope with them by now, not die in droves,’ said Graham.

‘You saw the memo … it’s supposed to carry off those who’d have died in the next few weeks anyway. I’ve not seen much sign of that,’ pointed out Andrew.

‘I’ve arranged for a post mortem on my Mr Salmon. His family swears blind there was nothing wrong with him and insisted,’ said Graham staring at the clear liquid of melted ice at the bottom of his glass. ‘Want a refill?’ he asked getting to his feet.

‘No thanks,’ replied Andrew also standing. ‘I’m supposed to be playing a half of golf with Professor Fallon from the university. Maybe he has a theory about these deaths.’ Andrew left the small room distractedly, apologising for bumping into Sister Johnson as he walked through the doorway.

‘He seems to be somewhere else,’ observed the Sister, pouring herself a glass of juice.

‘Golf,’ said Graham cheerfully. ‘Bit of a bad day today,’ he observed.

Sister Johnson, a plain practical woman in her mid fifties, dropped into a low wooden-armed chair opposite the doctor. She gave her colleague an appraising look before replying. A married man with a passion for his work, she had known him for nearly five years. His dark eyes were closed as if composing himself as he stretched his long thin legs across the floor in front of his chair.

‘I’ve never known so many people die in ER in one week,’ she said in a low quiet voice as if afraid to admit failure. The warm air stirred by the fan wafted a few loose strands of grey hair from beneath her white starched cap.

Graham opened his eyes to look at her, surprised by her tone. ‘We can’t save everyone,’ he said to placate her.

‘We didn’t save anyone today at all. The mortuary’ll be complaining soon. Forty people have died this week. It doesn’t happen like that,’ she said sorrowfully.

He sat upright and patted her on her knee. ‘You did everything you could for each of them. I saw you. You have nothing to reproach yourself with.’

Sister Johnson looked close to tears as she smiled back at him. 'When will you have the results from Mr Salmon's post mortem?' she asked to deflect his patronising look.

Graham sat back again, sighed and said, 'tomorrow hopefully. I can't understand it at all. He had all the symptoms of a mild stroke. We should be arranging his rehabilitation at home not his insides on a pathologists scales.'

Sister Johnson didn't care for his mortuary-speak and grimaced. She finished her drink and left the room mumbling about getting back to work.

~*~

'I've arranged the funeral for Friday at 11 o'clock,' said Hayley over the telephone to her sister in Woodley, a small but posh village ten miles south of Norleigh.

'I just can't believe she's gone,' said Bridget, obviously still overcome with the news of her mother's death the day before.

'I keep remembering little things about her … they just pop into my head unbidden,' said Hayley, leaning back on the sofa, resting her head on a cushion, she wafted a *Homes and Gardens* magazine in front of her face to try to cool down. Bridget just said 'hmm' so Hayley expanded.

'When she took me for riding lessons - she didn't just drop me off and rush off to get on with the next task as the other mothers did. She introduced me to the trainer and held the pony while I stroked his head. Then she helped me to mount, explaining what I needed to do to sit on comfortably.'

'She was like that when I first went to ballet,' said Bridget, her voice sounding stronger. Always the more delicate of the sisters, she had become a graceful dancer. 'She helped me lace up my shoes, walked me to the handrail and watched from the back while I attempted my first steps.'

Hayley could hear the smile in her voice. 'She always understood where boyfriends were concerned too, do you remember, all those years ago?' Bridget repeated her 'hmm'. 'Do you remember Steve … or was it Chris, I can't remember now. My first proper boyfriend anyway … the first I kissed. I brought him home to meet mum. He was terrified … only about twelve I think. She was bottling pears; he'd never seen anyone do anything like that before and thought she might be a witch. She sussed him out straight away and gave him some ice cream. I think he became better friends with her than me after that.'

'I remember when I told her I was pregnant with Josh. She was so over-the-moon but still told me all the things I should expect from being pregnant – what to eat to stop morning sickness, all the ups and downs and mood swings – I could talk to her about anything and nothing ever fazed her.'

Hayley fell silent at this phrase which summed up her mother.

'How's dad?' Bridget asked after a few moments reflection.

'Pulling around, but he'll never be the same again. They spent so much of their lives happily together.'

'It was so sudden … no warning. What did the doctor say?'

'He thinks she had a heart attack although the monitors were contradictory. They have to do an post mortem as she had no history of heart disease; we should know for certain later today or tomorrow … not that it makes much difference … she'll still be dead.' Bridget was startled by the coldness of her older sister's comments. 'Sorry,' said Hayley after a pause. 'I've got to the *want to blame someone* stage and the doctor not being able to instantly tell me what I want to know is annoying me.'

'Would you like me to come over and look after dad for a bit? I've got time off work.'

'No thanks Bridget, but he would like to see you if you can come around later … I know he'd like to talk to you.'

'I'll come once I've picked Josh and Kit from sailing on the lake … about four.' They concluded their conversation, both feeling numb and empty. Life without Joan was unthinkable. So full of life, never letting aging pose a problem with plenty of hobbies, lots of country walks, a healthy diet and looking after her three grandchildren to keep in touch with the young.

Bridget's Discovery pulled into Milton Kerr's driveway just after four o'clock as promised. She jumped out and strode to the door still wearing a pale green vest top and khaki shorts as the day was as hot as ever.

'Help me get dad to the hospital!' shouted Hayley as she opened the door. 'He's just collapsed. I think *he* may have had a heart attack.'

Alarmed, Bridget, suddenly wide eyed and as white as a sheet, helped her sister to support Milton's slim frame to her car.

'What happened?' asked Bridget. Milton groaned and moaned as she reversed the car then sped off as fast as she could.

'I found him collapsed on the kitchen floor with a spilled glass of water beside him. I think he may have heat stroke which has caused a heart attack,' replied Hayley.

'Why haven't you called an ambulance?' Bridget demanded, narrowly missing a woman pushing a pram across a zebra crossing.

'Emergency services say they're at full stretch and wouldn't be able to get to him for an hour, so could I bring him in,' explained Hayley holding onto her father on the back seat as the vehicle swayed from side to side. 'You're going to lose your licence!' she exclaimed.

'I'd rather that than my dad!' shouted Bridget over her shoulder.

Milton gave a soft gasp. 'You'll be all right Dad,' said Hayley as soothingly as she could, trying not to sound as panicked and nervous as she felt. He gasped again - a more rattling unpleasant sound - stiffened and then went completely limp in her arms.

'NO!' she screamed.

Bridget slammed on the brakes then managed to control the large car enough to get it near the kerb as passing vehicles sounded their horns in protest. Ignoring them she said, 'I'll try CPR,' and climbed onto the back seat as Hayley made room for her. 'Help me lay him on his back,' she instructed as Hayley slowly backed from the car, leaving her sister to work on their father's body.

A police car drew up behind them. 'Magnificent display of illegal driving back there, madam; in a hurry?' asked the tall bulky young policeman in shirt sleeves.

Hayley ignored his patronising tone and without taking her gaze from Bridget's life saving efforts, answered dully. 'My father's just had a heart attack. We have to get him to the hospital.'

The policeman's demeanour changed instantly when he saw Bridget. 'Can you drive while she carries on with that?' he asked, jerking a thumb at her. Hayley looked at him and nodded.

'There's no point,' said Bridget softly. 'This isn't making any difference. He's gone.'

Hayley crumpled onto the policeman's chest. He gave her an embarrassed pat on the back and suggested, 'I'll give you an escort to the hospital in any case madam. You keep going.' He helped Hayley into the driver's seat then with sirens wailing and lights whirling, they set off, arriving at the hospital just ten minutes later.

Despite her pessimism, Bridget had carried on working on Milton's unresponsive body. The main entrance was blocked with far too many people trying to get in. Concerned, the policeman led them around to the rear of the hospital directly to the mortuary. He realised this wouldn't be pleasant for either woman, but would be better than trying to get their dead father through a scrum. However, the scene was almost as busy at the back of the hospital.

'These ladies have brought in their father,' he explained to the orderly who answered the bell at the mortuary door. 'What the hell's going on around here? Has war been declared?' he asked, puzzled by the large number of weeping people wandering around the rear of the hospital.

The orderly smiled sincerely at a tearful Hayley and Bridget and arranged for a trolley to take Milton's body from the back of the Discovery. 'Something's happening to all the elderly people in the area ... heat stroke it said on the news.'

'Really?' said the policeman, thinking of his old mother in her flat the other side of Norleigh.

'Yes,' said the man, helping his colleague wheel the trolley through the plastic flaps which served as doors. 'If you could help me with the paperwork madam,' he said to Hayley, leading her to the counter overlooking a small grey office with a desk, three chairs and a large filing cabinet. Dutifully, Hayley answered his questions, but couldn't help thinking that just two days ago, both her parents had been alive and well, and looking forward to a holiday in Malta.

The policeman hovered in the shade outside the rear of the tall dark building trying to call his mother on his mobile phone. She didn't reply but he managed to get hold of a neighbour who said she was fine, just pegging her washing out in the yard so wouldn't have heard the telephone.

Relieved, the policeman caught sight of a familiar figure with a camera and Dictaphone. 'Daryl,' he called. 'What's this about old people dying? You been frightening everyone again? Why's there such a hive of activity here?' he quizzed but his smile dropped when he saw the anguished look on the journalist's face.

Usually Daryl Verner, a man who made Columbo look tidy, was the life and soul, but today he was white faced and frowning. 'This is something really scary Jason,' he replied seriously. 'Perfectly healthy people are keeling over and dying within minutes. I've never seen anything like it. It's like ... like ... a biblical plague or something.' He shook his head and wiped his brow with his soiled sleeve.

Jason looked back at the hospital. Years ago he had been on duty when a coach had crashed on the stretch of A1 motorway close to town and fifty four people had been rushed to the hospital in a fleet of ambulances and police cars. Fifteen had died at the scene or over the next few days. The hospital was overstretched and at its busiest at that time although it normally catered well for the twenty thousand people who lived in the town and surrounding area. Now it seemed to be bursting. People were being brought in by ambulances or in relatives cars, but were dying before they got here and the mortuary would soon be unable to cope.

He rubbed his hand over his hot, flushed face and returned his attention to Daryl. 'It's the heat, right,' he said, telling rather than asking. 'Older people can't cope with the heat. I got mum a fan so she'd keep cool. That's right. Isn't it?' he pleaded.

'How old's your mum Jason?' asked Daryl, doing some mental arithmetic.

'Sixty two,' he replied wondering why he'd been asked. 'Not really an old person at all.'

'I'm fifty eight,' said Daryl and he turned to leave, mopping his brow again before taking off his crumpled sweat stained linen jacket and holding it by the hook over his shoulder.

Jason watched Hayley and the distraught Bridget leave the mortuary not knowing they had a second funeral to arrange. Hayley acknowledged him with a quickly dropping smile as she helped the sobbing Bridget into her car, and drove her home. He sighed then returned to his patrol car and left for his mother's flat.

The traffic was odd today. Certainly a lot more people were around the hospital than usual and most of them had the same lost look as Hayley and Bridget. Distractedly people moved about town on foot or in cars. A few more horns blasted, more people shook fists and swore at other motorists, but he could be imagining it. Maybe that was the heat too; causing stress and making people lose their tempers.

He arrived at his mother's flat half an hour later. Her washing on the whirly bird in the communal courtyard was almost dry already. She lived three floors up so he collected it for her to save her coming down again, not that she minded the stairs, saying the exercise was good for her. For such a tiny woman, many people wondered how she managed to produce a strapping son like Jason. Immensely proud of him, she told her neighbours about every little detail of his professional life – the bits he told her - knowing it would be spread through the neighbourhood, complete with embellishments.

He knocked on her front door and opened it with the laundry basket balanced on one knee. 'Mum,' he called. 'I've got the washing in for you. It's dried to a crisp already. Mrs Knox said you were hanging it out when I phoned earlier.' Surprised at not having a response to his welcome, he grew more concerned. Usually she knew he was coming up the stairs before he reached the door.

'Mum,' he called again worry creasing the corners of his eyes. He put the basket on the kitchen table. The window was wide open with a warm breeze flicking the light white curtains, as was the window in the living room, and the bathroom.

'MUM!' he shouted when he reached her small single bedroom. She lay across the neatly made bed, her eyes and mouth open and her hands clutching at her chest, obviously dead. Jason, even in his anxiety and panic, was still professional enough to notice the fan he had left her was switched on and the thermometer embedded in a piece of Welsh slate on her dressing table told him it was only a comfortable 23°C in the room, not enough to kill her surely.

He telephoned his mother's doctor's surgery, but that was closed with only the emergency number on the answer-phone message. He telephoned the hospital but the switchboard was swamped and he couldn't get through. Suddenly, he sat down on his mother's bed next to her, and began to cry, helplessly wondering what he could do.

After a few moments of indecision and thinking of Hayley, Bridget and their father, he carefully wrapped his mother in her best coat and carried her gently downstairs to lay her on the back seat of his patrol car and drove her to the mortuary.

The same orderly as before met him at the door. His tired face looked strained as he tried to maintain a professional countenance, but all he wanted to do was get home and not have to deal with this nightmare any more.

Jason completed the paperwork and asked to speak to a doctor. The orderly used an internal telephone to the staff room to see if anyone was available. Sister Johnson, who sounded as if she had been sobbing, said Dr Dixon was on duty in ER if Jason would like to speak to him.

Jason found Dr Dixon in the ER waiting room, talking to a bereaved couple following the death of their aunt although they didn't look as upset as the two sisters he'd dealt with earlier. 'Doctor, my mother died this afternoon. I think she had a heart attack. Have you any idea why all these people are dying?'

'Straight to the point constable,' he said with a smile. Jason didn't smile back. 'Sorry. Tactless of me.' He ushered Jason to a chair in the corner of the waiting room full of anxious relatives. He spoke quietly. 'I take it your mother was in reasonable health and took care of herself,' he suggested, Jason nodded. 'I'm sorry, but we just don't know what's happening. In hot weather, we get a few elderly - and I mean elderly people - dying from the heat, but this is out of proportion.'

'My mum had her fan on ... her flat wasn't that hot,' explained Jason quietly. 'Probably cooler than in here.'

Graham nodded. 'It's been going on all week and the papers are saying it's the heat because we can't think what else it could be. This high pressure system is keeping hot dry weather over Europe. We've had it for over a week now and it also means the night air isn't cooling down which just makes a bad situation worse. When a person's body temperature regularly exceeds 40.6°C they can get hyperthermia if they're not looked after, which leads to confusion and they stop acting rationally. It can start off as heat exhaustion with heavy sweating, rapid breathing and a fast weak pulse as the body tries to thermoregulate itself.

'We're performing autopsies on as many people as we can, and hopefully we'll get an answer in the next couple of days, but to be honest, at the moment, the sustained heat is the most likely cause. But the hospital system just can't cope with this many people dying at once, so it's slowing things down.' He patted the policeman on the shoulder. 'I'm so sorry about your mum, Jason. Call in and take tomorrow off. You need a break. You can't do anything else for her now.'

Jason smiled reluctantly, knowing he had to be satisfied.

~*~

When she got home Hayley made a long cool Pimm's with slivers of strawberry. She'd driven Bridget home to be with her husband and children, and taken a taxi home. Bridget had been inconsolable and far more upset than Hayley would have thought possible. Although she hadn't been as close to her parents as Hayley, both of them dying within a day and then having to contemplate two funerals had deeply upset her.

Hayley absently watched the traffic moving slowly passed her front garden but put her tall glass down with a start when she saw the unexpected familiar blonde head of her daughter Alexis behind the trimmed privet hedge.

Meeting at the door, they embraced warmly. 'I didn't expect you to come home!' Hayley said as she pulled away from Alexis to give her a good looking over. Her tanned pretty face looked tired and red as if she'd been crying. She dropped her bulging rucksack onto the hall floor and followed her mother to the living room. The windows were all open wide, but hardly a breath of air stirred around the house.

'When you told me they'd both gone, I couldn't believe it. And then Tom said his grandmother died this morning too, I just wanted to get home and find out what's going on.'

'Tom?' queried her mother. 'You don't mean Mrs Higginson from gran's bridge club do you?'

'Yeah,' agreed Alexis, flopping into a soft pale green sofa, resting her elbows on her knees and putting her face in her hands. 'She just got these pains in her back – her kidneys a neighbour said - and was rushed off to hospital, but died before she got there.'

Hayley sat next to her and put a consoling arm around her shoulders. 'Something's going on,' she murmured, breathing heavily.

'What do you mean?' asked Alexis looking at her curiously.

Hayley patted her knee. 'Mum was taken ill but … died shortly after we got her to hospital. Then earlier today, dad suddenly collapsed while getting a glass of water. I couldn't get an ambulance because they were all busy so Bridget and I took him in. He … died in the car, but Bridget tried to revive him. It didn't work so a policeman escorted us to the hospital. When we got there it was chaotic. People have been dying all day. The doctors didn't really say much and the Press is blaming the heat wave. Everyone's helpless ... It's so awful,' she concluded, finally breaking down with quaking sobs into her handkerchief.

Alexis put her arm around her and gave her a hug, offering what comfort she could, but frowning and trying to puzzle what might be causing all this misery. As a fourth year medical student at Sudcliff University, she had studied geriatric medicine last year, but nothing covered this as far as she could remember. From what she heard on the news, people were having heart attacks, strokes or various organ failures, but why would so many be dying? Some should survive with modern equipment and medical knowledge. It didn't make any sense.

'They said on the news there've been power cuts in Westwater this morning with all the extra demand with people using fans and air conditioning to try to keep cool. Shops and offices are the worst affected apparently. Barclays Bank in the High Street had to close because staff couldn't cope with the heat,' explained Alexis, still with an arm around her mother's shoulder.

'I know,' agreed Hayley sniffing, appreciating her daughter's attempts to help her. 'Mrs Archer next door says she's got a great big crack appeared across her living room ceiling – apparently the foundations are drying out and shrinking already.'

'And there've been those forest fires in Portugal and the south of France.' Alexis rested her forehead against her mother's head and said sadly, 'other people are in the same boat as us, if not worse off. Life goes on Mum. We've got to get used to them not being around ... But I'm going to miss them.'

~*~

Dr Andrew Bragg never arrived at his game of golf. On his way to the links, he noticed two speeding ambulances weaving their way through traffic, as well as a police car escorting a Discovery in the direction of the hospital. Conscience pricked and he returned to work.

He found Graham in the ER waiting room and overheard the end of a conversation with a young couple. 'We'll have an answer for you tomorrow, but for now, just go home and think about the life your gran had and be grateful she didn't suffer.' Andrew thought this a bit patronising, but the forlorn pair turned and left, arms around each other having nodded and given Graham a brief smile.

'"We'll have an answer tomorrow?"' repeated Andrew as he joined his tired and anxious looking colleague.

'There has to be an answer somewhere. All this death must have an explanation.'

'You look like you could do with a break. Let's catch up over a coffee then I'll give you a hand,' said Andrew leading Graham to the staff room and made them each a much needed drink.

'Tell me what's happened since I left – it looks like war's broken out somewhere.'

Graham sighed and leaned back in his chair, giving a long stretch. 'When the first lot started to arrive earlier this week, I agreed with the general feeling they were suffering from the heat and their hearts couldn't take the strain.' He sat up, elbows on knees, twirling the cup of coffee in his hand. 'But while they're hooked up to the monitors, heart rates might be up, but rhythms seem OK.' His friend listened.

'We had results back from the path lab for two who died on Monday. Tissue samples from heart, lungs, liver were all fine, except for the usual wear and tear you'd expect in the over sixties and some unusual tissue growths.' He sat back again and sighed. 'We'll need more results, but ... and I know how daft this sounds ... it seems they just wore out and died.'

Andrew chuckled at this but Graham's expression didn't change. 'You're not serious!' he said disbelieving. Still Graham looked white and drawn, not finding anything to laugh at.

Andrew thought for a moment, remembering Joan Kerr the previous day. 'The woman who died first thing yesterday; she'd just collapsed for no apparent reason. She faded before my eyes. I've seen patients die before, but it was like someone ... just turned her off.' Graham nodded. 'What's happening around here?'

Graham shrugged and rose from his seat. 'Let's get back to the war zone,' he said and left the room. Andrew, thinking hard, followed.

~*~

Thirty miles south of Norleigh in the Sudcliff General Hospital's Pathology Department, scientist Kate Jordan asked, 'are you looking at today's samples from ER?' She adjusted the focussing wheel on her microscope to fine tune the image of a sliver of heart cells. She sat back, flicked a stray strand of dark hair around her right ear and frowned. Her colleague Hugh Old simply grunted and carried on peering through his microscope at his own sample.

As it had no windows, the white laboratory felt like a well lit cave. The walls were lined with books, computer screens, X-ray light boxes, cupboards full of bottles and small boxes. Various pieces of machinery and equipment performed analytical tasks quietly in the background.

'This is the fourth or fifth one I've seen this afternoon and they all look identical,' she continued despite Hugh's lack of response. 'I'm beginning to think the mortuary staff are having a joke and just sending different slivers from the same person.'

Hugh, surprised by her attitude, rolled his swivel chair over to her screen to see what she meant. 'Here's the one I've just looked at from a man and here's one from a woman ... see what I mean?' She produced the two samples side by side on her computer screen for Hugh to compare. Hugh pushed his black rimmed spectacles up his nose and stared at the screen, his mouth open slightly as he thought. Kate's forehead was still furrowed and Hugh looked equally puzzled.

He rubbed his black stubbly chin. 'They do look similar.' His voice sang with his Welsh accent.

'It looks like the growth of fibrous or connective tissue, you know, desmoplasia. That's usually only associated with malignant neoplasms - a cancer which evokes a fibrosis response when it invades healthy tissue. But according to their notes, neither of these people have been diagnosed with cancer,' explained Kate.

Hugh nodded and pointed to a particular area of the screen. 'Whatever it was must have happened very quickly. They both seem to have undergone a sort of metaplasia. The delicate heart membrane cells have been replaced with hardier ones but they seem to have lost their function. That's not good.' He sat back and thought for a few seconds. 'Something really nasty much have happened to make their cells change like this; whatever it was must have been bad enough for the original cells not to be robust enough to withstand the new conditions, so changed into another type more suited.'

'I thought metaplasia only occurred as the result of reprogrammed stem cells in the organ's connective tissue being nudged along a different differentiation pathway,' suggested Kate. 'You know, like dough in a bakery being made into a cottage loaf instead of a bloomer,' she added for clarification.

Hugh smiled at her quaint analogy and nodded. 'Neither of these two died of a heart attack as such.' He rolled back to his own computer and put a different sample under his microscope; a liver sample. 'I'd be glad if my liver looked like this now let alone when I'm his age,' he said, giving Kate a quick smirk.

Kate and Hugh had worked together for two years, his first proper job since completing his university education, and although they got on well, he got the impression Kate saw him more as a younger brother than a potential life partner. Hugh liked rugby and during the winter months he played open side flanker passionately every weekend for his local side, the Wilverton Wasps. As a consequence, he was a burly young man with less than perfect ears and a slightly squashed nose. Kate, slim, well groomed and approaching thirty, enjoyed less aggressive forms of entertainment than physical sports, preferring art and music.

'These bone marrow samples from the same patient don't look good though. Look at this.' Hugh had got her attention and she rolled her chair to his desk and looked at the liver sample showing on his screen. 'This man was seventy five years old,' began Hugh, reading the notes which accompanied the samples and then pointing at the screen. 'His heart, lungs and liver all look reasonable. He should be cutting the grass not pushing up the daisies, but look at this.' He changed the image on his screen to show a section of bone marrow. It showed clumps of immature cells of unequal size and abnormal shape.

'There're signs of anisocytosis and poikilocytosis,' said Kate pointing respectively to the odd sized then the odd shaped cells. 'And hyperchromatism,' she said, pointing to extra large cell nuclei in a few of the cells.

'This looks like dysplasia - you know, the expansion of immature cells, with a corresponding decrease in the number and location of mature cells. High grade dysplasia like this represents an advanced progression towards malignant transformation and eventually cancer.' He threw the clipboard onto his desk. 'Treatment should have been straightforward, but he hasn't even been diagnosed.'

Kate shot him a disapproving look for his outburst, but Hugh felt frustrated not angry and it showed on the rough lines of his face.

'OK. So far this week we're getting larger numbers of people dying than is normal. We're going to have to dig deeper to find out what's killing them,' said Kate straightening up and wheeling her chair back from his desk.

'People are dying ... fact,' she said counting points on her fingers. 'What we've found so far seems to indicate a lot of older people are walking around with undiagnosed conditions ... although the pathology of their symptoms suggests it shouldn't be enough to cause death necessarily. That would seem to imply that whatever it is must be rapid like an infection. It could be a virus, but would a virus be that specific.'

'Or it could be the heat wave,' said Hugh under his breath.

Kate ignored him. Thinking of her third point, she touched her middle finger. 'It might be a toxin or poison. It could be a chemical agent or something of that nature that's causing cell damage.'

Hugh pointed out the obvious flaw in this. 'Why are only elderly people affected?'

'Only elderly people so far as we know. It could be something determined by age ... affecting weaker people.'

'There's nothing particularly wrong with the three people we're talking about here so I wouldn't describe them as *weaker*.'

Kate nodded in agreement. Puzzled by what was going on, she was thinking out loud, using Hugh as a sounding board. 'OK ... there's something about older people which this chemical agent affects ... it might be beyond organic.'

Hugh smiled and turned back to his microscope and looked at a heart tissue sample from Mrs Danson, Jason's mother. He tried another one but as well as the wear and tear he'd expect from someone in their sixties, the sample showed the same rapid cellular transformation. 'You keep thinking Kate ... that's what you're good at,' he said.

Kate clocked him around his head affectionately with the clipboard and returned to her desk. 'We're missing something,' she muttered and could just hear Hugh mumble 'obviously' in the background.

Chapter two

Monday 10th August 2015

Nigel Atkinson, the recently retired manager of the Norleigh branch of Barclays Bank, had told his wife Jessica the night before that he wasn't feeling well and would have an early night and a lie in, so when he didn't come down as usual by seven thirty for his breakfast, she wasn't worried.

She'd been feeling tired herself but had never been the sort to resort to bed rest, and ploughed on. She'd already completed the pile of ironing from Saturday's washing and was relaxing for a few minutes with a cool glass of fruit juice, reading the newspaper, before getting dressed smartly for shopping. The heat wave continued to dominate the headlines although the gloomy economic climate crept in at the bottom, and a possible split between an actress and her footballer husband covered the second page. Jessica didn't bother reading about the various continued Middle Eastern quarrels reported on the subsequent pages.

As she read through the report of the highlights of the Canadian tennis championships on page twelve, the telephone rang. She placed her glass carefully on its coaster and answered. 'Hello Mum,' said the cheerful fluty voice of her daughter Greta, a primary school teacher. 'Did you enjoy the party at the vicarage yesterday?'

'Yes thank you dear. You have no idea the scandalous stories one picks up at these social occasions.'

'Such as?' asked Greta genuinely intrigued. 'Is there a story about the vicar and his mistress?'

'She's his fiancé, not his mistress, you wicked girl,' said Jessica crossly. 'That wasn't the sort of scandal I meant.'

'Come on Mum. I haven't been to school for weeks, I need some hot gossip.'

'Well,' began Jessica, casting a glance towards the stairs to make sure Nigel wasn't just coming down to hear her passing on unfounded stories. 'Mrs Taylor did say she had heard from a friend that *Mrs* Benson from the florist is not only unmarried but her two boys have different fathers.'

'Oh I know all about *her*,' said Greta sounding disappointed. 'She picks the boys up from after school club - buxom and blousy with a different bloke in tow each week.'

This took the wind from Jessica's sails.

'Have you heard the news?' asked Greta on a different tack.

'Yes love. I was listening to the radio when I was ironing earlier,' replied Jessica. 'What a shame about Mrs Danson; such a helpful soul in the parish.'

'And Mr Salmon. He always had good local produce. I hope his grandson takes over the business; he's a better head on him than the rest of the family.'

'I expect your father will be seeing something of him in the next day or two; I'm sure he'll speak to him before he sees someone at the branch - he'll need advice.' Suddenly feeling tired, Jessica leaned against the breakfast bar and watched blue tits pecking at the peanut feeder hanging from her cherry tree.

'Is dad about? I'd like a word with him about my trip to Germany,' said Greta. Jessica cupped her hand over the mouthpiece and called upstairs for Nigel.

'He hasn't heard me,' she advised her daughter. 'Not feeling too good yesterday after the party so he's having a lie in. I'll just go and wake him.'

Leaving Greta holding on, Jessica climbed the stairs stiffly and went into her husband's bedroom. 'Greta's on the phone Nigel,' she said, shaking him.

At once she knew something was wrong. Nigel was unresponsive, stiff and cold. She bent closer and could tell immediately her husband was dead.

Wide eyed and stunned, she backed away from the bed with her bony hand to her open mouth and made a shocked startled gasp. She stumbled downstairs swiftly and reached the telephone. 'Greta! Something terrible ... Your father is ... dead!'

A pause from the other end indicated Greta had trouble grasping this. 'What did you say, Mum?'

Pulling herself together at her daughter's reaction and calming slightly, Jessica explained as best she could. 'I've just been to try and wake him, but he's cold. He must have died in the night.' The horrid thought that she had carried on as if everything was all right while her husband lay dead on his bed made her feel sick; the cooling iron caught her eye and she began to sob.

'I'll call Dr Henderson and I'll be there as soon as I can,' said Greta, hanging up. Jessica slumped onto a kitchen stool and began to cry in earnest.

Greta and Dr Henderson arrived together half an hour later. Greta comforted her mother while Dr Henderson examined Nigel's lifeless body. He joined them a few minutes later and Jessica explained that Nigel had felt unwell the night before.

'Did he take anything?' asked the doctor, a broad honest-looking man.

'No. He just had a mug of Horlicks like normal even though it was a warm night. I looked in on him when I went to bed at half ten and he was snoring peacefully so I didn't disturb him,' Jessica explained calmly enough although the sentence was punctuated by the occasional sniff. 'I left the window open too, so he had fresher air. Should I have closed it? He didn't catch a chill?' she asked anxiously.

'No, he didn't catch a chill,' said Dr Henderson frowning. Nigel had seen him a few weeks before with pains in his back and other symptoms which he had diagnosed to be an infection of his kidneys. A course of antibiotics had sorted that out, so with no reason why his patient should have died, he would order a post mortem. Knowing how stretched the hospital was already, this wasn't a pleasant thought.

Leaving him to make the necessary arrangements Jessica telephoned her son Ewan. 'What did the doctor say?' he asked disbelievingly.

'He thinks it may have been a complication following the kidney infection ... possibly blood poisoning or something. We won't know until after the ... post mortem.'

'I'll be there as soon as I can,' said Ewan, hanging up. Jessica knew it would take him over an hour to travel from Manchester and spent an unhappy time wandering aimlessly around the house, absentmindedly tidying books back onto shelves, straightening cushions and pictures, and tearfully folding Nigel's freshly laundered clothes and putting them away in his wardrobe.

Ewan arrived in time for lunch. Jessica had prepared cold chicken salad. No one felt hungry, but her children made an effort for her.

Greta had spent the morning at the hospital and described in a quiet voice what she had witnessed. 'There're so many families going through what we're going through. It puts things in perspective somehow,'

'If that's supposed to make me feel better because my dad's just died,' said Ewan hotly, 'I'm afraid it hasn't worked.' Jessica touched his arm to calm him. 'Sorry Mum,' he said softly. 'I just can't believe he's died from an infection; the antibiotics were supposed to have cleared that up.' He sounded exasperated.

'Most of the people who've died this last week have been … elderly,' said Greta, with a quick glance at her creased and lined elderly mother. 'I get the general impression the doctors think it's because it's so hot, but there're a lot more people dying than they would expect.'

'That isn't especially comforting either,' snapped Ewan, stabbing a wedge of tomato with his fork.

'It may take some time before they find the definite cause,' said Greta calmly. She'd been so stunned by what she witnessed – large numbers of grieving relatives, frazzled nurses, worried doctors, and a gathering throng of journalists as the story gained momentum. 'The journalists seem happy to think it's down to poor hospital administration, but I don't think that's fair or helpful.'

'Why not?' asked Ewan crossly. 'What did Dr Henderson do for dad except give him some tablets and tell him to lay off the whisky? If he'd examined him properly rather than a cursory inspection, dad would still be alive. This isn't a trivial matter Greta!'

'Ewan please,' said Jessica, touching his arm again, still trying to sooth him. With his slim frame and already greying temples, he looked much like his father.

'Dad recovered from his kidney infection, didn't he Mum?' asked Greta without waiting for a reply. 'Dr Henderson tested him for an infection, treated the symptoms and cured his patient. If something else occurred he wasn't aware of, you can hardly blame him.'

'Yes I can! He should have been aware of any further complications … or possible side effects of the drugs,' said Ewan angrily. 'Why are you sticking up for the man who practically killed your father?'

'Don't be ridiculous, Ewan!' snapped Jessica. Ewan looked angrily at his mother, his brow furrowed deeply. 'Your dad had complete faith in Dr Henderson and was grateful his kidney trouble cleared up … he'd been in a lot of pain with it. He was fine yesterday, just overdid it cutting the lawn and tidying the vegetable patch while it was so hot, that's all.' She paused and played with her uneaten chicken. 'I expect they'll find he had a heart attack. At least he died peacefully in his own bed,' she concluded firmly, and Ewan had to be happy to smoulder in silence, looking crossly between his mother's resigned face and Greta's emotionless one.

While Ewan tried to cool off walking around the shaded part of the garden, Greta, who had the same small boned body and long horsey faced appearance as her mother, helped Jessica with the washing up. 'He'll be all right once he gets used to the idea of dad being … gone.'

'I know. He's angry; wants someone to blame. I can understand that. I've felt like that all day, but tried to keep myself occupied. I'm so glad you went to the hospital … that was a big help. Thank you.' She patted Greta's hands

'It was awful,' Greta admitted. 'I don't mean just being with dad … that was bad enough, I mean seeing all those other people and the doctors looking so helpless. It was like the aftermath of a train crash or something … you know; when there're more people than they can cope with. Hopefully it'll cool down soon and things'll get back to normal.'

'I miss him,' said Jessica and began to cry again. Greta comforted her mother as best she could staring tearfully out of the kitchen window, wondering if she would ever be happy again.

~*~

'You're sure about this… you're not just trying to make me happy?' asked David Thomas as his sister Catherine explained to him their father Arthur had just died on his way to Westwater Hospital.

'David!' she said scolding, but quickly qualified what she'd just told him. 'Yes, he's dead. No, I'm not trying to make you happy … but I must admit I'm not especially sad about the news myself.' She paused and played with a curl of her reddish brown hair as she lay back on her cream well padded sofa. 'He was at the Westwater Museum arguing with one of the guides about a Crimean War exhibit and just fell across the case.' David, sitting in his own small front room in Comfortby just a few miles from his actress sister's smart new house in Eastdell, smiled. 'The people at the museum thought he'd had a heart attack or something, but the ambulance took ages to get there.' She paused again, musingly staring at the large ethereal black and white photograph of herself above her marble mantelpiece.

'He died happy then,' said David venomously. 'Arguing with some poor sod and sounding off on one of his pet theories. Belligerent to the last.'

'They'll miss him at the school,' said Catherine without too much conviction. She imagined the staff and pupils would be glad to see the back of the quarrelsome, opinionated, miserly old goat.

'Like they'd miss a dose of the Black Death. Are you going to arrange the funeral or would you like me to?' he asked as if he might enjoy the prospect. 'I'll let his old regiment know ... they can provide an honour guard, all togged out in their uniforms ... and the old farts at his Masonic Lodge. You know what I think is so dreadful?' he waited but Catherine only said 'hmm?' 'Mum wasting all those miserable years of her life to die of Alzheimer's last March. If he'd died twenty years ago, she'd have been free of him.'

'You're just saying that. You don't know he brought it on.'

'Of course I do! Mental cruelty ... that's what he did to her ... and us. Just as well we were young and strong enough to get away from his poison; we've mixed with normal people and've been able to live our own lives. Do you think you'd've had such a successful career if you'd stayed at home any longer?'

'He was ... good to me ... when I was out of work,' Catherine said unconvincingly.

'He treated you like dirt, criticised you from trying to make a go of it, constantly told you to become a teacher like him and practically turned you out of the house after a couple of weeks.'

'Mum was supportive,' she said weakly.

'Mum still had all her marbles then and at least tried to stick up for us ... but it was always such a battle. None of us should ever have had to go through being treated like that. To be honest,' he said hotly, 'I'm not sure I want to bother wasting my time arranging a funeral. They can leave him in a ditch somewhere and have his bones picked clean by crows.'

'I'll arrange the funeral,' said Catherine, although she silently admitted David's solution appealed. 'I'll send an e-mail around the family once I know the details. Do you have a contact for Aunt Isabel?'

'Yes. How can a brother and sister be so different?' asked David. 'Aunt Isabel is one of the loveliest women I know. I'll phone her … I'll be polite, don't worry.'

'Sad would do,' said Catherine as she got to her feet and walked into her lavishly appointed Schreiber kitchen and switched the kettle on. 'Do you suppose it's because of dad that neither of us married?' Tall, slender and talented, she had served her time in repertory companies and a couple of commercials, before winning a part in a TV detective series. She supplemented acting with modelling for clothes and for artists.

'Or just because you never found the right bloke,' suggested David. 'You didn't exactly have a great role model for the ideal domestic soul mate.'

Catherine thought about this for a moment or two. 'I have to admit whenever I've got close to someone, the thought of how dad treated mum was always in the back or my mind … as a kind of demon warning me off.'

'Or you just prefer one night stands … you hussy!'

Catherine laughed. 'That explains your long list of lovers, does it?'

'I work unsocial hours and have sacks of coal under my eyes.'

'And a paunch.'

'No need to get personal. You're the glamorous stage and screen star. You pull more often than I do … More opportunity.'

'I just never felt I could take anyone home and introduce them to dad. Is that an awful thing to say?' she asked, taking her mug of camomile tea back to the sofa.

'Yes. It's awful to feel so sure your father would've been rude and embarrassing to your friends that you couldn't expose them to that danger ... Sums him up beautifully. What are we going to have carved on his headstone? *Sadly missed, but not by us*?'

'You can't even say he was kind to animals. He beat the dog black and blue and threw out all mum's garden bird feeders the day she went into the nursing home.'

'How about *Loathed by all who knew him, Hell will surely spit him out*?'

'Perhaps we should leave that to the masons.'

'They're all as bad as him, rigid Victorian fossils, as bigoted, sexist and conservative as they come.'

'I meant *monumental* masons. But you could be right ... They'd probably be more polite. I'll be in touch when I know the details. It might be a while with all these people dying in the heat wave.'

'I'm in no hurry. I don't want to take a day off work so if you could make it early morning, that would suit me best.'

'I'll let you know.' They hung up and both continued what they had been doing before Catherine had been informed of their father's death.

~*~

Walking through the bustling corridors of Norleigh Hospital between ward visits with Graham Dixon, and to get his mind off the latest relatives he'd had to speak to, Andrew Bragg asked, 'how's Joanne taking to you living here twenty-four-seven?'

'Asked me to wear my name badge next time I come home so she knows who I am, cheeky cow,' replied Graham affectionately. 'I think it might be because of the beard I'm growing,' he added, rubbing his darker than normal chin. His tall frame and lean features still commanded attention and faith in any relatives he spoke to, to say nothing of patients and staff.

'In a way I'm glad Sharon and I split up. At least she's found someone who can comfort her after her mother died. I'd have been too technical and interested in her as a case study.' Andrew wiped his handkerchief across his damp forehead as they reached the geriatric ward.

Orderlies were removing yet another shrouded body to the morgue and as the trolley rolled by Graham snagged the patient's chart and walked beside them. He put it back as they left the ward and then returned to Andrew saying in a low voice, 'another one saying symptoms of heat stroke ... dehydration, racing heart.' The two men exchanged a look and left again, making their way to the ER staff lounge.

'You don't suppose it could be some clinical trial or something do you?' asked Graham.

Andrew thought for a moment. 'How do you mean?'

'You know. It could be some sort of comparative study where a group are given standard treatment and the other half the new drug.'

'New drug for what? People have died of a range of things.'

Graham thought for a few minutes. 'Maybe that's the problem. The new drug has serious side effects and affects different people in different ways.'

'You're clutching at straws,' said Andrew with a smile. 'This many people in one area - in fact the whole country apparently - couldn't all be involved with a drug trail.' He thought again. 'I suppose it might be some drug that's already tested and approved which is having some sort of delayed reaction. Maybe the researchers will find out if there's a link … They'll ask what medication people have been taking.'

'OK. Have you heard anything more from the path lab?' asked Graham.

Andrew stirred his umpteenth strong black coffee and handed one for his friend sitting on the couch next to him. 'In the last few days I've had two notifications with liver failure, four heart failures, and six complications with bronchus and lungs. I was almost pleased when I had a young chap die following a motorcycle accident – it made a change. How about you?'

Graham sighed deeply and let his head fall back to rest on the back of the seat. 'Two strokes, an aortic aneurism and a pneumonia. I've a feeling that's not the whole story.'

'I was thinking of popping down there when I get a minute. I'd feel more confident passing information on if I knew it was true.'

'You doubt it too?'

Andrew nodded. 'Let's go now, hear what they have to say.'

Graham sprang to his feet with instant energy, taking Andrew by surprise, but he got to his feet more sedately and putting his mug down, joined his friend to visit the laboratory on the basement floor of the hospital.

'Afternoon,' said a surprisingly young looking woman. She didn't look especially concerned at being interrupted as she glanced at them over the top of her fashionable black rimmed spectacles which enhanced her small round face, darkened her brown eyes and her red lipped mouth. Her name badge declared her to be Dr Sarah Hastings, Supervising Pathologist.

'Afternoon,' said Graham, taking the lead but wondering how to broach the subject tactfully.

Andrew leapt in, saving his friend the trouble. 'Afternoon, Sarah. We're concerned about the large numbers of people dying during this hot weather.' Dr Hastings raised a pencil thin eyebrow. 'Can you confirm the results you're getting are accurate or ... are these just symptoms of something else?' he asked, beginning to wish he hadn't been so bold.

Dr Hastings stood up from her desk letting her chair role back on its castors and Andrew noted she was shorter than he expected. 'Let me show you the mortuary,' she said, brushing passed him and waving Graham aside with the back of her hand. The two doctors exchanged a glance and followed her. She pushed open a pair of swing doors and walked through a slatted plastic screen. The air filters were on maximum, but as the racks and any other conceivable surface were full of bodies, they weren't as effective as they would normally be.

'Good God!' exclaimed Andrew, quickly putting his handkerchief over his nose and mouth.

'All these haven't died in the hospital have they?' asked Graham, covering his face in a like manner.

'About half, I should say.' Dr Hastings, apparently oblivious to the smell, walked to a small office in the corner near the back door. 'Jenny from Admin is having a hell of a time just keeping up, but I've asked her to do some analysis for me.' Dr Hastings pressed a few keys on the computer and opened a spreadsheet. She scrolled down for the information she wanted, highlighted a particular column in yellow then gestured to her guests to look at what she'd found.

'I don't understand,' said Graham after a few moments of studying the data. 'This is showing everyone who has died of the heat during this last couple of weeks has been over the age of sixty.'

'That's what it's showing,' confirmed Dr Hastings. She studied the two men, taking in their puzzled expressions. 'Hadn't you noticed that amongst your patients?'

'Well yes,' admitted Graham. 'But I thought it just happened I was seeing the older ones. I didn't realise that *everyone* was over a certain age.'

'This can't be natural,' observed Andrew, glancing at Dr Hastings. 'Are you still sure your notifications are right?'

Dr Hastings closed the spreadsheet and brought up other records showing notifications of death for various people. 'From what I can gather from colleagues and the autopsies I've done myself, the majority of these people were reasonably healthy shortly before death … well perhaps not healthy but certainly fit enough to survive a bit of hot weather. Hardly any of them show particular symptoms, certainly nothing in common between them all. They just died ... suddenly. As we have to produce a cause of death, we've gone with the cause which either fits the symptoms exhibited or from any defect found on tissue samples … Things like unusual cell structure, cell proliferation, lesions or signs of organ enlargement. If I hadn't done some myself, I'd be as sceptical as you are,' she added astutely, making the two men feel uncomfortable.

'It's not that we doubt your findings … It must be difficult with the sudden increase in volume you've had to deal with,' said Graham tactfully looking into the room full of shrouded bodies. 'It's just we're finding it all hard to take in. Now I've seen this …' he gestured around the room, 'it's sort of easier to understand.'

'Really?' said Dr Hastings as she led them back to her office. She regained her chair and gestured to a couple of battered wooden wheel-backed chairs next to her window for the doctors to sit on. 'I don't like to speculate without information.' She leaned forward, her elbows resting on her desk and hands clasped under her chin. 'This is outside my experience.'

She glanced quickly at the telephone. 'I've contacted a friend who runs the pathology lab at the Manchester Royal Infirmary. He tells me they're dealing with a similar situation there. He's a renal specialist and says they're getting numbers of people with anaplasia. It seems rapid tumors are forming from undifferentiated cells, although he hasn't been able to identify a trigger mechanism … not for such a wide group of people, any way.

'Despite what it says in the papers, hundreds, possibly thousands of elderly … if you can still be thought to be elderly at sixty … have died this last few weeks and while the heat is being blamed, it can't possibly have caused all those deaths.'

'There were thousands of deaths in France ten or twelve years ago put down to heat stroke,' pointed out Andrew and instantly wished he hadn't.

'The temperatures in this country, while hot, especially at night, are not as high as those. People who live alone or don't have relatives close by to look after them are the ones who would normally be expected to succumb. We're getting couples. We're getting people from nursing homes that have round the clock attention from nurses who know all about heat stroke, and how to identify and treat it. Admittedly we are not used to such prolonged heat as in France, but you both know it's not the heat which is killing all these people.' She glared at them. They didn't think it was the heat, but having someone, the same someone who had been signing reports saying it was, came as a shock.

'What do you think it is then?' asked Andrew bravely.

'I don't know,' admitted Dr Hastings leaning back into her chair as if exhausted. 'I've sent some tissue and blood samples to the Environment Agency lab. They have different equipment to us and will be able to test for other toxins or agents which might be responsible. Hopefully they'll find something.'

'You think this could be something in the environment?' asked Graham startled.

'Why would it only affect people over a specific age?' asked Andrew sceptically.

'I don't think anything until I get more information. I'm just trying to find out what's causing the problem.' She sounded tired, almost defeated.

Graham and Andrew exchanged another look. 'We'd better be getting back to ER,' said Andrew. 'Thank you for being so honest with us Dr Hastings.'

'You'll let us know as soon as you find anything?' suggested Graham. Dr Hastings nodded absently and returned to her computer. The two men left without another word.

~*~

'I've used two new pads of Death Certificates this week already,' grumbled Norleigh's Registrar, Sean Dalton, down the telephone to his colleague in Sudcliff. 'I'll have to get a new nib for my pen too … this one's wearing out.'

Oliver Nicholson, the Sudcliff Coroner who'd been forwarding Notifications of Death for Sean to process smiled at his friend's understated and irrelevant take on the current chaotic situation. 'Ever the practical man,' he observed. 'I wanted to ask you whether you think I should be calling for inquests on any of these deaths.'

'Should you be doing?' asked Sean his Scots inflections lilting through the question. 'I thought you had to be satisfied the deaths were from natural causes *before* you sent me any Notifications.'

'That's not what I meant,' said Oliver sitting upright at his desk and playing with the magnetic beads of the executive puzzle on his desk. 'The deaths are natural in as much as they're not caused by anything which usually comes under unnatural. But what's happening can't be natural, can it?'

'You watch too many Sci-Fi films. There isn't an alien spaceship hovering above the atmosphere blasting death rays down killing everyone, you know.'

'It's not killing everyone, just a select few.'

'You're the one who decides if an inquest's required. Equally, you'd be the one who has to explain to the doctors, the relatives, the police or whoever why you're wasting everyone's time and money arriving at the same conclusion you had at the start.'

Oliver was silent for a few moments, wondering. 'You know this would be a perfect time for someone to murder an elderly rich relative, don't you?' He felt Sean was nodding.

'You read too many detective stories too,' Sean observed dryly. 'If you feel an inquest would help in any of these cases, feel free. I think you'd be wasting your time. Admittedly not many of those who have died during this heat wave have had any long term illnesses, but as they're all still getting on a bit, it's not really a big surprise.'

Oliver wondered if Sean really was that callous or if he was trying to dissuade him from his doubts. 'What do you suggest I do? I've been in touch with other coroners around the county; this is happening all over the place.'

'I know,' said Sean. Oliver pictured him lounging back comfortably in his large leather chair, not especially bothered, except for needing a new pen nib. 'Unless the doctors don't think this will blow over once the weather cools down, I don't see what you can do. A public enquiry could be set up I suppose, but I'd wait if I were you.'

Oliver was not especially pleased at his friend's lack of support. 'I suppose you're right,' he said grudgingly. 'I'll wait another couple of weeks and see if things cool down. It just feels like I'm presiding over a twenty first century plague.'

~*~

Outside the Lavender Café just off Norleigh High Street, Hayley Watts gazed absently into the faces of passers by while she slowly stirred her bowl of puddled ice cream with a vertical spoon. Alexis looked at her mother carefully; her long dark hair was wound on top of her head and secured with a wooden clip. Her tired red-rimmed dark eyes, free of make-up for a change, were hidden behind a pair of Ray Ban sunglasses.

'Mum,' she began softly, gently touching Hayley's hand to bring her back from wherever she'd mentally wandered off to. 'They're together. You know granddad would never've been able to live without grandma.' It was the only thing of comfort she could think of to say. She knew how much her mother loved her parents and to lose them both so quickly wasn't something she could get over in five minutes.

They'd been at the funeral directors. Because Joan had been one of the first to die that awful week, her funeral had been arranged readily enough, but even though Milton had only died a matter of hours later, so many others had died in between that normally they would have had to wait another week. However, the undertaker had said that as Joan and Milton would be buried in the same grave, they could also share the same funeral. Hayley had actually caught herself thinking this was great, but had burst into tears immediately afterwards and had spent most of the last couple of hours crying. Alexis had to be the tower for her mother to lean on and after expressing gratitude for the thoughtful and practical help Mr Cahill the undertaker had managed to provide, they'd left. As Hayley hadn't wanted to go home they'd meandered about the shops, unsuccessfully trying retail therapy.

Sitting quietly with two bowls of ice cream neither particularly wanted, they rested and watched the world go by. 'I keep thinking of the little things they'll miss,' said Hayley hoarsely. 'Sparrows, dahlias, chocolate sundaes. I know it's daft, but they're the things which make life worth living, not owning a big house or earning lots of money.'

Alexis sighed and nodded in agreement. 'I'll miss the way granddad always gave me praise no matter what I'd managed to do. He helped me learn to ride a bike, taught me how to drive, got me interested in science.'

'Mum taught me how to cook and sew, dad taught me the Latin names for all the plants in the garden.'

'Grandma was always so helpful with school plays; making my costumes, listening to me learning my lines for hours, patiently correcting me. She was a saint.'

'She loved you,' explained Hayley simply. 'My grandma - her mother - was just the same when I was a child. I'm sorry you never knew her. A gracious Edwardian, brought up to be a lady and made sure we learned her lessons. I think Joan was her favourite daughter, and then she had me and Bridget. She'd have loved you ... She liked girls.'

'Grandma was so self-sufficient. I know I've said this before, but I really don't think granddad would have lived long without her anyway, even without this heat.'

'He asked her to marry her on their third date, you know,' said Hayley proudly. She happily thought of her father being astute enough to spot how perfect a young woman her mother was and had snapped her up quickly.

'I hope I find someone like granddad one day,' said Alexis softly, thinking of the young men she knew and realising none of them fitted the bill ... not yet anyway. They fell silent again, pondering the two people who had been cornerstones in their lives.

Hayley sighed. 'I can't keep feeling sorry for myself like this. It said on the radio this heat has killed people all over the country. We ought to start a support group ... Survivors of the Great Heat.' She smiled, not feeling the least bit jocular. Alexis smiled and stood ready to leave. She wanted to be home and amongst the familiar objects she knew and could relate to - to be private in her grief and less on show.

As she left, she apologised for bumping into a man who looked as tired and worn as she felt, and she wondered if he had also lost someone dear recently.

Ewan also apologised for getting in the tall young lady's way. He and Greta had decided to get some air and spend some time away from their parents' home before returning to the task of sorting things out. He sat opposite his sister with a fresh lime and soda for each of them.

It felt like months ago but it was only this afternoon Greta had suggested Jessica should have a lie down after lunch as she seemed worn out. Hearing her sobbing quietly they'd checked on her after an hour. A little later, she'd called out, apparently with a pain in her stomach. Greta had given her an indigestion tablet, aware her mother had hardly eaten anything since breakfast. This had soothed and quietened her for a while, but she'd woken again asking for the doctor. Before Dr Henderson had arrived, she had lost consciousness and Ewan had telephoned for an ambulance. She died on the way to the hospital.

Sitting outside the café with the late evening sun shining onto his face, Ewan felt nothing; an empty void. Greta had tried to talk but as she got little response from him, she lapsed into introspective silence, watching people walking by and looking around at the other café patrons. She knew Hayley Watts by sight and guessed the girl opposite was her daughter as they looked so similar. Judging by their vacant expressions they were going through the same as Ewan and herself. Feeling united to them, she had only just stopped herself from going over and condoling with them, expressing sympathy and hoping for some in exchange, and was glad when they left.

Ewan sighed and stretched. He'd been tense all day and hadn't been at his best in the hospital. His feelings for Dr Henderson's perceived lack of care for Nigel had risen unchecked to the surface and boiled over. He'd ranted at the paramedics that the ambulance had taken too long to get to Jessica and that they should have found it easier to travel quickly through the town centre in the middle of the day.

Greta had tried to calm him but it only made him worse. He then started on the sister who was trying to take details about Jessica. 'What does it matter what her bloody maiden name was. SHE'S DEAD!'

'I need a walk,' he announced getting up and leaving the table.

After a few seconds hesitation Greta joined him as he strode towards the river. She grabbed a couple of unwanted bread buns from the table. 'We can feed the ducks,' she said handing him one of the firm crusty balls. 'Do you remember feeding the ducks when we were little?' she asked. Ewan only grunted. Greta ignored him but carried on talking as it helped her to come to terms with losing both her parents and hoped it would help Ewan calm down eventually too. 'Playing on the swings and the roundabout,' she said smiling. 'You remember the time you went flying and grazed your knees?' she asked. Another grunt.

Undaunted she carried on. 'Scrumping for apples in Mr Wenlock's orchard.'

'Blackberrying in Wilton Quarry,' said Ewan softly after a few moments' silence.

'Building sandcastles on Blackpool beach,' added Greta, entwining her arm with his. They walked more slowly now, approaching the river bank.

'Climbing trees at gran's,' said Ewan beginning to feel more relaxed about the situation.

'They might be gone,' said Greta quietly, giving his arm a squeeze, 'but they're not forgotten. As long as we can remember them, they'll always be with us.'

Ewan felt this sentiment a bit cloying, but if it helped Greta feel better, he let it go. Anger flamed again, but simmered quickly enough. He'd realised while shouting at the nurse that it wasn't her fault and no matter how much he ranted, raved and stamped his feet, nothing would bring either of his parents back.

As they walked along the river's edge, breaking pieces of bread to toss to the swans and mallards, they heard a rumble of thunder in the distance. 'Finally,' groaned Ewan. 'Hopefully this will clear the air and cool things off a bit. No one else will die of the heat.'

'We'd best get back to the car before it starts,' advised Greta. 'It looks as if it might be a bad storm.' Lightening flashed across the darkening sky and thunder rumbled again. The first drops of heavy rain made them increase their pace and they made it to Ewan's car parked not far from the café before the downpour really got going. The gauge on the dashboard showed the temperature dropping rapidly from thirty three degrees to a much more agreeable twenty two. Despite everything, they exchanged a happy smile and drove back to their parents' home, spraying water high into the air as the rain came down in stair-rods.

Chapter three

Friday 4th to Friday 11th September 2015

Victor Ibbs, a round unhealthy pasty faced man walked into the bar of The Colourman Inn, the pub first on the left from the offices of *The Westwater Illumination* newspaper, and propped himself comfortably next to his friend and colleague Corin Lister. Both men finished cigarettes despite standing next to a warning sign indicating such an act was illegal. Victor blew out smoke and stubbed out his offending white stick of tobacco when he saw the frown on barman Pete's face. Corin followed suit. Younger, slimmer, fitter and ambitious, his sights were set higher than a provincial weekly.

'I like Friday nights,' Corin began. 'Pop down to the green tomorrow to watch Westwater Eleven get their final drubbing of the season from whichever cricket team happens to be passing, go to a club in the evening and get plastered and with any luck laid, then wake up in an unfamiliar bed on Sunday trying to remember the young lady's name. Cooked breakfast at the Cocked Hat café and fall asleep watching the grass grow. Can't beat it.'

'That rain'll have ruined your chances of watching cricket tomorrow I should think,' said Victor before giving way to a hacking and body racking cough. He took a reviving slurp of beer.

'You should go easy on the cancer sticks, Vic,' said Pete reprovingly as he placed newly washed pint glasses above the bar.

'You get your cut off each packet I buy from your wretched machine. You should be grateful,' Victor replied nastily before coughing once more.

Corin patted him on his shoulder affectionately and smiled at Pete. 'Perhaps another drink to whet his whistle.' Pete pulled two more pints and the friends took their drinks to a table tucked away in an alcove. The pub was a dreary Victorian pile which only those who preferred dark corners and graffitied toilets could love. Its position close to the two large newspaper offices in the city made it enough money to keep going in its un-modernised state.

Corin frowned as he unstuck his hand from the table and leaned back in his chair. 'You've heard that the Mayor was taken ill last night,' he began relating what he had heard in another, cleaner modern pub earlier in the day. 'Caught with his trousers down on top of a girl half his age ... Lucky sod.'

'He died you know. Fancy going that way do you?' asked a smiling Victor with a cough.

'Can't have been much fun for the girl, but I expect she got paid lots ... or will do for her story, with all the gory details.' Corin smiled and drank his pint.

Victor wasn't a good colour and looked to be having trouble breathing. 'Don't suppose you've been suffering from the summer heat like all those other old people last month, do you?' Corin asked thoughtfully.

'I'm not old!' chastised Victor before coughing again and putting a hand to his chest. He drank some of his beer which seemed to make him feel better. 'And I'm not suffering from the heat,' he added, wiping sweat from his brow. 'Just got a bit of a summer cold I expect.' He coughed again.

Corin shrugged seeing his sympathy was unwelcome. 'Seems odd that many people dying from the heat though, don't you think?' Victor was too tired to bother replying and his lungs really hurt. He kept quiet, rubbed his chest and finished his pint.

'Another?' he asked Corin, who shook his head. Pete brought another pint for Victor and took away their empty glasses.

'You think the big papers are wrong and there may be a story behind all those deaths, do you lad?' asked Victor to break the silence.

Corin shrugged again. 'Dunno ... might be. Lots of people still died after it cooled down. I think I'll call it a night. Get some beauty sleep ready for the onslaught tomorrow night,' he said with a grin. He stood and left, calling good night to Pete as he went through the chipped dark wooden doors.

Victor was alone in the pub. The Friday night rush had finished an hour before the journalists had called in for their traditional end of week relief and catch up with gossip. He returned to lean on the bar and watch Pete putting things in order.

'Not much of a pub this, is it?' he observed. Rather than be offended, Pete merely smiled. His fondness for the place had diminished when the brewery had been less than keen to update anything. It was just a job now. 'Still,' Victor added with a halitosis grin. 'At least you've got your regulars.' Pete smiled again and hoisted a crate of seldom needed orange juice onto the bar ready to stack into the fridge.

Victor began to cough once more, but this time he didn't stop. After thirty seconds Pete looked at his customer who was turning purple. He poured a glass of water for him quickly, but before Victor could reach for it, he collapsed to the bar floor, gasping for breath. Alarmed, Pete ran round to see if he could help; loosening Victor's shirt collar and laying him comfortably on his side. He then telephoned for an ambulance.

Once they'd arrived after ten minutes, the paramedics gave Victor a shot of adrenaline and stretchered him into the ambulance. Unconscious, Victor rode to the hospital with the paramedics working to get his heart going. By the time they had reached the hospital, it had become clear he would not come round again and was declared dead on arrival.

Corin discussed Victor's death on Monday morning. His weekend hadn't gone according to plan. The cricket had been cancelled due to a waterlogged pitch, the girls in the club had thought him too old so he had slept alone in his own bed and the Cocked Hat was closed for refurbishment. He hadn't felt like watching the grass grow and had walked around the Millennium Park instead. A lot of miserable looking people seemed to have the same idea and despite the duck's antics, he'd gone home to watch *Apocalypse Now* on DVD again.

'He wasn't well on Friday night; had a bad cough. Is that what killed him?' he asked his boss, editor Bill.

'The hospital just said he had a heart attack brought on by poor diet, lack of exercise and smoking,' said Bill, a portly man in his fifties, who had recently been told to lose weight by his own doctor. He put down the bacon bap he was having for breakfast and thought perhaps he ought to listen to his doctor's advice after all.

Corin smiled at the gesture. 'You're going to take up jogging, Bill. Lose a stone … or three?'

'Cheeky sod.' Bill wiped his mouth on his shirt cuff. 'All those deaths due to the heat … Why don't you see if there's a story in amongst them … Someone famous, infamous or even really boring. Do a profile on some relatives …

Communal grief, that kind of thing. It's topical and gives something people can relate to. By Wednesday,' he added and picked up his bap again.

Corin left him to it and thought about Victor. He'd known him since he got his job on *The Illumination* and had spent time getting to know him. Victor had been up and come down, as he described it. He'd worked at the big London papers but had returned to his roots. Corin, reading between the lines took this to mean he hadn't been a huge success and returned to his natural level. Still, he was good enough for this particular local weekly and did high-quality stuff on business failures, warehouse fires and other disasters. Now, as a statistic of those who had died during the summer, he was part of a story himself.

Corin thought about the task Bill had suggested to him. He could start by interviewing hospital staff but felt they might be either defensive or hostile and definitely overworked, so perhaps he should try some relatives first.

He parked his Astra in the small car park behind the row of shops on Spring Street and walked slowly towards Trott's Hardware. The street was lined with lime trees suckering from their bases; their leaves still a vibrant green, but with a hint of autumnal yellow or brown here and there.

A well built young man was arranging boxes of dishcloths, multicoloured plastic coated washing lines, and inter-stacking Tupperware boxes on a trestle table in front of the window.

'Morning,' ventured Corin in a friendly tone. 'Are you Melvin Trott by any chance?'

'Yes,' came a rather hostile reply. 'Who wants to know?' asked Melvin, straightening to his full six foot height.

Corin held up an appeasing hand. 'A friend of mine died on Friday night … breathing problems caused by too many cigarettes according to the nurse.' He gave a short barked laugh. 'That means I'm in the same boat as you mate. Your father died recently didn't he? During that heat wave.'

Melvin positioned an incongruous stack of red bladed snow shovels next to the door and stared into space. 'This place was his pride and joy. Lived over the shop, came downstairs to work. Went to the Cash and Carry and other suppliers and that was it.' He focused on Corin. 'Your friend old was he?'

Corin had never thought of Victor as old, but he nodded. 'Sixty two.'

'Dad was sixty one. It's his birthday next week. We were going to watch the Albion at the Hawthorns, first home game of the season. Don't feel like it now'

'You could still go … as a tribute,' suggested Corin softly.

'Not the same on your own is it.' Melvin pulled down the mauve and blue striped awning over the window to keep off the already bright sunlight and led Corin into the shop, switching the light on at the back. He dusted the counter and absently hung up some packs of rechargeable batteries on the wall behind it.

'How's your family coping?' Corin prompted.

'Gone to pieces a bit. It was so sudden… such a shock. I think my sister Madge is feeling guilty 'cos she said she took him for granted … expected he'd always be there.' Melvin fell silent, deep in thought. 'He was so fit and healthy, nothing ever wrong with him … not even a cold. He shouldn't have died just like that.'

'They're saying people were dying because of the heat. Well it's cooled down a lot since last month. Hopefully that will be and end to it.'

'Heat,' said Melvin dismissively.

'You don't think that's right?'

'Of course not!' He slammed his fist on the counter making a small display of packets of vegetable seeds slide over. He rearranged them as he continued. 'Why would so many people die from the heat when it was just as hot, if not hotter than that last year? It wasn't that hot inside here anyway. Why were they only older people? Why not children or dogs and cats? It's not because of the heat,' he said firmly.

'My friend Victor had a bad cough, said his chest hurt him, but he'd been fine up until Friday evening. What do you think's causing the problem?'

'Something in the air probably … Like a virus or poisoned gas.'

'We'd have heard if there'd been a chemical leak or something, and wouldn't that affect everyone, not just older people?' observed Corin.

'Could be terrorists setting off dirty bombs … you know, Arabs. They're doing funny things to each other in the Middle East. Probably come up with something new and nasty.' Melvin shrugged. 'Maybe people over a certain age are more susceptible.'

'That's what they said about the heat.' Corin offered. He decided to buy a bag of brass cup hooks seeing as Melvin had been responsive. 'I'm sorry about your dad; go to the match. You know he'd appreciate it. Hopefully whatever it is'll stop now its cooler, and no one else will have to feel the way we do.'

~*~

'It's the second job I've had cancelled this week,' said builder Magnus Unwin over his mobile phone.

'It'll give you a chance to get started on improving *our* patio,' replied his wife Bryony cheerfully. 'I'm sorry to hear about Mrs Trott though; she was a nice lady.'

'He's died too,' said Magnus starkly.

'Both of them!' said Bryony sharply. 'Just like Mr and Mrs Ridgeway ... That's awful. Their poor families ... It must be terrible for them.' Neither of them spoke for a few moments then Bryony continued, 'I'll see you at tea time.' She hung up and replaced the handset in its charging cradle. Thoughtfully, she collected her list, shopping bags and hand bag, and drove into Westwater.

The sun was bright and warm, blackbirds and sparrows darted about the hedges used to mark the parking bays in the main car park. Sainsbury's didn't seem as full as usual for a Thursday as she wandered absentmindedly around. With hardly a queue at the checkout, she remarked on this to the girl bearing a name badge saying Sophie.

'It's been like this for the last month, since we had that hot weather,' answered the girl. 'Not so many old people about now. They've been knocked up with various ailments or ... some of them have died,' she gulped and made brief eye contact with Bryony. Bryony looked around the store and realised that Sophie was right. Normally when she came in during the day she would be manoeuvring her trolley around a few women with toddlers, young couples dividing the job between them or discussing the merits of competing produce, but always reams of old ladies chatting and in the way, and several ponderous old men peering at labels. Hardly any one in the shop was older than herself.

From Monday to Wednesday Bryony worked as a pharmacist in Boots the Chemist further down the High Street so she knew a lot of the older generation of Westwater. Usually she would bump into at least a few moving up and down the aisle in the store or along the street. None of them were around today.

'Fifty two pounds thirty,' repeated Sophie. Bryony was brought sharply back to the mundane reality of life and paid for her groceries with her card. Packing the bags into the boot of her Clio, she decided to walk into town and see her son Martin.

With this being a fresher bright sunny day, the street should have been bustling. Apart from the mums with pushchairs, teenagers lounging amongst the raised flower beds and men making deliveries, she particularly noticed the absence of anyone over about sixty. Bryony reached Baxter's Travel where Martin worked, and walked in. Typing on his computer, he didn't see her straight away, but his subconscious recognized a potential customer and alerted him.

'Hi Mum,' he said getting to his feet and giving her a brief kiss on her cheek. 'How are you?' He stood back and looked at her drawn, concerned face. 'What's the matter?' He motioned her to one of the pale purple padded chairs opposite his desk and he sat down in his own swivel chair once more. The office was brightly decorated in sunny warm yellows and oranges, and the racks on the two opposite walls groaned with sunny brochures for holidays 2016.

'Nothing's the matter ...' she paused, knowing that wasn't quite true. 'Well not with me anyway,' she added, fading.

'What do you mean?' he asked, wondering if there might be something wrong with Magnus instead.

'Your dad phoned an hour ago and said he'd had a cancellation at Mrs Trott's about the work she'd asked him to do on her bedroom. Both she and her husband have died now and their family didn't know what they'll be doing with the house. That's on top of the work for Mr Ridgeway being cancelled too – you know the work on an extension and conservatory – because he and his wife have died in the last couple of weeks,' she paused, frowning again.

'He's a good builder. He can pick and chose his jobs. Don't worry,' said Martin comfortingly, thinking his mother might be concerned about the money.

'It's not that Martin,' she said looking at him. 'Haven't you noticed there aren't many old people about at the moment?' Martin shook his head being more the sort of person who concentrated on himself and his own concerns.

'I've just been around Sainsbury's,' she explained. 'The checkout girl said they weren't very busy because a lot of old people had died after the heat in August or were still ill because of it.'

Martin smiled. 'Is that all you're worried about. They said in the paper it's because it got too hot at night or something ... put a strain on people's hearts and they couldn't sleep properly ... It happens a lot, especially on the continent. Nothing to worry about.' He patted her hand comfortingly, but Bryony wouldn't be appeased.

'It's not as simple as that ... Don't you see?' she said gesturing to the plate glass door and window. 'There are no older people outside,' she turned back to Martin. 'How many pensioners have you had in the last week coming in to buy their trips to Spain for the winter?' This pulled Martin up straight. 'How many phone calls have you had from bereaved relatives cancelling reservations already made?'

He thought for a moment then realised what she said might be right. 'It'll pick up again once they're all feeling better. Nothing like the hope of a nice holiday in the sun to cheer you up.' He smiled at his mother, finding a flaw in her argument.

'It's been hot and sunny here!' she said gesturing again towards the sunshine brightening the street outside the shop. Having glared at him for another few moments she changed the subject. 'Are you and Paul coming around this evening? Your dad wants to try the new barbeque.'

Martin smiled again. 'Yes, he's really looking forward to it. He wants a go on dad's lathe and to try out his new chisel set.'

'He's too young to be using that lathe,' said Bryony shaking her head with a smile.

'He loves it. The Young Apprentice dad calls him.'

'Be round at six if you can make it.'

After Bryony had left, Martin did a bit of research on his computer. This time last year he'd sold thirteen month-long trips to Spain, Portugal or the south of France. This year he'd sold five, and two of those had been cancelled over the last couple of days when relatives advised him their loved ones had died during the heat wave. He'd also cancelled four holidays to Italy, one long haul to Australia and five to various parts of the United States, all because the purchaser had died recently. He dug a little further ... Yes; surprisingly they'd all been over sixty.

He sat back and brooded for a few minutes, but his introspection was disturbed by Daphne Porter, the buxom dinner lady from the St Luke's Primary School his son Paul attended. 'Majorca again Daphne?' he asked, as she plonked herself into the seat vacated by Bryony and with a beaming smile, handed him her dog-eared copy of the brochure she and her husband Kevin had thumbed through the night before. Regular as clockwork, Daphne arrived at the beginning of September hoping for a last minute bargain to her favourite resort. Martin found what she asked for and noticed it was only half full this year. He did some nifty work with his keypad and found she could upgrade to a smarter hotel along the beach for the same price if she was interested. Daphne was very interested, her bright little eyes twinkled in her chubby face and Martin had to work hard to dispel the unpleasant thought of her in a bikini.

When she had gone away satisfied with her superior holiday, Martin expanded his research to foreign resorts and destinations and was surprised - if that was the right word seeing as he found what he expected - that many winter resorts were less than half full.

The rest of his day was quiet with the odd enquiry, the odd booking and the odd sensation something was wrong. He collected Paul from his neighbour where he spent the after school hours playing with his friend Dylan. Martin, a widower since Paul was three, had raised Paul, now ten years old, with help from his parents and neighbours.

Despite his early misfortune, Paul was a cheerful happy child who had plenty of friends and an inquisitive, observant, curious and noticing nature. 'What's the matter Dad?' he asked as they later drove to his grandparent's house for tea.

'Oh ... I was just thinking,' replied Martin absently, giving Paul the briefest of reassuring smiles.

'About what?' asked Paul not put off so easily.

'Nothing much ... just people don't seem to be going abroad as much as they were. I'm getting more bookings for England and Scotland now ... and Wales of course,' he added. Paul seemed pacified by this and they talked about the kite he had made with Dylan and how it had flown for a few metres before crashing down unto the grassy bank in the park.

Once they arrived on the still warm evening, Martin handed over a bottle of merlot to Bryony while his father Magnus showed Paul his new cordless drill with sanding attachment – he could have a go on the lathe after the barbeque. While Magnus and Paul were engaged with machinery, Martin and Bryony sat on the low wall of the patio, waiting for the barbeque coals to heat up, sipping wine, enjoying the balmy weather and chatting quietly.

'That buddleia's had plenty of butterflies this year,' observed Martin, indicating the tall wispy orange sweetly flowered shrub in the corner by the shed, covered in red admiral, peacock and tortoiseshell butterflies, as well as dozens of hoverflies and bees.

'I bought that plant from Mr Trott - about fifteen years ago it would be now. I didn't think it would outlive him.'

Martin sagged, hoping his mother wasn't going to pick up from their earlier conversation. 'He'd be proud of it, no doubt. Is his son taking over the shop do you know?'

'Melvin has, yes. His other son Trevor has his own joinery business.'

Martin nodded. 'Daphne's going to Majorca again. I couldn't persuade her to try another island, but she managed to get an upgrade, which pleased her.'

'Have you seen the paper this evening?' asked Bryony, reaching across to pick up *The Westwater Illumination* she had delivered each Thursday. Martin shook his head, wondering if the subject had just been changed.

'There's a piece here by Corin Lister about all the deaths supposedly due to the heat.' Bryony flicked the paper so the relevant column was uppermost. The face in the photograph next to the article showed a middle aged man with large bags under his bleary eyes, a receding hairline toning to grey, a long nose leading to thin lips parted in a faint smile. The caption underneath stated it was Victor Ibbs, 1953 to 2015. The article below wasn't the expected obituary, but a questioning piece about whether the large numbers of deaths attributed to various natural causes might in fact have more to do with the Government's declining support for the National Health

Service, or perhaps the incompetence of its staff and the horrifying number of undiagnosed fatal illnesses. Corin, obviously affected by the death the previous week of his colleague and friend, barred no holds. He continued reflectively.

Victor, not only a journalist of considerable merit and critical acclaim, was first and foremost a human being, something of importance and he, like all those who have died within the last month or so should be mourned and grieved for, not allowed to simply become a statistic in a major countrywide catastrophe.

Martin read this to himself and gave a brief glance at Bryony then carried on. *To visit a busy hospital and be told that not only your friend was probably dead but the staff had not been able to complete his paperwork, and then minutes later to discover his unattended body covered in a pink cellular blanket - a not very clean pink cellular blanket - on a trolley parked in a corridor next to the gents toilets, leaves one feeling less than sympathy for the strain and tension nursing and doctoring staff must currently be under.*

Martin frowned at this and looked again at Bryony who simply motioned for him to continue. *Where will our society be without the likes of Victor to pass on his experience and pearls of wisdom? Without the Victors of this world, who will offer me fatherly advice and tell me how it was in the old days? Who will voice his opinions in tones of ridicule and scorn? Who will have the patience to get things done that the rest of us are too busy to do? Who will praise me for a job well done? Who will make me questions my decisions and choices? What am I going to do without him?*

To all those people who feel as I do about someone you have lost in the last few dark weeks of this terrible summer, I offer you my condolences and the hope for better times to come. I challenge the Government and scientific community to come up with a more convincing and less British answer than blaming the weather.

'Powerful stuff,' said Martin when he had finished the piece. 'I've not known him write anything like that before ... He's usually quite light hearted.'

'I expect he'd have found it difficult to be light hearted about his friend's death … especially as he was one of so many,' said Bryony contemptuously.

'You two been reading that newspaper column have you?' asked Magnus as he joined them with Paul who had wood shavings in his hair and attached to his T shirt.

'He expresses an interesting point of view, don't you think?' said Bryony provocatively.

'He's grieving for his friend and using the paper to articulate it,' observed Magnus.

'He's accusing the hospital of killing all those people,' said Martin, tossing it onto the table in front of him with vigour.

'Do you imagine the Trott or Ridgeway families feel any different?' asked Bryony in a superior tone. 'They're suffering the loss of a loved one ... or two ... and have become part of something greater.'

'It's the same with any natural disaster ... people lose loved ones and suffer grief but are not alone,' said Magnus, hoping to keep Bryony from getting too overemotional.

'You think what's happened is natural?' she queried.

'Well ... obviously ... it's because of the heat,' said Magnus doubtfully.

'It's cooler this week than it's been for ages ... those thunderstorms cooled things down, especially at night ... but people are still dying. It's more like a biblical plague.'

'You think this is all an act of God,' scoffed Martin.

'Of course not,' said Bryony impatiently. 'I'm saying if it's not the heat there's another explanation.'

'It might just be an experiment,' said Paul who had been quietly listening to his family arguing. 'You know a mad scientist ... like in the Marvel comics ... and it's got out of hand or something's escaped,' he said enthusiastically.

All three adults stared at him, surprised he had taken part in the conversation. 'It's not something from a comic Paul. This is real life,' said Martin dully.

'I think we'd better get cooking now,' said Magnus, 'the coals are hot enough.'

~*~

The following afternoon, Dr Prudence Richards the Senior Pathologist, pushed open the wide swing doors leading to the Sudcliff General Hospital's Pathology Department where scientists Kate Jordan and Hugh Old were working on the latest samples collected by their colleagues. The number of deaths had reduced from a torrent to a trickle and the mortuary had reorganised into a system which processed the corpses more efficiently. Criticism from the likes of Michael Quinn, Corin Lister's equivalent on the *Sudcliff Daily Scoop,* and various other authorities had meant basement storage had been commandeered and cleared as it was cool, dark and better fitted for purpose than hospital corridors. Staff worked reduced daily hours but seven days a week to clear the backlog and prevent another build up.

'I've heard from Sarah Hastings, my colleague in Norleigh, with a report from the Environment Agency,' Prudence said without preamble. With thick lines of steel grey in her dark hair tied in a large bun, and her white coat, she was drained of any colour she might otherwise have had. Her tall erect heavy posture and large thick-rimmed spectacles added to her air of authority.

Kate and Hugh looked around at her, startled. 'Dr Richards,' said Kate, 'I didn't hear you come in.'

'What have they found?' asked Hugh hopefully.

'No toxins, poisons, artificial chemicals ... As this phenomenon is countrywide, they've checked it's not in the water supply or anything airborne. As it's affecting such a large number of people over a wide area it's unlikely to be contaminated food, but they're checking milk and dairy products. They can't find anything in common to the deceased that might have caused this ... There's a whole range of life styles and religious observances. They've had no reports of slippages, seeps or large scale unwanted dumping,' she finished, looking up from the notes on her clipboard.

'The thing is ...' began Hugh, pausing as if worried what he was about to say was too controversial.

'What?' asked Prudence impatiently after a moment's silence.

'Well ... could it be something internal, if it's not external.'

'What do you mean?' asked Prudence sharply.

'Biological not environmental.' His two colleagues simply stared at him uncomprehending. 'If we can't find anything outside the body … heat, poisons or whatever … perhaps it's something inside the body.'

'People all over the country have died. We've analysed thousands of tissue samples. We've found anomalies but nothing common to all,' pointed out Kate.

'Maybe we need to look deeper,' said Hugh.

'Deeper inside the body?' queried Prudence.

'You mean inside the cells like its some sort of cellular breakdown?' asked Kate incredulously.

'Or genetic,' suggested Hugh sheepishly.

'But it can't be genetic. All these people are different, not related. Why would it be genetic?'

'Until we look, we won't know,' said Hugh with a shrug.

Prudence stood quietly thinking. 'I'll see if I can get some time allocated to this kind of research … for elimination purposes,' she said spinning around with a swirl of white coat and strode from the laboratory.

Kate and Hugh swapped a quick glance. 'I know it doesn't seem feasible,' Hugh began defensively, 'but we've found strange things going on in the tissue samples with no apparent cause.'

'We should be looking further outside rather than going deeper inside. Just because you're a biologist doesn't mean there has to be a biological answer for everything.'

Hugh looked mildly offended at this suggestion. 'They've had a look for environmental factors,' he said defensively.

'Only a few. There could be a thousand unusual things in the atmosphere or water supply which could kill people and we haven't looked for or been able to trace yet.'

'No there couldn't,' said Hugh shaking his head. 'You're over dramatising the situation.' He swivelled back to his microscope and looked at the latest liver sample which had once been a part of Sylvia Greggs, a retired local dancer. 'She drank a lot,' he muttered.

‘Enough to kill her?’ asked Kate with a sceptical well-shaped eyebrow raised.

‘No,’ admitted Hugh. ‘She died from a collapsed lung.’

‘Why are you looking at a liver sample then?’ asked Kate, looking up from her own sample.

‘Looking for a pattern. There must be something they all have in common.’

‘At the minute … the only thing they all have in common is they’re dead.’

Hugh shot Kate a glance. ‘This is getting to you, isn’t it?’ he asked, feeling the change in his colleague’s mood.

Kate slouched back in her chair and gave a deep deflating sigh. ‘I feel so helpless,’ she said softly tossing her pen onto her desk. ‘A month ago, I would look for cause of death in people and believe it gave comfort to the bereaved to know what it was.’

‘And now?’ prompted Hugh when Kate didn’t continue.

‘And now I can only find a real cause of death in one of three cases ... there’s so little to go on with most of them. I’ve never had to deal with this many in so short a space of time.’ Hugh saw the lights pick out a tear trickling down her cheek. ‘I don’t know if I can carry on doing this for much longer.’

Hugh leapt from his chair sending it whirling across the tiled flooring and strode to her. ‘Let’s have a break, grab a coffee or have a walk to the park for an hour.’ Kate turned sad eyes onto his big face. ‘We’ve been working eight days straight; we deserve an hour off in the sunshine.’

Kate smiled and rose from her seat; some fresh air would be welcome, even though it wouldn’t change anything and the slide she had been looking at would be as unhelpful when she got back as it was now.

Hugh bravely took Kate’s hand as they walked around the park half a mile from the hospital. Kate didn’t seem to notice or if she did, took it as a gesture of friendship rather than anything more. She wistfully walked along sighing regularly.

‘Penny for them,’ said Hugh softly.

Kate smiled at him and swung his hand. ‘I watch the people walking around this park and look at their faces. I see melancholy, distress, loss.’

'You're reading too much into it. Look at those kids over there,' said Hugh pointing across to where two young boys were trying to get a small remote controlled boat to leave the shore of the lake. 'They look happy enough.'

'Have you seen the lady they're with?' put in Kate with a nod at a woman watching the youngsters from a bench only a few feet away. She gazed absently into the middle distance, her face completely blank of expression or emotion, her greying hair untidily pulled back into a straggling pony tail; her hands limp on her lap, shadows from the tall trees lining the path stripping across her.

Hugh gave the woman a dissatisfied glance. 'You're jumping to the conclusion she's lost someone near and dear. Just because you've got caught up in this tragedy, doesn't mean everyone else has.'

Kate let go of his hand and they walked a little further rather stiffly together. Swallows and house martins twittered to each other overhead. Bees buzzed around the lime trees. Sparrows chased each other noisily around a rhododendron bush. 'The rest of the world seems to be carrying on as if nothing has happened,' observed Kate softly.

'Nothing has happened. This situation will sort itself out; we'll get to the bottom of it and find someway of preventing it. Don't worry. We always do ... eventually.'

'You think this will all be solved by the wave of a magic wand?' said Kate sceptically. 'Something's happening; something which has never occurred before and is affecting everyone's lives,' she said passionately. 'Take off your blinkers. Look around you. See what other people are going through.' She waved an arm expansively taking in a middle-aged couple quietly walking along the path talking softly to each other, a group of teenaged girls sitting on a blanket comforting a grief stricken friend, a bunch of boys one of whom was bouncing a football while his friend told a story about how his grandfather played in the park as a child too.

Hugh looked at her and tried to think of something to say which would take her mind off things. 'They say people are suggesting all kinds of home remedies to help solve the problem; mostly involving having lots of sex, smoking to excess or plunging into cold baths twice a day. I don't think I'd mind the first, but wouldn't be keen on the last,' he said with a chuckle. Kate didn't move or say anything, just sat in disapproving silence.

Hugh looked around. 'Let's go back. Maybe a walk in the park wasn't such a good idea.'

'Supposing it's nothing more than a scientific puzzle doesn't detract from the effect it's having on everyone. That's not going to go away,' said Kate firmly. 'It's our responsibility as scientists to find out what's caused this disaster and give people some answers.'

Hugh, not wanting her to think him unfeeling replied, 'why do you think I worked through the weekend? Why do you think I know the old gal on my slide didn't die from emphysema? Why do you think I want Dr Richards to cover as much research as we can afford no matter how unlikely?' Kate stared at him, surprised by his outburst. 'I want to find out what's causing this and stop it,' he said earnestly. 'I just thought you could use a change of scene. Perhaps I should have taken you to a movie and dinner afterwards.' He glared at her defiantly.

'Are you asking me on a date?' she sounded surprised.

'Yes … if you'll come.'

Kate raised her eyebrows and watched the two little boys run to their grandmother with their dripping boat. She smiled at them both and ruffled their hair then put the boat in a carrier bag and all three left, the boys running on ahead and returning like puppies. 'OK,' said Kate. 'Nothing too violent though and I'd like to go to Hamilton's Restaurant on the High Street.'

Hugh blanched slightly - Hamilton's was expensive. 'Sure. Let's get back to some analysis.'

~*~

Corin Lister had his own way of analysing what was going on. His first column had been from the heart but to continue his investigation he needed other people's points of view. He contacted the colleague who entered births, marriages and deaths in *The Westwater Illumination* and wrote a computer spreadsheet of all those who had died in the last six weeks and by whom they were lovingly remembered. He then matched telephone numbers, called a few and arranged interviews with those who said their loved one had died suddenly with no warning or prior illness.

The afternoon sun burned as hot as ever as he met Frank Neville at his garage. Frank had reorganised things since officially taking over from his father, so tyres were stacked in their racks, tools were in place on the pin board, and the whole place looked more professional and less haphazard.

'Your dad was sixty one. That's right isn't it?' checked Corin from notes on his pad.

'What's that got to do with the price of wing-nuts?' asked Frank crossly, hefting two oil canisters nearer the doorway. 'He was as fit as a boxer's bulldog, never had a day's illness, never smoked nor drank to excess, took plenty of exercise and fresh air. He should have lived another ten years at least; his dad did.'

Corin wondered why there was a general hospital at both Norleigh and Sudcliff ... everyone he spoke to said their dead relatives were fit and healthy.

'Some people go just like that,' said Corin provocatively.

'I can't believe dad just died from a stroke. There was nothing wrong with him ... even the doctor said it was only a small blockage when they'd done the autopsy.' Frank's strong oil streaked face creased into a frown. 'Can't think why they blamed a stroke if there was nothing wrong.'

Corin seized on the point and said quietly, 'supposing they didn't really know what killed him and just said that to pacify you?'

'Well it hasn't pacified me!' said Frank belligerently. 'I don't believe that's his cause of death and that's why I had him buried not cremated like he wanted to be.' He stopped moving things around and stood squarely looking at Corin. 'One day someone'll sort this out and I want to prove he died from some mistake at the hospital or whatever. He shouldn't have died!'

'You think the hospital should be blamed?' asked Corin pleased he hadn't brought up the subject.

'I don't know,' said Frank, his box-like frame collapsing like a burst balloon as he sighed. 'He wasn't ill but he's dead. There's no reason why he should die in hospital - they looked after him - so there must be some other reason,' he said thoughtfully.

'Got any thoughts on what that might be?' probed Corin.

'Could be anything,' said Frank his patience wearing thin. 'Pollution, global warming, the Russians ... Hell! Little green men from Mars for all I know. I only know he shouldn't have died.' Frank brushed passed Corin and disappeared into a rear storeroom, indicating unmistakably the interview was over.

As Corin had other people to see, he left Frank to it, but he had a clear idea this man also felt something was being covered up.

His next interview was much calmer and took place in the serene suburban surroundings of a bungalow in Summerton three miles out of the Westwater town centre. The dark stained wooden gate opened onto a brick path with lavender and Michelmas daises either side leading to a pergola of dangling pink roses framing the doorway. The plump young woman who answered the door had a pretty face with a button nose and sparkling blue eyes. Corin wished they were meeting under other circumstances, but you never know what might happen.

'You're Corin Lister aren't you?' said Rosie Foster as she held the door open for him. The bungalow was as neat inside as out. The hallway with the lounge to the right and the main bedroom to the left, led further to a second bedroom and the bathroom, ending in the neat kitchen with tidily arranged jars of tea, coffee, pasta and rice. The gleaming microwave sat quietly next to the gleaming kettle. As expected, the work surfaces were spotlessly clean; he could have eaten off the floor, had he been offered anything.

'I'll make us a coffee then we can sit in the room,' said Rosie, filling the kettle from the shining cold tap and collecting two mugs, a cafetiere, milk and sugar onto a tray adorned with ducks in a row. Corin insisted on carrying the tray and Rosie led him to the living room.

As a journalist, Corin noticed things and gained impressions. 'Someone's a good artist,' he said, genuinely pleased with the array of original watercolours around the walls. Scenes of Scottish Lochs and Cumbrian Lakes filled the wall opposite him while behind were botanical illustrations, a still life of tropical fruit and a portrait of a beagle.

'My brother Wesley's an art teacher,' explained Rosie pouring the coffee.

'He's good.'

'I know,' Rosie said tartly. 'You wanted to talk to me about dad,' she said, getting straight to the point while putting the coffee pot down and handing him his mug.

'Thank you,' said Corin, adding three sugars and stirring his drink. 'You lived here with him, is that right?' He'd already asked her that on the telephone but was just breaking the thick layer of ice.

'Dad was a long distance lorry driver; he worked for Stephenson's. When mum died about ten years ago, he asked me to come and live here. Seeing as he was away so much, it seemed to make sense to share the house. I work in Tesco's on the deli counter, Wesley teaches at the High School and my other brother lives near Salisbury - he has his own plumbing business,' Rosie explained, quite unnecessarily and without prompting. Corin made notes.

'Dad came home last Friday night saying he'd eaten something which didn't agree with him and he'd go straight to bed. I gave him some bicarb which usually does the trick when he's had a dodgy pie at a transport café, but he got much worse and about two in the morning, I had to call an ambulance.' Rosie stopped here and stared blankly out of the front window, absently noting she needed to fill the empty feeder hanging from the bird table.

Her voice became dry and emotionless. 'He was in great pain when they arrived and got him into the ambulance. I travelled with him, holding his hand all the way. They took him into Accident and Emergency and I waited. It was hardly any time before the doctor came out and said … he'd died.'

Tears slowly escaped from the corner of her eyes and fell unchecked. Her voice even duller than before continued, 'I couldn't believe it. He'd been fine the day before. He said he hadn't eaten anything except an M&S chicken pie from the motorway service station. I couldn't believe that would have done him any harm.'

'Did the doctor say what killed him?' asked Corin so softly as to be barely audible.

'They did tests and an autopsy,' said Rosie finally wiping her tears. 'They've told me he had a perforated ulcer.'

'You don't believe that, do you?' said Corin in a tone nearer his normal voice.

Rosie shook her head. 'He'd have known if he had an ulcer and would have done something about it.' She looked at the portrait of the beagle. 'I told the doctor that. He just said he might not have known about it if he'd eaten anything bad during the hot weather. But mum died of stomach cancer so he was very conscious of anything like that.'

'How do you feel about the diagnosis?' Corin asked, watching Rosie closely.

She curled the handkerchief between her fingers. 'I've spent the last week washing, cleaning, and rearranging the furniture. I've weeded and tidied the garden. I've packed dad's things up ready to go to a charity shop. All I want to do now is understand what really killed him and know why the hospital doctor lied to me.'

'You think he lied to you?' said Corin, looking at her sharply. He'd been looking around the immaculate room, noticing telltale impression marks on the carpet where a table had once stood, yet here was another person who felt the medical profession was hiding something.

'I don't know,' said Rosie listlessly, her hands going limp on her lap. 'I can't think why they wouldn't tell me the truth, but I just got the impression he was telling me something just to get rid of me. The hospital was very full of people.' She looked at Corin for the first time during their interview. 'Do you really think all those people died because of the heat, or are they just saying that to make us go away?'

Corin looked straight into her eyes, seeing the unanswered pain and grief, the sadness and loss, the helpless, hopelessness he saw when he looked in the mirror. 'No I don't think all those people died from the heat, but I intend to find out why they did die.'

'Then why are you asking me about dad. Why aren't you asking the doctors?'

'Because they'd just fob me off. The more relatives I talk to, the more stories I hear of people not believing what they've been told, the more pressure I can bring to bear to get at the truth.'

'I look forward to reading about it,' said Rosie with the first smile he had seen on her pretty face. She looked ten years younger as her short curly blonde hair caught the sunlight from the open window.

'I'll leave you to your housework and packing,' he said rising. 'Thank you for the coffee and your point of view. It will be most helpful.'

'Find out,' said Rosie, closing the front door behind him as he left with the scent of roses in the air.

Chapter four

Monday 12th October 2015

The Prime Minister Norman Bateman wore a sombre dark grey suit and black tie as he sat behind his vast oak desk to make the announcement to the world. Reading the autocue from the screen in front of him he said in a dark grey voice, 'it is my unfortunate duty to inform you of His Most Gracious Majesty's death. King Charles the Third died last night following a brief illness. My condolences and sympathy go to the family and household. The funeral and national day of mourning will be held on Thursday and I will be advising you later today of the final arrangements. Thank you all and may our prayers this day be with Prince William - now King William the Fifth - and the rest of the Royal Family. The King is dead. Long live the King.'

The silence following this speech was a contrast to the normal flurry of activity in the room in Number 10 Downing Street when a political broadcast was being made. Instead of the bustle of officials and crew shushing each other then dismantling things and putting the room back as it was, everyone stood completely still, absorbing what the Prime Minister had just told the country. They knew before hand what he was going to say, but having it literally broadcast in front of them made it true if equally unbelievable.

Every man and woman in the room had been born during Elizabeth's long reign and while they had not expected Charles to last for as long, they hadn't anticipated another state funeral quite so soon. The Queen and Prince Philip had died during 2013 within a few weeks of each other – the Year of Loss, Prince Andrew had termed it.

'Well,' said the director. 'That's that. Thank you Prime Minister. Not a pleasant task.'

'No. I didn't think I'd be the one to make that announcement. I have meetings to attend. Gentlemen ... Ladies ... If you'll excuse me.' Bateman stood tall at a lean six foot three and walked elegantly from the room. Mutterings followed him until the door was closed and with relief, he exhaled a breath and walked slowly and thoughtfully to the Council Chamber.

At Buckingham Palace, staff bustled around putting long worked out and familiar arrangements for the funeral into action. It would most likely be eleven o'clock on Thursday morning, the only question being whether the Archbishop of Canterbury would have recovered from his cold; the Archbishop of York was on standby. Like the BBC TV crew, they were all Elizabethans and having briefly discovered what life was like under Charles' influence, they now had to prepare to serve William as King.

Mr Bateman poured himself a glass of water from the crystal carafe and took his seat at the middle of long grey oval table, joining Donald Sharp his Deputy Prime Minister and Chancellor John Mahon who sat opposite. Light glistened from the gilded chandelier and the ornate clock ticked softly on the side table, as he reclined into the red upholstered chair.

'You look as if you could do with something stiffer,' observed Sharp dryly, a squarely built silver haired man in his mid-fifties.

'I could,' Bateman acknowledged, 'but we have important work to do and I need my wits about me.' He coughed and took a drink of water.

'What was the cause of death exactly?' asked Mahon. 'He wasn't ailing from anything that I'm aware of.'

'He had a severe stroke last night around eight o'clock and never recovered,' answered Bateman. His two companions fell reverentially silent.

'Right,' said Bateman, pulling himself from his reverie. 'I've had a report from the Environment Agency saying it's sure nothing environmental caused the deaths in the summer. Also, the British Medical Council confirms it can't have been the heat wave as the deaths have continued to a lesser degree, although it may have been a contributing factor in some cases, but by no means all.'

His two ministerial colleagues looked at each other. 'Is this the most important thing we have to discuss today?' queried Sharp. 'Surely we should be looking into continuing governing until Prince William … I mean *King* William is in a position to take over.'

'I spoke to His Majesty half an hour ago. He will follow one complete week of mourning, but be available for official duties following that. We continue with governing as before.'

Again the two ministers swapped a glance. 'That being the case,' said Mahon leaning forwards and interlocking his fingers on the table, 'we have the debt crisis, racial rioting in Leicester, the situation in Ethiopia, Saudi Arabia and the rest of the Middle East ... and His Majesty's funeral to discuss. Should we really be spending valuable time discussing the summer's medical issues?'

'Been to your golf club lately?' asked Bateman sitting back and raising his eyebrows at his colleagues. 'His Majesty's funeral will be the fourth ... no fifth I've been to this month already. How about you?'

Sharp looked thoughtfully at the Prime Minister. 'Old Bill Travis, Sandy Maxwell, Jim Booth. I've been to quite a few funerals too.'

'What are you saying?' asked Mahon picking up on Sharp's depressed tone.

'The older generation of our population is dying off. From what I gather from the President, it's happening in the States too ... and France and Germany. Something is killing people over a certain age much more quickly than is natural.'

'What are we supposed to do about it?' asked Mahon indignantly. 'I'm a finance man, not a health expert.' His clean shaven chin and closed cropped blond hair gave him a school-boy appearance, possibly why Bateman felt an urge to give him six of the best.

'There've been grumblings in the Press,' admitted Sharp. 'We need to be seen to be doing some sort of investigation. I wouldn't want to be the one to stand up in front of a news conference and say we haven't a clue what's going on and nor are we doing anything to find out what is.'

'Quite,' said Bateman. 'It may or may not be important in the grand scheme of things, but it's important to the electorate. They want an explanation of why their grandparents are keeling over like nine pins.'

'I suppose it would be one up on the Germans if we got to the punch first,' mumbled Mahon.

'Very patriotic,' said Bateman with a smile. 'So any suggestions as to what else we could do?'

'Check out space dust, solar winds, cosmic rays,' muttered Sharp insincerely.

'It could be Iranian bio weapons, or dodgy Chinese merchandise,' said Mahon. His fellows looked at him surprised. 'They could be emitting something lethal from the paint or plastic.'

Bateman looked as if he'd hoped for something more substantial but had received the sort of answer he'd come to expect. He sighed and motioned for his secretary, who'd been sitting quietly near the door, to take a memorandum. 'I want reports from each government department as to how this problem of excessive deaths during the summer affected them - whether literally through staffing or from adverse correspondence etc.'

His secretary scribbled then paused, expecting more. 'At the next Cabinet meeting I need reports from Works and Pensions, and the Treasury Secretaries as to how it's affecting us financially, with projections for the future,' Bateman added after a pause.

'May I just clarify?' asked the secretary, politely. A small mousey man looking as one would expect Uriah Heep to look. Mahon was surprised he didn't tug his forelock and proclaim himself to be ''umble'. 'These reports from each department, what are they reporting on?'

Bateman rolled his eyes. 'Each department is to investigate anything within their sphere which might have caused the deaths of unrelated people across two continents.'

'Forgive me, sir,' said the secretary, 'but how could the Justice Department, for example, investigate the summer deaths?'

Bateman looked at him as if he didn't wish to be bothered by trivialities. 'Suppose all those who died received a summons, parking fine or something which may have spread a virus. Get them to use their imaginations.'

'That would include King Charles, would it?' asked the secretary slyly.

Bateman shot him a scornful look. 'Don't be ridiculous man! The King's death has nothing to do with the deaths in the summer.'

'Forgive me, sir,' said the secretary, 'but the King was over sixty and died suddenly without having shown any previous sign of illness … much the same as many victims of the summer … incident.'

Bateman was speechless with anger at this suggestion. Finally able to contain himself he simple bit out, 'just get them to report any noticeable effects.' The secretary bowed and left the room.

Bateman watched the door close, breathed out heavily, then leaned forward and rested his hands on the table looking businesslike. 'Now for the funeral.'

~*~

Sean Dalton, Norleigh's Registrar, and Oliver Nicolson, Sudcliff's Coroner, met for lunch at the Green Garden, the most expensive restaurant in Sudcliff. Sean's seared steak was medium rare with a delicious and syrupy red wine sauce, while Oliver's lemon chicken was roasted to perfection, the sauce had wonderful piquancy, and his knife slid effortlessly through his potatoes.

'Shame about the King,' said Sean after a pause of a few minutes while both men chewed appreciatively on their lunch and looked around at their fellow diners. 'I liked the way he handled environmental issues.'

'It was always difficult for him … coming from a privileged position but telling us lesser mortals what we should be doing,' agreed Oliver.

'Led by example … up to a point,' said Sean.

With a forkful of chicken on its way to his mouth, Oliver introduced a new topic. 'You know there've been more of the benign, pre-malignant neoplastic cell growths in the majority of the autopsies carried out over the last few weeks.' His keen birdlike appearance gave his words authority. Sean scowled as if he didn't wish to discuss other people's insides while filling his own already ample stomach.

Oliver ignored him and continued. 'The growth of cells appears extremely rapid, almost unnaturally so, and it's not coordinated with the normal tissues around it. It seems the growths persist in the same excessive manner as earlier in the summer, and no evidence of any causal stimuli has been found, certainly not a heat wave.'

'I've heard most are not progressive … They haven't developed into full blown cancers,' agreed Sean. 'Certainly few were diagnosed as such prior to death.'

'The reports I've seen suggest growth is usually dependent on a single population of cells - clones descended from a single progenitor cell. One of the doctors suggests it's implying the same genetic anomaly amongst the victims.' Oliver chewed thoughtfully. 'How on earth could that happen?

'The egg-heads'll sort it out; there're enough of them looking into the problem,' said Sean confidently. He folded his stiff linen napkin neatly onto the table beside him and ordered the dessert menu. He felt indulgent and ordered passion fruit trifle and a coffee liqueur, while Oliver plumped for orange and saffron syrup cake and a glass of brandy - he was taking the afternoon off to visit his aunt in Westwater and needed some Dutch courage.

'Even if this phenomenon has something to do with the deaths, it's still odd having the older generation dying off like that. You suddenly feel more aware of them ... by their absence, if you know what I mean,' he said, thinking of Aunt Amelia and her several hundred thousands in property and investments.

'Can't say I miss them much ... All those little old ladies crossing the road slowly and old men in flat caps crashing their cars into immobile objects.' Sean smiled. 'What came of that inquest you decided to hold in August?'

'Nothing concrete. The verdict was vague ... cause of death likely to be natural but of unknown origin. At least it's official and was open to public debate. I don't think anyone was especially pleased or inspired.'

'I did warn you,' said Sean, waving a knowing finger at his colleague. He drank the last of his coffee. 'I'm off,' he concluded getting to his feet. 'You can pay.'

'My expense account is bigger than yours,' acknowledged Oliver, much to Sean's annoyance, and after settling the bill, they both left; Sean to his office, Oliver to Westwater, via a taxi, to see about his inheritance.

~*~

Dr Prudence Richards was in yet another laboratory. She mused on how much of her life had been spent in large cold rooms with sinks, gas taps, glassware and the strong smell of chemicals. In a dimly lit office to one side of this particular laboratory, Professor Fallon was hunched over his computer, frowning. A few years older than Dr Richards, she had known him since she had begun her scientific career as a laboratory assistant at Cambridge. Back then he had only recently achieved his professorship and had been young and enthusiastic, ready to change the world. A straggly man with dull grey hair sticking out like a scarecrows, his coat had many coloured stains, the laces from his loafers hanging loose, nicotine marking his fingers, and his general aura of untidiness all lent itself to all clichés about mad professors. His genius could not be faulted however, which is why Dr Richards stood on the threshold of his office waiting patiently.

After a few moments he became aware of her presence and looked over the top of his dirty glasses. 'Pru,' he began unpromisingly. 'Long time, no see.' He managed a mischievous smile.

Prudence rolled her eyes. She would normally have shown anyone who called her Pru the full name on her badge, but didn't bother on this occasion; she knew it would do no good and she needed Ian's help. 'The large number of deaths which occurred over the summer,' she began going straight to the point as usual. 'I'd like you to do some deeper research into what might have caused it.'

'I thought the Prime Minister did a good job letting us know about poor old Charlie, don't you? All those years as understudy and only made it a couple himself.'

Prudence thought this irrelevant and continued as if he hadn't spoken. 'We've managed to eliminate likely chemical or airborne causes, so think we should look deeper for an internal reason.'

'When the Queen died a couple of years ago, she was over eighty. King Charles was a little older than me.'

'I understand this phenomenon has also caused problems on the continent and in the United States. I haven't heard of anywhere else, but then I don't have time to watch much news.'

'How old are you?' Ian asked. Anyone overhearing them might think they were on different telephone calls.

Prudence took a deep breath and finally answered his question. 'Fifty five,' she said with a sigh.

'I'm sixty. I expect to be dead by the end of the month,' he said cheerfully. Prudence looked shocked and opened her mouth to speak but couldn't think of anything. He continued; 'I've been in touch with the Registrars of the four surrounding counties. People have either died at home, at work or in hospital, but we're now getting to the stage where we can name all those people alive today who're over sixty.'

His pale grey eyes washed over her searching for a reaction. Did she already know? Was she worried about anyone close to her? Was she really only thinking of the bigger picture?

'I'm lucky enough to work in a hospital where after the initial shock of having people dying in droves, we've arranged a system to cope. I'm well aware of the age group of those who've been affected. What I want to do is discover what caused it and stop it,' she said.

'Before you die too.'

'Before anyone else dies.'

They looked at each other for a few moments, like sparing cockerels. 'I have thirty-odd years of experience, you even more. We have to find out what's going on before we're affected …'

'Or there won't be anyone else around to solve it … That's what you're thinking.'

Prudence nodded and fell into a chair propped in front of a filing cabinet, unaware of the dead spider plant tickling the back of her neck. 'I'm trying not to let my juniors see how worried I am. I'm talking to colleagues working at various agencies to trace what it might be within their field of expertise – biological, chemical, radioactive, even extraterrestrial. It could take a while to analyse everything before we identify what's causing the problem.'

'And then we have to think of a way of combating it,' concluded Ian. His voice had changed from its normal gruff argumentative tone to something smoother and more reassuring. 'Who else have you got looking into biology?'

'Dr Peter Yeoman,' said Prudence getting back some of her normal assurance.

Ian raised a thick grey eyebrow. 'Yeoman Toeman he's known as. Full of bright ideas and promises … not good at seeing them to their natural conclusion … Says anything to get another grant.'

'He's got better as he's matured. Anyway, there aren't many people who could do what I'm asking. Can you help?'

''Course I can. What have you got for me?'

Prudence bent to pick up the cool box type carrier just outside of the door which proclaimed to contain human tissue samples. 'These are from a selection of people who have died at various times over the last three months.'

'None of His Majesty's I suppose.'

Prudence ignored him and carried on. 'Here's the list of details which matches each sample. If you can find anything in the DNA which might give us a clue, I'd be eternally grateful.'

'Assuming eternally isn't longer than the end of the month,' said Ian with a grin.

Prudence sighed, gave Ian a brief smile then left.

He opened the box and looked through the small boxes of samples and the card index for each. He scrubbed up, dressed in a green paper disposable uniform and entered his air controlled laboratory. He began preparing the first sample, a piece of heart muscle from Mrs Danson who supposedly died from heat stroke. While working he listened to Radio Two. Just after three o'clock the news explained to him that the Duchess of Cornwall had died shortly after one o'clock, apparently as a result of the shock of Charles' death the day before. As if nothing had happened, Ian carried on working knowing time was against him.

~*~

'Such a shock hearing about Camilla like that,' said Millie Hallam to her friend Jane as they listened to the radio behind the reception desk of the Grand Hotel in Eastdell. Eastdell was a small mostly Georgian town north east of Sudcliff once famous for its wool and cloth trade, but it had declined considerably in recent decades. With a good twice weekly local market, it had a wide range of local rather than the usual high street brand shops. The Grand Hotel was the most prominent building in the central market square but had run to seed.

'Not really,' said Jane, filing her nails. 'She was older ... wasn't she?'

'What's that got to do with it?' said Millie horrified. 'The poor woman had just lost her husband. It's hardly surprising.'

'My gran died just after granddad died. They said that was shock.'

'She wasn't one of those old people who're dying, was she?' asked Millie, forgetting about the Duchess.

'No. They died a couple of years ago. Has anyone you know died of this thing in the summer?' asked Jane, blowing her nails and rubbing the debris off onto her skirt.

'My neighbour was rushed to hospital, never came back, and the bloke in the fishmongers where Grant gets his haddock died then too. He died just like that,' she said, clicking her fingers. 'There wasn't anything seriously wrong with him before that as far as I know.'

'Glad I'm not over sixty,' said Jane who then paid attention to the two men who had just dropped their briefcases and suitcases on the floor beside the counter. As they were regulars Jane dealt with them competently enough.

Millie retreated to the small office behind the desk and checked her e-mails. One was from her daughter Ida. *Need to borrow the car for party this evening - pick you up at six. Did you see the Prime Minister had been taken to hospital, suspected heart attack? Can I borrow your red top for this evening?* Millie clicked onto the BBC website for an update on Mr Bateman. To her great surprise, she found the lead article was explaining Mr Sharp would be taking over following the death of the Prime Minister less than an hour ago.

'How does it know?' she asked Jane who came in to see what had kept her friend from returning to the desk.

'How does what know what?' Jane asked.

'How does it know how old people are?'

'What's *it*?'

'Whatever's killing everyone over sixty. How does it know they're over sixty?'

Jane shrugged. 'There can't be an *it* because lots of people are dying. It's just coincidence.'

Millie gave Jane an incredulous look. 'How can you say it's coincidence? There must be a reason for all these people dying.'

'Why must there?' queried Jane. 'Why does everything have to have an explanation? For all we know God's decided there are too many people on the Earth and anyone over sixty is to be terminated.' She said the last word in a blood curdling voice and smiled.

'How old are you?' Millie asked through narrowed eyes.

'Thirty one.'

'I bet you wouldn't be so flip if you were fifty nine.'

'Might be. Might be fed up with life by the time I'm fifty nine and be glad to go.'

'Don't say that!' said Millie hotly. 'You've got lots going for you, you have.'

'Like what?' asked Jane curiously.

'That bloke you've got; your figure, your looks, and your health. Lots of things,' Millie trailed off weakly. 'Got anyone you care about who'd miss you if you died?' she added to complete her argument.

'*That bloke*,' Jane said, curling her fingers around the words, 'might miss me, but he'd find someone else quick enough.'

'I'd miss you,' said Millie, patting her shoulder and making Jane smile.

'Pity about Bateman. I voted for him,' said Jane nodding at the computer screen still showing details of the death of the Prime Minster.

'Grant did too. I'll get him to get some meat on the way home from the surgery. I need cheering up,' said Millie reaching for the telephone.

'Must be weird being married to a dentist,' muttered Jane. 'I'd always be worried about what he's thinking when I smile at him.'

'He thinks the same thing every other man does when I smile at them,' said Millie with a cheeky grin. Jane raised an inquisitive eyebrow. 'How far will I go?' Millie concluded in a breathy whisper.

Jane's jaw dropped but another guest distracted her and life returned to normal.

~*~

Sharp, now Prime Minister rode in the back of the black chauffer driven Jaguar with his new Deputy John Mahon. The plane trees lining The Mall were shedding golden and russet leaves across the road, blown about by a high wind. 'I know he'd been under a lot of strain with making decisions about the economy and the escalating threat in the Middle East, but I didn't think Norman was ill at all.'

'He worked fifteen or sixteen hours a day, wore out two secretaries and a valet,' said Mahon in all seriousness. 'It'll be hard to follow him.' This he said looking straight at his colleague as if considering whether he thought Sharp was up to it.

Sharp sat back into the red leather upholstery and ran a finger down his black tie - he'd been wearing black ties a lot lately so had several. Their journey to Buckingham Palace wouldn't take long but neither man was looking forward to the interview. 'How do you offer condolences to a man on the loss of his father while congratulating him on attaining something he had been groomed for all his life?' he asked.

'Are you going to pursue this idea of Bateman's of discovering the source of why so many older people have been dying?' asked Mahon, almost adding as Bateman was one, but choosing not to.

Sharp frowned and nodded. 'I'll make sure the Departments carry on looking, but I still don't think of it as a priority. It could end up being a colossal waste of money just when we're short. Anyway,' he gave Mahon a grin, 'they'll be fewer pensions to pay out.'

He continued. 'I've heard from the Transport Department saying it's meant large numbers of driving licences being cancelled and the price of second-hand cars has dropped ... there being more of them.' Sharp absently stared out of the window. 'And the Diplomatic Service has reported a lot of their men - and women - abroad have died too; serves them right for employing old codgers as diplomats.'

'Quite a few other heads of state have died in the last few weeks,' said Mahon softly. 'We're not the only ones having state funerals.' They both fell into contemplative silence again for a few moments.

'You've not heard from the Fraud Squad? asked Mahon.

'How do you mean?' asked Sharp who'd been thinking about whether he could pick and chose which foreign funeral to go to – he fancied the Maldives.

'With all the pensioners dying in such large numbers, it's hard to keep up with the paperwork,' Mahon explained, pleased he knew something his superior didn't. 'People are still claiming and collecting pensions for people who died months ago. It could take a while to sort it all out.'

Sharp scowled. 'What is the world coming to?'

The car rolled through the gates of Buckingham Palace and glided towards the entrance. 'God, I wish I was anyone else just now,' muttered Sharp. Mahon found himself nodding in agreement as a lithe young man opened the doors for them to alight.

~*~

Ida collected Millie from the Grand Hotel at six o'clock as promised and they dropped Jane not far from her flat.

'Hi Mum,' said Millie's son Will as he stooped to kiss her cheek. 'You look nice,' he added with a gentle smile as he regained his full height.

'No you can't,' said Millie as she slammed the door behind her with her foot. She shifted the shopping she was carrying to a more comfortable position and led him to the kitchen.

'Can't what?' he asked, running a hand through his thick shaggy brown hair.

'Whatever it is you're creeping round me for,' said Millie with a fond smile as she unpacked packets of pasta, olives and tinned tomatoes and put them in the cupboard.

'That's mean and presumptuous,' said Will sulkily, pouting. 'I only wanted to borrow the car for the evening.'

'Is that all?' said Millie as if it were the easiest thing he could ask her for other than a spare kidney. 'Ida beat you to it and asked for the car this afternoon.'

'She could walk, it's not far … to the club,' growled Will.

'Bloody cheek!' replied Ida, helping her mother put bleach and washing powder under the sink. 'Where do you want to go in mum's car?'

'There's a debate at Uni this evening,' said Will enthusiastically. 'Some of us have decided we'd like to go.' He paused, looking shyly at his feet. 'Alexis Watts said she might come along.' Millie and Ida both straightened to look at him. 'They're going to debate why so many people died in the summer, why it seems to be starting again and what we think they should be doing about it.'

'Alexis. I see,' said Millie with a wry smile. 'Bit up-market for you isn't she?'

‘She’s a *friend*,’ said Will, colouring to letter box red.

‘Also pretty and from a rich family. Good for you son.’ Millie reached up and patted him on his shoulder. ‘You still can’t have the car. Bike or go on the bus.’

Grant Hallam walked through the front door at that moment and called hello to the rest of his family.

‘Dad, can I borrow your car this evening?’ asked Will before Grant had got as far as the kitchen.

‘He has a date with Alexis Watts,’ teased Millie, giving Grant a kiss on the lips. ‘How have you got on today?’

‘If I have many more cancellations I shall have to start taking on National Health patients again,’ said Grant with a sigh as he filled the kettle.

‘Is that still because of older people? I thought that had all stopped now its turned colder,’ said Millie surprised. She started to prepare a Bolognese sauce with the minced beef Grant had brought to go with the pasta.

‘That’s what the debate is about this evening. It’s open to anyone; you should come too, Dad,’ said Will suddenly impassioned.

‘What debate?’ asked Grant.

‘At the Uni. There’re people from various organisations going to give their opinions and then we present further questions and make suggestions of other avenues to explore. No one knows what it is and with the royals dying, it’s become more important again.’

‘Sounds interesting. How about it love?’ asked Grant.

‘I’ve got art,’ said Millie, shooting a quick glance at Will.

‘Ida, would you be interested?’

‘Not really Dad. I’m going round to Sharon’s this evening to work on a maths project.’

‘This before or after you go to the club?’ asked Millie slyly. Ida blushed and looked at her shoes.

‘Oh, what geniuses we have produced,’ said Grant with a smile. ‘I’ll give you a lift son, and we can pick up Alexis too.’

With supper finished and cleared away, the suburban Eastdell house emptied of its dwellers. Having driven a winding route to collect Alexis from her lodgings in Comfortby on the other side of Eastdell, Grant found a parking space outside the Hall at Sudcliff University with difficulty. 'Seems very popular this debate,' he pointed out as Will spotted a space. Sodium lights cast an orange glow over the area as they joined the thread of people heading towards the brick buildings.

'It means a lot to people, to know why their loved ones have died like that,' said Alexis softly.

'Sorry love, I didn't mean it wasn't important,' said Grant turning to smile at the girl, 'but I wasn't expecting this many people to come.'

They managed to find seats at the back of the main auditorium which seated five hundred. On the stage far below, five people were sitting staring back at their audience. The University Chancellor, presiding over the meeting, rose and introduced each delegate and the debate began.

First to speak was Dr Prudence Richards from Sudcliff General Hospital who also headed the national medical research team. She explained what the medical evidence showed, or rather didn't show, so far.

A short red faced man from the Environment Agency stood after Prudence had finished, explaining what work the Agency had done to trace anything in the air or water supply which might have caused illness or death, but again reported nothing had been found.

Following him was Martin Hayton, Conservative MP for Eastdell who said the issue was not bound just to Eastdell or indeed England, but was also evident in many continental countries, and the United States. He also confirmed that Mr Bateman had instructed heads of all ministerial departments to send any findings to Downing Street, which Mr Sharp would be continuing.

The fourth speaker was the Reverend Rupert Hilliard, vicar of Comfortby, who put forward what the Church of England was doing in the crisis, mostly conducting three or four funerals a day, offering counselling to the bereaved, and giving practical advice and help to those left to sort out the affairs of the deceased.

At the end, the Chancellor stood and asked the floor for questions. After the initial barrage during which he ignored everyone until they quietened down, he methodically pointed to people with a baton and asked if they had a question.

'My question is for Dr Richards,' said a young looking man, smartly dressed in a shirt and tie, but revealing jeans beneath his jacket when he stood to pose his question.

'Your name sir?' asked the Chancellor.

'Dr Pete Yeoman,' replied the young man. Prudence peered at him over the top of the glasses she was only wearing to give the impression of professionalism. 'My question is what is being done to investigate possible disease vectors, air borne plague, or even bio-weapons?' A murmur swept across the auditorium like a verbal Mexican wave. The Chancellor glared everyone to silence.

Prudence stood and walked slowly to the lectern. 'As you know Dr Yeoman, autopsies carried out since the summer crisis have shown no consistent evidence of any known disease, whether natural or man-made. It would be foolish and irresponsible to start rumours that it might be due to any kind of terrorist attack.'

'In which case,' he continued, 'are you looking for traces of *unknown* diseases, such as induced by prions, for example?'

Dr Richards had a feeling he was leading her somewhere, but with five hundred people waiting for her response, she couldn't do anything but answer. 'Professor Fallon is investigating the possibility of cellular disorders.'

'Professor Fallon, the theoretical geneticist?' he asked, knowing the answer.

'I believe he was your professor when you studied here, Dr Yeoman. He still holds his position and is well respected at the University.'

'Well respected ... but out of date,' said Dr Yeoman.

The Chancellor stood. 'We'll have another question, Dr Yeoman, and will people kindly restrict themselves to one question and not start a conversation!' A ripple of laughter followed him as he raised his stick once more to choose another questioner.

'Young lady in green,' he said, thinking she looked safer.

'Alexis Watts. My grandparents died in August,' she began, having risen to her feet at the summons. 'My mother and I would like to start a support group for grieving relatives such as ourselves. Could anyone suggest how I go about that?'

Martin Hayton stood and jumped at the lectern, grateful to be able to answer a question positively. 'That's a marvellous idea Miss ... Watts. If you contact my secretary at the constituency office, she can put you in touch with the right people. I think you'll find small groups have already been set up in other parts of the country, and possibly a few unofficial ones amongst neighbours.' He nodded and regained his seat feeling pleased with himself.

The Chancellor wielded his pointer again and it rested in front of a dark young woman in a long black leather coat, who stood confidently. 'If I read the poster correctly, this is supposed to be a debate,' she said.

'Quite right. Your name madam?' asked the Chancellor.

'Eartha Zull. *The Eastdell Reporter*. From what I can gather, this assembly doesn't know what's going on, neither does it know what to do about it.' A ripple of agreement and lots of nodding heads filled the pause she left. 'Is there to be any overarching plan in finding out what caused all these deaths?'

Prudence rose again. 'The medical profession is currently best placed to manage any plan. As I explained, I've been working with various colleagues in this town, at county level and nationally. Tomorrow, in accordance with the late Mr Bateman's wishes, I'm attending a meeting with the Minister of Health, and together with other leading medical professionals, we will confirm a coordinated programme of research.'

'How long is that going to take to set up?' asked Eartha, ignoring the Chancellor's wish to point at someone else with his baton.

'As research is currently ongoing, it will merely be to sort out gaps and overlaps. A matter of days,' replied Prudence optimistically.

'And when will we have an answer?' asked Eartha.

'That depends on how long it takes us to find the cause,' said Prudence in her best headmistress voice.

'How long is a piece of string,' said the buoyant Chancellor. 'Thank you Ms Zull. Next.' He continued to find victims and the debate continued for another hour, but as no one could really answer any questions other than with negative generalisations, it was wound up without a resolution. Grant and Will took a quiet and thoughtful Alexis home.

'I'm sorry they couldn't be more helpful, but at least you put your question,' Grant said as he walked her to her door.

'All those people trying to sort it out and all I want is someone to comfort me,' she said looking at her shoes. 'I feel so selfish.'

'Nonsense,' said Grant. 'You've lost two very precious people; people you've known all your life. You can't expect to forget them as if they'd never existed. Of course you need comfort and you've recognised that many other people do too, and all credit to you.'

'Will you come in?' asked Alexis. 'I've got some proper coffee somewhere.'

Grant shook his head saying it was late and he didn't want to keep Millie waiting, although in view of what they'd just discussed, it seemed cowardly. He and Will drove home.

Georgina, Alexis' flatmate lay languidly on the sofa, staring into space. She hadn't heard the door open or Alexis' whispered conversation. She sat up straight when Alexis slouched into the room and dropped onto the sofa beside her. 'What was the debate like?' she asked as if trying to stir herself, but failing.

Alexis explained, 'assuming everyone was telling the truth, they don't know why so many people died this summer, but apparently it's started again.

'I'm sorry about your uncle, Georgie and how you feel about his death. I wished I could do something to help you, so I asked about support groups.'

Georgina smiled a grateful smile. 'Studying is the best cure for me. I know that's what he'd have wanted ... why he supported me. I only get melancholy like this when I'm home ... which isn't fair on you,' she said, giving her friend a hug. 'That's why I was glad when you said you were going to the debate. Unfortunately it meant I spent the evening brooding instead of doing something more positive. I must try harder.'

'You're doing marvellously. I'm bushed. I'm for bed. Don't stay up too much longer.'

Alexis left for her bedroom across the hall, leaving Georgina to relapse into her silent reverie once more, not even stirring when she heard Alexis softly crying in her room.

~*~

Having left the debate early when he realised nothing new was being put forward, Corin Lister drew up in his Astra and parked outside the warehouse of Neil & Son's Limited, importers and exporters of machine parts. Despite this warehouse being situated in deepest Eastdell and him being a Westwater reporter, he had arranged to speak to security guard David Thomas after nine o'clock.

'You're one of the few people I've spoken to who'll admit they didn't get on with the relation who's died,' said Corin honestly.

'Well either everyone else is lying ... or I'm just really unlucky with my choice of father,' said David calmly as they walked and talked. The moonlight was drowned out by the security lighting of the warehouse yard.

'You're Catherine Thomas's brother aren't you?'

'No, I can't get you an autograph ... or a date,' said David lifting his torch to check a window at the back of the warehouse.

Corin smiled. 'Isn't this place alarmed?' he asked suddenly curious.

'Of course it is, but it's a big site. Neil's prefer the personal touch.'

'How long have you worked here?'

'Twelve years ... just about.'

'Enjoy it?'

'It's a job. I thought you wanted a story?'

'Sorry ... just getting a flavour of your character.' The cold air distilled their breath as they walked in silence for a few moments.

'You say you held your father responsible for your mother's early death. What exactly did he do?'

'All the time they were married he belittled her, found fault, picked holes, complained. She couldn't do anything right no matter how hard she tried. She gave up in the end, switched off and didn't bother any more. I could tell you the day it happened.'

Corin looked at David and encouraged him to go on.

'I came home from school and found her sitting at the top of the stairs staring into space. Dad had very old fashioned ideas so she was a housewife and mother; never allowed to have a job or any hobbies which didn't directly benefit the family … you know like sewing and cooking. She didn't join any clubs or groups and didn't even go to church or anything like that.'

David checked a door and shone his torch through a window. 'I don't know if he ever hit her … he certainly hit me and Catherine often enough … for minor discretions mostly. We didn't do anything major … he'd probably have whipped us to death,' he said with a smile.

'Anyway I came home to find her sitting there at the top of the stairs. Dad would be home shortly after me … he didn't stay at school to work, he always did his preparation in the living room and we had to be quiet and get on with our homework and not watch telly … that was for him to watch wrestling, boxing and war films on.

'She didn't move when I spoke to her, didn't blink when I touched her … she just sat there and stared.' David rattled another door to check it was secure. 'When dad came home his dinner wasn't ready, not even a pot of tea brewing. He created merry hell saying he went out each day to earn money and all she had to do was make his home clean and provide him with meals. She'd come downstairs by this time, but just stared at him as if she'd never seen him before and didn't understand what he was ranting on about.'

David stopped looking and checking, standing still in the floodlit courtyard with a blank expression on his face. 'I was scared stiff. I had no idea what he was going to do to her - or me come to that - if she didn't get him his tea ready. He ranted a bit more and then noticed she hadn't moved or spoken. He grabbed her and shook her … no response. I chipped in she was ill and needed a doctor and he clouted me round the ear hole for being cheeky.' David smiled ironically at this memory.

'Catherine came home from the girl's High School just after that … she'd used the bus. She agreed with me that something was wrong with mum and we eventually persuaded him to call the doctor. She was diagnosed with Alzheimer's and the doctor said he'd never known a case of deterioration so badly or so quickly.'

David checked the last door on his round and headed back to his cosy office where he made a cup of coffee for them both.

'A few years back she died in the nursing home she'd lived in for ten years. They must have been the happiest of her life. She was cared for, fed and looked after.

She had friends and visitors. She could make things and look after the birds. She fed the birds when she went home for visits.

'Catherine left home as soon as she could and went into acting. I got a job here. Mum got a bit better, had moments when she knew who and where she was. She helped Catherine a lot when she was out of work, not that that was very often.

'We both feel if she'd married someone else ... someone normal ... she'd have had a happy life and probably still be alive today.' He stood and swilled his remaining undrunk coffee down the sink.

'I hated my father ... I will always hate my father, not for anything he did to me ... I probably deserved it, right little tear away I was at times. But he killed mum and he tried hard to ruin Catherine's career. She's never had a stable relationship because she's scared all men might turn out to be like him.'

They walked out of the door towards Corin's car. 'I hated my father. Print it if you like - it makes no difference to me.'

Corin drove home eternally grateful he had had a generous and understanding father and reflected that Mr Thomas, though a relic, was probably typical of men a hundred or so year's ago. He shuddered as he parked his car and locked his front door behind him, glancing briefly at the top of the stairs.

Chapter five

Tuesday 15th to Sunday 20th December 2015

'You know,' said Mick Quinn as he propped up the bar of The Colourman in Westwater, 'I'm getting sick of writing obituaries. You'd think they could parcel it out a bit.'

Quinn wrote for the *Sudcliff Daily Scoop* and had been interviewing the widow of Sudcliff Rangers rugby club manager who lived in the posh end of Westwater. With him on this occasion was his scruffy colleague Daryl Verner of similar late middle age and stocky build as himself, and Dustin Timms and Corin Lister from *The Westwater Illumination*, which as a weekly paper was not a real competitor and the journalists from both papers were often seen to mingle. These two younger men swapped a glance and smiled. 'You don't do obituaries do you,' noted Mick.

'We do profiles, and I agree, there seem to have been rather a lot of those over the past few months,' said Corin.

'I've been getting to know the history of the Royal Family quite well,' Daryl said confidently. 'What sort of King do you think William's going to make?' he asked generally.

Dustin shrugged. 'Only been doing the job a couple of months, give him time.'

'Must still be in shock from losing those closest to him; everyone who could have given him proper advice.'

'He'll have advisers,' said Corin.

'A lot of the court elders have gone too of course,' replied Daryl. 'It's not just the crowned heads which have rolled; most of the top jobs are vacant now their occupants have snuffed it.'

Corin winced at his choice of words. 'Have you heard anything about Government reports that they still haven't a clue what caused it all.'

'No,' said Mick. 'But I've heard this thing was global, not just a European problem, the older generation's died off everywhere in the world, as far as we know.'

'That must effect poorer countries even more than this one,' suggested Corin, thoughtfully replacing his glass on the bar. The others looked blankly at him. 'Other cultures who look up to their elders and don't just sweep them under the carpet once they get old and embarrassing like we do.' The others exchanged knowing looks; he was off again.

'Think about it. Many Western countries have much larger older populations, so the loss of a generation had less impact initially, except the usual passing on of land, wealth and title as elsewhere; just earlier than anticipated. People feel sorry about it but appreciate the long lives these people have led.

'In Third World countries, life may be more rustic and simple, but they've lost cultural wisdom. The elders whose advice and council has been heeded for thousands of years have gone, leaving a vacuum for the younger generations to fight amongst themselves for and determine leadership. Some rural communities who respect their elders are severely traumatised ... Chinese, African tribes and Indian villages.' Corin paused before adding a startling fact. 'You know, I read somewhere a few years ago the Chinese population was aging since they started that single child thing. I think it said sixteen per cent was over sixty years old. If that's true, they've lost sixteen percent of their population. That's nearly two hundred *million* people have died in China since the summer ... the size of the population of the United States.' This thought took a while to sink in and silenced the most cynical of reporters for several minutes.

'He's right,' admitted Mick quietly. 'As well as having to deal with all the extra deaths, if you read foreign reports, there's much more turf warfare and civil infighting going on even than ten years ago. Arms traders must be doing a roaring trade.'

'It's odd how things have changed here over the past couple of months though,' said Daryl softly after a few moments ponderous silence. 'Money's shifted from one group of people to their children in larger amounts and earlier than normal. Some groups have suffered - ones you mightn't think of at first like charities who rely on retired volunteers, nursing homes and geriatric wards obviously, and pension funds – it must be really hard to sell pensions these days,' he laughed and the others agreed. 'Other businesses have thrived though; funeral directors and the churches for starters, then builders and solicitors. Bizarrely, with some people retiring earlier, they've left gaps in the employment market, creating jobs as well as having more money to spend on home improvements and holidays, white goods and leisure.'

'They say international co-operation has taken an unexpected turn for the better and trade's improved,' added Mick with a grin.

'We're importing even more food than usual though. It seems a lot of the farmers in this country were over sixty,' added Corin.

'So what's happening to all their farms?' asked Dustin, struggling to keep up.

'The land's passing to their children – or to their bank – and being sold. We'll live to regret that,' predicted Corin

'You hope,' said Mick quietly into his beer glass before draining it. Corin shot him a concerned look.

'But generally, from what we've been saying, it's not actually that bad a thing that people aren't living to be ninety or a hundred ...,' stated Dustin. Three surprised faces greeted his comment. 'The Government's paying out less in pensions, less demand on the National Health, there are more jobs for younger people, but some businesses are suffering as a consequence. There're fewer people in the world to feed and fewer people at home burning coal and gas so global warming's decreasing ...' he paused. Mick handed him another pint. 'Thanks mate. All I'm saying is, unpleasant as it may be to lose loved ones and colleagues, is it really that bad in the grand scheme of things?'

'Does anyone else find his attitude disturbing or is it just me?' asked Corin, looking around the table.

'It's disturbing,' said Daryl, 'especially for anyone not far from reaching sixty. Makes the phrase *your contract is terminated* take on a whole new meaning.' The others laughed, except the frowning Corin.

'You don't seem to appreciate the social consequences of losing a whole generation.'

'We read your piece after Victor died,' said Daryl. 'We know how you feel about it.'

'Just suppose it was the other end of the age scale ... what if it had been children who'd died off ... would everyone be so calm about this thing then?' This gave the others food for thought and it was clearly an indigestible idea.

'Just because it's people who've lived their lives and are nearer the end anyway doesn't mean they aren't entitled to live out those remaining years without being picked off by ... this thing,' said Corin firmly. 'If children had died, we'd be petitioning Parliament, staging rallies, blockading research laboratories until they came up with an answer ... and a solution.'

The others exchanged a worried glance, each having a horrible feeling Corin was right. 'I'm not going to sit back without so much as a murmur and accept that everyone over a certain age has been wiped out. I intend to do something about it.' He fell silent, scowling. He finished his drink and left his colleagues to consider what he had said.

'He's a bit sensitive,' said Daryl pointing his glass at the closing door.

'He's a frustrated poet,' said Dustin; 'needs love and understanding. He's probably right though.' He followed his friend, leaving the older *Daily Scoop* men to continue drinking in rueful silence.

Dustin caught up with Corin as he reached his car. 'You're doing too much work on this death business. See if you can get transferred onto the sports section; there's some good football matches coming up soon and no players have died from this thing.'

Corin smiled at his friend as he started the engine. 'Nice try, but I'm fine. I want to know just what this plague was ... in case it starts again.' Dustin removed his hand from the roof as Corin drove off and with a sigh, turned to find his own car.

Jim and Valerie Cahill left The Colourman at the same time, following Dustin a short way down the road before turning left at the traffic lights and travelling another few miles home in the suburbs of Summerton.

'You should really take a holiday,' said Valerie, as they got out of the car in the newly extended double garage and took the few bags of shopping from the boot. 'You've hardly stopped working for the past four months. Take a week off now it's Christmas.'

Jim sighed and followed her into the recently refitted kitchen. 'I'd feel I was letting people down if I had to put them off. Some people have to wait weeks as it is.'

'You're worried people are going to these new fast funeral outlets rather than having a proper service,' chastised Valerie. 'You're making a good enough living to take a week off, surely.' Leaving her doubtful husband to put the shopping away, she walked to the cottage next door to where Judy McVey had been looking after her children.

'It's only me,' she called as she walked in at the back door to be jumped on by a boisterous yellow Labrador named Suzie.

'I'm in here,' said Judy, popping into the kitchen and ducking back into the small side room she used as her office. 'Come on Suz, leave the nice lady alone.' She beckoned the dog over and Suzie trotted to her happily, had her head ruffled then went straight back to Valerie, tail thumping on furniture and doorways throughout. 'Daft animal.'

Valerie gave her a warm smile and greeted her children; Frank, a joyful ten year old, and a more sedate Holly aged six. 'You haven't been any trouble I hope?' asked Valerie, looking for a negative answer.

Both children shook their heads and Judy said, 'little angels, as always.'

Judy finished shutting down her computer and joined her friends around the kitchen table where the children finished off milk and digestive biscuits. Even though Judy had been doing her a favour at short notice, Valerie wondered how she would get them to eat their tea.

'Have you got everything sorted?' Judy asked.

'Yes. We've seen the planners, did the shopping and had a word with Wayne at the Colourman; his father Pete only died a couple of weeks ago, poor man.' Valerie stopped there, not wishing to discuss the town's deceased in the children's presence – they got enough of that at home.

'You two pop and make sure you've left the living room tidy while I have a word with Judy about our loft,' she added, pointing the children in the right direction.

As anything they needed to discuss about the loft conversion she was designing for the Cahills could safely be discussed in front of the children, them being banished made Judy lean forward, anticipating something juicy. 'I'm worried about Jim,' was all Valerie said softly.

Judy, a little disappointed, sat back again. 'What's wrong with him?'

'Oh nothing major. He's feeling the strain, I can tell.' She paused and let her finger follow the grain of the beech worktop. 'He's used to dealing with bereaved relatives, but he sees so many each day … and his office is open six days a week, and then he goes in on Sundays to catch up. I'm just worried. I do what I can but I'm working too and he won't take a holiday because he says he'd be letting people down.'

After a pregnant pause, Judy asked, 'is there anything I could do to help him?'

'Well,' said Valerie. 'I did just wonder if you could try to drag the loft thing out a bit. Ask his opinion for things so he's not at work so much. What do you think?'

After another pause in which Judy tried hard to rationalise what Valerie had just said, she replied, 'I don't think that's a good idea. For one thing I have my reputation to uphold and I don't want him thinking I'm slow and inefficient, and for another, it would mean he was away from the office more and would probably get more stressed at letting people down. If you're looking for a solution, that isn't it. Why not hire a secretary? It's about time he had one.'

Valerie's face changed from despondency to joy as Judy's solution progressed. 'That's a great idea. Why haven't we thought of it?'

'Maybe because Jim doesn't want anyone interfering and he's worried he'd waste precious time showing someone what to do.'

Valerie nodded agreeing with everything Judy suggested. 'We could get someone really efficient and who knows lots about computers. That'd be great!'

Valerie collected the children from the tidy living room where they had been helping to decorate the Christmas tree, and feeling much happier as she left her friend's house, they protected themselves as best they could against the cold hard rain and ran home next door.

In the office which had once been the dining room Jim was catching up with some paperwork. His established family run funeral business had been doing nicely before the unexplained events of the summer, and now as winter began to set in, things were going very well for him. Rival firms were springing up, that was true and even Valerie had jokingly predicted Tesco would be offering a funeral service before the end of the year. However, he liked to think he was a professional and people respected the years of tradition he and his firm offered.

The larger garage, new kitchen, and the planned loft conversion were all evidence that as usual not everyone suffered when disaster struck. Builders and designers benefited, as well as kitchen manufacturers and carpet fitters. He mused how the economy was a complicated mix of triumphs and failures, each balancing out the other when Valerie burst in on him.

'You need a secretary!' she announced loudly before he had chance to register the return of his family.

'Please tell me you aren't thinking of offering up for the job,' he said half joking.

Valerie pulled a face and instructed the children to wash their hands ready for tea. 'Of course not. Judy has it all sorted. We need someone who can do spreadsheets and things on computers, and will be so efficient you won't need to worry about the paperwork any more.' She gesticulated towards his cluttered desk.

'Great minds think alike,' he said with a wry smile and handed her a copy of that evening's *Daily Scoop*. His forefinger pointed out a ten centimetre square advert asking for a secretary to join an established funeral directors, ability to use the complete Microsoft package essential. 'I've been in touch with the Job Centre as well. Apparently, with lots of nursing homes closing, there's a glut of suitably qualified administrators on the market. I should find someone I like and can do the job well.' Valerie smiled. 'I'm already seeing a woman from Eastdell's Grand Hotel, later this evening.'

~*~

Corin could have done with an administrator to help him sort out the large pile of notes he was acquiring. He wouldn't let go of his crusade to find out what had been the true cause of Victor's death and having failed to rouse various officials into revolt and spend more money to find out why an entire generation had been killed off worldwide in less than six months, he decided to attack from a different direction. He collaborated with Dustin Timms on some research for a series pieces for *The Westwater Illumination.* The previous week they had simply listed all the film stars who had died since August, followed by a list of retired sportsmen and women, although admittedly they tended to die younger and that list wasn't as long or as impressive. Pop stars, other musicians and artists followed that selection.

Having spent a lot of time working on that, Corin returned to the effects this garnering of the senior generation was having on the chaff left behind, for which he needed Dustin's help.

'We need a plan of what the articles will cover … whether they'll be general tales of how people are fairing, or whether it's more specific … you know … divided into categories; politics, finance, commerce, education … that kind of thing,' outlined Corin. 'What do you think?'

'Wouldn't it be a good idea to run this past Bill first?' said Dustin with the impression of someone who didn't want to waste his time.

'He gave me a broad brush assignment when this all kicked off.'

'For a week, three months ago. OK, how about we start gathering information, see what we've got then decide on format.'

Corin considered this for a few moments. 'No offence mate, but that's why you'll never get off the back pages. You need to plan, map out the article then gather your information.'

'Ah, see what you mean. How about weighing up the pros and cons of each style?' asked Dustin, determined not to be the one to make a decision.

Corin glanced at his friend and raised a quizzical eyebrow. 'Not good at sticking your neck out are you? OK. A general article might end up being a bit muddled, confusing and not really getting the point across, whereas a categorised one might seem a bit school bookish. Saying that, I'd rather it was structured, professional and made it easier to research as we'd have a goal ... a word you should understand,' he added with a twinkle.

Dustin smiled and leaned forward onto the beer-stained bar at The Colourman. 'What do you want me to do then?'

Corin looked across at Wayne. 'How about you start with health workers and try to get a mix ... those who've been at the sharp end having to deal with families,' he gave Wayne another quick look. '... and those who've been in the background or have quitted,' he said quietly.

Dustin followed Corin's shifty glance and hunched lower over his pint, moving closer to his friend. 'OK. What about you?'

Corin stood straighter and leaned away slightly. 'I'll start with businesses which have done well; funeral parlours, speak to the odd vicar. Then I'll look at businesses which have crashed.' He chinked Dustin's glass. 'This is going to be one hell of an article.'

While Corin got in touch with various vicars throughout the area, Dustin revisited the obituaries and selected a few names of people who had died in hospital recently so when he approached the medical staff he was prepared. He contacted Norleigh and Sudcliff hospitals and cleared it with the managers, then met with Corin the next day for lunch to compare notes.

'Finding someone who admits they haven't been able to cope with all that's been going on and is willing to say so in print might be difficult,' moaned Dustin. 'The doctors and nurses I've arranged to see seem a bit cagey.'

Corin nodded although he'd been reasonably successful. 'Getting anyone to say dealing with death on a daily basis has become routine and doesn't affect them is going to be hard, but these people have to be tough. I'm seeing a few undertakers today ... I'll have to be my usual tactful self so as not to rub them up the wrong way, but they are the obvious ones to benefit from all this. You keep going with the nurses.'

Dustin sighed and returned to his list. Sister Johnson from Norleigh Hospital where the deaths had first come to public attention in the summer was at the top. As she had since transferred to the maternity ward, with a career change perhaps she might make a good subject.

'Yes, all right,' she said with a tired voice over the telephone when Dustin asked to meet with her. 'I finish at three. I'll see you after that. Where would you like to meet?'

Dustin bought some bread and they each sat on a park bench feeding the ducks and pigeons. 'You've moved jobs; when was that?'

'Beginning of November. I just couldn't cope anymore with the tidal wave of people coming in with the dead or dying. I think it's slackened off a bit now, mostly because they're all dead I should think,' she said in a dreary end-of-her-tether voice.

'So maternity any better … not got a tsunami of pregnant mum's swamping you then?' asked Dustin with a grin, trying to cheer her up a bit.

'No,' she said softly.

Her voice was such a contrast to how it at been a moment before that Dustin checked to make sure it was the same woman. Her face had relaxed from its stern deep lined frown and now looked ten years younger. 'You OK?' he asked.

'If I tell you something … something weird I've noticed, will you promise not to use my name or ever say where you got the information?' She looked sincerely into his eyes.

Dustin was taken aback. If Sudcliff United's manager had asked him that, he'd have known he was going to be told something exclusive about one of the team which the board wouldn't want him to hear. In that case his instinct would have been to say 'yes' instantly. But here he was talking to a nurse about death. He stared at her, wondering what Corin would do but found himself nodding in any case.

'We've only had eleven births in the last couple of months,' she paused and Dustin was convinced she was going to say they all had six limbs and antennae, but she continued, 'and no new pregnant women have reported or been referred since September.'

Dustin looked at her, waiting for the punch line. 'That odd, is it?' he asked eventually.

Sister Johnson looked rather crossly at him as if he was a barbarian. 'Do you know how many women on average are pregnant at any one time in a town this size?' she asked gesturing widely around the park. Dustin looked over his shoulder. He would normally expect to see two or three women in various stages of pregnancy walking the park, even on a cold December morning. There were none. He shook his head.

'Roughly four percent or about eight hundred. No women have become pregnant in the last three months. I spent yesterday phoning fertility clinics to see why they hadn't referred anyone to the obstetrics or antenatal clinics. They said they hadn't had any successful fertilizations and hadn't been able to determine why.'

'Bad batch of sperm?' suggested Dustin. 'Or maybe the heat affected things back in the summer.'

Sister Johnson gave him another one of her impatient looks. 'Even without fertility clinics, teenage girls get pregnant all the time. We haven't had any of those referred either.'

'Maybe they're all being good and wearing condoms,' joked Dustin.

'You are an idiot!' said Sister Johnson hotly, getting to her feet. 'You call yourself a journalist. A story's staring you in the face and you just sit there making stupid remarks.' She rose and marched swiftly away. Dustin, feeling like he had been slapped, eventually took out his mobile and called Corin.

'You bloody fool!' was Corin's initial response in a similar tone to the one the Sister had used. 'If you were any kind of reporter you'd have taken notes and thought about it afterwards. Why didn't you ask her more about it rather than disbelieve her?' He tried to calm down. 'We'll meet up and discuss this ... and I need to give you some lessons in interview technique.'

They met at Corin's flat as he didn't think they should talk in the pub. Dustin told him all the nurse had said while Corin drew a thought diagram on a sheet of A4 paper. 'What the hell is going on?' he asked himself out loud. Dustin shrugged not grasping the significance.

'Don't you see?' Corin whispered sharply. 'The old have all died off and now we find no babies are being born to replace them!'

'But that's impossible, surely?' said Dustin justifiably. 'And anyway, it's only one hysterical nurse's view. You don't know if it's true or if that's the case everywhere. You're jumping to conclusions.' *Which is not like you*, he thought.

'OK. This is a distraction from our original plan, and if true, a major scoop in a different direction.' He secretly wished he had interviewed the nurse but thought it would be a bad idea to pursue it at the moment. The hospital would want to hush up something like that to prevent panic, assuming, as Dustin said, it was true, which meant it was unlikely to get into the public domain just yet. He could sit on it until after Christmas and concentrate on the job in hand.

'How have you got on with your dysfunctional families?' he asked to persuade Dustin he was over his irritation.

'I've found one chap - who would like to remain anonymous - who claims he was on the verge of bumping off his old man to get some money when he keeled over and died anyway, leaving him several thousand in his will. He says bookies must be doing well out of this generation thing with all the people who suddenly have lots of money to gamble. I wonder if anyone has thought to open a casino in Westwater or Norleigh. Perhaps we should see if the Council's got lots of extra planning applications coming in.'

'That's on my political list. You stick to the family side for now. I'm going to see a few bank managers to get a feel for how investments are going.'

'Can't you just look at the stock market?'

'This is a people piece Dustin; we need the personal touch. We'll meet again in a couple of days.'

With the door closed firmly behind him, Dustin felt he had been thrown out of the flat, and also that Corin was still angry about the baby thing, but he just didn't believe it. He suddenly had an idea for a more familiar angle he could question people from, and with this genius level brainwave activated, he drove back to the office.

~*~

Dr Prudence Richards and Dr Pete Yeoman walked swiftly down the basement corridor at Sudcliff Hospital heading towards the laboratories where the initial analysis of tissue samples was conducted. Staff also took responsibility for looking for potential DNA or genetic connections.

'A lot of the organ damage noted in autopsies has been hyperplasia associated with the enlargement of the organ. Under usual conditions, you'd expect to see such a proliferation as a normal response to some abnormal condition; chronic inflammation, or some hormonal dysfunction, or perhaps compensation for damage or disease elsewhere,' explained Pete, using his hands to emphasize the difference.

'I know,' said Prudence firmly.

'What I mean is, these are obviously not *usual* conditions. Some force, whether it's internal or external is causing the problem.'

'I'm glad you've told me that, it would never have occurred to me otherwise,' said Prudence sarcastically as she pushed open the swing doors to the laboratory. 'Good evening Sarah,' she said as she came to a halt at the desk where Dr Sarah Hastings, visiting from Norleigh, was working on the statistics.

Sarah smiled a response, but it dropped when she saw Pete. 'Hello,' she said, uncertainly.

'Could you show my colleague here what you showed me earlier?' Prudence asked, pulling a wheeled chair to sit next to her friend.

'You mean the anaplasia?' asked Sarah, adjusting her screen and bringing up a picture saved from her work earlier in the day. The screen showed an image from a slice of stomach lining but several of the cells were gigantic compared to their neighbours. 'These are stem cells which have failed to differentiate into their correct mature cells and have just carried on growing. You see the size of the nuclei ... and this cell has three nuclei. You can also see how the other parts of the cell are coarse and clumped. This sliver came from a section which had sheets of these things inside it,' Sarah explained to Pete who nodded, scowling. He had seen other such samples in other laboratories.

'So we're looking for something which is causing devastating and rapidly forming cancer type tumours. The cells are practically destroyed so quickly that death is inevitable.' Both Sarah and Prudence nodded at his assessment. 'How are we doing with looking for a likely cause?' he asked.

'That's what I want you to help with – looking into the DNA of these extraordinary cell responses,' Prudence said and Pete nodded, smiling.

Sarah chipped in. 'You *do* think it could be some sort of genetic mutation?'

'Certainly.' Pete sucked in a breath through his teeth. 'There're plenty of possibilities,' he said looking at the ceiling for inspiration. 'It could be some sort of somatic mutations ... you know, so called acquired mutations, which involve non-reproductive cells and which aren't usually transmitted to descendants, as is happening here. Or it could be something like slipped strand mispairing.'

Sarah looked confused so he sat on another swivel chair and continued his explanation. 'During DNA replication of the new strand from the template something goes wrong with the process and when it's all put back together again, the part that's been replicated ends up in a different spot. You could end up with insertions or deletions as a result of that too. Like someone chops a ladder in half, takes some rungs away from one side then joins it back again so the ladder's now shorter on one side and you fall off the top.'

'But it would still need an initial cause,' pointed out Prudence. Pete nodded.

'So this could be the mechanism for killing people, but it would need a trigger to get it to work,' said Sarah for clarification. Pete nodded again.

'There could be a genetic *reason* for all the older generation dying, but as it affected so many people right across the world, it can't of itself be the *cause* of the problem. Something else set it off. We have to find out what and stop it,' said Prudence.

'Could this also explain why there are so few conceptions these days?' asked Sarah.

Again Pete adopted a thoughtful posture, looking at the ceiling. 'It could, potentially. Assuming it's something like deletions which are removing one or more parts from the DNA strand. Like insertions, these mutations can alter the reading frame of the gene and are generally irreversible.'

'Theoretically, if this was happening to women trying to conceive, it might either affect the eggs or sperms directly. Mutations may be present in all subsequent reproductive cells produced,' suggested Prudence.

'Or if a mutation is present in a germ cell, or in the foetus even, it may give rise to the mutation being carried in all of its cells. That's where hereditary diseases come from after all. Until we know what's causing the genetic mutations, we won't be able to answer that question,' said Pete matter-of-factly.

Both women looked glumly at him and he scratched the side of his nose. 'We'd best get looking again,' he suggested and walked across to a vacant desk and computer. Prudence and Sarah exchanged a look and Sarah left for her own research project at Norleigh.

~*~

Louise McVey met her daughter Judy for lunch in the Blackberry Café on Eastdell High Street. She ate a large slab of chocolate cake while Judy had Christmas pudding with brandy sauce.

'What's the matter, Mum?'

'Why do think anything's the matter?' said Louise shortly.

'You're eating chocolate cake. It's like catching the Pope in bed with a nun.'

'Don't be vulgar.' They exchanged a smile. 'I needed chocolate and a carob bar just wasn't doing it for me.'

'Are things still not going well?' asked Judy, with genuine concern, pausing with a spoon of pudding en route to her mouth.

'Half my clientele have died, of course things aren't going well,' Louise snapped, but apologised straight away. 'Sorry. I'm working on an advertising campaign to entice a younger audience into my shop. If the bloody medical profession would get their act together and find out what caused the geriatric deaths, I could suggest to people what they could take to make sure it didn't happen to them. But when they see supposedly healthy people dying in droves, they hardly rush to health food shops to have some of the same. I blame the Government. If I hadn't got that bit of money from dad … I don't know what I'd be doing now.'

Judy, feeling slightly uncomfortable as her interior design business had taken off since the summer, played with her remaining Christmas pudding and didn't look at her mother. 'I've read that people are coming up with all kinds of theories and potential remedies. Maybe you could play on that a bit?' she suggested.

'What do you suggest? I advise people to carry garlic amulets around their necks or rub themselves in vinegar?' Louise sounded fraught.

'Or keep a rabbits foot under their pillow, and eat lots of porridge,' said Judy with a grin. Louise didn't see the funny side and they lapsed into silence once more.

'So you're busy I understand … when you're not looking after neighbours kids.'

'They're really great and I don't mind. Jim pops round and helps with anything I need doing around the cottage so it's very mutual.' Judy sat back in her wheel-backed chair. 'Have you heard from Dan recently?'

Thinking this was to change the subject, Louise sighed and answered, 'I haven't heard for a while. He did say he might go abroad for Christmas. I wish he didn't feel I'd pushed him away, but his life style is rather at odds with my own ideals.'

'He's a bloke,' said Judy as if that explained everything.

Louise nodded. 'Barry'll be around; he'll probably be working over Christmas though. A chef in a large hotel is likely to be busy. Has he said how this death business has affected the hotel trade?' she asked.

'I met him in town last week on his day off. He said they were quieter than normal, even for this time of year; fewer people at Christmas parties, but it gave him time to be creative and their specials are more elaborate,' Judy replied, smiling at the remembrance of her elder brother's enthusiasm. 'Would you like me to try to think of an advert you could use to drum up more business, perhaps not mentioning the word *health*?'

Louise smiled at her daughter's offer. 'Thanks. I haven't managed to come up with anything thrilling. Maybe another approach is called for.' She stood to leave, putting on her padded black coat and wrapping a long purple scarf around her neck. 'Make it quick though.' She kissed Judy on the cheek and left.

As she walked home, Judy called Dan on her mobile. 'You have to sort this feud with mum soon, you know. She's going through a bad time and needs our support.'

'She's a first class hypocrite and knows it,' came his broken reply.

'Where are you?' Judy asked frowning, holding the telephone away from her ear as it crackled at her.

'At granddad's,' said Dan becoming clearer. 'Just stepped outside, he doesn't ... didn't have good reception here.'

'Why are you there?' asked Judy concerned he was poking his nose in. She had reached her front door and with the telephone crooked under her chin, let herself in.

'There was a break-in last night,'

'WHAT!'

'Nothing too serious … The TV's gone and some of his better LPs, but no real damage.' Judy gasped. 'The policeman who came over said they're getting a lot of burglaries at houses where the owners have died and they've been left unoccupied while the solicitors sort out the legal stuff.' Judy had to sit down when she heard this. Losing her granddad was bad enough without this sacrilege to his property as well.

'Don't tell mum,' she said quietly.

'I think if you remember why you phoned you'll find that's unlikely.' Dan took a deep breath of cold December air and calmed down. 'Mum has high ideals and I don't see why I have to share them. If I want to pollute my particular temple with drink, drugs and lots of women, that's my business. She can be high priestess in glorious isolation … I like company.'

'Just keep out of the papers. I'm helping her with an advert to get more people to visit her shop so I'd prefer if you weren't the story next to it in a magistrate's court for possession.' She sat back in her sofa, Suzie lying across her lap. She stroked the dog's velvety ear absently. 'Would you like to come here for Christmas,' she said softly.

'Going to Spain,' said Dan, walking in circles around the small courtyard at the back of his granddad's house. 'Taking Rachel with me,'

'I don't need the details, thanks,' said Judy. 'How's your job doing?' She carried on stroking Suzie who snored gently. 'Has this generation thing made much difference to you?'

'Other than granddad dying and having to sort out a burglary,' he began angrily but calmed down. 'We don't sell a huge number of computers to the over sixties, and those we do tend to need a lot of after sales input. Judy …' he said earnestly, 'I'm going to live my life the way I want to, regardless of how mum feels. I suggest you do the same. See you.' He disconnected.

Judy stared at her mobile for a few seconds then put it down on the table in front of her. With teary eyes, she looked around the living room of her cottage filled with her favourite things; striking hand thrown pottery, beautiful watercolours, delicate glass figurines. What did they all amount to in the end? Did it really matter whether she had a successful business or not? What could more money buy that she really wanted? What did she really want? Tears flowed down her cheeks and she answered softly, 'I want granddad back, I want Dan and mum to stop squabbling, I want Barry to be happy.' She slumped back into the chair and Suzie, disturbed by her sudden movement and conscious of her misery, licked the tears from her face to comfort her. Judy smiled, rubbed her faithful companions head and kissed her. 'Thanks,' she said and got up to take her for a bonus walk.

~*~

Having entered the Blackberry Café shortly after Louise and Judy had left it, Millie Hallam feeling important, added three sugar cubes and stirred her espresso, and smiled at Dustin. 'It came out of the blue really,' she began. 'I wasn't thinking of changing my job, but my friend Jane left after she'd got off with this bloke – one of our regulars – and I thought there wasn't much wrong with a change of scene.'

Dustin smiled his friendliest smile – a sort of leer - and Millie, put off slightly, sipped her coffee and glanced out of the café window. 'Mr Cahill's very nice, and his wife.'

'Your husband OK with you going to work for an undertaker?'

'He's a dentist; he doesn't mind what I do.'

'What about your kids?'

'They're grown up and looking for jobs of their own. It makes no difference what I do. I could be a stripper as long as I served up tea on time.'

'I'd like to see that,' said Dustin without thinking. Millie gave him a surprised, but not unfavourable look and he carried on, blushing to his earlobes. 'You'll have contact with the bereaved relatives, I suppose?' Millie nodded. 'You don't have a problem with that?'

'I've had years of experience dealing with people,' she said sitting erect as if in her brief interview once more, then added more softly, 'and I've personal experience to draw on; my parents died years ago in a car crash in France.'

'So you don't know anyone who's died of this thing that killed off older people then?' he asked after a pause.

'Neighbours, friends … not relatives, no.'

'So how would you say it's affected you?

'Well ... at the hotel we'd noticed a drop off of mid-week pensioners, but they never want any extras and complain a lot so were no real loss to anyone, if you ask me.' Dustin laughed, Millie scowled. 'Now I'm going to be with Mr Cahill I can see things differently.'

After a pause Dustin prompted with, 'how?'

'Well, I mean death ... it's just another phase of life isn't it ... one you keep to yourself.'

As this was far too profound for Dustin, he looked blank, shook his head briefly and asked, 'what's Mr Cahill spending all his extra earnings on then? Holidays in Madagascar? Bought a posh new house with a pool? Sent his kids to public school?'

Millie looked scornfully at Dustin, finally realising why she was having this interview. 'Mr Cahill hasn't had so much as a weekend off since August, that's why he wants a secretary. He's had an extension to his house designed by his neighbour and used local builders to do the work, and his kids go to the same school as mine did.' She drained her cup dramatically. 'If you want dirt on him, you'll have to find someone who doesn't admire him.' She pulled on her coat. 'But I don't think you'll be able to find anyone.' She left the café, banging the door behind her.

Dustin sighed and finished his own drink. 'I'm going to stick to footballers,' he said as he donned his cap and left to apply his earlier brainwave idea on the real world.

He arrived at the Willow Park stadium, home of Westwater City Football Club and the offices of Bob Thompson the manager. They had conversed on many previous occasions about the wellbeing of the forward's left knee, the goalkeeper's dislocated shoulder and the ground staff's inability to clear snow from the pitch. After his female failures, Dustin was sure this was the right line of attack.

Bob Thompson was a former player, not a star especially, but solid enough in the defensive. He'd worked his way from back room boy to manager over a career of thirty plus years and was settled at the club. A few scares along the way including a dodgy decision to buy an Inter Milan star well past his sell by date, making Paul McCrery captain when no one liked him and opposing the board's decision to extend the ground for corporate boxes had left a cynical old pro who knew how the world worked better than most.

Extracting a half-full bottle of single malt from the bottom drawer of a filing cabinet behind his desk and two tumblers from the top drawer, Bob poured Dustin a measure and himself a double. 'You really working with Corin Lister on this old people's death thing?' he asked, incredulously.

'Sure,' responded Dustin a little hurt he should not be thought a serious journalist. 'You've lost three directors and the chairman. How's that left you with running the team?' Dustin asked proudly, feeling this bit of research made him sound every bit as professional as Corin.

'Not my problem,' was Bob's rather brief reply. 'The Board has to sort that out. I run the players; they're all under thirty five so I've no worries.'

As this took the wind from his sails, Dustin countered with, 'how old are you though Bob?'

Bob was silent as he swirled the amber liquid around his lead crystal glass. 'Far enough away from sixty not to worry about it. How about you?'

'Forty three,' replied Dustin with a gulp. 'Hasn't this thing affected you at all?'

Bob lowered his head, rolling his chins around his neck then said, 'we've had to find a new milkman, and half the kids who used to come and watch us with their granddads don't come any more.' Dustin looked disappointed as he took another sip.

'We've had more of a problem with security,' he began again and Dustin perked up. 'After the regular night-watchman died, we've had a couple of younger men at the job but either they're really useless or the youth of today is getting braver. Scaled the walls over the back and had a bash at digging up the pitch. They got frightened off, but they'd graffitied the walls on their way out.'

'What did they say?' asked Dustin, pen poised.

'Something about the chairman being more use now he's dead.' Dustin laughed. Bob frowned. 'Have you heard about what they did in the graveyard?'

'No. What? Which graveyard?'

'Behind St Mary's,' explained Bob jerking a thumb over his left shoulder. 'Someone decapitated a chicken and smeared the blood all over a headstone.'

'When was this?' asked Dustin, concerned he hadn't heard anything about it.

'Last night. The vicar came round earlier to see if either of these new lads had seen anything, but as usual they hadn't noticed a thing,' he said scornfully.

'Blood smeared on a gravestone,' repeated Dustin. This was more like it. 'Any idea whose headstone it was?'

Bob looked at his guest wondering why *The Illumination* had sent him to do this interview. 'Miss Este Heath, spinster of the parish. Died about ten years ago … rumoured to have been a witch. Hence the chicken I should think.'

'You mean someone sacrificed a chicken to old Este as part of a ritual?'

'No, you mean that. I'm just answering your question,' replied Bob in his matter-of-fact tone. 'Look Mr Timms, I'm a busy man. Unless you want to talk to me about having to cancel matches so players can attend relative's funerals, sponsorship being withdrawn as the owner's businesses are wound up, having to employ twice as many ground staff because the one man who knew how to run this place has died or the struggle I've had to find a new physio who my touchy feely players are happy with, then I think you should leave me to it.' He picked up a pen and began writing on a notepad.

Dustin, recognising a dismissal when he heard one, rose but at the door turned. 'What was that about a physio? I thought you had a young woman.'

'We do. She's on maternity leave.'

'I thought no one was getting pregnant these days?' said Dustin surprised.

'What do you mean?' asked Bob, frowning.

'Oh, nothing,' said Dustin, realising what he had said. 'Good luck getting out of your troubles.' He opened the door, walked through and closed it behind him, leaving Bob still frowning at his desk.

Chapter six

Wednesday 17th February 2016

'I can't get used to Mr Black dying like that,' said Daphne as she swabbed the corridor with an extra wide mop. She squeezed it into the bucket and covered another section of Eastdell's St Luke's Primary School entrance hallway.

'He was due to retire at the end of this year,' said her husband Kevin, his arms folded across his muscular chest as he watched her from the safety of the doormat.

Daphne's long florid skirt swished from side to side as she moved back and forth with the mop. 'I hope Gladys gets better soon; I don't mind doubling up for a few days, but it's been nearly a week now.' The mop disappeared into the dirty water as she reached the end.

'Which one's Gladys?' asked Kevin looking puzzled.

'The old fat one; needs two coffees and four fags before she starts anything,' said Daphne with venom. She walked across the cleaned floor with the bucket and handed it to her husband. 'Tip that down the drain, love.' Kevin obliged as they walked together out of the front door and round to the back of the school.

'She's supposed to have had a heart attack but I expect it's just wind.'

'How old is she?' asked Kevin, suddenly interested.

'Late fifties, early sixties ... Oh my God! You don't think she's got this thing do you?' Kevin shrugged. 'I bet she has. I bet she's going to die and I just said horrible things about her!' Daphne's face scrunched into a picture of desperate horror and she sniffed.

'Come on love,' said Kevin, putting the bucket down and an arm around her broad shoulders. 'It's not as if you're a close friend or anything.'

Daphne shrugged him off and blew her nose on a small tissue. 'Don't say that; it's unkind. It's almost as if you wished her dead.'

'Of course not!' said Kevin, thinking this innocuous conversation had gone far enough. 'How about we go to the pub and play darts this evening?'

'Darts! ... Darts!' cried Daphne. 'Poor old Gladys is about to pass over and you're talking about darts!'

'Just trying to cheer you up, love,' said Kevin defensively.

Daphne's burst of emotion concluded abruptly. 'You are good to me, Kev; always thinking of my comfort.' Having put the bucket and mop away in the cleaner's cupboard, she went to the staff room and picked up the two heavy bags of shopping she had collected during her lunch hour and carried them to their car. Kevin, unhindered by groceries or anything else, walked in front and opened the boot for her to drop off the shopping, then got into the car.

'How many of the staff has died here now?' asked Daphne as they drove away from the schoolyard with the energy saving LED street lights giving a clean pale blue glow to the world.

Kevin sighed, wishing they'd left the subject at school. 'Including Mr Black, that'll be four – Mrs Robinson, Miss McDonald, and Miss Boxer.'

'I wonder how the teachers manage. Double up I suppose like I have to. And now the Headmaster's gone … I can't think what's going to happen to the place.' She glanced back over her shoulder glimpsing the low brick wall as they turned the corner into Main Street.

'You're too attached to it. Leave work at work Daphne. Why don't you think about where you want to go on holiday this year? How about a change from the Med?'

Daphne smiled thinking about the great hotel they'd stayed at last September and how the children had enjoyed the pool. Thinking of the children, however, made her think about their childminder. 'I do miss Mrs May.'

Kevin rolled his eyes. 'Belle's great with them though isn't she, and not far away.'

'Belle's running a business and doesn't have time to look after other people's kids ... Not properly anyway. I'm sure Stuart'll pick up bad ideas playing in their backyard.'

'Errol doesn't keep the guns at the newsagents!' said Kevin exasperatedly. 'He's got a shop for that, all legal and well secured, so stop twittering about the kids getting ideas about guns.'

Daphne ground her teeth, but as they pulled up outside Williams' Newsagents, she could see Carl and Stuart waiting for them. She got out so they could climb into the back seat, quickly spotting Carl had a cut above his left eye and Stuart had a rip in the back of his sweatshirt. 'You two been fighting again!' she yelled loud enough for the whole street to hear.

'No Mum,' said Carl defensively. Long and bulky for a nine year old, he had his father's dark hair and eyes. 'Fell over playing statues.'

'What's your excuse!' demanded Daphne of her youngest son.

'He grabbed me as he fell over,' said Stuart unconvincingly.

'I've just been telling your dad how worried I am about you two being at the newsagents, and you spend all your time fighting!' She slammed the door closed and Kevin drove home as quickly as he could.

'Peace at last,' sighed Belle to her eighteen year old daughter Nerys.

'I like those boys; they're fun,' she replied.

'Not if they have to be picked up at the door by *her*.' Belle closed the door against the cold February air and shivered.

'Do you really need to take kids in after school?' asked Nerys after a few minutes of silence while Belle restocked her display of first aid supplies.

'They needed someone after Mrs May died, and with so many old people gone, I need all the money I can get.'

'Has it really made that much difference?' asked Nerys, putting the *Hello* magazine she had been flicking through neatly at the back of the pile.

'Old people ... retired people, had more time to read papers, and were more likely to walk down to the corner shop for a few odds and ends and a bit of company than your younger person. They're out at work all day and shop in the supermarket at the weekend. A lot of them get the news off the Internet anyway.' Nerys nodded. 'Besides, they seemed to have smoked a lot more too,' added Belle. 'Where's your brother off to this evening? We ought to be getting tea on.'

'He's gone to that new flute teacher he found after Mr Armstrong died, but she's the other side of town. The bus won't get back till after seven. He said not to bother with his tea; he'll get something from the chippy on the way home,' Nerys informed her, walking from the shop to the house part of the building.

'Whop some fish fingers under the grill while you're in the kitchen,' called Belle after her. Nerys grunted assent. Belle looked at her watch; only five thirty and already dead - a word used a lot lately. When this thing - as people termed it - first started in late summer, Belle had tried to attend the funerals of her more loyal regulars, but after a while it became too much of a burden for her both emotionally and financially. She had to pay someone else to mind the shop and as takings were always borderline staff became a luxury she could no longer afford. She had to let Shelia go; Shelia who had worked at the shop when her father had owned it. Shelia's was one funeral Belle had attended.

'Are we having Microchips?' called Nerys from the depths of the house.

'Yeah,' called back Belle. 'I'll bring a new bottle of sauce.' She turned the sign so it read *ring for attention*, then bolted the door.

'Hi my darlings,' said a cheery voice from the back of the house as Belle made her way to the kitchen and the smell of cooking. She popped the bottle of tomato ketchup on the table which Nerys had just finished laying, and gave her husband Errol a big hug.

'What's the matter with you, my love?' he said tunefully. He looked concerned as he pulled away from her and peered at her at arms length.

She patted his chest and sat at the table while Nerys dished the fish fingers and chips onto waiting plates. Errol gave her a hug and a kiss then sat down too.

'Have you heard that Town is in trouble again?' asked Errol as he tapped the bottom of the sauce bottle to encourage the red fluid out of it.

'Eastdell Town is always in trouble,' said Belle in a resigned disinterested tone.

'This is serious. They're saying gate numbers are down so much, they'll have to start selling players if people don't come to watch.'

'They pay them too much anyway.'

'They cut wages and gate prices back in November to help the situation, but it's still made no difference.'

'If they were more successful ...' began Nerys, but realised this was a mistake as soon as she started.

'They're higher in the league than they've been for years. They've played some really good games just lately, and scored almost as many goals as Chelsea. It's not that that's keeping people away.'

‘What then?’ asked Belle hoping Errol’s favourite subject would be finished soon.

‘The chairman’s saying it’s because old folks aren’t around to take the kids to matches and fathers have other things to do at weekends.’

‘So they’re saying it’s because of this thing are they? How convenient.’ Belle said bitterly.

‘You said you were suffering because of it, why shouldn’t the football club,’ pointed out Nerys. ‘Is it having any effect on your business Dad?’ She rose and cleared away the plates, replacing each with one of warmed treacle tart and ice cream.

‘Being a gunsmith is quite a specialised business,’ said Errol, leaning back on his chair and appreciating his daughter’s grasp of the situation. ‘There’re plenty of sportsmen and marksmen to do business with. More people have money these days; it’s time they’re short of.’

‘How do you mean?’ asked Nerys with interest.

‘Inheritance,’ he replied simply. ‘People are getting money earlier from their elders now.’

‘I wonder what caused it … this thing,’ said Belle with a far away hopeful look on her face.

‘The Government’s got people looking into it, but I don’t know if it’s stopped. Have you heard of anyone dying recently?’ asked Errol

‘The headmaster at St Luke’s died earlier this week. They’re running out of teachers now as well as vets,’ said Belle

‘Vets!’

‘And farmers,’ said Nerys. ‘I read in *Farmer’s Weekly* they’re worried about the number of older farmers who have died with no one to take their farms on. We could end up with a food shortage or having to import more … It could get expensive.’

‘The price of farms will become cheaper, encouraging more people to have a go at it,’ suggested Errol hopefully.

‘But they’ll not have experience. That’s what the article suggested the Government should do … more grants and subsidies to encourage people into farming. But they said they'd not have experience so they suggested setting up mobile training or self help groups for people to share knowledge and best practice.'

'Like they'll have time for that,' said Belle sceptically.

She retreated to the shop to dust the shelves again while Nerys washed the plates and tidied the kitchen. 'Do you know what research the Government's conducting?' she asked.

'There's a Dr Richards in charge ... co-ordinating everything for the Medical Research Council,' explained Errol. 'Rather than looking for a single cause, they're looking for possible combinations of things.'

'How do you mean?' asked Nerys, wiping the inside of the microwave.

'Well ...' began Errol on tentative ground and not sure of his facts. 'They don't think it's a specific toxin like pesticide or something, so now they're looking to see if it might be a combination of say car fumes and a chemical ... like the smog in Los Angeles.'

'I see,' said Nerys wiping her hands on a pink fluffy towel and leaning thoughtfully against the sink. 'But why would that kill a particular age group?'

'Probably because their resistance is lower ... something like that,' offered Errol vaguely.

'I've read some people think it's Martians shooting death rays from the sky, slowly killing people off from space.'

'I think the Medical Research Council say it's unlikely, but as they don't know what it is, they can't rule it out,' said Errol with a twinkle in his eye. He gave his daughter a quick kiss on her forehead and went to the living room to watch the *One Show*.

Nerys unpropped herself and went to her room, switched on her computer and sat for a few minutes in silent contemplation waiting for it to complete its start up processes, then she Googled *age death theories* and *medical research.* The expected explanations were listed in various orders, with one or two conspiracy theories that it was all a Government plot to save money on pension payouts.

The widespread perception that from the end of the autumn to present there had been a lull in the number of deaths of the over sixties was not borne out by the statistics. Globally, the death rate amongst the over fifty fives – the age of unexpected natural deaths was lowering - was steady, with regional peaks and troughs, although no specific pattern had been identified.

The World Health Organisation had issued a number of statements since August which had become less certain, less confident and less optimistic as time went by. It appeared to be struggling to come to terms with the thing as much as everyone else was and claims of being not far from finding the cause had diminished inversely with the number of eliminated causes.

Nerys then looked for potential non-medical causes which definitely brought her into the twilight zone of suggestions; nerve gases, nuclear accidents, chemical plant disasters, prehistoric diseases escaping from melting glaciers, trees emitting arsenic vapour, God / the Devil needing more souls in heaven / hell. She noticed that no matter what was suggested, the same barrier came up each time. Why was the thing killing older people and not whole communities?

Nerys gave up after an hour and joined her father in the living room. 'How are you getting on with your studying,' Errol asked, quietly watching her as she entered the dimly lit room. With light brown straight hair cut neatly to highlight her ears, he remembered thinking she had pixies ears when she was born.

'Mocks start in Thursday, but I'm ready I think.' She paused as she fell onto the sofa next to him. 'I miss Gerry.' Gerry White had been her English teacher until he had died, suddenly and dramatically in front of his A level class. Most of them had freaked, seriously, and now needed counselling, but Nerys had calmly called for an ambulance and informed the headmistress what had happened.

'You did well, my love,' said Errol giving her a hug.

'Mum thinks this thing has stopped and it'll just fizzle out like a 'flu virus, but I don't think it's going to do that, do you?' Errol shook his head. 'Gerry was only fifty eight and he hadn't been ill or anything, not even a cold.' She looked up at her father with watery eyes. 'When's it going to stop?' she asked so softly Errol strained to hear her, even though he was sitting with his arm around her.

'I don't know love, but someone will sort it out soon ... they're bound to.' He hugged her again and kissed the top of her head as he had done so often when she had woken from a nightmare as a child. From her resigned body language, he got the feeling she didn't believe him.

~*~

'I just don't believe it,' said Greta Atkinson with the *Norleigh Herald* in her hand. She jumped to her feet and reached for the telephone, dialling her brother working in Barclays Bank in Manchester.

'Ewan Atkinson,' said the distracted voice at the other end.

'Hi, Ewan. Have you heard ... Dr Henderson's died,' she said. 'He died last night in Norleigh Hospital, apparently of a heart attack.'

Ewan, who still bore a grudge, resisted the temptation to say *good* and said instead, 'I'm sorry to hear that. Dad always liked him.' He thought for a moment. 'Why have you phoned to tell me at work? ... Not that it isn't nice to hear from you.'

'He was only fifty five or fifty six. He wasn't elderly by any stretch of the imagination.'

'Are you suggesting he was killed by the same thing that killed mum and dad?'

'He was fit and healthy, nothing wrong with him at all, just like mum and dad,' agreed Greta. 'This thing is starting to kill younger people too, don't you see,' she sounded more excited than worried.

'Don't be silly ... You're jumping to conclusions. The Government said it was fatigue and strain brought on by the hot summer which killed all those people.'

Greta couldn't believe her ears. Ewan had been so scathing and sceptical in August, was now defending the pathetic excuses trotted out by a medical profession who didn't want to admit it was being beaten by an unknown enemy.

'You know they haven't been able to find out exactly what it is yet and until they do, when anyone dies suddenly, we assume it's this thing. And besides, they've devised tests for it now,' added Ewan blithely. 'They check for all sorts of poisons, allergies and disease symptoms in a couple of days. If they don't get a result, they add you to the list of statistics for *death by unknown agent*. It's an unofficial cause of death, like old age.' He sounded so smug and pleased with himself he left Greta speechless.

'I'll have to go,' he said. 'I'm meeting a big client in a few minutes. He inherited half of Northamptonshire and would like help with investments and advice on a major building scheme he's got in mind; should be worth a bob or two in fees and commission.'

'I'm pleased someone is doing all right out of this thing,' said Greta snidely.

'Sorry about Dr Henderson, but it's not as if we were bosom buddies or anything. Speak to you next week, after my big killing.' He hung up.

Greta winced at her brother's choice of words, but put the telephone back on its wall bracket thoughtfully. Maybe she had been dwelling too much on the sad aspects of this thing and she should be thinking more positively. Money and property were now in the hands of younger, potentially more vibrant people, who might make beneficial use of it, creating jobs in England rather than opting for holidays abroad. Perhaps that was the silver lining Ewan seemed to have discovered but she was too dazzled by the light of truth to see.

It seemed he had come to terms with the loss of his parents far quicker than she had. Maybe loosing his temper had released it all at the beginning – that and he lived away. She lived in her parents' house, surrounded by the things they had loved. She had toyed with the idea of selling the house, but she couldn't stand the thought of all the upheaval when she was happy here. Maybe it didn't matter if they had different approaches to dealing with grief. She looked around the room at the familiar Royal Worcester ladies she had received for graduating, the gold plated carriage clock Nigel was given when he retired from the bank, and the neatly embroidered tablecloth Jessica had sewn while pregnant with Ewan. This was her home, moving to another house wouldn't solve anything or drive away any ghosts - mostly because she didn't want them driven away.

Greta collected a shopping bag and her purse and walked to Tesco halfway down Longfield Road. She picked up a bag of flour, a tub of margarine, half a dozen free range eggs and a pot of glace cherries then arrived at the delicatessen counter to select some ham for sandwiches. 'I'll have two hundred grams of the Yorkshire ham please Rosie.'

'Miss Atkinson,' said Rosie with a gasp. 'I was just talking about you this morning to our Wesley,' she said, her tongs hovering over the tray of ham.

'Really,' said Greta surprised. 'What could you have been talking about me for?' Although she had known Rosie for many years via the shop, she had never considered her more than an acquaintance.

Rosie turned scarlet, right to the roots of her curly blonde hair. 'I'm so sorry. I didn't mean we were gossiping or anything,' she said, the tongs still hovering. 'I was just saying how you're in the same position as me, living in the same house after your parents died.'

Greta nodded. 'I was just saying to Wesley – he teaches art at the High School, very good he is. Anyway, I just said I wonder if you've packed up your parents stuff and if you've ... found anything.' Her blush deepened and she finally picked up three slices of ham and weighed them.

'You've found something while sorting through your father's things?' asked Greta with curiosity.

Rosie, still red, asked if two pounds fifty two was all right. Greta nodded and their transaction was completed. 'Yes,' said Rosie wrapping the ham and sticking a bar-coded price label on the front. 'I really don't know what to do about it. Wesley says to throw it away and forget about it, but I don't think it's as easy as that ... I mean it *is* art, it might be worth something.'

'What are you talking about?' asked Greta, somewhere between impatient and intrigued.

'Can't discuss it here,' whispered Rosie casting a late furtive glance around her. 'Could you pop round one evening and I'll show you?'

Greta was taken aback by this. She couldn't understand what Rosie could expect from her if her brother was unable to convince her. 'All right,' she said hardly believing she was accepting this odd request. They arranged to meet that evening, and Greta went home to make cherry cake and ham sandwiches, wondering what she'd agreed to.

Greta arrived at Rosie's neat bungalow; the climbers around the doorway bare, dormant and in need of a trim. 'Thank you so much for coming around. Into the living room if you please.' Greta followed her hostess's guiding hand and sat on the sofa in front of which the coffee table was spread with a cafetiere and plate of blue foil wrapped biscuits, temptingly waiting to be pealed.

'Have you packed stuff away and given it to charity shops then?' asked Rosie, not beating about any bushes.

Greta, still getting her bearings and admiring Wesley's watercolours came back to the present. 'I have … mostly, yes. I have to say, I found it rather harder than I expected and there are still some parts I haven't been into, especially the loft.'

'Oh the loft!' said Rosie, rolling her eyes and unwrapping a biscuit. She pushed the plunger on the coffee and began to pour. 'The loft was the worst and where I found the dodgy stuff. Wesley and Albert helped sort that out though so I didn't get too involved. They're both respectable and took it all to the police, so it was all above board.'

'I'm sorry,' said Greta looking bewildered. 'Why were the police involved?'

'This is to go no further of course,' said Rosie leaning forward and whispering, 'but my old dad used to keep stuff in the loft he'd nicked from his lorry, and then sell it off in the pub.'

'How do you know that?' asked Greta her voice rising with her incredulity and her eyebrows.

'Bloke in the pub asked me if I had any of my dad's stuff and could he help me shift it,' she said, sitting back and nodding to confirm the truth of the statement. 'I said I hadn't a clue what he was talking about, but I had a good look around to see if what he said might be true.' She started on another biscuit.

'The thing I want to talk to you about was in his shed, but there were loads of other things in the loft. I didn't even know he could get up there as he always told me he had a dodgy back and couldn't climb step ladders. Should have thought that one through though as he had to climb onto his wheel rim to get into his cab, but there you are … he was my dad and I never doubted him. Makes you think though, doesn't it … we all have our secrets.'

Greta chewed thoughtfully on a delicious mint chocolate biscuit and wondered what on earth Rosie had to show her. 'I'll fetch it, shall I?' she jumped up and disappeared out towards the kitchen before Greta had time to respond.

She returned a few minutes later with a large framed oil painting covered in a rough grey blanket. She propped it against the unlit gas fire and removed the blanket, checking it was the right way up before stepping back and 'admiring' it.

The picture showed the most disgustingly awful nude painting Greta had ever seen, not that she'd seen many. The background was dark and indistinct but the red haired woman – probably - sat astride a wooden chair, facing the back of it. A red velvet cloak half covered the chair and the figure which looked uncomfortable with its right arm resting on the chair back, and the left arm dangled in front giving the shoulder a stooped appearance but managed to conceal anything which might offend anyone of a sensitive nature. The breasts were firm and rather red, though not large, adding to the problem with determining gender. In the foreground were tossed various garments none of which followed the perspective or scale of the rest of the picture. The whole thing was covered in grime from the shed, and as she watched, a small spider glided to the floor on the end of a gossamer thread.

'Well,' began Greta, not sure how to finish. 'It's unusual,' she decided in the end.

Rosie smiled taking it as a compliment. 'Dad did it. Although I don't know when; there's no date. Must have been before I moved in or I might have noticed him sneak a whopping great canvas up the path.' She smiled. Greta felt envious that this woman could feel such tenderness for her father so short a time after discovering he was, well, a bit of a rogue. 'What should I do with it, do you think?'

Greta had been dreading this question, but remembered that the sensible brother Wesley had told her to bin it. 'I have to say I don't really like it very much,' she paused wondering how to qualify that. 'It's probably too modern for me ... I'm a Constable and Turner fan myself.'

As she feared, Rosie's face fell but she examined it more closely. 'It's not really very good is it? I suppose it was his first go and that's why he didn't do much else.'

Greta thought about this for a few moments and leaned forward to look at the brush or rather palette work. 'I don't think it could have been his first attempt at painting with oils; the work is too confident, assured, as if he's familiar with the medium. He's not worked areas too much, everything is regular and even. His choice of colours … and possibly subject aren't great, but there's nothing wrong with his technique. Are you sure you haven't found anything else? You said you found it in the shed. Have you cleared it?'

Rosie had been warming to Greta during this speech and said she hadn't really ventured further than the door to reach for the mower and the odd gardening tool she needed. His real shed was further back. This painting had been beside the folded deck chair near the door, that's why she'd seen it.

'I ought to rake everything out and see if there are any more. Would you like to help?'

Greta thought about all the things she would like to do on a cold dark February night and looking through someone else's garden shed for the possibility of finding a lost masterpiece was not high on the list, possibly not even *on* the list. 'OK,' she found herself saying.

Rosie, torch in hand, led her across the starlit back garden path to the shed looming in the corner. Twice the size of a normal garden shed and on unlocking it, Greta could see straight away why Rosie hadn't done anything about it. Like the children's game *Pick Up Sticks*, just pull the wrong thing out and the whole lot would fall on her.

Floodlit by the back door security light, wrapped in warm coats, scarves and gloves, the two women began their bizarre search for treasure. Rosie was systematic and took things from the front and placed them at the far end of the garden, leaving the path clear to the house. Surprisingly quickly they sorted garden tools in one pile, woodworking in another, general maintenance in another, *Dandy* and *Beano* comics near the backdoor, and unidentifiable things in the general rubbish pile, by far the largest.

'Here we are,' called Rosie triumphantly from the depths of the spider ridden back of the shed. She reappeared with an easel and a congealed box of oil paints, knives and brushes. 'The pictures are at the back. Could you give me a hand?'

'I wonder why all this stuff is at the back. It looks as if he hasn't done anything for years,' observed Greta. They moved four covered canvases onto the remaining patch of lawn and under the harsh security light, they took off the covers.

'Oh my God!' cried Rosie, horrified.

'Oh my Lord!' agreed Greta, trying hard not to laugh. 'Are they all nudes?' They uncovered the others. If Greta had thought the first one was bad, these were dreadful and only vaguely anatomically correct.

'Are those two doing what I think they're doing?' asked Rosie in a loud whisper.

'I have a horrible feeling they are,' agreed Greta her hand over her mouth, stifling a smile. Rosie looked truly shocked and she didn't want to make her suffer more than she was already.

'I wonder if this was done from life, or a photograph?' asked Rosie. Greta thought it wasn't done very well from either. Rosie lifted the picture so the harsh light shone on it even more strongly. Her face broke into a more amazed stare. 'I think I know who this is!' she squealed, pointing at the female figure, lying back arched apparently in the throws of ecstasy. 'That looks like Mrs Salmon, the greengrocer's wife … going back a few years, obviously, but that's who it reminds me of.'

Greta peered at the picture frowning. Thinking they would probably be the only people to look at the woman's face, but she did think it looked a bit like Mrs Salmon, but as it wasn't particularly clear, she wasn't prepared to make any accusations.

'I wonder who the man is?' said Rosie, turning her attention to him, but his face was buried in the woman's ample bosom and no other distinguishing features could be seen.

'Why would dad want to paint this subject?' she asked, but Greta felt she couldn't possibly answer. However, Rosie looked at her as if expecting her to understand.

'Perhaps … these were done after your mother died and this was his way of expressing her loss,' she hazarded. Surprisingly Rosie seemed to like this idea.

'What will you do with them?' asked Greta, hoping she would destroy them.

'Put them back and leave them to decay quietly, just as he's doing,' said Rosie thoughtfully. 'If it helped him then, it will help me now to understand him a little bit more.'

Greta raised an eyebrow and helped Rosie restock the shed in a more orderly manner, leaving a pile of rubbish which she would need a mini-skip for.

I hope my father never had to solve his inner issues in such a manner, she thought as she drove home an hour later, ready for a long hot bath.

~*~

Just as Greta and Rosie had begun to delve into the back of the shed, Nerys and Ross Williams waited at Eastdell bus station for the number five which would carry them to within a few hundred yards for their mother's shop. Ross a lanky sixteen year old, kicked at the wall beside the bench while Nerys finished texting a friend about their evening's entertainment.

'They're going to put the prices up again next month, did you hear?' asked Ross dropping onto the seat beside his sister as she closed her phone. She pulled up her coat collar and rubbed her gloved hands together.

'Who are putting up what prices?' she asked distractedly, hoping for an early response to her text – she might have to pop back to Boots if her friend had used all her gold nail varnish.

'The bus companies are putting up the fares … increasing price of fuel they say.'

Nerys looked at her brother surprised he should have heard something like that if she hadn't. 'Where'd you get your info from?'

'In the *Eastdell Reporter* this morning. That Eartha Zull – great name – has been doing a bit about the issues raised by the global dying off thing.'

'What does that have to do with the buses getting dearer?'

'For one thing there are no old people with bus passes anymore so the Council isn't subsidising buses as much and for another, even though demand for fuel has gone down 'cos older people aren't driving everywhere, oil companies aren't producing as much, keeping prices high.'

'You're well informed,' said Nerys still surprised.

'It's important,' replied Ross with an earnestness she had never noticed before.

After a moment's reflection she asked, 'why?'

'If all the older people really have died, that changes our society ... not just locally. Things won't be the same.'

'Are you saying putting the bus fares up is just the start?' she asked with the hint of a laugh in her incredulous voice.

'Obviously,' said her brother climbing onto the bus and handing over his fare. 'They say car sales have already dropped dramatically and another Nissan factory in Japan is closing. The Toyota plant has already closed. Sales to India and China have been hit most as older people there were the ones with the money.'

'Surely their children have inherited money the same as here.'

'They already have cars.'

'Yes ... I suppose they would have. I'd heard there were problems with sufficient fuel for trucks too. Is that part of the same thing?'

Ross, who was studying Geography as well as Economics GCSE knew the answer to this and spouted like a reference book. 'We reached peak oil about seven years ago but the rate of use increased until last summer. We're using up stocks faster than we can pump, refine, distribute and locate other sources. Heavy industry has lost a lot of expertise and financial backing in the last few months which will take time to replace, if it's possible.'

'The Mediterranean War hasn't helped. I suppose it takes a lot of skill and effort to extract oil.'

'It's not just the extraction. There's transporting, separating, refining, processing and distributing. They have to find the stuff in the first place which takes years of geological research, then there's getting financial backing, gathering all the necessary equipment together before you can think of pumping any oil from the ground.'

'And we're running out.'

'Yes. The thing is,' said Ross with fervour, having giving the topic many hours of sleepless thought, 'we're so dependant on supplies of oil and gas for modern agriculture techniques, a fall in global oil supplies will cause spiking food prices and future famines. Current population levels are growing too fast and to achieve a sustainable economy and avert disaster, the global population would have to be reduced by at least by two-thirds. As the older generation's died off, it seems as if it's already happening, naturally.'

'That seems harsh,' said Nerys interested despite herself and unused to having a lengthy philosophical conversation with her younger brother.

'Have you any idea how many things we use petroleum for besides fuel?' Ross sounded smug when he asked the question. Nerys shook her head on cue.

He ticked things off on his fingers, neatly negotiating dismounting from the bus and thanking the driver in the process. 'Plastics, pharmaceuticals, lubricants, fillers, gums, adhesives, cosmetics, detergents, electrical insulation, dyes, pesticides, film, nylon, perfume, synthetic rubber, man-made fibres, toothpaste, upholstery, wax, drugs and creams like Vaseline, anaesthetics, antiseptics ... and so on.'

Nerys accepted the list thoughtfully. The absence of older people around the town was more obvious each day as the evening light lengthened. A plantation of house sale signs led the way up their street and she noticed another boarded up shop for sale – the lighting specialists – which was not being taken over by the deceased proprietor's family.

They separated once they entered the newsagent's and she sat back in her familiar living room chair and in spite of the text message saying she could borrow her friend's gold nail varnish, she was far from happy. She'd picked up the late edition of *The Guardian* Errol had left beside his favourite chair. *Fuel Crisis: Nationalisation of Transport and Agriculture Imminent* read the front page headline. The article pointed out that crude oil being extracted and distributed wasn't matching demand. Imports of oil and gas were not only becoming more expensive, but the likelihood of their long-term sustainability was becoming a major concern. Food production would be affected, at home and abroad. Air travel was likely to be disrupted.

Nerys remembered hearing that initially after this thing started back in August, the economy had began to boom. Instead of money and other assets being retained by a few fossils reluctant to part with it, it was in the hands of offspring keen to see some action before it was too late. World trade flourished and things began to look brighter.

King William, with Queen Catherine by his side, led the way as ambassadors for United Kingdom businesses, accepting invitations from leaders in all corners of the world, riding, sailing, shooting and eating their way through other countries hospitality. Having listened to Ross, Nerys reflected and knew it couldn't last, although she would have expected it to be rosy for longer. The spending power of the grey-haired was missing. Charities had lost their volunteers, coach tours had all but ceased, baby-sitters were harder to find. Where had the people with money and time to spend it gone? Why had they gone?

The UK economy had become dependant on exports of aerospace manufacturing, pharmaceuticals and motor parts. This anticipated fuel crisis could affect the other major industry - tourism, and by association, the retail industry. A shortage of sugar was mentioned as a footnote.

She read through the article Ross had pointed out to her from the *Eastdell Reporter*, finding Eartha had listed some of the potential causes of the thing which was apparently continuing to kill people, including bio-weapons centred on some as yet unknown disease, some sort of ecosystem collapse which only affected certain members of the population or external influences such a gamma ray bursts or the ever popular alien attack.

Nerys folded both papers away in the magazine rack and slowly climbed the stairs to her bedroom to get ready for going out. She'd get mostly ready then pop round to her friend's to do her nails, but somehow, the appeal of a night out had evaporated.

Chapter seven

Thursday 26th May 2016

'That was probably the worst funeral I've ever been to,' said Kate, slinging her shoulder bag on the floor beside her desk, sinking heavily into her swivel chair and burying her face in her hands. Hugh had driven her back to the laboratory while she sniffed and dabbed her tearful eyes. 'I didn't realise how much I respected and depended on Pru Richards. How are we going to manage without her organising everything?' She sounded desperate and depressed.

Hugh, also regaining the seat at his desk, loosened his black tie and undid the top button of his unfamiliar shirt. He stared blankly at his computer screen and muttered, 'I don't know. I suppose we carry on following her plan until we hit upon something.'

'That doesn't look like it's going to be any time soon,' said Kate hotly, pushing her dark curtain of hair out of her face as she re-emerged into the stark brightness of the overhead strip lights, her face white and pale, her eyes red from lack of sleep and crying.

'Mostly because you're looking in the wrong place,' said a sharp voice from the doorway. Startled, both Hugh and Kate turned to look at the newcomer. Dr Pete Yeoman pushed himself off the door jamb where he had been watching them and strode into the laboratory, his hands in his pockets.

'I don't remember seeing you at the funeral,' said Kate churlishly. 'Why are you here?'

'I was at the back. I want to point you in the right direction so you're not wasting your time and this country's resources.' He leaned on the edge of her desk, staring, in Hugh's view, threateningly into at her face.

Hugh moved protectively towards Kate. 'Just why do you think we're wasting our time and you're so right?' he asked caustically, his Welsh accent heightened.

The two men stood and squared up to each other above Kate who looked up like a frightened rabbit, wondering what they might do next. Hugh didn't feel at all threatened by Pete physically, considering him a scrawny little wimp, but neither was Pete put off by Hugh's bulk.

'Have either of you reviewed Professor Fallon's work since he died?'

'Professor Fallon? He worked on genetics. We're looking for a disease which causes massive cellular damage,' said Kate calmly from below them.

'Are we?' asked Pete looking down at her. 'Arc we indeed? What if it's not a disease, not in the conventional sense?'

'What do you mean?' asked Kate curious.

'Read Fallon; see if you come to same conclusions I have.' He turned and left the laboratory.

Kate and Hugh swapped a quizzical glance. 'Do you think we should take any notice of him?' asked Kate, wondering if she should at least have a glance at Fallon's papers.

'Which bit? Professor Fallon worked on genetics for years; he knew more about it than any man alive. We're not going to become experts and find a serious flaw just by having a quick flick through his notes.'

'No, but Pete Yeoman is also a geneticist, also a genius … if Pru Richards is to be believed; an arrogant one, but a genius.' Kate pulled her chair up to her desk and started up her computer. She wiped her eyes and blew her nose, thinking like a scientist once more.

'The one thing we can do for Pru's memory is find out what this thing is and stop it. She worked across the board, not just looking for a disease. Perhaps that's what we should do.'

'We should leave other avenues to people who know what they're doing,' complained Hugh, turning on his own computer.

'I don't think Pete Yeoman would have bothered to come here to tell us we're barking up the wrong tree unless he had a reason.'

'He would if he has some crackpot idea and no one'll listen to him … but he thinks they'd listen to you,' said Hugh over his shoulder.

Kate pulled up references to Professor Fallon's genetics research and started to try to filter out anything which didn't relate to the current crisis. After only a few minutes however, she realised she didn't have the expertise to do that without knowing a lot more about genetics. She blew out a breath and began at the beginning with Hugh grumbling he now had to do her workload too.

Pete was not simply relying on Kate finding something in Fallon's papers, but like Pru, was trying various avenues. In The Colourman pub, Wayne poured him an orange and mango J2O with ice and he joined Corin Lister and a young lady he didn't know, at a far table by the window.

'I still can't get used to coming into places like this and there being no scruffy old man at the end of the bar talking to his beer,' he said as he sat down.

'They're saying lots of places like this are closing for that very reason. Regulars have died and not enough new people are coming in to make out of the way places viable any more,' explained the young woman.

Corin looked from her to Pete. 'Pete, this is Phoebe Gilligan from *The Daily Scoop*. We're working together now.'

'Isn't that sleeping with the enemy?' asked Pete with an amused look on his face.

'We're not sleeping together,' said Phoebe hotly. Corin shot her a look and all three laughed.

'So why have you two teamed up?' asked Pete, sipping his juice.

'Our papers are merging,' explained Corin. 'The circulations are dropping off, as is the number of journalists. We just can't continue to support all the papers in this area.' Pete nodded seriously.

'My colleagues Mick Quinn and Daryl Verner both died last month, both in their mid-fifties ' said Phoebe firmly. 'After we'd attended their funerals, the remainder of us met to decide what to do and proposed a merger as the best course for everyone.'

'I just can't accept what's happened in the last ten months. About a quarter of the population has gone and they're still saying they don't know what's causing it,' observed Corin, somewhere between sad, angry and frustrated. Pete stiffened and sat erect. 'You know something, don't you,' asked Corin sharply. 'Is that why you wanted to see me?'

'Got a scoop for us, Dr Pete?' asked Phoebe archly, giving him a glorious girly smile. Pete looked at her scornfully and the smile dropped. 'Sorry,' she said apologetically.

'Did you go to the funeral of Dr Prudence Richards this morning?' Pete asked.

'Didn't see you there,' observed Corin.

'I didn't want to cause a scene. Many of my ... colleagues don't approve of me and feel Dr Pru didn't either,' he took another sip of juice, apparently hurt by the injustice of this scepticism.

'That's not the case, I take it,' suggested Corin, paying all his attention to Pete.

'I have a theory, which I outlined to Dr Pru. She was reluctant to believe me, but I'm amassing proof.'

'Why reluctant? I'd have thought if you have an answer to this, she'd be pleased, to say the least,' said Corin intrigued.

'Let's just say my proposal didn't make her a happy bunny.'

'So what you've found isn't going to make people eternally grateful and shower you with gifts,' suggested Corin.

'You could say that. It's the sort of thing I don't want to discuss with colleagues let alone the Press until I know for sure what I've found is right.' He sat back and looked around the deserted bar. 'This place gives me the creeps,' he added.

'You fancy something to eat?' asked Phoebe. The two men looked at her and nodded. 'My place for a bowl of pasta, how does that grab you?' She gathered her bag and stood without waiting for a response. Corin and Pete followed her in Corin's car; Pete didn't drive and would take a bus home.

Following Phoebe's small Peugeot, Corin tried subtlety to get Pete to open up. 'Dr Richards was co-ordinating the whole research effort, wasn't she?' Pete nodded, looking out of the car window at neat suburban gardens coming into flower and wondering how much longer they would be there. 'What angle did she have you looking into?'

'I'm as geneticist, as you know. She didn't ask me to look for alien invasions,' snapped Pete.

Corin felt he had had his knuckles wrapped and withdrew his hands from the top of the steering wheel as an involuntary response. 'So you're supposed to be looking for a genetic solution to this thing then?' he asked finding it hard to believe, still sure it was something environmental.

Pete continued to stare out of the window, irritated at coming up against another sceptic. He reflected that Kate had showed more promise and would probably make a good choice for associate; nice ankles too.

Parking places were much easier to find on side roads these days and they successfully found one only yards from Phoebe's house, a Victorian mid terrace with a miniature front garden set back from the pavement and guarded by a firm iron railing. 'It's started again,' she said as they joined her in her living room. The room was remarkably modern with a fancy JVC entertainment system and large LCD TV. This showed a BBC reporter outside a hospital with a throng of other media and relatives coming and going like ants from a disturbed nest.

'*The number of deaths recorded during the last three days has risen to rates similar to those encountered during the worst periods last August. One fact is certain; there is no heat wave this time*,' he concluded, looking grim. The picture cut back to the glamorous blonde in the studio. She was new. Possibly, Corin thought, to distract people from what she was saying.

'*Thank you Alistair.*' She turned from the screen to her left and sitting so she could show as much leg as possible and still be decent before the watershed, leaned to the right and explained, '*I'm joined this evening by MP for Eastdell, Mr Martin Hayton.*' The camera panned to show the cherubic face of the familiar minister who would shortly be announced as the new Chancellor thanks to the death of Simon Robinson - together with about twenty colleagues - earlier in the week.

'*Mr Hayton,*' began the blonde, her red talons rested gently on a clear plastic clipboard, and as her left shoulder drooped towards the camera those who were interested could see her dark pink bra had delicate lace around the top. '*We appear, from what Alistair has just reported, to be experiencing a further attack of this mysterious phenomenon. Is the Government any further forward in determining a cause, and more importantly, finding a solution?*'

‘*Thank you Pamela,*’ said Hayton, the perspiration on his top lip picked out by the studio lights. ‘*I’m glad you asked me that.*’

‘I’ll bet,’ said Pete. ‘He’s drawn the short straw of who has to face the public and either lie his head off or tell the truth.’

‘There’s not much point in lying if people carry on dying,’ said Corin.

‘Shush!’ said Phoebe loudly, waving her hand for them to sit. They sat on the sofa while she sat on the edge of a chair next to the empty fire grate. All leaned forward, listening intently.

‘*… following the research scheme devised by Dr Richards last year. Results so far have mostly been of elimination, I’m sorry to say, but the more we eliminate, the more we’re honing in on the true cause all the time,*’ Hayton concluded, sitting back and smiling benignly at Pamela.

Pamela, to give her credit, didn’t look impressed. ‘*Please will you give me specific examples of things which have been eliminated, Mr Hayton,*’ she said in a school mam voice he couldn’t possibly refuse.

‘She’s taken lessons from Jeremy Paxman by the sound of it,’ said Phoebe with a grin.

‘Shush,’ said Corin and Pete together. Phoebe tutted and rolled her eyes.

‘*We’ve eliminated the majority of environmental factors … and don’t forget this is a global phenomenon so if it were environmental, it would have to be something like volcanic ash carried around the globe in the stratosphere … But it’s not,*’ he finished weakly.

‘*Anything else?*’ asked Pamela, now sitting upright thus disappointing cheap thrill seekers.

‘*On the same token, it’s nothing in the water supply or any damage to the sewerage system,*’ he added, perspiring still more.

‘*How about disease options*?’ asked Pamela, the bit between her teeth.

‘*Well, Pamela,*’ began Hayton, ‘*teams from the Medical Research Council and research staff from various countries have been working on different disease vectors so we can eliminate them as fast as possible. We can confirm it’s not a new strain of influenza, or anything else which may have derived from other species, or*

Ebola or bubonic plague, and it's nothing which might relate to unsanitary conditions such as typhoid or cholera.'

'I can't believe he just said that!' said Pete, but was shushed by the others.

'*Do these research staff feel they may be closing in on the target?*' asked Pamela in such as way she thought the answer would definitely be no.

'*Not yet, but there have been some interesting developments with work on cosmic rays*,' said Hayton as if that was marvellous.

'I can't listen to any more of this,' said Pete rising and making for the door.

'Sorry,' said Phoebe. 'I shouldn't have turned it on - just a habit I'm afraid.' She switched the set off and Pamela and Hayton vanished. She made her way through an arch to the kitchen and plugged in her kettle.

'Cosmic rays?' asked Corin, a sceptical eyebrow raised.

'Richards was asked to come up with a system which would encompass anything which might possibly impact on people living on different continents, and other than air and water, the only thing which we are all exposed to is cosmic radiation. It's not actually as daft as it sounds.'

'So why did you say you didn't want to hear any more?' asked Phoebe a bit miffed at having to turn off the programme just when it was getting interesting. She measured pasta into a saucepan and rummaged for a jar of sauce.

'I think I know what the answer is, but I know they'll never believe me,' said Pete, still standing near the door.

'So how could cosmic rays be killing specific people?' asked Corin. 'Why anyone over sixty … or anyone over fifty as it seems now?'

'That my friend,' said Pete, 'is a very good question. Thanks for the offer of food, but I've lost my appetite,' he added as he turned the handle and departed.

Corin and Phoebe exchanged a glance then Phoebe turned the TV on again. 'Other than saying he's right several times, he didn't actually tell us anything, did he?' asked Corin, just to check he hadn't missed anything.

'No. Full of himself, if you ask me. Probably got the boot and wants the world to know about it.' Phoebe dished up the pasta and gave Corin a bowlful and a spoon as he flicked through the channels. All news broadcasts were taking place outside hospitals or mortuaries. 'How old are you Corin?' she asked quietly without looking at him.

'Nearly forty. Why?'

'I hope they get this sorted before it gets to you,' she said just as softly, reaching over to give him a peck on his cheek. Corin noticed as she sat back in her chair that she wore a similar bra to Pamela.

Pete didn't go home, but took the bus back to Sudcliff Hospital and the laboratory where he hoped Kate would still be working. As he walked through the Emergency ward, he noticed the people waiting around had different expressions to those of last year. Then, they had been frantic, terrified, worried. Now they looked resigned almost expectant. He found he couldn't meet their eyes.

Taking a less picturesque way to the laboratory, Pete found Kate carefully studying something on her screen. Thankfully she was alone. He'd had enough of sceptics for one day and Hugh was a large one.

'You look glued to that thing,' he observed as he strolled into the room. He swung Hugh's chair around and pulled it across to sit next to Kate. 'Have you heard the news today?'

Kate nodded, having given him a smile of acknowledgement. 'I just can't believe it's started off again ... All over the world too. It's like something triggered it and off we go again, another few million people dying in the next few weeks. Joy,' she said helplessly.

'I didn't want to say anything in front of your hairy friend, but I can help point you in the right direction, if you'd like a hand.'

Kate looked at him with utmost incredulity. 'How can you just sit here calmly? If you think you know what's going on, you should say so.'

'OK. It's genetic,' he said simply.

'No it's not,' said Kate instantly. 'It can't be because we're all different.'

'No we're not,' said Pete holding up his forefinger and thumb with a small gap between. 'The bit that makes me Pete and the bit that makes you Kate is tiny, miniscule, titchy. All the other bits of our DNA which make us human are huge. If it's one of *them* that's gone wrong, we're all in trouble.'

Kate didn't believe him, he could tell, so he went a bit further. 'Professor Fallon worked on DNA in the nineties and he did some interesting bits of manipulation.'

'Lots of people do, what's so special about what Fallon did?' asked Kate still sceptical but interested.

'He was working on extending life.'

'So are lots of people,' Kate repeated, thinking if this was all he had, he was mad.

'He succeeded,' said Pete. Kate frowned, doubtfully. 'He succeeded in making human DNA which could survive for twice as long as normal DNA.'

'Why haven't we heard about this?' asked Kate her frown deepening.

'It only worked on DNA molecules in the laboratory, not in a living person. He started with mice and frogs. When he altered their genes with the corresponding part of their DNA, all the specimens died, but they died at a medically earlier age than their actual age in terms of days.' Kate's jaw dropped. 'He managed to make animals younger, but not to live longer.'

Kate looked more thoughtful now, the furrows smoothed. 'Why do you think this had anything to do with what's causing all these people to die?'

'I think he did manage to get it into humans. I've found an obscure record which says he treated a woman who had terminal breast cancer and agreed to be a living test tube. He manipulated her DNA so she reverted to an earlier age, thus curing the cancer.'

'But that would be the most remarkable medical breakthrough! A genetic cure for cancer using the patients own cells!' Kate sat back open mouthed and contemplated this news. She then noticed the look on Pete's bland face. 'OK, Fallon didn't receive the Nobel Prize for Medicine and put cancer hospices out of business. What happened?'

'The woman died a few weeks after leaving the clinic. The cancer didn't return but even though there was no apparent cause of death, she died.'

'No cause of death? But there must have been ...' Kate trailed off, suddenly realising what Pete was suggesting.

'Whatever he did for that woman has somehow begun to affect everyone else.'

'That's impossible. You can't change someone's DNA externally. Except at conception, it can only be altered in a laboratory.'

'Laboratory Earth,' sighed Pete. 'Ever heard the expression?' Kate nodded. 'Pru Richards had research done on everything. Cosmic radiation levels spiked last August and didn't drop again until the end of October. They've risen again recently.' He let that thought sink in for a minute. 'Our ozone layer is being depleted by all the chemicals we shove in the atmosphere. Who's to say our DNA isn't vulnerable to external forces which might affect specific nodes in our genetic makeup? Do you know what proportion of the population has died from a sudden unexpected cause of death, just something doctors - like yourself - felt was nearest to the most probable cause?'

Kate slumped down in her chair. 'You have no proof of this as such, do you? It's just a theory.'

'I've no proof, but I'm trying to find it.' He pulled his chair closer so he could rest his elbow on her desk. Their knees touched briefly until Kate moved.

'You told Pru Richards about this didn't you?' asked Kate. Pete nodded. 'What did she say?'

'She didn't like the implications and couldn't pass it higher up the food chain.'

'Implications?'

'The human race is doomed ... we're all gong to die Kate, all of us.' He bent forward and kissed her on her cheek, then turned and left, wheeling Hugh's chair back into place first.

Shocked, Kate was too numb to move and her brain stopped functioning. She sat motionless staring at a small dark rubber mark on the laboratory floor.

~*~

'You were a bit too vague with your responses to Miss World,' suggested John Mahon when he and Martin Hayton met at 10 Downing Street for their afternoon reappraisal session. 'People will get suspicious if they think we're holding something back.'

'I only told her what I knew. You're the one who knows all the secrets these scientists are discovering daily,' said Hayton in a hurt little boy voice. 'Who's putting all these theories together?' He looked straight at Mahon. 'Who's going to tell the people once we know the answer?' He wasn't a scientist, but he knew with all the great minds working on the problem throughout the world, someone would get there soon, if they hadn't already.

'In this country, now Dr Richards has died, we're relying on them all to report to the Minister of Health. Mind you, they don't seem as keen to talk to her as they did to Pru,' observed Mahon dryly.

'Threaten them with cutting their budgets.' Hayton smiled and sipped his strong black coffee.

Mahon gave his junior colleague a worried look. The turnover of MPs was rapid these days and hastily arranged by-elections were cropping up everywhere as local members died. Constituency parties had twigged and were starting to recruit younger people – idiots most of them, Mahon thought to himself.

The Health Minister Pearl Leith, MP for Westwater joined them and poured herself a glass of mineral water. Her emaciated face looked chalky in contrast to her flame red hair cascading down her bony back. The dark suit hung from her as if still on a coat-hanger and the bones of her ankles protruded above her neat black court shoes at the end of long thin legs. Mahon considered she was not a picture of health, but had at least started medical school ten years before so knew more about the science the experts were churning out than most of his Cabinet.

'Have some cake,' Hayton couldn't resist saying.

'Thank you, no. I had lunch before I came in. I can't get used to trains being practically empty these days.'

'That's the sort of thing we need to discuss,' said Mahon, moving towards the dark grey table which took up most of the space in the room. 'Gaps are appearing in our society and we need a strategy to fill them.'

'Gaps?' queried Hayton sitting next to his leader while Leith took a seat to Mahon's right.

'Initially it was in farming, which after a bit of massaging of farm and food prices has almost sorted itself out. We now have lots of enthusiastic people managing farms who haven't a clue what they're doing, but plenty of other people on hand to give advice, some of it actually useful.

'The problem is the situation is mirrored all around the world. Food shortages are beginning to appear as farmers die off and are not replaced. We need to secure food supplies here by supporting farmers, small holders, market gardeners and the like with subsidies if necessary.'

'I see the flaw in this glorious plan. How do we pay for that?' asked Hayton, taking his new position as Chancellor of the Exchequer seriously.

'This is going to be the unpopular bit. We can't divert funds from the scientific investigation into this ... thing, so we have to cut elsewhere. Pensions payments have been frozen, winter fuel payments stopped, public transport subsidies cut back, housing projects cancelled as they're not needed any more and we have to cut back on the military.'

'You're suggesting reducing military spending?' asked Hayton, astonished.

'The war on terrorism has all but stopped with all the in-fighting in the Middle East. They've been devastated by this business just the same as we have,' explained Mahon.

'And war mongering religious bigots have been replaced by hard headed young fools out to prove a point,' said Hayton firmly. Leith just stared at both of them, paler than ever.

'Have you tried to buy a gun recently or ammunition?' asked Mahon.

'Of course I haven't,' replied Hayton hotly.

Mahon continued on a different tack. 'Another thing which is suffering worldwide besides farming is mineral extraction and the supply of raw materials. Expertise and skilled workmen are being lost in all industries right across the board. We're going to start running out of stuff before long.'

'Surely people know how to mine things. It's not as if only geriatric miners existed before this.'

'People who managed and ran these places were generally older. Fewer of the younger generation are able to take over straight away, not having the training. Mistakes and accidents are happening all the time. People are being killed and thousands are leaving mines to take over farming which now pays better and is locally essential.'

'So regardless of whether gross manufacture is in place, if they're not getting the raw materials, they're not producing the goods,' clarified Hayton. Mahon nodded. 'But surely bright eyed entrepreneurs are queuing up to take over mines which are no longer operating?' he queried with a note of incredulity to his voice.

'Yes,' agreed Mahon, 'but there are so many mines and similar operations to choose from, they aren't all being worked, and as I said, as following any plague, labour is in short supply so wage demands are higher making products dearer and in some cases more marginal and less favourable. Only minerals which pay well such as iron and copper are being extracted rather than the more difficult but equally essential ones like aluminium.'

He sat up and pulled his notepad towards him. 'We're here to discuss budget cuts and come up with some ideas to put to the Cabinet.' He looked at his colleagues. 'Let's start with the military and work our way out, shall we?' Leith and Hayton both scowled, knowing the response they would get from their Cabinet colleagues.

'It's such a sore subject,' began Leith. 'There's genuine concern that unless we find the real solution to this thing, the newspapers are going to speculate even more about germ warfare, bio-weapons or nuclear attacks. We may even need the military to quell rioting if people's minds aren't put to rest soon.'

'What's the latest report on finding the cause?' asked Hayton, putting Leith under the spotlight.

'We're expanding more into genetic work, although how that could affect so many people I'm afraid I don't understand,' said Leith.

'You don't need to understand it, as long as they're doing something,' said Mahon.

'So ... cutting the Army's budget ... presumably a lot of top brass have ... died recently and we won't be paying pensions to their widows, so why not just reduce the size of each of the forces proportionally to the population?' suggested Hayton.

'Marvellous,' said Mahon. 'That's the military budget sorted. Is there any way we can save on the health budget?' he asked, turning to Leith.

'No,' she said simply, 'if you want us to keep investigating ...'

'The investigation process is to be funded separately. I was referring to the Health Service budget,' said Mahon.

'Well,' she began promisingly. 'Obviously geriatrics has been reduced, and for some reason maternity and paediatrics are less demanding of late, but people are still suffering from normal illnesses and accidents just as they did before. Almost a third of the population has died, and one of the more expensive thirds too, so I could let you have ... a third,' she offered tentatively.

'Marvellous,' said Mahon again.

'Are we intending to do anything about reports from poorer areas of the country where things aren't going quite according to plan?' asked Leith.

'Poorer areas?' asked Hayton as if he'd never heard of such things.

'Some people are becoming desperate and drugs barons are making further inroads into certain elements of society, and finding new markets,' she explained. Hayton frowned, but Mahon shifted uneasily. 'People who have had a sudden loss of income and subsequent life style shift are struggling, and many are being medicated. What happens when the medication runs out? In some areas, it's like the aftermath of the Wall Street Crash in 1929, or after natural disasters like the Christchurch earthquakes.'

'Are you suggesting this thing is affecting crime?' asked Mahon.

'The Home Secretary informs me crime per head is on the increase, despite the decrease in population. It may just be more crime is reported as people are more aware of their neighbours and what's happening around them,' she replied, her superior manner grated on Mahon.

'Personal property is definitely being targeted,' he agreed. 'Vigilantes, people defending property with guns is on the increase too. Citizens are either taking the law into their own hands or resorting to protection rackets. We may have to take back law and order from local authorities and come up with some sort of civil defence mechanism.'

'Another thing ... the major supermarkets have reported apparent hoarding of dried and tinned goods. It seems not everyone is convinced we shall be able to determine a cause for the thing and do something about it ... before it's too late,' said Leith.

'I've heard reports of increased vandalism against religious sites,' chipped in Hayton, as if to show he had his finger on the pulse. 'Wiltshire police are mounting a guard on Stonehenge.'

'Graves have been desecrated and monuments vandalised. Red paint, or possibly blood was smeared on the statue of the St Michael at Coventry Cathedral, amongst others,' admitted Mahon, reluctantly.

'You think this might be some new religion ... or anti-religious cult?' asked Hayton.

'People need an explanation for what's happening around them,' pointed out Leith. 'If we don't give them one, someone else will, be it the newspapers, scientists or religious cranks.'

'I'd better call another Press conference ... make a statement,' said Mahon, closing the meeting by getting to his feet. 'Give me what you can Leith, and I'll try to smooth the troubled waters. Get specifics from the Home Secretary; pin point which areas are having problems. We'll offer aid and draft in more police ... or military if needed.'

'In spite of their budget cuts,' said Hayton quietly as he too rose.

'The people need some sort of hope, some sort of Messiah to follow. See if you can find someone ... doesn't matter what sphere ... sport, leisure, science, whatever.' Mahon left the room striding tall and confidently down the corridor.

'He's as worried as hell,' observed Hayton.

'He's the man overseeing the breakdown of our society.'

'That's a bit gloomy.'

'It's realistic. We haven't a hope and he knows it,' said Pearl Leith as she walked towards the stairs.

~*~

'It's funny how many people feel the need to have a firearm these days,' said Errol Williams as he took the Mossberg pump action shotgun back from Louise McVey.

Without showing any sign of having heard him, she asked, 'how many cartridges do you get in the box?'

'Twenty five of the 12 gauge. I have smaller hand guns which you might find more suitable for your purpose,' explained Errol, aware of the blank expression on the woman's face.

'My purpose?' asked Louise after a moment or two. She looked at him for the first time since she had walked into his shop in Eastdell, not far from her home in Comfortby. She had pointed out the shotgun and asked to hold it. She'd felt its balance against her shoulder and looked along the barrel peering down its fourteen inch length before admiring it once more while Errol explained how the magazine was loaded.

'I imagine you need it for defence ... keep away intruders. There're lots of dodgy people about.'

'Yes,' she agreed absently and paid for the shotgun without considering anything else.

'Have you used a shotgun at all?' he asked, doubtfully.

'My husband took me clay pigeon shooting one Christmas,' she replied, vaguely. Having completed the licensing paperwork, she left with it in its shoulder carrying bag and a box of cartridges in her handbag.

'Odd,' said Errol to himself after she'd gone. He didn't know Mrs McVey at all, except that she owned the health food shop. He'd noticed it was boarded up the last time he'd been passed it, like so many others. She must have taken her stock home and run the business from there, as people did nowadays. It made it more difficult for shoppers not having everything side by side on one street, but it kept overheads down.

Louise drove around in her Clio for a while, the unpacked loaded shotgun on the passenger seat beside her, eventually pulling into the small private car park behind Boots in Westwater.

'You'll get clamped if you leave it there, love,' advised an obliging passer-by as Louise got out of the car, dragging the gun towards her.

'Thanks,' she replied without interest.

She walked into the small branch of Boots, the shotgun hanging beneath her coat beside her, and made her way to the pharmacy at the back. 'Hello,' she began. 'Do you have anything for depression?'

Bryony Unwin turned to look at her as she finished moving filled prescriptions into a more orderly fashion. 'I'm sorry. Have you seen your doctor?'

'I'll fit him in later. I just wondered what *you* would recommend.'

'Perhaps you should talk to someone first, before resorting to medication.' Bryony looked more closely at Louise, but as she was next to the counter, she couldn't see the gun. Before her stood a middle aged woman, her greying hair escaping from its combs at the back, dark sleepless rings around her tired eyes, the sagging pale cheeks of someone not eating properly and a listless posture telegraphing her need for help.

'You want to talk?' asked Louise in a tone which suggested she was indifferent to the answer.

Bryony helpfully looked at her watch. 'I'm free for lunch in half an hour. I could talk to you then.' She smiled benignly.

'I won't be around then,' said Louise.

'I'm sorry to hear that.'

'Neither will you,' said Louise as she pulled up the shotgun and shot Bryony in the chest.

The explosion from the gun was followed by a moment of shocked silence then the howling screams and a mad scramble for the doors as the rest of the staff and customers tried to get away from the mad woman with the shotgun. Bryony's body lay in a heap against the bloodstained wall behind her, covered in tablets and capsules, with orange liquid from someone's medication dripping down the front of her white tunic. Her wide eyes still stared forward in surprise and her mouth hung slightly open.

Louise looked with satisfaction at her handiwork, turned and left the empty shop. The sound of sirens bounced from the walls of the high street shops. She carried the gun beside her once more and with debris from boxes and prescriptions in her hair and on her clothes, she casually walked down the street as if nothing had happened.

She continued until she reached the doctor's surgery. In here, she didn't wait to ask for an appointment or any remedy for depression. She shot the solid receptionist as she sat at her desk, then the practice nurse in the back as she tried to get away. Having reloaded, she shot three people who came from the examination rooms to see what was going on.

While reloading again, she left the surgery. By this time the police had got their act together and had closed the street off and waited for her behind parked patrol cars. 'Lay the weapon on the ground and come out with your hands in the air,' commanded a voice through a loud-haler.

Louise ignored the voice and carried on walking back to where she had parked the Clio, the gun still beside her. She walked towards one police marksman and away from two others. Surprised by her calm demeanour and unusual reaction, they were unsure what to do, so merely kept their guns trained on her and let her pass. Frightened voyeurs stood quietly behind the police, hands covering mouths, tears rolling down cheeks, faces pale, as they watched a woman who had lost control, seek vengeance on those she felt had wronged her.

She made it back to her car - which hadn't been clamped - without anyone trying to stop her. 'I'm afraid I can't let you leave madam,' said a young policeman standing next to the bonnet. 'You've killed half a dozen people. You can't expect to just walk away.'

'I don't,' she said, placing the gun beside her as she got into her car and put it into reverse.

'I'm placing you under arrest,' the policeman found himself saying, a desperate tone in his voice.

'No you're not,' said Louise quite calmly. 'I'm leaving and you can't do a thing about it.'

Two of the three marksmen arrived just as Louise drove off, one getting a shot at the car, but the other told him off for firing with all the people about.

Sirens pursued Louise down the road as she drove rapidly towards Norleigh. By now the news of the murders had got onto the radio and someone had identified her. Judy, from the comfort of her cottage in Summerton, almost choked on the biscuit she was eating when the news was broken. She tried calling her mother on her mobile but it was switched off. She tried the home landline number but it went straight to the answer-phone. About to hang up, not wanting to waste her breath on a machine, she stopped as she heard the message. '*Hi, I'm sorry I can't come to the phone. Actually I'm not sorry. I'm not sorry about anything. I've given it some serious thought and quite honestly, none of this is worth it. Leave a message if you want to, but I won't get back to you.*' Judy couldn't believe the total despair and misery in the voice. She knew her mother's business hadn't done much better even with the advertising campaign, but she was still trading and things had apparently improved since she'd moved to her house. She'd appeared happier there, being able to look after the garden and her birds, but it seemed that hadn't been enough.

Louise still felt remarkably calm and self-assured when she screeched to a halt outside Norleigh Hospital. Taking the shotgun, she walked through the reception area, along a few grey tiled corridors and through a set of swing doors marked *Private, Doctors only*. By the time she reached this point, the police had begun to empty the hospital of those who could move fast enough and followed her to the doctor's lounge. They found her pointing the shotgun at Dr Bragg. On the floor with a wisp of smoke curling from the hole in her chest, lay Sister Johnson. Dr Dixon knelt beside her body, looking up at Louise.

'What the hell did you do that for?' he demanded as he got swiftly to his feet. 'She's been working tirelessly soothing the sick and suffering, comforting the bereaved and ministering to the dying ... Why?'

'She was next ... It's my turn soon. You'll be going in a few months. Do you really want to waste your time here, pandering to that lot,' Louise jerked her head back the way she had come through the wards. 'Get out while you can,' she said, pointing the gun at the two doctors. 'Live what little life you have left. See the world while it's still here.' She cocked the gun and held it up ready to shoot. The two men backed away, getting through the door and running down the corridor.

'What's she done?' asked the same young policeman from Boots' car park.

'Shot Sister Johnson ... for no reason whatever,' complained a tearful Dr Dixon.

'You get back. We'll take over,' the policeman commanded and nodded at his two armed colleagues to get down the corridor. They crept along either side wall, stealthily making their way towards the lounge. A thunderous boom shattered the unhealthy silence and both marksmen froze then cautiously moved towards the smoke filled doorway.

Louise, what was left of her, lay across the dead body of Sister Johnson, her face blown off by the close blast from the shotgun.

Chapter eight

Tuesday 9th August 2016

'You know people spend a lot of time reading the list of deaths in the newspaper,' Belle Williams observed to Errol as he read the back page of his choice of *The Westwater Illumination,* the remaining regional newspaper.

'Yeah,' he said, not listening.

'Well, have you noticed the lack of corresponding births?' she asked.

'Yeah,' he said, getting his cue wrong.

'Is it noticeable in yours too?' she asked, her voice quickening as she reached to grab his paper.

'Oi!' he cried. 'I was in the middle of that!'

'You were at the end of it,' said Belle, pealing off the back page to return to him while she hunted for births, marriages and deaths.

Nerys, topping a piece of toast with a smear of strawberry jam leaned over her shoulder to see if her mother was right.

'None,' said Belle triumphantly. 'No births. I've been looking over the last couple of weeks. No births have been reported at all.' She sounded thrilled.

'No births,' repeated Nerys, her toast wavering and in danger of dripping a strawberry onto the tablecloth. 'But that's not right surely.'

'Unless the papers have all decided not to report any – there are none in the nationals either,' confirmed Belle.

Nerys put her toast on its plate and took *The Daily Telegraph* from her mother, looking for anything which might mention this odd fact. Finding nothing, she looked back through *The Illumination* to see if Corin Lister had anything to say. He'd become even more belligerent and controversial over the last few weeks and would probably get the sack soon, she thought. His article in this week's offering was on the likely repercussions of the defence cuts to our NATO commitments and the consequences to vulnerable Third World countries.

'Lister says there're huge numbers of refugees travelling the globe in search of sanctuary as dictatorships spring up in South American and African countries and military coups are becoming more common. There's nothing here about no babies being born though. Maybe it's just a seasonal lull,' suggested Nerys, unconvinced.

'People don't reproduce in spring like sheep you know,' said Belle, surprised at her daughter. 'There's something weird going on. I just hope it's got nothing to do with this thing.'

'Why would it have anything to do with people dying?' asked Nerys, genuinely puzzled.

'Well ... you know ... it might have,' said Belle vaguely. She plucked the sports page back from Errol, put *The Illumination* back together and handed it back to him.

He picked up *The Telegraph* and read an article about the problems in oil fields. He summarised for them. 'It says here that after some of the Middle Eastern oilfields were attacked in the Mediterranean War, the petrochemical plants have seeped oil and leaked gas leading to explosions and toxic fires, belching smoke and fumes miles into the atmosphere. This isn't a nice list: "*benzene, ammonia, heavy metals and sulphur stored and transported under high pressure and temperature systems, are creating pools of hot corrosive liquids and acid rain.*" Good heavens; "*static electricity from the pipes and lightning has resulted in fires and the acid rain will eventually cause global environmental devastation and the deaths of many plants, animals and birds.*" That's jolly!'

'They're saying with the majority of the affected oilfields abandoned or destroyed, the world isn't producing enough oil to last the next couple of years, let alone a few decades,' commented Nerys quietly.

'You wouldn't have thought a war ... so bloody and quick ... could have left so much devastation,' said Errol equally softly.

Fears for the Third World War hadn't materialised after the series of up risings and revolutions were quelled within a few months of springing up, having begun in 2011 and kicked off again in 2013 in the North African and Middle Eastern countries ringing the Mediterranean. Fortunately the United States held off joining in, thus delaying Europe's involvement and some of the ugliest conflicts of the twenty first century thus far were settled internally, but with shattering environmental consequences, and potentially leaving a long term fuel crisis.

Ross emerged at the doorway still in his pyjama bottoms. He rubbed his eyes sleepily. 'You need a paper round,' Belle observed and poured him a cup of tea.

Ross yawned widely, stretched theatrically, and plonked into the chair next to Nerys. He finished her piece of toast and began to butter a slice of his own. 'This is all very functional and conventional; the whole family sitting around the table eating breakfast together. We must try harder to give our neighbours something to gossip about,' he commented. Errol clocked him affectionately around the head with the paper.

'Any good news in the papers you'd like to share?' Ross asked, chewing.

'The financial section goes on about the lack of imports,' advised Errol.

'Didn't know you read the financial section,' Ross said with a smile. 'What sort of imports?' he asked, spreading another slice of toast with jam.

'White goods mostly; electrical stuff like washing machines and microwaves.'

'Carpets and furniture too,' added Nerys pouring a second cup of coffee.

'Stuff for houses; that makes sense,' said Ross nodding. 'House building's stopped and people must already have all the stuff they need. It's probably just things that break and need replacing Comet is selling now.'

'It's hell trying to get a plumber these days. Have you heard?' noted Errol.

'What do you need a plumber for?' asked Belle.

'Leaking pipe under the sink at the shop. Bloke down the street did it in the end; I was sick of mopping and buckets everywhere.'

Nerys was looking through *The Illumination* again. 'Had you heard that St Mary's church at Comfortby is closing?' The others shook their heads and looked blankly at her. 'The vicar, Mr Hilliard died a month ago and the Church Commissioners have decided to try to sell the building. Apparently they'd hardly anyone coming to services even before he died once all the old ladies had gone. It says the verger was the only one turning up for services.'

'Pity,' said Belle. 'It's a nice church. I suppose someone'll convert it into a house or craft centre or something. It's not that big a building, or that old.'

'I can't really say I'd thought of turning to religion after this thing started,' observed Errol. 'I mean, all they try to do is get you to stop listening to the scientists for explanations just because they don't seem to be able to find anything. They're saying we should stick with divine intervention and all live blameless lives.'

'That doesn't really hold water with all the popes, bishops, priests and clergy who have died,' observed Ross wryly.

'They say we should all be helping our neighbours both physically and spiritually, and not losing self control in despair about what's happening or resorting to blaming everyone else,' said Belle.

'They didn't help that woman who went round shooting everyone in May,' said Ross.

'I know, but churches have been offering comfort and a listening ear to some people's fears and expectations, as well as giving practical advice and help with funerals and things,' said Nerys, rather defensively.

'There're plenty of new religions cropping up too, have you heard?' asked Ross. His mother didn't like the glint in his eye when he mentioned this.

'How new?' she asked worriedly.

'You know; communes and cults with people preaching about clean, simple living. They're probably making lots of money out of people scared stiff of dying,' explained Ross.

'I've heard some of these cults involve sacrifices, like witchcraft and stuff,' said Errol then added with a quick glance at Belle, 'probably lots of free sex now you say no one's getting pregnant. It's no longer the act of procreation, it's simply for pleasure.' Belle was as shocked as Errol hoped she'd be, but his children took it in their stride.

'There's more alcohol and drug abuse again, more escapism into 3D games and fancy dress partying with role plays,' said Nerys blandly.

'And hunting's started up again … hunting people as well as animals, whether the hunters are on horse back, on motor bikes, in four by fours or even on foot. They use all sorts of weapons too … dogs, guns, or crossbows,' said Ross.

This held up the conversation for a few minutes as each reflected on what they had been discussing. 'This is a bit heavy for first thing in the morning,' said Belle quietly.

'Just repeating what's in the papers. You can ignore it but it won't go away. Things aren't what they used to be,' observed Errol philosophically.

After another pause, Ross asked in his sweetest voice, 'is it all right if I go round to Jimmy's this morning Mum?'

'Jimmy?' she frowned in an effort of remembrance. 'Oh yes, Jimmy. I should think so. Don't be a nuisance. I know his mum's not well.'

'She's better than she was and likes help around the house,' he said between mouthfuls.

'Oh, so you can help Jimmy's mum around the house but I have to follow behind you with a broom I suppose,' said Belle crossly. Errol smirked behind his newspaper.

'What's wrong with Jimmy's mum?' asked Nerys.

'She was in the car when her dad has his heart attack … Drove her into a wall; she's lucky to be alive. Got a broken collar bone and two fractures in her left leg. She'll be a while before she's on her feet again,' explained Belle.

'So it's all right if I go round then?' asked Ross again, bringing them back to his original point.

'Come back here for lunch, don't make too much noise or cause any problems, don't worry the neighbours, don't play music too loud and don't … '

'All right Mum!' said Ross. 'I promise I'll just go round, sit perfectly still and breathe really softly.' He rose and left to get showered and dressed.

'Saucy little bugger,' muttered Errol folding the paper. 'He's only going round there 'cos her fancies Jimmy's sister.'

'How old is she?' asked Belle with mild interest.

'She's in my year,' said Nerys. 'You know her; the red head … works Saturday mornings at the hairdressers.'

Belle gave a puzzled frown then her eyes widened as she realised who Nerys meant. 'Her!' she said appalled. 'My baby and that girl!' she added hotly her face turning puce. 'That fast and lose trollop and my little angel!' She turned to Errol who looked amused. 'You have to do something Errol. You're his father.'

'Too right love,' he said getting to his feet and kissing his wife's forehead. 'Just glad I'm not hers.' He left to get ready for work leaving Belle doing goldfish impressions and Nerys clearing the breakfast table with a broad grin.

Jimmy's red haired sister ushered the two boys out of the house shortly after Ross arrived saying her mother needed peace and quiet. 'Got some bloke coming round, I should think,' gruffed Jimmy. 'Let's go to the park.' They collected a skateboard each as well as a football and sauntered to Eastdell Park half a mile away.

'Isn't that those Porter kids your mum looks after?' asked Jimmy, pointing his skateboard at Carl and Stuart, playing on the roundabout.

'Fancy a knock about?' yelled Ross.

'Sure,' said Stuart enthusiastically, running towards them just behind Carl. Being asked to play football with these older boys was a dream come true. Jimmy and Ross exchanged a glance, but both felt this would pass the time until something better presented itself.

Jimmy, once he'd warmed up by skilfully dribbling the ball out of Stuart's reach, did tricks with bouncing the ball on his ankles and knees, then passed it to Ross who performed a couple of passes with Carl then Stuart, then kicked the ball hard into the distance for the younger ones to chase.

The ball arrived at the feet of Dan McVey, holding back Suzie who strained against her leash to get at the ball and play with the children. He did the honourable thing and kicked it neatly back to Carl, who muttered thanks and dashed back to Jimmy and Ross.

Dan's other hand was still clasped to that of his young wife Rachel who was doing her best not to cry. The breath of fresh air Dan thought she needed didn't seem to be doing her any good. 'We'll just keep trying,' he said for the umpteenth time. 'The doctor said there's nothing wrong with either of us, so it's just a matter of time and patience.'

'We've been married for two months,' replied Rachel as if Dan wouldn't know that. 'It's not as if we haven't been trying,' she added, sniffing.

Dan tried hard not to smirk. He'd enjoyed all the trying and wasn't sure how he would feel when they finally succeeded. Perhaps Rachel might go off the idea of children if she didn't conceive soon. Perhaps she might become ill during her pregnancy and not want any more. He gave her a hug and pulled Suzie away from a disgusting looking bag of mouldy chips that had missed the bin. A blackbird zipped across the path with a beak full of drooping worms. A robin sang proudly in a branch above their head's declaring his territory. A couple of mute swans on the lake gracefully danced around each other, giving every indication of being in love, followed by a flotilla of four cygnets. Rachel's tears flowed.

Despite his mother Louise's infamous killing spree in May, they had continued with their early June wedding as planned. His sister Judy had understandably been in a poor state and had still not really recovered from the shock. Her neighbours Valerie and Jim Cahill had done what they could to help her over the worst part – keeping the journalists at bay, the gossips with vicious tongues saying madness was inherited, and being shunned by just about everyone else. Her design work orders were cancelled but for a change not because anyone had died from the thing – except indirectly thanks to her own mother.

Consequently, Dan found himself surrounded by wailing women. He tried to make them happy but it was a struggle at times. He enjoyed working on computers more than ever; they didn't have emotions, just crashes and power-outages.

'We'll go back to the doctor and get him to check again,' suggested Dan as the only thing he could think of to make Rachel calm down.

She tightened her grip on his hand. 'I'm sorry love,' she hiccupped. 'I just expected to be pregnant by now. I never thought it would be this difficult.'

Dan sighed as they left the park, and drove home to Sudcliff for lunch, making their way back via Judy's house to return Suzie.

~*~

Hayley Watts, still in her horsehair white wig and barrister's black gown, met Alexis for lunch in the Norleigh High Court dining room. She sighed as she took her seat, having kissed Alexis on the cheek first.

'Not a good day?' suggested Alexis, browsing the menu.

'Busy,' replied her mother. 'It's just over a year since both my parents died and my client is claiming self-defence for shooting the young man who tried to break into her recently deceased father's house. The Prosecuting Counsel claims it was hardly self defence as she had a loaded revolver on her at the time.'

'How're you going to get her out of that?'

'I shall claim it's a sign of the times. Everyone has loaded revolvers under their pillows these days. The young man thought the house was empty but she was staying overnight because sorting out her father's things and boxing up paperwork was taking longer than expected. She heard the breaking window in the pantry and sorted him out.'

'She didn't kill him did she?' asked Alexis, horrified.

'No, just winged him. He ran off, got himself repaired at the hospital. His brother said he should be able to get her put away – actual bodily harm. All very Christian and forgiving. God I'm tired.' She looked it too with dark rings around her eyes and a sallow complexion.

'Why don't you take a break Mum? You need time for yourself.'

'Too much to do. Property defence cases like this are more common these days, and its not just houses. Business premises seem to be fair game for young criminals these days.' Hayley removed her wig and slid off her gown, folding it neatly over the back of an empty chair.

'James, my senior clerk died yesterday. He was only forty five, like me,' she explained quietly. 'I'd have closed up, if I hadn't been booked for court today. He just collapsed while handing me some case notes. Had an aneurism right there in court. Never recovered.' She stared vacantly out of the leaded window for a few seconds, Alexis barely breathing across from her.

They ate their simple lunches of locally produced lettuce and tomato salad and egg sandwiches with only a few words about the weather being hot and dry again and Alexis' practical work at Norleigh Hospital in preparation for her finals. Hayley paid for the meal, redressed herself appropriately and returned to the fray, while Alexis went back to the hospital.

An hour or so later the paramedic joked, 'I didn't know aneurisms were catching,' as he wheeled the trolley into the Emergency Room. Dr Andrew Bragg frowned at the man who apologised and left swiftly, having helped to transfer the inert body onto a trolley. Alexis' hand went to her mouth as she failed to stifle a scream, and then promptly fainted.

On the bed lay the freshly dead body of her mother, Hayley, still in her wig and gown.

~*~

'I sent Alexis home in a taxi, poor kid,' explained Dr Bragg as he made himself and Graham Dixon a camomile tea each in the staff lounge at Norleigh Hospital; coffee was too expensive for the staff lounge. Graham accepted his mug languidly as he continued to lie back in his chair quietly staring at the cracks in the ceiling. He'd been offered counselling following the traumatic event of Sister Johnson's murder in May, but had refused saying it would take him away from work and where he was needed, and claimed he'd dealt with things like that before. He had dealt with people who had been shot, but not on the receiving end. Over the last three months he'd become quiet and thoughtful, often brooding.

Andrew opened *The Daily Telegraph* a previous occupant had left on the low table and flicked through the depressing pages. He read that despite the Chancellor dropping interest rates to virtually zero making investment capital cheaper and the stock market more appealing to investors, this still wasn't happening and the economy had slowed to a crawl. The finance reporter speculated this was due to huge uncertainty and lack of faith in the future. Andrew felt people were too busy or too sceptical to believe in financial institutions any longer.

He threw the paper down and joined Graham in contemplating the ceiling. 'I didn't think I envisioned any of this when I took up medicine,' he said softly, mostly to himself. Graham murmured something Andrew couldn't make out but took to be a question.

'I thought I'd be curing people, making them better, cheering up relatives and bringing babies into the world.' He sighed again. 'Now I'm dispatching people and ordering death certificates like there's no tomorrow and haven't delivered a baby for over six months.' He sat up. 'Don't you think that's odd?'

'You're in ER not Maternity. Not odd at all,' said Graham, sipping his drink and wincing. He pulled himself upright with an effort and went to add another spoon of precious sugar.

'You've noticed there haven't been any new pregnancies then?' asked Kate Jordan making herself an herbal tea as Graham stirred his camomile and returned to his seat. She'd spent the morning in a meeting of pathologists at Norleigh and was grabbing a drink before heading back to Sudcliff.

'Not especially. Why is there a problem?'

'I don't know if it's a problem, but it's mentioned in a couple of papers,' replied Kate, leaning against the cabinet next to the kettle and looking at the tired doctors. With her hair tied back in a pony tail, her blouse collar sticking up from her white coat and her shoes less than shiny, she gave the impression of someone who didn't spend a lot of time in front of a mirror.

'You're looking a bit rough these days,' observed Andrew.

'Pot calling the kettle black,' said Kate with a grin, readjusting her collar and admiring Andrew's less than immaculate presentation. 'Dr Chambers must be spinning in his grave at the thought of you two looking like a couple of tramps have wandered in and pinched a white coat each.'

Graham looked at Andrew in his prone position, noticed the unshaven chin, the spiky hair, the crooked tie and smiled. 'A couple of tramps,' he acknowledged.

'So how come you've noticed no babies have been born if you're working so hard to find out what's killing everyone?' asked Graham to divert attention from his scruffy appearance.

'We do biopsy work too and get samples from babies who've died at birth or become ill shortly after birth. We haven't had anything for months. I checked with Maternity at Sudcliff and here; neither has had any new referrals for months now. It seems few women, if any, are getting pregnant around here.'

'No one is getting pregnant and reporting to Maternity,' clarified Graham pedantically.

Kate smiled at him. 'Do you know if the Ministry are doing anything about it?' Both men smirked. Kate groaned. 'I mean investigating. I've not heard anything official, but rumours are starting that it's probably a worldwide phenomenon. Have you heard anything?'

The two doctors exchanged a glance and both shook their heads, but were interested. 'I'll just clarify,' said Graham reaching a long arm to the phone on the table beside him and asked to be put through to Maternity. He had a brief conversation with the ward sister. 'She says you're right; they've had no actual births since April and no referrals from GPs since last year.' He let this information sink in for a moment or two. 'She says they've been dealing more with paediatrics overspill than births. More children are left unsupervised these days – no grandparents to babysit – and are having more accidents.'

'That means no one has conceived around here since last July or August. That can't be coincidence,' said Andrew. Suddenly both he and Graham got to their feet and purposefully left the lounge. 'I'll check with Eastdell, you check with Westwater,' he said.

Kate, on leaving the room with her mug added, 'I'll try other counties too.'

As she reached the laboratory, she logged on to a vacant computer and began typing an e-mail when the telephone rang. She looked around the deserted laboratory and picked up the receiver. 'Is that you Kate? They said at reception you might be on this extension. It's Pete, Pete Yeoman,' said the high floaty voice. Kate hadn't spoken to him for a while, nor given a lot of consideration to what he was researching. 'Is there any chance we could meet up?' he asked. 'I've something to tell you ... well tell someone and I'd rather it was you.'

Pete wasn't on Kate's list of favourite people, let alone anywhere near the top so she was reluctant. 'Can't you just tell me now? ... I'm busy.'

'I'd rather see you in person and I have data I need to show you. I want your advice,' he added softly.

Unsure now, Kate had another go. 'Look Pete, if it's really important you should be taking it up with Miss Leith, the Minister. I just work in a lab and I've already got too much to do.'

'I'll buy you dinner. It may be my last chance,' said Pete, evidently not to be put off. 'Pick you up at seven,' he added. 'I know where you live.' He hung up.

Kate found this last statement disconcerting, but tried to put it out of her mind. If she got a free dinner, she might as well meet him, listen to him, repeat her advice about who to talk to, and then go home.

She sent her e-mail to her regional colleagues and a couple of other hospitals asking each if they had also had a dearth of conceptions and lack of births then made a move to return to Sudcliff. Hugh was in holiday in Ireland, playing rugby with the Wilverton Wasps and wouldn't be back for three days and she was surprised how much she missed him, occasionally finding herself turning to look at his empty chair, as if surprised by the lack of mumbling and low level swearing she normally got from his corner.

Leaving the laboratory at five thirty gave her just enough time to get home, grab a quick shower and make herself presentable for Pete. It wasn't a date, but she didn't know who else might be at the restaurant. Wearing a long turquoise blue dress with a plunge neckline, she was climbing into her three inch heeled sandals when he rang her doorbell.

Pete looked her up and down, eyes wide and said, 'you look nice,' at which Kate glared. 'Sorry, I mean beautiful. I just wasn't expecting you to have gone to any effort.' He nodded appreciatively. 'You look great, really great.'

Kate had had enough compliments by this time and moved him aside while she locked her door and followed him to the kerb where he had a taxi waiting. 'I didn't think you'd want to go by bus,' he observed as she made herself comfortable. They travelled in relative silence for ten minutes, randomly mentioning what a bright day it had been, Hugh's holiday, and Pete's hoped for holiday cycling around France, by which time they arrived at the Rustic Basket in Sudcliff, Pete's favourite vegetarian restaurant.

After swiftly perusing the menu and finding the food sounded surprisingly tasty, Kate chose a spinach and mushroom risotto and Pete went for pasta. 'You said you couldn't talk to me over the phone. I assumed you had something to show me on your laptop,' Kate said, getting straight to business.

'No, I've brought you a hardcopy summary of my findings so far and I'm not sure whether to publish or not as it's not complete. My problem is finding peers … most of them are dead, which is kind of ironic when I tell you what I've found.' He handed over a bulging manila folder secured with a couple of red elastic bands.

'Go on then,' said Kate after she had sampled and approved the organic chardonnay the waitress offered her.

'Did you read Fallon?' he asked, expecting her to say no.

'I started, but as I only did one term on genetics it didn't give me enough of a grounding to understand what Fallon was working on.'

'Fallon was working on a project to extend life,' stated Pete, leaning forwards and looking earnestly into Kate's eyes.

'You told me. He didn't do a very good job,' said Kate, half joking.

'No, he didn't,' agreed Pete. 'He made a right mess of things.'

The waitress brought a carafe of water and bread rolls for their soup. 'What do you mean?' asked Kate, concerned and tearing a bread bun in half, scattering poppy seeds across the white tablecloth.

'He did the opposite. He shortened life.' The soup arrived. 'He caused this,' stated Pete emphatically.

Kate dropped some bread into her locally sourced cream of tomato and swirled it around. 'How?' she asked.

'Have you heard of telomeres?' asked Pete, leaning forward again, talking quietly. Kate shook her head. 'Telomeres are long regions of repetitive DNA at the end of chromosomes - the structures in your cells which contain the genes. Humans have twenty three chromosomes. The telomeres protect them from partial degradation each time a cell divides ... like the end of a shoe lace that keeps it from fraying,' Pete explained. Kate nodded.

'With each cell division, the telomere shortens slightly which limits the cells to a fixed number of divisions, suggesting telomeres are responsible for aging on the cellular level and setting a limit on lifespan. Telomeres also protect cells from forming cancers by ensuring cell death.' Pete had some soup and a mouthful of bread but he had Kate's wrapped attention. 'Many aging-related diseases are linked to shortened telomeres. Organs deteriorate as more and more of their cells die off. Fallon was working a various drugs which would activate the enzymes which stimulate telomere production, the theory being this would extend life.'

'I remember you saying he actually tried it,' said Kate softly.

Pete nodded, 'but there's also other research to show that extending telomeres may actually shorten rather than extend life.'

'So what did he do ... Are you suggesting he's responsible for everyone over sixty dying?' Kate couldn't get the disbelief out of her voice.

'Over fifty,' corrected Pete. Kate acknowledged this pedantry with a glare.

'I'm suggesting he succeeded in encouraging the enzymes which make telomeres, but it had the opposite effect to what he was expecting.'

'Do you have proof? Come to think of it, how could he have started something which affected all parts of the world simultaneously?' Kate was not convinced. The main course arrived while Pete composed his answer.

'I have Fallon's notes and the conclusions he was working on when he died. He wasn't far off publishing his findings,' Pete smiled at this. 'Ironic really; his major breakthrough and it could mean the death of every human on the planet.'

'Did he name this enzyme which has turned on everyone's telomeres?' asked Kate crossly stirring her rice mixture vigorously.

Pete watched her demolishing her meal as he swirled his pasta on his spoon with a practiced hand. 'It's one found naturally in the body. He hadn't worked out a way to increase it, but discovered it was increasing anyway although he couldn't work out why it had suddenly begun to activate.'

'You have?' asked Kate.

Pete smiled. 'I might have, but I'm still got a few vital pieces missing - the trigger mechanism for one - so I'm not close enough to tell everyone yet. I just want to know what you think about what I've found so far.'

'Like I said on the phone, tell the Minister,' said Kate. 'You need to show what you've got to other competent specialists and see if they agree with what you've found ... they might not be expert geneticists, but you know how peer review works.'

Pete nodded then pointed at his empty plate he informed her, 'they do really good ice cream here; all local organic and natural flavours made on the premises.'

Kate patted her tummy and breathed out. 'I'll have a pause and then give the strawberry one a go.'

'Have you heard the Americans are working on clone research to see if they can find a cure?' asked Pete provocatively.

'How would cloning help to find a cure?'

'Remember they don't know about my research so don't really know what they're looking for. Creating pure stem cells may flip the DNA back to where it should be.'

'But if, as you believe, something is making these telomeres increase in activity anyway, mending things genetically isn't going to make any difference, is it?'

Pete shook his head. 'I don't think so, no; a) they have to find the cause, b) they have to find a potential cure, c) they have to run tests to see if it works, d) they have to find a way to get it to every human, or at least a decent sized group. Personally I doubt they have the time … even if I told them to look at telomeres, it wouldn't make any difference.'

Kate frowned and leaned forward again to play with the flower arrangement, noticing how cold the petals of the carnation felt. 'You seem remarkably calm for a man who's predicting the end of the human race,' she observed, looking straight into his eyes for any trace of a reaction.

Pete sighed and his face took on a resigned look. 'I've been looking into this for months now and I've become used to the idea.'

'You think there's nothing we can do about it?' asked Kate leaving the flower alone and giving Pete her undivided attention once more.

'Not in the time we've got left. I imagine we ought to be planning for what sort of world we'll leave for our children to inherit, bearing in mind they'll still be children when they inherit it.'

'You think the process will slowly work down from oldest to youngest?' asked Kate, thinking of it as a philosophical exercise.

Pete took a breath. 'That seems to be what's happening which would be logical. The oldest have fewer telomeres and are more likely to suffer from unaccountably rapid damage to all types of organs … which is what you've been finding with your autopsies isn't it?'

Kate nodded and fell silent for a few minutes. Their ice cream arrived as she looked around the restaurant at the few other midweek diners. 'Have you heard that women are no longer becoming pregnant?' she asked watching a young girl staring dotingly into her partners eyes.

Pete smirked. 'That sounds like heaven.'

'Why?'

‘You can have as much sex as you like and you won’t have to worry about the consequences.’

‘That seems a might selfish,’ chastised Kate. ‘If there are no births, the human race really is doomed.’

‘Sorry,’ said Pete insincerely. He leaned forward so they were closely facing each other. ‘I thought we’d just been talking about how the human race is doomed anyway. What’s the point in having babies if their parents and older siblings are going to die and won’t be around to look after them?’

‘You’re suggesting this disease is being kind - killing at both ends? How do you know this phenomenon isn’t just a blip and new babies would be immune to it?’

‘It isn’t a disease. It’s a genetic disorder and it’s affecting everyone, everywhere. We’re both dying now only we can’t feel it. I’m thirty nine; I don’t expect to see forty one.’

‘You think it could happen that quickly - within the next couple of years?’ Kate was horrified.

‘To wipe out everyone will probably take longer, but we may only have three or four years left. With that knowledge, how would you want to change your life?’

Kate sat back and thought about this. ‘You’re vegetarian and you don’t own a car to save the planet. Do you think it’s worth it?’

‘As far as we know, this phenomenon is only affecting humans,’ pointed out Pete. ‘There’s no reason why we should stop trying to save the planet and leave it in good order for the rest of life on Earth once we’ve gone.’ He smiled. ‘Leave the place as you’d expect to find it, as my old mum used to say to get us to clean the bathroom.’

‘Very noble,’ said Kate with a smile. ‘Hmm. This ice cream is to die … for,’ she said, the another spoonful halfway to her mouth. Pete looked at her and they both burst out laughing.

~*~

Across town in the bedroom they shared with their numerous toys, some of which actually worked, Carl Porter whispered to his younger brother Stuart on the bunk below, ‘that Jimmy and Ross are OK, aren’t they?’

'Yeah,' agreed Stuart.

'Do you suppose dad'll let us go to the shooting range with Ross's dad if we ask him right?'

'Dunno,' said Stuart honestly.

'It'd be cool,' murmured Carl, lying back on the bed and thinking about all the baddies he could shoot once he knew how a real gun worked. Making two fingers into a gun, with one eye closed, he made exploding noises.

'Do you reckon City'll be able to replace Bob Thompson all right?' asked Stuart who was dwelling on the death of his favourite football team's manager and the consequences this might have on the stock of still highly paid talent the new man would have to bring to order. 'He'd just got them winning. Now someone else'll have to start again.'

'Don't worry,' said Carl helpfully. 'Lots of teams are losing their managers, trainers and things. Dad says they're going to have to tighten up.' He didn't understand what that meant, but neither would Stuart.

It didn't make Stuart feel any better, but he thought Westwater City might be able to take advantage of the situation if they were fast enough. He lay back and sighed.

'It's a pity Mr Lassiter died last week; I enjoyed games with him, he's a good referee. Dad went to his funeral and said there were loads of people there,' said Carl.

'Mum says people don't go to funerals much now because they're so common ... you have to pick and chose,' advised Stuart sounding grown up, 'otherwise she'd be at funerals all the time and never get any cooking done.'

After a lapse in conversation Stuart asked, 'do you think Ross's dad will let us fire one of his guns, or are we too young?'

'You're too young; I'm two years older than you,' Carl pointed out in a superior tone.

'That'll mean you'll die before me,' said Stuart honestly.

'You'll not manage once I'm gone,' said Carl smugly.

'Mum and dad'll look after me,' said Stuart getting concerned.

‘They’ll have died long before either of us,’ replied Carl nastily leaning over to look down at his little brother. ‘So you’d better get used to having me as boss around here.’ He lay back smiling, listening as Stuart began to cry.

‘You boys should have been asleep half an hour ago,’ said Kevin’s voice, his muscular frame silhouetted in the doorway of their bedroom. ‘Why’re you crying Stuart?’ he asked, a note of concern entering his voice. Daphne hovered in the doorway behind him as he knelt at the side of his son’s bed.

‘He’s upset ’cos City’s Bob Thompson died,’ explained Carl.

‘No I’m not,’ said Stuart hotly, wiping his eyes on his sheet. ‘You said mum and dad were going to die and leave you in charge.’

‘Whatever made you say a thing like that?’ asked Daphne coming into the room and turning the low-energy nightlight up to brighten the room.

‘All the older people are dying Mum,’ said Carl matter-of-factly. ‘We were just talking about what we’d do when you and dad go.’

Surprised at his tone and apparent lack of concern, Daphne said, ‘we’re not going to die and leave you with no one to care for you. Don’t be silly.’

‘It’s what all the kids are talking about at school,’ said Carl. ‘They’re saying we won’t have to go to school when all the parents are dead.’

This left Kevin and Daphne speechless for a moment.

‘You stop talking and get to sleep, both of you,’ said Kevin firmly. ‘We’re not dead yet and you still have to do what we say.’ He turned down the light and left the room. The boys settled down and soon fell asleep but their parents were not so fortunate.

‘You don’t really think all the kids in school are discussing what’s going to happen if all their parents die do you?’ asked Daphne incredulously.

‘He didn’t say if,’ observed Kevin, ‘he said when. They’re expecting everyone to die off.’ Daphne was horrified by this thought. ‘A lot of teachers have died in the past few months, and other staff. It’s hardly surprising they’re talking about death; it’s all over the news, all over *Coronation Street*; there’s no escaping it. Even the caravan site we wanted to go to in Cumbria is closed because the owner died and his son can’t get enough staff to run the place.’ Kevin sat miserably on the sofa, a can of beer held loosely in one hand and the TV remote in the other as he flicked unseeingly between various Freeview channels.

Daphne, with tears welling in her eyes sat next to him and hugged his arm. 'I don't want to live without you?' she whispered.

'According to the boys, that shouldn't be a problem,' said Kevin with a grin.

Daphne poked him in the ribs. 'It's not funny. Our children are planning what they're going to do when we're not here to look after them. Don't you think that's frightening?'

'I think that's sensible and shows a certain degree of maturity,' said Kevin as if proud of his boys.

'I can't think about our boys having to fend for themselves; it's too horrible.'

'At least they're being practical and talking to their friends about it. Hopefully they'll be all right when the time comes.'

'When the ... time comes!' stammered Daphne. 'You don't seriously think we're going to die because of this ... thing do you?'

'Can't see why not,' said Kevin calmly, swigging the last drop from his can and settling on a programme about building super motorbikes.

'That's awful,' said Daphne, truly appalled.

'Why?' asked Kevin sincerely. 'As soon as you're born the only one sure thing that's going to happen to you is you're going to die. I like the thought of knowing it's probably not going to be too long.'

'But I don't want to live without you,' said Daphne again quietly. 'You want to leave me all alone?' she asked tearfully.

'Don't worry love,' said Kevin, putting a comforting arm around her. 'We're both the same age, we'll not be long apart. The good thing is the mortgage will get paid off by the insurance and the boys'll have the house with no debt. Always look on the bright side.' He kissed her chubby cheek, but she carried on quietly sobbing into his shoulder.

When he got bored of building super motorbikes, Kevin flicked across the channels again until he saw a portion of the news which made him stop and listen.

'*...despite premiums being paid on time, both the Counties Insurance and the Friendly Insurance Companies are saying they can no longer pay out on mortgage insurance payments against death due to anything other than accidental causes. It's likely other insurance companies will follow suit. Mortgage lenders are having discussions with the Chancellor tomorrow*,' the attractive brunette newsreader said, tidying her papers and staring into the camera with a look which suggested she didn't have a mortgage and therefore nothing to worry about. She moved swiftly onto the sport headlines – Bob Thompson's funeral had been well attended – and the weather – tomorrow should be another hot and sunny day, although thundery outbreaks were likely by the end of the week.

Kevin was too stunned to move and Daphne had fallen asleep. Carefully moving her off his shoulder, he rummaged in the bottom drawer of their tallboy where they kept CDs, DVDs and important paperwork and found the life insurance cover for the mortgage. The small print clearly stated either party could terminate the agreement with thirty days notice.

'Shit,' said Kevin softly to himself. The building society would still take their mortgage repayments from him, but would probably want some reassurance that when he died, his offspring would be capable of taking over the borrowing should his insurance company fail to cover the debt. He felt less confident of dying anytime soon and wondered how they could pay off the mortgage as quickly as possible.

He had a sleepless night.

Chapter nine

Thursday 21st March 2017

The meeting felt informal, more informal than it was, largely because it was held in the main drawing room at Chequers, the state home for British Prime Ministers since 1921. Pearl Leith liked being Prime Minister and making use of as many of the facilities as she could. The meeting was intended to sound out various department ministers outside the Cabinet structure as to how they felt things were going in the country and whether she, as head of the Government, should be doing more about it.

She looked around the group of people in their thirties responsible for the fate of the nation and smiling inwardly, wondered what Churchill would have thought of them, these children just out of short trousers.

'Things are tough, there's no denying it,' started Adele Irving, the Education Secretary, a small mousy woman who blended so well with the pale brown suite, she was only noticeable when she opened her mouth.

'It's tough for everyone, not just teachers,' protested Mike Sefton the newest Local Government Secretary. His northern edge wouldn't be blunted and he'd have struck out for what he could get, no matter which department he headed.

The tall thin Transport Secretary, Steve Croft, unwound his long legs and reached for another digestive. 'My department should be renamed Lack of Transport if things carry on in the Middle East as they're doing at present.' A few chuckles greeted this observation.

'They're devastating huge areas and spreading pollution all around the world,' added Hazel Harrison the Environment Secretary on her first visit to the Prime Minister since winning her by-election a couple of weeks ago. 'If it carries on for much longer, all the rescue missions and cleaning up packages in the world won't save anything. We'll all die from chemical poisoning, let alone …this thing.'

That silenced the room, except for the sipping of mint tea, munching of digestives and rain pattering against the window.

Pearl decided to bring the group into some sort of order. She would make notes, but no minutes would be taken; it was more a chat, an appraisal, a gathering of feelings. No agenda had been set, but they each knew what they had to discuss.

'This country isn't fairing too well following the deaths of so many of its older citizens,' she began baldly. 'So I want to hear some positives and work out a way we can come out of this mess and give people hope.'

The four ministers exchanged a glance. Pearl had been Prime Minister since December when Hayton had died suddenly from what was diagnosed as deteriorated kidneys. The thing had killed off everyone over fifty and was apparently working methodically through people in their forties. Although Pearl felt she was doing as well as could be expected in her role, the majority of her Cabinet didn't agree, but would never say so. No one else wanted the top job.

'I know the Home Secretary couldn't be with us today, but I do feel the breakdown of law and order is causing as many problems as anything else,' suggested Adele timidly.

'People are taking the law into their own hands, protecting themselves and their property with guns and knives. Vigilantes are everywhere. I've heard tales that lynching is common place,' said Mike. He didn't seem keen on bringing this point up, but it was the one thing his Local Government Department had specifically asked him to mention.

'I know it's becoming a problem in some areas … areas where we've had trouble before this thing happened, but we're looking to increase the number of Military patrols in the worst affected areas,' Pearl explained.

'People only see troops as a threat and it makes them more agitated. They're not solving the problem, just making it worse,' said Mike, not to be fobbed off.

'As you say, the Home Secretary isn't here, nor is the Minister for Defence, so we'll keep our talk to present departments only, shall we,' said Pearl, coldly and firmly.

'Well, the main problem in Education … apart from the lack of teachers - in some areas, schools have had to close - but where they're still running, teenagers in particular are becoming even more belligerent and less respectful than usual. Absenteeism is rife as they roam the streets in gangs, which may tie into the problem with people protecting their property,' said Adele, holding up her hand and closing her eyes, ready to stifle protest. 'I'm not going any further down that line, but you must see all parts of society are linked and can't be dealt with as isolated pockets.'

'I understand, but that isn't why we're here,' said Pearl. 'Continue.'

Adele, wondering why they were there, continued. 'As class sizes reach mammoth proportions, younger children seem less controllable and more susceptible to the influence of older children as they have fewer mature role models. A lot of them are orphaned and are being brought up as best they can by older siblings or neighbours where they're lucky enough to find someone willing. They're in shock, traumatised; some are in denial about the whole situation. They need skilful handling from trained child psychologists and there just aren't enough of those to go around. '

'Have you any suggestions?' asked Pearl, her voice the consistent glacial calm it usually was.

'Mix age groups within classes so older children are asked to behave more responsibly in front of younger ones … They could set examples.'

'As you've just explained most of them are causing the chaos and mayhem dogging the rest of the community, I doubt that would be a bright idea,' snorted Mike.

'Well perhaps younger children could be taken to work with adults rather being left in large groups feeding off each other's neurosis? Another issue is malnutrition … the majority of them are eating badly and infrequently. School dinners need to be made free for the ones with no parents and no family income.'

Pearl nodded sceptically, making a note on an electronic pad. 'We'll leave those as suggestions for now. Perhaps get your Department to look at feasibility studies,' she said to avoid arguments. 'What's happening in Local Government we should be aware of … besides the death of staff of course?' she asked, turning to Mike, fingers poised over her notepad.

'Well,' began Mike sucking in a deep breath. 'Where to start?' He looked at the moulded ceiling for inspiration then began, making Pearl wish she hadn't asked.

'I know you said apart from the staff, but that's one of the big issues isn't it. Despite what people think, it takes a lot of staff to run a council and we seem to be spending most of our time recruiting these days. It's virtually impossible for anyone over or near forty to get a job unless they're already holding one … people don't take them on if they think they're going to keel over any minute.' His colleagues frowned at this but he carried on regardless. 'Having said that, people are crying out for staff, it's a buyers market and people can change jobs quickly.'

'Regarding the actual work, one problem is the collection and disposal of waste. There're fewer people producing less waste, but it takes just as long to collect it with people being more scattered around towns and in the country. The incinerators are running at maximum but the power produced isn't going to the right places. We need to look at ways of making the National Grid more efficient,' he said addressing Hazel who raised an eyebrow and made a quick note on the paper notepad on her lap. 'Recycling's reduced as there's less plastic packaging and tinned stuff about so that's becoming more expensive to process too.

'The next thing is cemeteries ... chocked full, believe it or not. We need a more efficient way of disposing of bodies ... Crematoria can't cope either.

'Then there's the collection of Council Tax to pay for everything. Even though the number of services has reduced making it cheaper, with the banking system near to collapsing, the number of dodgers has risen. We just don't have the manpower to keep records up to date and people have worked out how long it takes us to check and determine who should be paying. Of course houses where it's just the kids living alone don't pay the tax in any case.

'Street cleaning, lighting and public toilets ... forget it, ain't going to happen,' he said crossing his hands in front of his chest. 'It'll not be long before you can grow potatoes in the gutters ... not that I'd want to eat them if you did. There just aren't the people about for maintenance ... Same goes for the refuse trucks.'

Pearl gave him a considered look, one which suggested she might be regretting appointing him as minister. 'Anything positive?' she asked softly.

He blew out through his teeth. 'Housing and most other building work has stopped, with only repairs and alterations being undertaken now. There're far fewer qualified electricians and plumbers around as the population becomes deskilled ... they may be computer literate but they're not practical. More evening classes on practical skills would be a good plan ... gives people something to do in the evening besides shooting each other.

'We don't have the number of homeless people to deal with we did a few years back … They're squatting in vacated houses as more become available … and there's quite a demand for swimming pools these days too … not sure why.' The others swapped bemused glances while he thought some more. 'Oh, and parking illegally has dropped off. On the downside I'm afraid, we've closed tourist advice places, art galleries, museums, national nature reserves and things like that due to lack of visitors and staffing problems.'

'Thank you,' said Pearl firmly drawing a line under him. 'Transport, Steve. What are your issues?'

Steve followed Mike's example and drew in a sharp breath and leaned forward before starting. 'With fewer people driving, whether private or commercial vehicles, we certainly don't need any more roads and the ones we have are wearing better with less traffic. It may become uneconomic to maintain both road and rail services and we're going to have to decide which is most practical in the long term.' He stopped and frowned as if not keen on having to make the decision himself.

'With the fuel crisis, air and shipping freight are getting prohibitively expensive to operate. Biofuels don't seem to be the answer as the countries which previously produced lots are now growing food crops instead. Consequently, imports and exports are becoming more expensive and suffering as a result.

'Public transport, while partly funded by local government,' he said, giving Mike an acknowledging nod, 'is becoming much busier than expected. People don't seem to like the necessary hikes in petrol prices and are abandoning cars left right and centre. It's just as well the population has decreased or we might not have enough buses to go around,' he smiled. The others glared at him for his callousness. 'Sorry,' he mumbled.

'With people not using their own vehicles, journeys are becoming shorter and out of town areas are suffering but smaller local community centres are regenerating,' he added sitting up straight indicating he'd finished.

'Thank you Steve. Environment,' said Pearl, looking at Hazel.

'Well there are some unusual things going on, probably relating to the reduction in maintenance systems intended for a much larger population.'

'What do you mean?' asked Adele before Hazel had a chance to explain herself.

'As Steve mentioned, town and city areas are gradually becoming deserted as people spread back into their local community or head for the country where it's easier to get food. Also the power reduction system of four hours on and four hours off is having a deleterious effect, however much it's preserving fuel stocks.

'One of the reasons we're having this meeting here is because of the flooding in London. That's becoming more common around the country as streams and rivers contained below buildings in cities - such as the Fleet River in London - are finding their way to the surface, following tunnels, drains, power lines and pipes, undermining buildings and carrying debris and rubbish with them. The pumps, which would normally keep everything dry above ground, are running intermittently so roads are collapsing leaving uncertain surfaces and craters. The longer they're left, the more dangerous cities will become.

'The cost of repair is beginning to reach excessive proportions and it seems to me the most sensible course as the population decreases, is to abandon the larger cities, or at least the worst affected low lying areas, and move to unaffected country districts or those built on higher ground.'

'The price of our ancestors building on flood plains and river valleys,' commented Mike with a smirk.

'The price of us continuing to do so after we'd realised it was a stupid thing to do,' said Pearl severely. 'Anything else Hazel?'

'The majority of main roads may be all right, according to Steve, but generally infrastructure is starting to decay through lack of maintenance. For the last thirty years this country has been geared towards having a population of between fifty and sixty million people. We now have around thirty million with the same amount of roads, canals, drains, sewers, water pipes, gas pipes and electricity cables to maintain and that's just not happening. As sanitation becomes a problem, more people will die through disease.'

'As if we don't have enough problems with people dying from this thing,' said Mike.

'While we're mentioning population, if I could just point out that figure is split two thirds adults to one third children,' said Adele, 'and the proportion is getting closer all the time.' That gave the small group pause for thought for a few moments.

'Returning to the gas supply,' continued Hazel, 'which has been a bit dodgy for the last few winters, will be even more unreliable next winter. I'm certain the Russians will keep it for themselves,' she explained to a general muttering of disapproval.

'I know the Press has been banging on about fewer farmers having to produce more food with fewer tractors running, meaning more labour is needed, but it's true. Over the last sixty years or so, agricultural production has become unsustainable because we've relied so heavily on machinery. The fuel crisis has just made a bad situation worse and more labour *is* required. We need to find alternative sources of power quickly, making use of heavy horses and oxen, but they don't grow on trees and require training just as people do. Dairy produce is getting more expensive as cattle and sheep are becoming restricted to marginal areas as they cost too much for upkeep and protection compared to crops which don't need a vet. People are defending their chicken coops and pig pens with shotguns. With less food imported from abroad for various reasons, we have to provide more of our own food in this country and we still have thirty million people to feed. We'll have to prioritise fuel use or we're going to struggle to get things organised and set up in time to survive the winter.'

Silence fell across the room as Pearl listened, taking in what her colleagues were telling her. She thought for a while, deciding what she should tell them. Discretion flew out of the window into the rain.

'As you know, once the full horror of this thing became apparent and we realised it was a global issue, the international community pulled together, helped each other with financial and practical support. However, it now seems the First World ... *our* world ... isn't able to cope with the continued death rate and loss of experience and knowledge. Our financial systems are collapsing with insurance companies and banks going bust up and down the country; no more mortgage lending, no more business lending, no more insurance, money has devalued and people are beginning to barter and exchange ... others to steal, loot and pilfer. We're back in the Middle Ages.

'As Hazel has so vividly pointed out, it has become apparent that those of us remaining in the First World can't feed ourselves without large inputs of fossil fuels, and still require food imported from the Third World. However, they are no longer exporting food to countries which can't pay for it and they're feeding their own people with real food, instead of cocoa, tobacco and bananas.

'We're relying more heavily on locally produced food which of necessity is seasonal meaning we will face problems if harvests aren't successful. The population has become accustomed to having whatever they want from the shops whenever they want it, and skills in preserving food for the future have been lost. We have to convince people our lives before this thing were unsustainable; education is going to have to play a vital role in this. We'll have to go back to rationing and turning flower gardens into vegetable patches like they did in the Second Word War. We can look forward to a painful period of adjustment.'

Total silence met this heart-felt statement from their leader and she gained a deal of respect for her honesty.

'The one good thing about this - and it probably shows how we should all have behaved before this happened - International scientific cooperation has increased with the free unhindered exchange of information and knowledge while the source of the problem is identified. Thousands of men and women are still working to find the cause and halt the process,' Pearl added.

'You've all given me food for thought and I'll collate something for the Cabinet meeting this afternoon. Safe journey home.' She stood and left the room.

'I'm really glad I got elected,' said Hazel. 'I get to hear first hand, from the horse's mouth that we're really in the shit.' She stood and followed her leader.

~*~

Phoebe Gilligan and Eartha Zull, reporters from *The Illumination,* sat on a stone seat built into an overgrown raised bed in the centre of Norleigh looking at the boarded up shop windows. 'Do you remember all the pigeons?' asked Phoebe, her hands limp on her lap as she leaned back casually. The rain falling on Chequers in Buckinghamshire hadn't yet reached this far north.

Eartha looked around her suddenly realising what Phoebe meant. 'Don't miss them much,' she said. 'They used to get under your feet looking for food and made a mess of buildings and cars.'

'I wonder where they've all gone?' asked Phoebe, not interested in the answer.

'Same place as the rats presumably,' said Eartha, stretching and getting to her feet. 'Come on, this isn't achieving anything ... we've got work to do.'

Phoebe struggled to her feet and followed her friend down the dusty High Street. The spring equinox had begun brightly, but quickly clouded over, cooled down and the rain was imminent. After a dry start to the month, this was a good thing. 'Do you remember shopping here?' she asked rhetorically. 'I loved that boutique. Sandy could get the most amazing things in. I've a feeling she made a lot of it herself. Very talented. I suppose all her old clients have died now. Everyone wears jeans these days. I wonder who grows all the cotton.'

'Jeans are looted from shops and sold on the black market like everything else,' said Eartha, 'just like all the food stolen from food stores and supermarkets. I'd kill for an orange,' she added with a smile.

During the day, the centres of towns like Norleigh were safe enough, as long as you weren't alone. Youth gangs of all races tended to operate at dusk and through until about midnight and then even they cleared the streets. The animals - packs of stray dogs and foxes - took over until dawn as if the different groups worked shifts. Shops, the ones which had survived competition from the Internet, had slowly closed and been boarded up, inviting fewer people into the shopping centres and malls. Pubs and clubs had to cope with escalating fighting, alcohol and substance abuse and many of those had closed too. Deserted places were inexorably being taken over by tough grass, sturdy weeds and intrepid tree saplings.

Phoebe had decided to have a look to see why some people chose to stay. They approached Charlie Salmon, still running Bruce's greengrocer's shop. 'Apart from the fact that granddad ran this shop all his life, believe it or not, there are still hundreds of people living here,' he explained. 'Some people have lived in towns all their lives, and just can't face the open country and the thought of the work involved in keeping a farm going.'

‘Where do you get your stock from?’ asked Phoebe looking at the seasonal produce he had; leeks, carrots, onions, broccoli and a couple of brace of rabbits hanging from nails by the door.

‘Some people sell their surplus from allotments and I have friends running a market garden not far from Eastdell. We meet half way so we’re neither of us using too much fuel.’

‘How do you cope with thieving?’ asked Eartha.

‘This,’ said Charlie opening his waistcoat revealing the butt of a pistol. ‘I used to leave it unloaded, just for show until some kids took a box of apples. It’s cleaned and loaded now.’

‘You’d use it?’ asked Phoebe intrigued how people had changed over the past eighteen months.

‘Sure. So would you. This isn’t a charity … although I’ll help people out as much as I can. I’m trying to survive just the same as everyone else.’

‘What happened to all the Tesco Extra stores?’ asked Eartha looking up and down the street.

‘They had trouble staffing the out of town supermarkets, but as fuel prices rocketed, they found fewer people going to them, or at least people going less often … bulk buying and stocking up.

‘Once electricity started becoming more intermittent and you couldn’t rely on freezers to store food, people needed local stores to get food they couldn’t grow themselves.

‘Some of the Extra stores must have been borderline as quite a lot of them have closed, but the grocer down there sells black market stuff for a price if you don’t ask questions. People still eat in cafes although the standard of food might be down a bit. The pawn broker does a good trade, again probably stolen stuff mostly. He’ll exchange things for food or fuel as well as currency. The chemist at the end – you have to ask for what you want at the grill at the front of the shop and he passes stuff through; he used to get broken into once a month at least. That’s it for around here. There’re one or two other shops on other streets, but most things are black market stolen goods passed around at hot markets.’

‘Hot markets?’ asked Phoebe.

'A market would spring up one day in an old theatre, an abandoned church, or a derelict house. It's mostly by chance where they'll be located but they put word out on local radio too.'

'And it's mostly stolen goods?' she clarified.

'They keep things in circulation for those who need them rather than being closed up and useless in dead people's houses. I've no problem with it.'

'I suppose you're right, although it takes a bit of getting used to,' said Eartha.

'Our societies changed and our beliefs and culture have to change with it,' observed Charlie, 'or we'll go the way of the dinosaur.'

They each exchanged a smile at this pleasantry. 'Well, thanks for your time. Good luck,' said Eartha and both women left, having bought a Cox's apple each.

'Where next?' asked Phoebe munching. They walked down the street to where she had parked her fuel efficient moped chained to railings outside a closed primary school. The windows had all been smashed, the walls graffitied and the swings ripped from their frame. It looked injured, hurt, forlorn. They left quickly.

A sharp shower caught them as they drove up to Norleigh Hospital one of the few centres still performing its function admirably. The sick and injured came here and were looked after as well as staff and resources would allow. Knowing the way, Phoebe and Eartha went to the doctor's lounge in the hope of finding someone off duty or at least having a quick break.

Andrew Bragg lay curled up on the dirty sofa, its stuffing poking through near one of its legs. He woke as they came through the door.

'I'm sorry for disturbing you, Doctor,' began Phoebe, but Andrew waved her down as he swung his legs onto the floor and wiped his hands over his tired bleary eyed unshaven face.

'What can I do for you ladies?' he asked, getting to his feet and stretching. His hair had thinned to near baldness, his former cubby face was sunken and thin, his glasses were crocked and dirty.

'We're trying to see how the latest series of deaths and the massive changes in our society is affecting people,' stated Phoebe, her voice nervously too high and loud.

'Is that all,' he joked. 'I'd offer you coffee but we don't run to such luxuries these days. I can do you nettle tea … good for the bladder apparently.'

'Thanks,' both women said at once.

'Are you sleeping here?' asked Eartha, her curiosity getting the better of her. A variety of clothes hung from a pole fitted across the far end of the room and toiletries lined the back of the sink.

'Not just sleeping; I live here,' he confirmed. 'Since … so many of my colleagues … have gone … its easier and more economical for me to be here. Everything I need is here … we have running water, a generator, food and medicines of course. I'm not using precious fuel getting to and from work. It makes sense.'

'Where do you get your medicines from?' asked Eartha.

'We built up large stockpiles when things started to seriously unravel last year. The major drug companies' realised things were going up the spout and actually gave drugs away. Unbelievable.'

'Great,' said Phoebe smiling at this bit of positive news. They all stood around the kettle. 'But if you're here all the time, that must mean you never get away, never get a break. Is that healthy?'

'I go for walks when it's dry. There're plenty of people about to talk to. We've set up a cinema for the patients and visitors. I can read and do research. I find it's actually a better system then it used to be … when everyone else was around.' His response while positive was tinged with sadness and regret. He obviously missed his friends, Graham amongst them.

'So how are things in the hospital generally?'

'We're still getting the usual patients … colds and 'flu, broken limbs, knife wounds, gunshots and more people coming down with dysentery and other infections … the usual for younger people.'

'Are you involved in the research at all?' asked Eartha.

'No. Never have been,' he advised them. 'Quite frankly I don't see it makes much difference knowing what's caused all the deaths. By the time we find a way to fight it - assuming we do - they'll be hardly any of us left to pick up the pieces.'

'Don't you think we'll fight it?' asked Phoebe softly, her face appealing.

‘Not in my life time,’ he smiled. ‘Suppose we make a breakthrough this year,’ he said authoritatively. ‘By then, everyone over thirty five will be gone leaving only a few thousand people who know enough about medicine or immunology to do anything about it. The world’s population will be scattered, fragmented. Our infrastructure is collapsing. It would take decades, generations to get back to any sort of civilisation we might have known.’

‘You sound like you don’t think it’s worth it,’ observed Eartha.

‘It is for those who have the fortitude and stamina to live in a world like that. I couldn’t, I know. I’ll do my bit for as long as I can, then it’s up to you lot … the young ones to inherit the Earth and make of it what you will. Think about it.’

A young woman in a soiled nurse’s uniform popped her head around the door. ‘Oh sorry Andrew, I didn’t realise you had company.’

‘No problem. We’d just finished.’

‘The girl in sixteen with the fractured skull is coming round. I think you ought to see her.’ Nurse and doctor disappeared from the lounge and Phoebe and Eartha left the hospital, their mood slightly gloomier than when they arrived, but the rain had stopped.

‘Is this article going to be worth writing?’ asked Eartha. ‘There’re enough end-of-the-world doom merchants about without us adding to the pot.’

‘Do you know Wesley Foster, the art teacher at Westwater High School?’ asked Phoebe. Eartha shook her head. ‘Let’s go and see him … he’s bound to be more positive.’

‘Why?’

‘He’s an artist - always looks on the bright side.’

They scooted passed a long line of abandoned burned out cars and through a hail storm as they reached the outskirts of Westwater – a small city where the infrastructure was deteriorating as the Environment Minister had described - and arrived at the High School. It had become a hostel for teenagers and young people whose parents had died, had been driven from their homes by money lenders, the fear of night gangs or an inability to fend for themselves.

The few teachers who were left had organised the school into dormitories in upstairs rooms using beds and bedding purloined from surrounding houses and flats, the kitchens were run by the children adapting various cultural cooking styles. The grounds and playing fields had been given over to growing potatoes, beans, cabbages, carrots, parsnips and any other seeds they could find in sheds and outhouses along with the tools and equipment needed to raise them.

A happy communal atmosphere had developed with new people coming and disillusioned ones leaving, keeping the population at around five hundred.

Phoebe made her way to the front entrance where all the bikes were chained up. Some older children had the time and energy for a knockabout at football. She and Eartha walked along the dimly lit corridor with its glass doors and windows showing various lower floor classrooms were still used as such, at least in the mornings.

Wesley was explaining to a class of twenty girls from ten to fifteen years old about the art of the eighteenth century. 'Portrait artists such as Reynolds and Gainsborough catered to the nobility and middle classes who wanted portraits showing how they got on with their lives and how they made things happen. Britain was then a world leader politically, socially and economically but portraits showed down-to-earth people, like we have today.

'Your work reflects on the times we are living through now in just the same way. We're here, working together showing what can be done if we put our minds, bodies and skills to a problem.

'Go into the playing field and watch the boys digging and planting. See if you can capture the purpose and belief in what they're doing. If you can't … it probably means your drawing Tommy Wilson and we all know he's only thinking of his stomach!'

The girls all smirked and chatted as they left the room, pads and pencils in hand, ready to seal a small moment in time onto the page.

'I'll probably get half a dozen matchstick men and some odd shaped vegetables, but it keeps them happy,' he said, turning to Phoebe and Eartha as they walked further into the vacated room. 'How can I help you?' he asked, smiling. A handsome well built young man of about thirty with a good tan which showed that even in March he spent a lot of his time outside.

'I didn't realise you still taught art in schools these days,' said Phoebe.

'You think it's a waste of time?' The two women exchanged a glance, thinking they might have been rude. 'It's not, as long as we hope to continue to be human beings and not degrade to savagery. It helps us remember the past, even if that's gone forever. It also helps them to relax, think about something else and gives them something to do in their down time.'

'So is art available to everyone?' asked Eartha.

'We rotate what everyone does here. They could be digging for an hour, writing essays on the Romans for the next, feeding the chickens and collecting eggs in the back gardens after lunch, spending a couple of hours on maths and geometry – that might come in handy – then relaxing with music, poetry and art in the evenings. We try to be holistic … It helps to produce well rounded citizens - which is what I'm aiming at personally.'

'You seem to have it all very well organised,' said Phoebe. 'Is this typical of schools these days?'

'I shouldn't think so. We - the few teachers remaining - decided to change it to more of a guided commune. We don't have a curriculum as such and as you saw, age groups are mixed; they help each other. We've found, admittedly through trial and error - mostly error - that this reduces the amount of antagonism, prejudice and bullying. There're fewer cliques or small gangs of children intimidating the others. Someone has a friend in each group they work with; there's less isolation and loneliness with the way we run things.'

'Is it really that successful?' asked Eartha sceptically.

'It has to be. There're only ten adults - people over twenty one - here. There's no way we could keep them all under control unless they did it themselves.'

'You don't think it's a potential powder keg if … all the adults went?'

'That, I think you'll find, is one of the problems which our society has been building up over the last twenty odd years,' said Wesley, shaking his head.

'How do you mean?' asked Phoebe.

'We've gone so health and safety mad over the last few decades that our children are protected by bubbles and wrapped in cotton wool.' The women exchanged a glance which Wesley spotted. 'I may sound like a preacher, but have we done them any favours? All they have is a long list of things they're not allowed to do. All children need to suffer some knocks and buffetings to get through life, otherwise they have no experience and no frame of reference to call on when things do go pear-shaped and they don't have a parent or teacher on hand to sort it out for them,' he continued. The women exchanged another worried glance.

'The more resourceful, the more intelligent and the more practical children will get through this, I'm sure. But the majority won't have a chance because they don't understand what's going on, or because they believe someone is going to ride over the hill at any moment and save them because that's what happens in the movies. I'm afraid the strong will overpower the weak, just as they have throughout human history and we'll revert to the Dark Ages. I'm trying to toughen the kids up a bit, get them used to supporting themselves, and more importantly sticking up for themselves. Natural leaders will rise, but for the sake of the others, I'd like them to be the right sort.'

'The right sort?' asked Eartha.

'Ones who look outwards, not inwards; ones who take the long term view, who can see beyond the next week or next month, the ones who can plan and organise. What we don't want are the self-centred ones with blinkers.

'When it gets to that stage with no adults, places like this might not be able to function. I don't know what will happen, but at least we've tried … and I think succeeded to give these kids something to live and hope for; something they can take with them when they leave.'

'Is this your work?' asked Phoebe as she noticed an oil painting on the back wall depicting a team of young children happily playing cricket beside a cabbage patch.

'Yes. I did that last summer after the school was closed and handed over to us. It sums us up nicely, I thought.'

Phoebe and Eartha both smiled in agreement. 'Do you still take in new kids if they turn up … I mean would have room for any more.'

'We've a small turnover of older ones leaving to try out the big bad world, and a few waifs and strays turning up when their parents or older siblings die. We'll find space for anyone who comes to us.'

'Mother Teresa would've been proud of you,' said Eartha with a smile. They returned to the entrance and said goodbye.

'This should be used as a formula for other schools really, not just confined to Westwater. We'll have to give it a good write up,' said Phoebe.

'I've a feeling few places like this would be so liberal, most would be like labour camps.'

'I suppose it depends on the personalities of the people running them; Wesley seems to have his head screwed on right.'

'Being tall and good looking doesn't do him any harm either,' agreed Eartha smiling. They rode off towards Sudcliff.

Alexis Watts and Will Hallam sat chatting on the concrete block announcing the entrance to Sudcliff University as Phoebe and Eartha drove up.

'I'm just saying I think he's doing a remarkable job considering,' said Alexis.

'Considering what? He's just the same as his mother. He has privileged access to transport so can travel to Africa and let us know what a dire state they're in ... like everything's rosy here.'

'You're just cross because he's a helicopter pilot and you'll never get the chance,' said Alexis scathingly. 'He's done great work here with his children's hospital charity.'

'He's only doing great things because he's the King,' said Will hotly.

'I'd have thought you'd like him more seeing you were named after him.'

'Not my choice.'

A large lorry rumbled by, the young soldier driving it waved acknowledgement as he passed, saluting Phoebe who moved her moped out of his path.

'What's he got in there?' asked Eartha.

'Library books,' said Alexis calmly. 'They're taking anything vaguely to do with medicine, genetics or pathology to the central Medical Research Council place in Oxford. They've gathered all the brains in one place so they can feed off each other in person rather than through the unreliable Internet.'

'I see. What are you two doing here?' asked Phoebe, removing her helmet and shaking her hair free.

'Just watching … and arguing,' Alexis replied with a smile at Will.

'What about?' asked Eartha the journalist in her sensing a story.

'Will here doesn't think the King's doing a great job. I do.'

'He's the pinnacle of an outmoded and decrepit system which no longer functions or performs. We don't need national leaders; we need regional or local heroes. We don't need government; we need support.'

'He has strong views on the subject,' explained Alexis softly, still smiling. Will gave an exasperated growl and Alexis laughed at him.

'What are your views?' asked Phoebe, sitting next to Alexis, with Eartha joining Will.

'I agree we probably don't need a government anymore, but the monarchy is traditional - a figure head which has represented us through a thousand years of our history. I think now, as things unravel, we should hold on to things like that. He's not a bad king either. He's been positive, visible, taken a prominent role and led by example. Admittedly Harry's been a bit wayward, but he always has been.'

'Where are you living?' asked Phoebe, that part of the conversation having been concluded.

'I live in my flat in Sudcliff, though I don't think I'll be able to for much longer,' said Alexis, looking at her feet.

'Her mum died last August and she still hasn't been home yet,' explained Will with such an expression of sorrow that Eartha gave him a double take. 'The house'll be a wreck by now.'

'Mum died on her way to hospital. She had an aortic aneurism while working in the High Court. I managed the funeral but couldn't face going home,' Alexis explained.

'Where will you go?' asked Phoebe.

'She'll come with me,' suggested Will on the spur of the moment. Alexis didn't react. 'But I expect I'll join a commune or something. It's the easiest way of getting protection and making sure you have food to eat.'

Having thanked the couple for their insight into the current situation and one potential future, Phoebe and Eartha headed towards Eastdell to complete the full circle of neighbouring towns in the district. 'Have you noticed there aren't many people out and about on the streets?' asked Eartha. The total journey had taken most of the day; the rain had cleared leaving a red streaked sky as the sun set behind them. Traffic was reduced to local delivery vans, occasional police patrol cars, furniture lorries outside emptying houses and a profusion of bicycles. Traffic lights and the rules of the road still operated and were generally respected. Accidents happened much less frequently now there were fewer people and fewer cars.

'Maybe they all have better things to do,' said Phoebe.

'I remember getting stuck on the one way system in Eastdell if someone was trying to switch lanes in a daft place … now you just sail through.'

'I take it you're not complaining.'

'Not me … It's just noticeable,' said Eartha. Once they'd parked in the town's multi-storey car park, apparently full until they realised a lot of the cars had flat tyres and no radios, they walked to the main shopping mall.

This area was much busier than any area they had seen. Perhaps it was the site of one of the hot markets Charlie had mentioned. Children from five upwards roamed around drinking from bottles, probably homebrew, laughing and chatting, just like malls in the old days. A lot of noise seemed to be coming from one area in particular so Phoebe and Eartha cautiously made their way towards the sound of music.

Above the racket of a diesel powered generator, dozens of gaming machines and video games were hooked up and had large groups of people gathered around them, enjoying letting their hair down and not worrying about tomorrow.

'Hi,' said Phoebe with a broad grin on her face as she approached one man. 'Does this happen here often?'

'Hi,' said the tall broad muscular man who was overseeing a couple of boys on a space shuttle flight simulator. 'No. Terry's brought his generator in so the kids can have some fun. Seems to be working,' he added with a smile.

'I'm Phoebe ... this is Eartha. We're from *The Illumination* getting a handle on how things are going since the last lot of deaths. It seems Eastdell at least is coping OK.'

'On the surface.' The man held out his hand to shake theirs. 'Kevin Porter. I used to work at St Luke's as grounds man. Once they closed the school - no teachers left - I started looking after other people's kids, trying to stop them from fighting and making a nuisance of themselves.' He looked around the room full of happy excited faces, concentrating on their tasks of blowing up aliens, flying faster than anyone else, winning a grand prix, escaping dragon infested dungeons or finding their way through labyrinths for hidden treasure.

'Seems to be working ... at the minute at least,' said Phoebe, still smiling as Craig almost fell out of the booth in an effort to turn the shuttle out of a nose dive.

'We have to keep coming up with different ideas which will suit a large group. Taking over malls for the day helps, but some of them are becoming dangerous places to play in.'

'The gangs you mean,' suggested Eartha.

'Not particularly. Structural damage caused through lack of upkeep. It doesn't take much of a hole in the roof for rain to get through, next thing you know half the building's collapsed. You don't want that on twenty of other people's kids, do you?' The two women shuck their heads.

'We've done football, cricket and rugby ... even had some pros along to help. We just keep them entertained for as many hours as we can, then send them back home.'

'Where are their parents?' asked Phoebe.

'Working in the shops and offices which are still open, electricians, builders and plumbers still work long hours, then there are those growing food; all kinds of jobs. A lot of these kids don't have any parents,' he said quietly so Craig and Stuart didn't hear him. 'I hope someone's around to do the same for my kids when I ...' He didn't finish the sentence, just ruffled Stuart's hair.

'So you're out here seeing what's really going on ... reporting it like it is,' he said.

'Yes. There are so many fantastic stories in the papers these days; half of them are just scare stories. From what we've seen today, things aren't anywhere near as bad as some of the things I've read,' said Phoebe.

'No. People are pulling together, overcoming the difficulties imposed on them and getting through this problem,' agreed Eartha enthusiastically.

'Have you any idea if they've found out what's killing everyone and if there's anything we can do about it?' asked Kevin.

The women exchanged a glance. 'I've not heard anything since they announced it was a DNA problem affecting everyone. I imagine they're still working on a cure,' said Phoebe, crossing her fingers behind her back.

'The Military were taking books from Sudcliff University library for the specialists in Oxford to use,' said Eartha helpfully.

'I doubt the answer's in a book,' said Kevin, watching Stuart manoeuvre the space shuttle with more subtlety than his older brother and bring it gently in for a safe landing.

A loud bang and a waft of acrid smoke came from the generator. The machines all stopped, the lights went out and the children groaned. 'That's it for tonight kids. Let's get you all off home safely … Into the coach,' called Terry from the back of the room, switching on his powerful torch as he gave instructions.

'You'd better come with us. Are you in the car park?' asked Kevin. Phoebe nodded. 'I'll walk you there. You never know.'

Once he'd made sure the two women had got going safely into the night on their moped, Kevin walked cautiously back to the coach park on the other side of the mall, ears pricked for any sound, whether from a rat, a cat, or worse.

Chapter ten

Sunday 24th and Monday 25th September 2017

'I've been to see my contact at the Norleigh Hospital laboratory,' said Phoebe Gilligan to Carol Nunn, her colleague at *The Illumination*. 'She's prepared to go on record this is a DNA problem which affects all mankind … and there isn't a cure.'

'Big surprise,' said Carol. 'The unfortunate thing is it affects all womankind too,' she added with a smirk. She knocked back her glass of black-market whisky in one go. 'Do you think anyone cares anymore? The scientists aren't going to be able to do anything about it … People have given up hope already if you ask me.' She refilled her glass and drank it off again - too quickly as some dribbled down her chin.

Phoebe watched her. Alcoholism and drug abuse had exploded over the last few months with the latest wave of deaths taking place. Prime Minister Pearl Leith - for what the position was worth - had banned not only the sale of alcohol but its production too. That didn't stop breweries and distilleries of course. If they could get the ingredients to continue making and distributing their product, they knew there weren't enough inspectors and police officers to do anything about it. People were making drugs from all kinds of plants and herbs, some medicinal in purpose, but most to try to obliterate what was happening around them.

'You could try doing something more constructive than drinking yourself into oblivion,' commented Phoebe quietly.

Carol looked at her through unfocused bloodshot eyes. 'How I meet my inevitable end is up to me. If you want to be all heroic and save the planet,' she said gesturing around the wreck of her front room, 'be my guest.' She had another drink and slipped off the edge of her sofa onto the floor, dissolving in a fit of giggles.

'There're people out there helping others rather than feeling sorry for themselves. Why don't you come with me and I'll introduce you to some of them?'

'Saints and martyrs … very biblical. Booking a place in heaven. Good luck to 'em. I'm off to the other place, thanks. 'S warmer.' She giggled again and took another swig from her glass.

'Well at least you'll burn quicker with all that booze in you. See you tomorrow,' said Phoebe getting to her feet sadly and picking her way across the carpet covered in the remains of half eaten meals, empty bottles and discarded newssheets. She took a deep breath once outside and listened to the peace and quiet of the bright Sunday afternoon.

She walked slowly back into Norleigh and reflected how some parts of the town still looked reasonably normal while others had died completely. The lack of fresh litter struck her as she tried to remember what the streets had been like a couple of years ago. No plastic carrier bags caught in the trees, no cigarette butts, no chewing gum adhering to the pavement, no sweet wrappers, no polystyrene trays with the remains of a curry spilling to be eaten by rats.

Food was sold loose now, not shrink wrapped preserving it for days against the ravages of aerial bacteria or fungal spores. People took their own containers to market, be they old carrier bags, hessian sacks or Tupperware boxes. Sweets didn't exist, unless they were homemade and none had sugar in them - it took too much precious energy to refine sugar beet or cane these days and England no longer imported sugar, tea or coffee.

Phoebe remembered an article, probably the last one Corin had written, about what the country imported and exported since the thing had begun; swapping coal for timber, wool for cotton and oats for wheat. Electricity production was a big problem; power stations were plentiful but there were not enough people to operate and maintain them, and scarce fuel to power them.

Because of this and other similar issues, the Military, with its personnel used to following orders unquestioningly, its intelligence network and organisational skills, had begun to rearrange the population, identifying gaps in manpower and taking people from areas of excess population and moving them where more were required. It sounded like a good idea but they were dealing with people not Lego bricks. Emotions ran high. Workers objected to being shoved around like chess pieces. They missed their homes and families, and it took time for them to adjust their skills to unfamiliar work.

The philosophical debate waged across all forms of media of whether it was better to eke out however many years of existence people had living and working happily where they wanted to be, or being forced to live longer where they didn't want to live.

Perhaps this was why so many of the houses Phoebe walked passed were empty; people had moved on to work elsewhere. The nation had moved from one of large numbers of independent people living separate isolated little lives, to one where they lived and worked for each other, for the greater good - like a hive of bees. At least that's what the leaders wanted the nation to do. Perhaps people were easier to control in larger groups than if scattered. Certainly, the Military presence was the only thing there seemed to be a surplus of these days; an expanding business with recruitment obviously working.

As Phoebe turned onto the High Street, a young man – why she thought this she didn't know, she would have been surprised if she had seen an old man – was hammering plywood boards over a shop's windows.

'Evening,' she said politely. Martin Unwin turned to her, a defensive startled look on his face. 'Business bad?' she asked noticing the name Baxter's Travel over the window.

Martin regained his composure and came down his ladder. 'With the fuel shortages people can't afford to travel far anymore. Most tourist attractions closed long ago. I've been organising bus passes and fuel rations, but even that's not worth keeping this place open for any more.'

Phoebe nodded. She held out her hand, sensing a story. 'I'm Phoebe Gilligan, from *The Illumination.* I don't suppose you fancy a chat over a cup of tea and a cake do you?'

Mia Salmon, wiping her hands on her already soiled apron, welcomed them to the Lavender Café not far from the boarded up travel agent. She smiled sweetly and lifted the long sheet of slate dangling from her waistband and used a stick of chalk to take their order.

'A pot of tea for two and a scone each please, with jam if you have any,' said Phoebe. 'You do boil the water thoroughly before you make the tea don't you?' she asked, genuinely concerned.

Mia looked offended. 'This is a class establishment. No one's got typhoid from drinking here.' She gave them a reassuring smile and bustled off into the kitchen, collecting a tray of crockery from another table as she left.

'Her mother Leanne died a month ago. She and her brother Charlie live alone in the house which once belonged to her grandfather Bruce who ran the greengrocer's just over the way,' said Martin pointing across the street. Phoebe followed his finger to *Salmon's Greengrocer* and recalled speaking to Charlie earlier in the year.

'You've heard about how we're burying people now, haven't you.'

'We're not,' said Phoebe coldly. 'We're incinerating them to produce power.'

'That's just a rumour,' said Martin. 'Probably started by the Press,' he added with a smile. 'I heard they're being shovelled into landfill sites.'

This stopped the conversation for a few moments as Mia arrived with a stainless steel tea pot of mint tea and two scones with a small jar of honey. 'Sorry, we don't have any more jam now, ran out a couple of months ago,' she said as she arranged the table for them.

Phoebe looked around the café. 'You're not very busy at the moment ... would you like to join us?' Mia looked surprised. 'Get yourself a cup and a scone. We can spread the honey a bit further.' Mia smiled and disappeared into the kitchen, returning a few seconds later with a plate and a mug.

'So what do you think of the curfew?' Phoebe asked them as she spread a meagre amount of butter on her scone before applying the honey.

'I suppose it had to come, although I'm not sure how Leith thinks she's going to enforce it,' said Martin, chewing his scone.

'Makes no difference to me,' said Mia. 'I don't go out after dark any more anyway.'

'How old are you?' asked Phoebe.

'Eighteen,' said Mia.

'Thirty three,' said Martin.

'Twenty seven,' said Phoebe. 'Which part of the situation we're all in bothers you the most?' she asked them both, finishing her scone and wiping crumbs from her hands onto her plate.

'Money,' said Martin without hesitation. Phoebe raised an eyebrow in surprise and invited him to explain. He leaned forward confidentially even though no one else was in the café. 'Money's lost its value. Cash still circulates; although where it comes from I wouldn't like to guess. People have to pay too much for what they want or need so barter … or steal.'

'Once the insurance companies went bust, it was inevitable the banks would follow suit,' said Mia sounding as if she were quoting something she'd read. 'Food for places like this is becoming harder to source all the time at a price we can reasonably charge people, but we still get customers and it makes us a living,' she said, gesturing around the café. 'Not sure for how much longer though.'

'People will always need feeding,' said Martin graciously. Mia smiled her thanks. 'And if they come here, they don't have to use fuel for cooking,'

'So Leith has imposed an unenforceable curfew to try to cut down on crime, mostly thieving, is that how you read it?' asked Phoebe.

'Once word gets around someone's died, people gather around their house like wasps at a picnic. A house can be stripped in a night if there're no relatives left to defend it … Even if there are sometimes.' He drank his tea. 'Personally I can't see the harm. The stuff would go to waste otherwise, and it's not as if a TV or laptop will be a huge amount of use to people nowadays with all the power cuts.

'I must admit I find my windup radio a big help,' said Phoebe.

'It keeps things like clothing in circulation and it's often the best way to get tools,' added Martin.

'Or things for the kitchen,' agreed Mia.

'What are you going to do now you've had to board up the business?' asked Phoebe.

'The travel agent has been closed for a while. I work at a market garden with a few mates – Charlie being one of them,' he said, nodding at Mia. 'Growing food is easy … making sure no one else steals it is the hard part.'

Phoebe nodded. 'What do you miss most about the old life?'

'Going out with my mates,' said Mia without hesitation. 'I miss dancing or going to the cinema.' She paused looking wistful. 'I wonder what happened to all those actors who don't make films any more.'

'They still make films; just low budget, not very good ones,' said Martin with a smile.

‘What do you miss about the old days?’ Phoebe asked him for completeness.

‘I miss my mum and dad obviously. I can see now why so many people have freaked out and killed themselves.’ He stared into the middle distance. ‘Mum was murdered by a woman who couldn’t take it any more … she blamed doctors and health people, at least that’s what they said at her inquest.’ He fell silent for a few minutes sadly looking into his empty cup. ‘I feel like I’m hanging around waiting to watch everyone I’ve known all my life go just like that,’ he clicked his fingers, ‘and we’re supposed to carry on like nothing’s happened.’

‘What makes you think we’re expected to carry on?’ asked Phoebe. Of all the people she had interviewed over the last few months when things had really started to unravel, she hadn’t come across this attitude before.

‘Everyone’s in the same fix, right?’ He looked from one woman to the other. ‘It’s not like when there was a disaster; say a major earthquake or flood or famine in Africa. This isn’t something which we can make an appeal for money or blankets and hope everything will be made better. The cavalry isn’t going to ride over the crest of the hill just in the nick of time and save us all. We can’t just sit around and be miserable grumbling about no TV and blaming the Government. This is it. We’re all going to die. Some people have just decided they’d like to be in control of the where and when and not wait for fate to decide their number’s up.’ He said all this quite calmly, rationally and sincerely.

‘You’ve obviously given this some thought,’ said Phoebe after a few moments of stunned silence.

‘A bit,’ said Martin. ‘I’ve been thinking about what’s going to happen to my son Paul when I’m gone.’

‘How old is he?’

‘Nearly eleven. I know he’s scared stiff. He won’t admit it. He either sits in his room all day waiting for the TV programmes to come on or plays escapist games with his friends. He hardly eats, and doesn’t do anything useful like reading maintenance books some dad’s make their kids do. He just does ostrich impressions - trying to pretend nothing’s happened and this is one long summer holiday.

'Why doesn't Leith do something about education instead of wasting resources on curfews?' he asked bitterly.

'Schools had to close when class sizes became unmanageable. Had you heard people have moved into the buildings now? Young people's communes; safety in numbers rather than risking living on their own … it makes better use of irreplaceable resources too,' said Phoebe.

'You sound distant, distinct, like none of this is happening to you,' observed Martin after a few moments contemplating her remarks.

'I'm a journalist. I have to appear aloof to get to the heart of the story. If I get too caught up, I can't do my job properly.'

'How do you print the papers?' asked Mia curiously.

'These days we just print sheets off and photocopy them, then distribute them around markets in exchange for food. Getting ink and toner is becoming a problem though so we're rationing how many we produce. Paper's hard to source too, except handmade which is too expensive.'

'You don't put them on the Internet anymore?' Mia asked trying to remember the last time she'd seen a working computer.

'People keep in touch with current affairs through CB radio rather than TV these days. The Internet - when people can get to it - is free access for information. I need to eat,' Phoebe explained practically.

'So how are you going to pay for this?' asked Mia thinking she ought to have been paid before now.

'Good old fashioned cash, if you'll take it.'

'Some markets still use money.' Mia smiled as Phoebe handed over two crisp twenty pound notes. 'These look wet,' she joked, but held them up to the light just the same, before pocketing them.

'So,' said Martin twisting his teaspoon between his fingers, 'what do you miss most from the old days?'

Phoebe pondered for a moment or two. 'I miss some of my colleagues.' She paused. 'Did you ever read anything by Corin Lister?' The others nodded; Corin had been considered the first crusader of this human disaster. 'He died a couple of months ago. You'd think with everyone else going, you'd not miss one person, but somehow his loss is greater than most.'

Phoebe was quiet again. 'The other thing I miss is shopping,' she smiled dreamily. 'Just popping down the shops and spending money on things I neither needed nor wanted. Retail therapy ... do you remember that?' She smiled at her comrades.

'I miss my car; being able to fill it with petrol and go where I wanted. No rationing, no travel permits. The open road, the potential for discovery, getting lost and finding myself again. That's what I miss ... freedom,' said Martin.

'I'm not old enough to miss anything,' said Mia, sounding miffed. 'I haven't really begun my life yet. I'm going to be the age group that gets hit hardest by this thing. You lot have at least lived a little before you go. I've just finish twelve years at school to find it was all pointless; preparing for a future I'm not going to get. At least your son hasn't got to waste his time in school; he can have a bit of fun while he has the chance.'

'Do you really see things as darkly as that?' asked Phoebe. 'You see this thing as unfair and you won't get a chance to enjoy what life you have left?'

Mia sank in her chair and her body went limp. 'No, I suppose I was just feeling sorry for myself. I miss my mum. She worked so hard for us, helped us with homework, made sure we were turned out well, grew up polite and went to Church each Sunday; all for what?' She sounded even bitterer than Martin.

Phoebe didn't know what to say and gave an awkward cough. 'I'm sorry,' she said eventually. 'I had no idea I'd stir up such dark emotions in either of you. Please forgive me,' she begged softly.

Mia smiled at her. 'You didn't cause this ... you're just asking us how we feel. I feel that I don't want to think about it because it's too painful, but you've made me admit I don't like things the way they are much.'

She stood, put their plates and cups on the tray and turned to carry them away. 'Thank you for making me realise this isn't how I want to spend the rest of my life, however long that might be.'

Phoebe glanced at Martin. 'Maybe this is like one of those Alcoholics Anonymous sessions where they have to admit they have a problem, face it and then do something about it,' he said with a smile. Phoebe thought of Carol alone in her flat with her whisky bottle. 'Maybe you should encourage everyone to face their demons and we'd all be a lot happier. Maybe this thing just boils down to an attitude problem.' He stood to leave. 'It's getting dark, can I escort you home?'

'Best offer I've had all day,' said Phoebe with a smile. Turning to the kitchen door she said, 'goodbye Mia. Thank you for talking to me.'

Mia joined them and locked the door behind her as she left. A police car was the only vehicle moving down the road - most likely the only one with petrol. It slowed as the driver saw them and he wound down his window. 'You just closing Mia?' asked PC Jason Danson.

Mia nodded. 'We're just leaving; we won't be long before we get home.'

PC Danson nodded. 'Don't take too long. We're keeping an eye out for a gang who've been on a looting spree this afternoon. A place like this would suit them down to the ground.' He nodded in the direction of the shuttered café. Looking up and down the deserted street, Phoebe noticed all the shops not boarded up and closed had security grills tightly fastened to them.

Wheeling his bicycle, saying goodbye and thank you to Mia as she was met at her door by Charlie, Martin walked Phoebe to her flat two streets away, and then continued riding through dimly lit streets where the lights still worked, or relied on his cycle lamp where they didn't.

Once he got into open country the night was star-lit black, with only a half moon. He made good progress as there was little motorised traffic and few people about on foot or bike. Being a silent night he was aware of sounds carried on the chilly air; a fox barking, an owl hooting. Behind him, he could hear another cyclist gaining on him. He glanced over his shoulder and saw a black clothed figure riding out of its saddle to increase speed. Feeling his pursuer had more energy than he had, Martin returned his attention to negotiating the bridge over the disused railway line when he felt a sharp prod in his back and fell sideways from his bike, hitting the stone wall with a jarring crump. The pursuer had caught him and pushed him off, slewing to a halt in front of him.

Dazed, grazed and angry, Martin got to his feet. 'What the devil do you think you're doing you idiot! Couldn't you look where you're going?'

The silent hooded figure merely walked up to him and punched him hard in his stomach, winding him and causing him to buckle helpless to the ground. The figure then kicked him savagely in the face and almost knocked him unconscious. With blood pouring from his nose and mouth, he could feel the figure going through his pockets, taking his wallet, his penknife, his house keys, his useless mobile phone.

'Give those ... back,' he struggled to croak, reaching out to try to prevent the figure leaving. The figure grabbed hold of his outstretched arm, pulled him to his feet and gripping his trouser belt, tossed him backwards over the bridge to drop fourteen feet onto the hard rail tracks below.

~*~

Once in her own flat, Phoebe locked her door and moved the bookcase to block it as she did every night after curfew. She then opened up her laptop and wrote the story of her encounter with two decent people whose lives had been wrecked by something inside their bodies they could do nothing about; something unseen which had also devastated the society in which they lived.

After midnight when she had finished it, she prepared to run off a couple of hundred copies, but also e-mail it to Pearl Leith. As unelected Prime Minster, she needed to know what people living through her grand social schemes had to put up with. She fell asleep to the distant reports of gunfire, screaming and a loud explosion.

At 10 Downing Street, Pearl Leith, looking at her thin face in the mirror saw dark rings under her eyes and knew she looked much older than her thirty two years. She would never admit she was in over her head and consequently reacted to every incident without planning, preparation or patience.

The following morning, she met with the Chief Constable John Warden, a man younger than herself and with little experience of riot control, Colonel Andy Burton who had seen action in Afghanistan and Libya and was popular with his men, and the latest scientific adviser Dr Kate Jordan who currently co-ordinated the country's research into the thing which was killing everyone.

Pearl poured herself a cup of peppermint tea and offered a cup to each of her colleagues. Looking out of the window into the almost deserted street below – the recent dry weather meant the streets weren't flooded for a change - she saw the armed sentries behind the razor wire barricade, uncertain whether they were to keep people out or in. 'Curfew breaks are becoming more common,' she said to John. 'Is there anything practical we can do about it, or simply adjust the rules to allow people more freedom?'

'An interesting suggestion,' John observed. 'The natural reaction is to tighten regulations, not slacken them.'

'I have a history in health, not force,' replied Pearl. 'I have a tendency to kindness which might be considered weakness, but after receiving an e-mail last night from an aggrieved journalist, I'm reconsidering our position.'

'The curfew works on adults, but not on kids and teenagers. They've a natural propensity to disobey authority. They walk across any lawn with a *keep off the grass* sign. We need another tactic to prevent our children from wrecking the country,' said John.

'I suppose talking to them won't work?' said Pearl hopefully.

'Probably not, but you could always try … appeal to their better natures.' John smiled wryly.

Pearl considered for a few minutes looking at her colleagues. The Colonel didn't look thrilled at being here and would rather be rounding people up and probably shooting them. Kate looked like she had a lot on her mind and wasn't paying attention. Only John looked calm, but then he wasn't responsible and just followed orders.

'Kate, I don't suppose there's any chance I can make everyone happy by telling them there's a cure on the horizon,' said Pearl her face a white mask in contrast to her red hair tightly coiled on top of her head.

'Not really. We've discovered this isn't a manmade phenomenon; we aren't blaming Professor Fallon anymore for what's happened.'

'Explain,' encouraged Pearl.

'We had thought Professor Fallon's work to extend life through manipulating parts of our DNA by increasing certain enzyme levels had actually done the opposite. But we've since found his work is coincidental to a natural phenomenon happening globally in the background.

'Human evolution has slowed,' Kate explained. 'We're essentially exactly the same as we were about ten thousand years ago. Now there are so many of us and we use medicines and technology to overcome biological difficulties, our ability to build up disease resistance in our genes has diminished. Death has stopped eradicating illnesses or disabilities … think of rabbits and myxomatosis or rats and warfarin … large numbers died but a few built up resistance and survived … We've stopped doing that and our immune systems have become weakened, our DNA is more susceptible to external influence.'

'We get the picture,' said the Colonel. 'What are you saying?'

'This planet is subject to our own generated radiation from nuclear explosions, testing and power production accidents, and vast amounts of solar radiation and cosmic rays. The build up of pollution has degraded the ozone layer and chemicals disrupt our protective atmospheric shell, allowing more of this radiation in. Even the magnetic field generated by the Earth's core isn't helping.'

Kate looked around the faces concentrating on her words. 'We have caused our own extinction by our modern way of life, by our willingness to over-consume and destroy our environment,' she watched as they all looked at her in horror. 'It's Newton's Third law: for every action there is an equal and opposite reaction. For the last sixty years particularly, we've blithely pumped all sorts of concentrated waste into the system expecting nothing to happen as a consequence. Well now we're suffering the opposite reaction … We've reached saturation point ... We have killed ourselves and our children.'

The silence was tangible.

'There must be something we can do,' said Pearl, her voice hopeful. 'This enzyme you mentioned, couldn't we still use that?'

'The enzyme doesn't do what Professor Fallon thought it did. It stimulates the telomeres – the end of certain DNA strands – but it's easily destroyed by the radiation causing the problem.

'Two of the nucleotide bases in DNA – cytosine and thymine – are most vulnerable to radiation. Longer-wave radiation can also cause oxidative damage. This damage can cause various forms of mutation. For example a point mutation in a sequence of DNA may result in a premature stop and possibly a truncated non-functional protein. It's like punctuation in the wrong place in a sentence so it no longer makes sense. When that alters a protein playing a critical role in the body, a medical condition can result, as has been recorded in autopsies by rapidly deteriorating organs and damaged tissue cells.

'Another type, the frame-shift mutation, is caused by insertion or deletion of part of a DNA sequence that isn't evenly divisible by three. As gene expression occurs in threes this can disrupt the reading frame, resulting in a completely different translation from the original. It's sort of genetic Chinese whispers - the original message becomes corrupted and useless with fatal results for the individual. The earlier in the sequence the frame-shift occurs, the more altered the protein product is.'

After a few moments of contemplative silence, the Colonel said, 'surely we can do something to prevent the radiation reaching us.'

'This is a global phenomenon. We'd have to shield the whole planet, which is what ozone and the atmosphere used to do.'

'Why are only humans affected?' asked John.

'Certain other animals are affected ... breeds of cattle, sheep and dogs for instance ... ones we've domesticated away from their natural strains. Wild versions aren't affected ... they must have built up better resistance.'

'But surely,' said Pearl who had been thinking hard, 'we've produced a lot less pollution over the last two years ... with fewer people on the planet. We're using less petrol in vehicles.' She looked at her colleagues. 'Won't that make a difference and slow the process down?'

Kate shook her head. 'Atmospheric scientists have been studying data from satellites and weather balloons from around the world. The chemicals in the atmosphere take at least decades to breakdown. The rate this thing is killing everyone off, we'll all have gone long before that. And the Mediterranean War pumped huge amounts of chemical waste into the atmosphere, and we're still burning fossil fuels to generate electricity.'

'Couldn't we build an ark or something?' asked Pearl. 'You know - a protective shell or live underground in communities of, say a couple of thousand people, to keep our civilisation alive.'

'Do you remember the Biosphere 2 in Arizona in the early nineties?' asked Kate, the others nodded. 'That was huge and took years to design and build. It required maintenance, self contained water purification, air filtration and waste disposal systems – all for just eight scientists to attempt to live for a year or so. It's a different culture to live in something like that. I don't think we've got time.'

'You don't sound very positive Dr Jordan,' snapped Pearl.

'Sorry,' said Kate surprised at her tone. 'I'm just reporting what I've found and giving advice. If you want to build a biosphere and put people in it, feel free. It might give people hope and take their minds off what's happening.'

'If we made it an international project and got help from around the world, wouldn't that make it more feasible?' asked John.

'How is the international situation?' asked Kate. 'I understood a lot of places are evacuating … moving to more hospitable climates.'

'Canadians are moving south … the winters are too harsh for them to manage without fuel, although several brave souls aren't going to be beaten by a bit of cold weather – the hardy pioneering types - and Australia is practically closed … fresh water has all but run out and the seawater purification plants are too expensive to run,' explained John.

Pearl nodded. 'Well, you can still put feelers out about the biosphere and see what response you get.' She looked around the table. 'Right, what are we going to do about these child gangs?'

'Give them what they want,' said Kate firmly.

'What do you mean?' asked Pearl thinking Kate had made her contribution about the science and should be quiet.

'You must remember what it was like being a teenager,' Kate said looking around the group. They had only left their own teens about ten or so years before, and now they governed the country. 'You felt the world was against you, life was unfair, no one ever listened to what you had to say, adults just told you what to do all the time.'

John nodded. 'We give them seats on government, a representative voice and talk to them about the problems our society faces and the decisions we're making.'

'You don't seriously think that will make a difference?' asked the Colonel incredulously.

'It couldn't do any harm,' said Pearl. 'How do we select whom to meet?'

'Get them to select representatives.'

'We need to be able to deal with whoever it is.'

'We need to show them they are part of this society, no matter how fractured or broken it is, and we need them to trust us. Imposing our representative is still telling them what to do. Let them chose.' Kate sat back feeling she had done enough. Being new to the world of politics, her feet were still well and truly in the real world, not the fantasy make-believe world inhabited by Pearl Leith who just wanted everything to be right again and pretend she was in control.

'John, contact four or five groups, ask them to chose a couple of kids to meet us.' Turning to Kate Pearl asked, 'do we meet them here or somewhere more neutral?'

'You make it sound like we're at war,' observed Kate.

Pearl looked at the Colonel who had a broad grin across his face. 'Some of us think we are.'

'Meeting here would show respect and look like we mean it,' suggested John.

'Whereas neutral territory might make them feel safer,' said Kate. 'Ask them where they want to meet. I'm not sure that's really the most important issue. We need to know what they want, explain what we want, and figure out between us how we're going to achieve it without lots of people getting hurt.'

'I think you should chair the discussion,' said Pearl. 'It's your idea and you seem to have a feel for what's going on.'

'I've been close to families around Norleigh since this began,' confirmed Kate.

'Shall we get back to the purpose of the meeting,' suggested Colonel. 'We still have about twenty six million people in this country to feed, provide water and power to, clothe, and move about in an organised fashion. How do we do that successfully without the right people in the right places?'

'Food production and distribution has to remain the priority,' said Pearl.

'I suggest we reduce everything to a smaller scale … keep things local,' said the Colonel, thinking of the situation like a continuation of the Military's current exercise and eager to expand those plans.

'Things have naturally become local as travel gets more difficult. Do you think we should be evacuating more isolated thinly populated areas where it's difficult to maintain food and communications, or should we leave people to cope as best they can?' asked Pearl.

'It's a kind of drift back to the country,' said John. 'I'd heard people are taking over abandoned farms and starting them up again. It's happening all over Europe, especially in the Netherlands.'

Kate nodded. 'I know the Military has already started to move people about, but we could find out where we have vacancies before offering anywhere, and then let them chose,' she suggested.

'You really don't like telling people what to do, do you?' asked Pearl.

Kate smiled. 'I don't like being told what to do any more than anyone else. We haven't got to the stage of imposing rule yet. I'm glad you've decided to reduce the curfew. It wasn't really working.'

'Not enough manpower,' agreed the Colonel, although he looked like he would prefer more control than Kate suggested.

'What about power?' asked John, feeling left out. 'I think we should be decommissioning nuclear power stations while we still have the expertise to do it, like the French are doing.'

'Why would we do that?' asked the Colonel. 'Surely we need the power they produce … or are you thinking they could be subject to terrorist threat or sabotage?'

'No,' said John, surprised he would need to ask. 'They're largely run automatically, but if anything went wrong and there weren't the right people to prevent an accident, the results could be catastrophic for the planet. It's a safety measure.' The Colonel looked taken aback at his reply.

'That's a great idea John, except the cost would be astronomical,' stated Pearl.

John looked at her, surprised. 'I thought governments have always had a budget set aside for decommissioning nuclear power stations?'

'There was. But it was never enough and nowhere near the amount needed to decommission all of them. Look into it John and see what can be done,' asserted Pearl.

'I feel we should be advising the Press and radio what we're doing on a more regular basis, so people hear about what's going on from us rather than through rumours. It should stop panic and grumbling, and make them less likely to form into their own vigilante groups or resistance units,' suggested Kate.

'You don't understand the political process very well, do you?' asked Pearl.

'I understand we are living in extraordinary times and I for one want to be able to walk home at night without the fear of gang attacks, burglars or anyone with a grievance throwing a brick through my window.' Kate looked around the small group. 'By keeping people informed of decisions and the reasons behind them, they'll be calmer and less likely to be belligerent or argumentative. All of us have to change our lives by huge amounts. That's bound to be painful. It's our job to make it easier,' she said firmly.

John nodded. 'How are things with travel and communications?'

The Colonel took this as being addressed to him. 'Infrastructure is a problem as roads become harder to repair adequately. Obviously, fuel stocks have stabilised with fewer people driving but they're not being replenished. As you know the Middle East has dissolved into civil war again with mass destruction of oil fields and huge areas of pollution. We won't be getting gas from the Baltic this winter as the Russian pipeline isn't being maintained or protected adequately, and apparently several places have had illegal junctions added as locals siphon off what they can. We're still mining coal to produce power, but it takes a lot of manpower.' He poured another drink of mint tea.

'Communication satellites are falling from the sky and are no longer being destroyed in a controlled manner. The likelihood of one getting through the atmosphere without burning up completely and destroying a major city is increasing all the time. Mind you, as cities become less suitable for habitation, that might not be such a big issue.

'More earthbound forms of communication are not doing so well. Telephone lines are not being repaired, nor mobile masts. The storms a couple of weeks ago did a lot of damage. The postal service is slow and haphazard and of course the Internet is still intermittently available for e-mail, Twitter, Facebook etc. The medium-wave radio and the Press are still the best ways of communicating with large numbers of people, if you can trust them to get the right message across, and to print and distribute it properly.'

'OK. I think we're there for today's meeting. Next week I'd like up to date figures on the death rate, confirmation there're still no births or pregnancies reported, and proposals for the meeting with youth groups.' Pearl closed down her electronic notepad, the one concession to a world of reducing technology she was loathe to part with, and drew the meeting to a close. 'I need a drink,' she muttered and walked to the drinks cabinet by the wall.

'Could I buy you a drink Dr Jordan?' asked the Colonel. He stood head and shoulders above Kate and was about twice as broad. 'I'd like you to explain the medical situation in more detail … see if we can't tease out a possible solution.'

Kate collected her paper notes and stuffed them into her bag and put it over her right shoulder. 'Thanks Colonel, but I really don't think there's anything anyone can do about the problem.'

'There's always a solution,' said the Colonel, opening the door to let her and John through, 'even if the solution doesn't come from where you'd expect.' He closed the door behind them.

Turning back to Pearl, 'you know you're just a figurehead and don't really have the faith of the people don't you?' he asked softly, his hand in his jacket pocket. Pearl, surprised he hadn't left with the others looked at him and frowned.

'You don't seriously think talking to the youth is going to make things better do you?' He walked to the cabinet to stand next to her. 'Things have got into such a state that the people don't need to be asked what to do, they need to be told.'

Pearl looked at him, with a puzzled frown still on her face. 'We live in a democracy even if our social structure isn't what it was. Our culture of freedom and personal expression must be preserved.'

'Our culture of freedom finished when this thing started killing everyone,' he said, pulling a pistol from his pocket and aiming it at her head. She looked shocked and startled as he continued. 'The Military is taking control. The country will be divided up and each section controlled by a Military unit. Land, possessions and skills will be made use of to the best advantage for each community. There will be purpose and direction, not discussion and inaction.' He removed the safety catch.

'Your resignation is accepted.'

Chapter eleven

Friday 19th April 2019

'It seems so wrong,' said Valerie Cahill tearfully to Ida Hallam, the daughter of her husband's secretary Millie who had died a year ago. 'All those coffins he built, all those funerals he arranged and attended. Hundreds of people he gave a dignified end to and what happens to him?' Her voice became harsh and offended. 'He just gets wrapped in a dirty sheet and poured into a communal grave with strangers without so much as a word said of him. It's disgusting,' she spat venomously.

After a pause for something new to say on the subject, Ida put her arm around Valerie and tried to comfort her. 'They don't use cemeteries any more, you know that. Communal cemetery pits are more efficient and if people aren't buried in the pits, their bodies get torn to pieces by wild dogs and foxes. It's the most humane way of disposing of bodies.'

'It's wrong,' began Valerie again and Ida sighed, deciding to make a cup of camomile tea. One of the last alterations Jim Cahill had made to his house outside Sudcliff before it became clear things were never going to improve was to install a wood burning stove which they could cook on. Ida moved the kettle onto the hotplate and within five minutes the water began to bubble, steam whistling purposefully.

While Valerie continued to rail bitterly at the world, Ida looked out of the window at the garden. The once neat lawns, herbaceous borders and rockery were now neat rows of beans, potatoes, cabbages, carrots and onions all showing shoots and signs of promise. Beyond the privet hedge in need of a trim with a family of colourful long tailed tits looking for spiders, she could see two men weeding the field. She returned to the laundry.

Since the overthrow in September 2017 eighteen months ago, the Military had taken control of supermarket depots with any stores in them, and medicines were distributed on a rationing system, the same as fuel. Few people used buses, preferring to travel by bike, pony or on foot. Barges glided down canals and horse drawn caravans bumbled up country roads. Land had been sequestered where no owner could be traced and small groups were set up all over the country. Towns were deserted except for parties gathering diminishing supplies of clothing, hardware, tools and equipment from abandoned houses, shops and warehouses. Money no longer existed; skills were the new currency. 'What can you do?' not 'what do you drive?' being the in phrase.

Farm museums around the country were raided for old equipment to use or copy, such as scythes, tine or chain harrows and hay rakes. Brewer's dray and shire horses were trained to work the land as tractors became harder to fuel and repair. The absence of skills was evident everywhere with only a handful of specialist around the country. Blacksmiths and farriers were as rare as fresh oranges but just as welcome. Tinkers travelled around selling salt for preserving, vinegar for pickling and spices for flavouring. No one asked where they got their stuff from.

People learned quickly, mostly from their mistakes, and became innovative. This wasn't an experiment in primitive living for a television programme such as *The Victorian Farm* on BBC2 a few years back - this was real. They used as much technology as they could to make their lives easier, gaining a wealth of knowledge from books. Libraries and second-hand book shops provided the gardening and agricultural texts people read as avidly as they once read *Hello* or Dan Brown. History was the most read subject on any farm, discovering how people had managed before tractors and combines, before everything was powered by diesel, electricity and gas instead of muscles. Reading about the different types of plough and the best way to use them saved groups many hours of fruitless hard work and helped to produce good yields.

Motorway service stations were meeting areas for the disillusioned and homeless young. Gaming equipment was powered by electricity generated using wired-up exercise machines. Shopping malls were dangerous unlit cavernous places occupied by rats and gangs. Reports of cannibalism helped to keep the innocent away.

The Military had devolved central government to local areas. Even counties were too difficult to administer and clusters of settlements, be they villages or communes worked together to produce and safeguard food, clean water and what fuel they could. Fortunately, due to Climate Change, the previous winter had been milder and wetter than of late, leaving land ready for new crops and the lack of Eastern European gas hadn't been as big a problem as many feared.

Colonel Burton, with advice from the few he trusted, drew up guidelines for communal life, advocating committees to ensure fairness and thus avoiding the likelihood of dictatorships or serfdoms arising. People having a hard time adjusting to the coup, read the guidelines but did what suited them best. Generally, if they didn't like the way a commune was run, they tried somewhere else. As time progressed however, groups became settled and less open to new people who would have to be fed and cared for and it became harder for people to travel far. Skills were still at a premium and if they had muscles, electrical, plumbing, carpentry, metalwork, medical or veterinarian knowledge, they were welcome.

Spring Farm, the farmhouse and fields beyond the Cahill's hedge had been taken over by a commune of young people. Ida's older brother Will had joined a similar community on the far side of Comfortby sharing his life with twenty other students in another farmhouse. After Jim's death a few months before, Ida had decided to stay with Valerie and her children, but was finding it a trial. Leaving Valerie to her own grief-stricken thoughts, she pottered about in the garden. Spring, with all its promise for the rest of the year, was a lean time. Fresh produce was in short supply so they relied on the remaining tinned food, dry stores and what they had been able to pickle or bottle from last year's harvest.

Kate Jordan and Hugh Old, having been released from their research duties by the Military had joined Spring Farm just after New Year. Hugh, strong, practical and good at getting people to work together, found life much to his liking. Kate, more cerebral and less well adapted to physical work, struggled. She settled for being an arbitrator of disputes, a counsellor, a shoulder to cry on. She wrote a journal of all that had happened in the past few years, including interviews with her fellows of their thoughts and feelings.

Former Tesco employee Rosie Foster and her brother Wesley were also part of the Spring Farm group. Wesley, being an art teacher, made the farmhouse into a haven for pictures and craftworks rescued from homes and galleries, and helped to design equipment from the resources available, improving technology they found around them, and the comforts of the house. Having experienced communal living at Westwater High School, he proved invaluable as he was already aware of some of the pitfalls which might arise and suggested ways of dealing with them. The school project had begun to fail when they realised the small area of land around the school couldn't support all of them and worse, their water supply became contaminated when an underground storm drain burst, seeping oily polluted water into the spring.

At Spring Farm, they un-boarded and swept all the chimneys and fireplaces in each bedroom and made use of coal stocks requisitioned by their Military personnel, and firewood from the adjacent woodland. They each learned how to milk the Golden Guernsey goats and how to use the butter churn. They built composting toilets, recycled dishwater and shower water in a greywater system and dug a freshwater well to the underground stream running beside the wood.

They washed their clothes and bedding in a rescued washing machine driven by securing a belt drive to an old bicycle and taking turns to pedal their laundry, using an old washboard and mangle to help when required.

Wesley built a seed drill following illustrations from a book for guidance. It consisted of a hopper arranged above a series of tubes set at selected distances from each other to allow the correct space between each plant for weeding and watering. A series of knife blades were in front of the tubes which cut open the soil as the drill was dragged forward. A sprocket dispenser dropped seeds in the ideally spaced rows without crowding or the need for thinning, and the seeds were covered without having to go down the line again.

Watching Hugh unhitching the horses from the chain harrow – another piece of equipment designed by Wesley - having completed work on the strip set aside for barley in the field beyond the farmhouse, Kate and Rosie stood in the kitchen pealing and eyeing old potatoes for the stew for supper.

'Did you ever find out anything about a relative or friend who'd died which shocked you?' asked Rosie with a smile.

Kate frowned, not sure what she meant. Rosie explained about her father's paintings and Kate smiled too. 'It's good you can accept his way of handling his grief without being critical or judgemental,' she observed.

'It's better than some. Greta Atkinson, the lady who helped me to look for the pictures,' explained Rosie leaning close to whisper, 'she found much worse about her father once she started digging. I'm glad she didn't live long after her discovery; I doubt she'd a happy life after that.'

'Why?' asked Kate, intrigued. 'What did she find?'

'Pornographic magazines tucked away in a corner of the attic,' said Rosie softly. 'They were in a box under a pile of other boxes, but by the dust, she could tell they were looked at fairly regularly; recent copies too.'

'Mr Atkinson, the old bank manager,' clarified Kate incredulously.

'The worst was he had photos of children too ... Naked children,' said Rosie with a look of disgust.

Kate looked at her friend wondering what to say but Rosie concluded, 'I'm glad it wasn't my dad.' They walked together into the yard with Rosie carrying the bowl of potatoes pealings. 'Why do you keep your journal?' she asked.

'You never know,' said Kate, not sure herself. 'Someone may read it one day and wonder about what kind of people we were.'

'You think someone will survive … and be interested.'

'Sure. Knowing where you come from is important.'

'How do you mean?'

'Well … because we're able to study history and a time when people once lived on farms such as this, we can find out what worked and what didn't and try to base our attempt on the most successful parts without having the pain of discovery ourselves; sort of learn from other people's mistakes.'

Rosie laughed. 'It's great having someone intellectual like you in the group … you keep us on our toes.'

'It works though, doesn't it,' said Kate smiling. Rosie gave the pealings to the Tamworth pigs as she walked passed the sty and Kate wandered across the yard and stood by Alexis Watts admiring the work in the fields.

'Hi. Have you heard if they're going to carry on with the research into combating this thing?' Alexis asked, flicking her long blonde waves over her shoulder.

Kate shook her head. 'I tried to argue with Colonel Burton, but he said it was a waste of resources. Either this thing would kill everyone or it wouldn't. He said it was too late to find a cure.' She sighed. 'I suppose he's right, but I've spent half my life researching things. To be told it doesn't matter stings somewhat.'

'It seems a bit short sighted if someone could've found something to counteract it,' observed Alexis with a jutting lip.

'There are still a few working on the problem in America, but other than that, they're "not contributing".' Kate curled her fingers in the air around the last two words.

She gave a wry smile and patted Alexis' hand. 'How are you settling in?' Alexis had left the commune in Sudcliff when they had started to burn books for fuel.

'I prefer it here,' she said looking around the yard with its clutter of buckets, dirty wellington boots, piles of logs, stray chickens, and the sound of Wesley planing wood in the workshop. 'There's a better mix of people.'

'How're you getting on with Ross?' Kate asked.

Alexis coloured slightly and whispered, 'fine. He's a nice quiet young man.'

Kate smiled and said no more.

'Break time's over,' said the man carrying another sack on his back. 'Give us a hand planting these, would you?'

'Sure Charlie,' said Kate, taking Alexis' empty mug back to the kitchen. Alexis walked towards the fields while Kate followed Charlie to the back vegetable garden to the sunny south facing side where they had already prepared the soil over the last week by digging it over and adding manure.

'If you could make the shallow drills with the trowel, I'll plant them so the necks are just protruding from the soil.'

'Are these onion sets?' asked Kate, vaguely remembering something her granddad mentioned one spring.

Charlie smiled and nodded. 'The sets increase in size and each forms one full-sized bulb by the time they're ready to harvest from August.'

Charlie Salmon had joined the group when his market garden had been taken over by the Military, its produce 'allocated' to those in most need, according to them. His use at Spring Farm was not only in having knowledge of growing seasonal food, but of being able to plan the rotation system for the crops, and the vegetable and fruit gardens. Turnips, clover and grasses were grown to feed the animals over winter, with a rotation of grain and other root crops – potatoes, carrots, parsnips, beetroot, leeks and Swede. Leaf crops of cabbage, asparagus, cauliflower, broccoli, spinach, sprouts, sweetcorn, beans and peas were grown in the fields close to the farmhouse, and onions, pumpkins, squashes and marrows were grown in the garden. The more intense crops of salad leaves, aubergine, cucumber and tomatoes of various varieties were grown in the greenhouse to extend their season.

Pests and diseases were the main problems as sprays were not only hard to come by but disapproved of by most of the residents who thought while they were at it, this survival game they were playing should be as natural as possible in the hope that would stem the flow of the thing which had killed everyone else.

'How are you getting on now?' Charlie asked her, working dexterously.

'I still don't feel I've really found my niche. I've a horrible feeling if the Colonel hadn't thought I may be useful, I'd've ended up with a bullet in my head like Leith.'

'Did he really shoot her?' asked Charlie curious.

Kate shrugged. 'No one really knows, but she's wasn't heard of after that meeting.' Kate stopped for a moment.

'You're a doctor,' said Charlie to change the subject. 'That makes you useful.'

'Thanks,' said Kate with a smile. 'But I'm a pathologist. I've never practiced as a doctor of the living.'

'But you're still one up on the rest of us and people like having you around. You know what's going on for one thing.'

'I did. Things have changed.'

'No one's died here for six months. Do you think it may have stopped?' Charlie stopped what he was doing to look at her.

'It's been shown in studies on telomeres that a diet low in refined sugars, rich in whole foods, fruits, and vegetables, with fewer calories derived from fat, and following moderate aerobic exercise, relaxation techniques and breathing exercises, gained a significant associated increase in telomeres,' Kate explained.

'Sorry?' said Charlie after a short pause.

Kate smiled and said, 'I mean our enforced change of life style to more physical work and no processed foods may be stopping the thing which has been killing everyone … or at least slowing it down,' she added softly. 'Our diet with fewer free-radicals from sugary high fat foods and with all this fresh fruit and veg is helping to keep us alive.'

'So the Military may actually be saving us all?' asked Charlie.

'Possibly, but don't tell the Colonel I said so.' They smiled and continued their task.

'I thought this thing was caused by a genetic problem,' said Charlie after another couple of minutes.

'Yes,' agreed Kate softly. 'The increased radiation we're receiving is damaging parts of our DNA which when it replicates to produce new proteins, isn't working properly. It either results in fatal tissue and organ damage or creates cancerous cells growths. Both appear so quickly they're hard to diagnose let alone treat.'

She and Charlie continued to work in silence until the whole sack had been planted.

Daphne Porter prepared the rest of the meal for the group in the kitchen, while her husband Kevin worked enthusiastically in the fields helping Alexis and Ross clearing the early weeds from the neighbouring strips of carrots, parsnips and potatoes.

'Can't say I've ever been very fond of parsnips,' said Kevin, pulling up a small chickweed as he went along his row.

'You like working with the horses?' asked Ross.

'Yes, I had a go at ploughing last month,' said Kevin proudly.

Ross had read up on ploughing and advised not to go up and down in consecutive rows or they would end up with ridges, but to space the rows out so the soil was turned in the same plane. The dip between two sections – a chain length apart, the length of a cricket pitch apparently - formed a furrow which acted to drain the field. It definitely worked. The ploughing equipment would be checked by a peripatetic blacksmith due to visit again next month to shoe the horses.

'The kids helped with sowing the grain crops.' Kevin gestured to the next field on the other side of the farmhouse. He paused for a moment in his task looking around him. The farm was about a thousand acres in the middle of the country with fields divided into Charlie's mixed rotation system, woodland useful for fuel, hazelnuts and somewhere for the goats and pigs to forage, hedges bearing blackberries and rosehips for autumn, and a small apple, plum and pear orchard where the beehives stood with the fruit cages.

After a long and occasionally heated discussion between the Military and the adult members of Spring Farm, a four field rotation system had been devised. Starting eighteen months before in September 2017 shortly after the coup, local houses and shops had been searched for any remaining stores, and vegetable seeds collected.

Harvesting of the standing crops and ploughing for winter ones had been done mechanically with the farms old combine and tractor while they still had the fuel. The cycle had started again in spring with each member of the commune from the youngest to the oldest, including the Military rotated from job to job so everyone would develop the necessary skills to work in any area. Specialists were tolerated and given leniency, but still had to work the fields, mending walls and fences, laying hedges or building hurdles, weeding everywhere, setting seeds in the greenhouses and keeping the house in good repair. The Military were no exception, but they were the only ones who had guns or knives. No one was unemployed or idle for long.

Haymaking had been the main team activity in May with the older members learning to use long handled scythes, while the children turned it and gathered it into stacks for fodder for the animals. These were the old rare breeds which had survived as their DNA was nearer to wild species than the ones bred by man and all but cloned for meat, milk, leather or wool.

Throughout the summer, everyone helped with weeding thistles, dock, dead-nettle, charlock, and corn cockle from the various crops. During August, the wheat was harvested with a sickle leaving long stubble, followed by scything the barley cut closer to the ground. The goats, White Faced Woodland sheep, the Dexter cattle and Dales ponies were then let onto the field to eat the stubble and manure the soil. Their meadow would be used for grain crops the next year.

The grain was threshed and winnowed with the chaff again used as fodder. Ross read that their grain would keep for several years if stored dry and vermin free. Being able to make use of large plastic wheelie bins meant they only produced flour laboriously when they needed it using a hand quern.

Last September the peas and beans were harvested. Most were dried but some was used to make a pottage as an experiment. Kept warm all the time and topped up with more beans and water; it was surprisingly tasty, especially after it had been fermenting for a week. Now another spring was here and the cycle began again.

'Have you noticed how clear the sky is nowadays?' asked Kevin, looking up and resting on his hoe. Thanks to Wesley's seed drill, they could hoe easily between rows.

'No vapour trails,' agreed Ross.

'No cars or aeroplanes,' said Alexis. 'You can hear birds singing for miles around.'

'Have you seen what we've done in the wood?' asked Ross, pointing to the top of the slope the large straggle of oak, sycamore, hazel, beech and horse chestnut.

'How do you mean?' asked Alexis.

'We've cleared a lot of the scrub for kindling and firewood, and started coppicing the hazel, ash and lime. We've even marked what we've done on a map so we know how old each stand is and when next to cut it.'

'Optimists,' said Kevin.

'What do you mean?' asked Ross sharply.

'Do you think this place will still be running in five years time?' asked Kevin doubtfully.

'If you don't think it will, why are you here?' asked Alexis moving to stand next to Ross as if offering support.

'We have to live somewhere and look after our kids for as long as we can. You don't seriously think this thing has stopped and we aren't all going to die?' he asked, looking over his shoulder to make sure no one else was listening.

'No one has died since I moved here – except Jim at the end of last year, and he was thirty nine, the oldest person around here. For all we know it's stopped now we aren't living such materialistic lives,' said Alexis.

Kevin laughed loudly. 'You're joking!' he looked at her incredulously. 'This thing's inside us; it's not some heaven sent retribution to make us mend our sinful ways – three Popes have died too remember! There were lulls before, and then people started dying again.' He looked around sourly. 'We're just here, biding our time until it gets us too.' He returned to his task in silence. Ross and Alexis shared a look and also continued, moving a few rows further from Kevin.

Ten year old Holly Cahill, having burrowed her way through the thin boundary privet hedge, joined Craig and Stuart Porter to remove stones from the wheat field under the supervision of Nerys, Ross's older sister.

'Are you coming over to play football later?' asked Craig.

Holly shrugged. 'Mum's not keen on me being out after five – she still remembers curfew.'

'Why don't you come and life at Spring Farm?' asked Stuart wiping soil from a large rounded stone before dropping it into the yellow plastic bucket.

'Ida says we can support ourselves with what's produced in the garden, and the Military say that's OK as long as we don't interfere with you lot.'

'Do you do any lessons,' whispered Stuart softly so Nerys wouldn't hear.

'Mum's a teacher so she's making sure we do reading each evening, to pass the time as much as anything, and she still wants Frank to carry on with his piano practice which he does till it gets dark,' said Holly. 'How about you?'

'We only have to read books which'll tell us how to grow things, how to mend machines and how to store stuff once we've collected it – harvested Rosie says.' The bucket was getting about as full as they could lift for now, so between them, Craig and Stuart struggled to the edge of the field - careful not to damage the short bright green crop - and emptied it onto a growing pile near the gateway.

Frank, Holly's older brother, was in the middle of the field using a catapult to scare crows and pigeons off the wheat seedlings. A harsh engine roar came from behind his family's house making him stop for a moment, trying to remember what the sound was. A cloud of dust heralded a vehicle moving swiftly along the dry gravelled road. The engine cut out and he heard raised voices and gunfire. Clutching his catapult, he began to run as fast as he could across the lumpy field, followed as quickly as they could by Holly, Stuart, Craig and Nerys.

The sound of shouting voices continued as well as noises of someone throwing things about. Through the thin hedge, Frank could make out the movement of figures rushing backwards and forwards. He heard rapid footsteps, doors slamming shut, and the engine roaring back into life. The dust cloud enveloped the white van he could see reversing at speed down the road again. A bullet narrowly missed his left ear as he pushed his way through the hedge. He dived to the ground and lay flat, panting and frightened for a few seconds, until he realised they had gone, whoever they were.

By the time he had got to his feet, the others, equally breathless and scared, had joined him.

'What's happened,' demanded Nerys. She looked around the garden noting it didn't seem to have been touched except the washing line had come down and the clothes lay along the path.

Holly squealed and pointed, breaking into a scream.

Nerys looked to where she indicated and could see feet poking out from under a sheet draped over the edge of the cold frame. She ran to look and discovered Ida with a bullet hole in her head, dead upon the path covered in the blooded laundered sheet and clothes she had been hanging out.

Stuart and Craig ran into the house to check on Valerie. They found her, also with a bullet hole in her head, lying face down on the kitchen floor. All the cupboards in the kitchen and larder were flung open and had been emptied of food, only a burst packet of cornflakes scattering over the floor remained.

'They've killed them and taken everything,' cried Craig to Nerys as she ran in through the back door, wet eyes wide with horror.

In the living room Frank and Holly were in floods of tears, failing to console each other. Having come to terms with their father's death as being part of the thing which took everybody, this was different; their mother being murdered while they were in the next field was too much for them.

Nerys took as much charge as she could under the circumstances. 'Run to the farmhouse and tell the Captain what's happened. The Military have radios. They should be able to catch whoever did this and have them … punished.'

Craig and Stuart, not wanting to remain in the house with two murdered women, darted off through the kitchen door and round to the road, running as fast as they could to the farmhouse.

Nerys covered Valerie's face and shattered head with a tea towel and slumped to the floor beside the body. She heard a click behind her and whirled around, startled. A stray dog had wandered into the house through the front door left open by the raiders. An emaciated border collie, its one-time glossy black and white coat dirty, matted and rough from living wild, clipped across the kitchen floor. It looked as warily at Nerys as she did at it, then trotted across the floor and began devouring the stale cornflakes. Nerys got to her feet and fumbled in a drawer for a carving knife. She didn't intend to hurt the animal, but she wasn't sure what it would do if it felt threatened. She slipped from the house into the garden, closing the kitchen door behind her and sighed with relief.

She heard the Captain's motorbike roaring up the road to the house and went around to the front to meet him.

'What's happened?' he asked, dismounting and flipping the bike stand out. 'The kids say someone's been shot.'

'Ida and Valerie have been murdered and their dry stores stolen,' reported Nerys succinctly, her voice trembling uncontrollably.

'Why the knife?' asked the observant man.

'There's a starving dog in there,' she jerked her head towards the house. 'I didn't like the look of it.' Suddenly, she felt ashamed of assuming the probably good natured dog might harm her.

'I'll sort it,' said the Captain, pulling his gun from his belt.

'Don't hurt it!' said Nerys sharply. 'It's just hungry.'

'Aren't we all,' said the Captain and stealthily pushed open the back door. He found the dog still in the larder, its full stomach making it calmer but it would like some water. It wagged its tail hopefully at him, but kept its distance.

Crouching down, but still with his gun handy, the Captain said 'here boy; let's have a look at you.' He offered the back of his hand for the dog to sniff. It came forwards and he was able to stroke it, noticing it had a collar and identity disc telling him he was called Sam and lived in Sudcliff, complete with the obsolete telephone number of his erstwhile owner.

'Well, Sam,' said the Captain, 'what have the bad men been doing today?' He looked at the bodies of Valerie and Ida, checked the stores and looked around upstairs which didn't seem to have been touched, and then examined the road where the marks of the vehicle screeching its getaway were patently visible.

'I'll report this to headquarters. We'll need to dispose of these two. You make arrangements.' He got back onto his bike and beckoned Sam to sit on his lap. Turning the machine carefully, he roared back to the farmhouse.

Nerys, still clutching the knife and with tears rolling down her grubby thin cheeks, wandered slowly after him with the distraught Holly and Frank, wishing she was dead in the house rather than being the one to sort out the sanitary disposal of her friends' bodies.

The murders stunned the little community; Daphne and Kevin looked after Holly and Frank while word was sent to Will Hallam at Comfortby about his sister's death. A soldier dropped him off from the back of a military motorbike two hours later. While their bodies were taken to Sudcliff to be disposed of in the sanitary communal graves, their memorial service was already being held with Kate reading a section from Hamlet, Act 1 Scene 3:

"'Give every man thy ear, but few thy voice;
Take each man's censure, but reserve thy judgment.
Costly thy habit as thy purse can buy,
but not express'd in fancy; rich, not gaudy;
for the apparel oft proclaims the man.
Neither a borrower nor a lender be;
for loan oft loses both itself and friend,
and borrowing dulls the edge of husbandry.
This above all: to thine own self be true,
and it must follow, as the night the day,
Thou canst not then be false to any man.
Farewell: my blessing season this in thee!"'

'Why that passage?' Will asked as the rest dispersed back to Spring Farm house.

'It seemed appropriate to Valerie and it'll give something for the others to think about, rather than the usual religious diatribe no one believes any more,' replied Kate abstractedly.

This surprised Will. 'You don't think people have any religious feelings any more?'

Kate, who had never been particularly religious herself replied with certainty, 'of course not. You think if there was a god who had created man in his own image he would let that image go through what we're going through?'

Will, contemplating his sister and Valerie for a few moments said, 'I have to believe they've gone to a better place … to make all this worth while.'

'They've gone to a better place all right. Out of this world where nothing can hurt or harm them ever again. They'll never be hungry, thirsty, sick or frightened.'

'They'll never be happy, laugh, or joining in with the rest of us,' he pointed out sadly.

'Yes they will,' said Kate assuredly. 'We'll all keep them alive … in here,' she said, tapping the side of her head.

Will looked into her eyes and could see she really meant it. Ida and Valerie had been neighbours and friends and she had cared about them, helped them, and had got to know them. She would remember them being happy, chatty, and kind. They would live on, as long as someone was around to remember them.

The group allowed Will to take Ida's personal possessions from the house she had lived in for nearly two years and had called home. 'We see death all the time,' Will said to Kate. 'You'd think we'd be used to it by now.'

'This is different,' said Kate touching his arm. 'Few people have been murdered since the Military took over … since Pearl Leith was killed in fact.' She fell silent for a few moments thinking of her last conversation with Leith.

'I know … we're all one big happy family now,' he sounded angry. 'Well someone isn't happy. Someone was prepared to kill for a few tins of tomato soup and some dried beans.'

'They'll find out who it was. It has to be someone from one of the gangs in Sudcliff or Comfortby. It has to be local.'

'That makes a difference how?' he asked angrily turning on her as she stood in the centre of the living room stripped of everything which the main community at the farmhouse could make use of, even the piano.

'The gangs have to be stopped to prevent this from happening to someone else,' said Kate firmly. She would not let this young man's hurt feelings overcome the bigger issues.

'We're all going to die anyway, what does it matter?'

'It matters to the people still alive and would like to live out the remaining time left to them in peace.' Kate said strongly. 'I know you're hurt and I sympathise ... but you're not helping.'

Hugh returned with Ross and Kevin to take the rest of the furniture from upstairs to the farmhouse. Will looked furiously at them and stormed out of the house, marching swiftly down the road towards Sudcliff, Kate followed him part of the way and watched him rapidly gain the end of the road.

Loading two mattresses onto a handcart, Hugh and Kevin watched as he reached the main road and turned left, disappearing behind an overgrown hawthorn hedge. 'I wouldn't want to be on the receiving end of anything he might do to whomever he gets hold of,' observed Hugh quietly.

Ross joined them looking worried and Hugh asked him what was wrong. 'I'm sure Valerie had a shotgun under her bed. It's not there now.'

The three men exchanged glances then turned the cart and wheeled it carefully back to the farmhouse, followed by a thoughtful Kate.

Over the radio that night, the Military reported large-scale gang warfare in Sudcliff and Comfortby. It seemed one gang had tried to invade another's territory and a violent struggle had ensued with several men being killed, some by close range shotgun pellets.

'How are things going in other parts of the world?' asked Kate tentatively as they all huddled around the radio set in the dining room, eighteen concerned souls wondering if their own biology would kill them before the gangs did.

'France is practically empty ... refugees have fled to Belgium and Germany, leaving what little they have to the gangs. Buildings in major cities in the States are being destroyed to prevent gangs setting up in them. They're running out of drinkable water in Jordan as well as Australia. The Middle East is still on fire and no one's heard anything from Russia or China for months,' reported the Captain, going against protocol by allowing the community to listen to the radio reports, but he knew they'd only worry if they didn't know. Now they could worry because they did know.

'Why are we bothering?' asked Mia.

'Don't worry sis,' said Charlie putting an arm around her shoulder. 'They won't come back here again; they know the farmhouse is too well defended.' He looked at the three armed Military personnel who watched over them.

'No. I mean why are we bothering to find out what's going on elsewhere? It's irrelevant to what happens here,' replied Mia, shrugging off his embrace. 'While I'm breaking my back removing weeds and stones from the crops, I'm not worried we haven't heard anything from Nepal for five months, I worried when it'll rain next. When I'm dressing a graze after someone's gone too quickly through the brambles, I'm not thinking the Sony Tower has been blown up, I'm hoping you won't get an infection.'

'Well, I for one need to know what's going on in the big bad world,' said Hugh. 'If some Ruskies got his finger on a button which means he'll launch his nuclear missiles, I'd like to know.'

'Why?' asked Mia again. 'So you can pray.' She looked incredulously at him 'You don't seriously think there's a god anymore do you? You big fool!' She leapt up and ran from the room slamming the door behind her as she left. They heard her pounding up the stairs. A few people gave the impression they might follow, but collectively they decided to leave her to it.

The Captain turned off the radio. Perhaps protocol was right after all. 'That'll do for tonight. I miss the Country and Western station myself,' he beamed brightly at them.

'You used to go to the Cabinet meetings before the coup, Kate,' said Rosie, quickly glancing at the Captain. 'What sort of things did they talk about?'

‘It wasn’t really the proper Cabinet, more just whoever happened to be in London at the time. I doubt there’s been a proper Cabinet meeting for years,’ said Kate modestly.

‘Yeah, but what did you talk about?’ asked Ross.

‘Well whoever was there would report what was happening in their department, mention any progress made in sorting out problems and discuss solutions for other ones. They had some good ideas at times, although I doubt many were put into practice.’

‘Such as?’ asked Kevin interested in politics for once.

Kate thought of a suitable topic for a few seconds then plumped for something she thought would be safe. ‘They toyed with the idea of building a dome or sphere for a number of people to live in which would keep out harmful radiation but where they could live sustainably for a number of years.’

‘How did they get on?’ asked Kevin without thinking the idea sounded rather fanciful.

Kate gave him a double take. ‘It wasn’t a practical option in the time allowed.’ She looked around the faces of the group. The children were wide eyed staring at her, the younger adults frowning as if not sure what they were hearing and the soldiers looked knowing. ‘Something like a cavern or an ark takes years of preparation if you’re going to have to live in it with no outside influence at all. It would have to be completely sealed, have a water supply, a sanitation system, fuel and air recycling systems, enough food for years. It would cost a colossal amount to set up and keep going.’

‘Like a nuclear bunker or something,’ said Ross. ‘They must have had those prepared for all the big wigs and top people since the fifties and sixties. Why couldn’t we use those?’ The others gave a rumbling assent to what they thought of as a reasonable question.

Kate was startled by this response, even with nods from the soldiers. ‘Those sorts of places are only suitable for small numbers for short periods of time and no one has actually lived in one to see if they work.’

‘Unlike living on a communal farm where we all work ourselves to death,’ commented Nerys.

Kate looked desperately around the group for a friend. Hugh was noticeable by his silence and apparently wanted her to come up with better reasons than she had so far for why they were toiling on a farm rather than living in a bunker.

'Life in a cave or sphere is not sustainable indefinitely. We'll have to wait decades for the harm we've done to the atmosphere to be repaired. With the healthier more physical outdoor lives we're living now, the thing has slowed,' she flushed slightly, remembering her conversation with Charlie that morning.

'What's happening to us won't be changed by hiding underground living off tinned rations and recycled water. We have to make the best of the life we have now, stick together and keep each other going. Wishing things could be different isn't going to help.'

The group mumbled, not liking to be preached at. 'I happen to know,' said the Captain as he leaned against the mantelpiece, his gruff voice penetrating the room and silencing them all, 'such an experiment was tried in America. A couple of hundred people sealed themselves into a nuclear fallout base in Cheyenne Mountain about a year ago. Initially, all communication ceased as soon as they closed the doors.

'Just after Christmas the doors were opened and a couple of kids ran out into the desert. They were fortunately spotted by a man hunting jack rabbits or they'd probably have died of thirst.'

'What had happened to the group?' asked Nerys keenly.

'They'd all died, except for the two kids. The water system had failed - got contaminated and they'd all come down with dysentery. Because the water was a closed loop and no more came into the facility naturally, they had no way of curing themselves other than water purification tablets. Once those ran out, they were sunk.'

This silenced the room as people swapped nervous glances and their previous appetite for being shut up abated swiftly. The group began to disperse to their various corners to do what they did after dark.

Kate approached the Captain. 'Was that true, about those kids?'

The Captain looked down at her. 'Could have been, I've no idea. I think I read it in a book once. Horror story … probably Stephen King.'

Kate gave him a startled look surprised he would lie to everyone like that and then smiled. He'd poured oil on troubled waters and no one would think they were in a bad situation again, not until the next bit of bad news.

'Good night,' said Kate, and taking a candle, went to the bedroom she shared with Nerys and Mia. She read for a while as the others slept, at the back of her mind wondering what else the Captain might have lied about.

The Military personnel remained in the living room and the Captain turned the radio on again. He thoughtfully scratched the top of Sam's head. The earlier mention of a finger poised on a nuclear button bothered him.

Chapter twelve

August 2019 to March 2020

Mia looked across the farm at half the wheat still to be gathered in and thought grudgingly of the other half waiting to be winnowed and chaffed in the barn at the back of the farmhouse. A tear trickled down her cheek. She sighed and thought again of Nerys's suggestion - no, insistence - they should leave.

Mia and Ross had argued that it made no sense to leave now. They should wait until the spring and then try to join another group, not leave their only food supply and place of safety they had called home for the past two years in the vague hope someone nearby would be willing to take them in. With the Military personnel dead Ross should be able to defend the barn and its contents easily enough with the help of the others. The boys – Stuart was twelve, Craig fourteen and Frank fifteen - were capable with their catapults.

Mia stood and stretched, glad of the warmth of the sun of her face, and the peace and quiet. Guilt crept in and stole the moment. She should be collecting eggs, milking the goat or feeding the pigs. Chores. Is that all she had to look forward to for the rest of her life, however long that might be. Chores and more chores.

Since the last few older adults had died within a few weeks of each other through June, things had gone down hill rapidly both in organisation and purpose. They quarrelled about who was in charge and who should decide what the dwindling group ought to do. The younger children had more work to do and had to do it unsupervised. Undernourished Frank and Craig in their early teens were not strong enough to harvest the fields by themselves and Holly, nearly eleven and Stuart though willing, were slow and clumsy gathering it in.

The sheepdog Sam had been useful fetching rabbits and sort of rounding up the sheep, but he wasn't trained and no one really knew what he should do. He left one night in July and no one knew where he went. Ross was accurate enough with the rifle but didn't have the temperament to use it on anything bigger than rats or crows. Nerys, the eldest by a matter of weeks, had elected herself as the new guardian and decision maker of the farmhouse - at least she thought she was. All they seemed to do these days was argue. Nerys's suggestion of leaving to find another group because they couldn't sustain the farm on their own had horrified everyone else. Running away Frank called it. Mia knew the rest of them had wanted to stay because it was familiar, avoiding their fear of the unknown world beyond; how their world had shrunk, she mused.

She packed straw into the bottom of her pail and went in search of eggs. The Sussex chickens had a large wire-encased run next to the barn. One of the few old fashioned speckled red hens which hadn't succumbed to the genetic disorders of other domesticated animals. Mia couldn't remember the last time she'd seen one of the highly bred Friesian cows, just their own utility Dexters. The Tamworths were one of the few breeds of pigs to survive, ones her medieval ancestors may have recognised. They'd have made themselves at home in the farmhouse too, finding it most luxurious, however much the young moderns decried its want of instant comforts they use to take for granted - running hot water, central heating, electric power, television.

Mia found half a dozen warm creamy eggs scattered in the laying trays set out for the hens and watched Craig lead the two horses, genial fluffy footed black Dales ponies who did a great deal of the hard work of the farm. Horses were as rare and valuable as the food they helped to produce. Tales from infrequent vagrant travellers spoke of horse thieves and night barn raids. Food was the new gold and hunger was the human driving force these days instead of wealth, power and ambition. Ownership didn't matter, no laws existed anymore, certainly no one to enforce them. Each community had its own rules and people rarely strayed from one to another of the randomly scattered settlements around the country.

With this in mind, following Nerys's suggestion, Ross had asked if they left the house, what would become of them? Nerys had countered with if they *stayed* what would become of them? She estimated the country's population would be around eight million by this time, with no one much older than twenty two or three. They should be able to find someone. Mia felt that if she was going to die anytime soon, she would rather die here in the known place she called home. A fleeting thought crossed her mind that she didn't know who the house belonged to. She'd turned up here two years earlier having been told to quit Norleigh by the Military commanders and she learned to live with the seventeen other people who had arrived to work on the land.

What would become of them? Perhaps these few scattered folks would survive here; keeping the human race going. If they left, they had no guarantee they would find another welcoming settlement; they hadn't seen any travellers all summer, not even the farrier. Leaving was a risk which Mia and Ross didn't feel was necessary.

Taking the pail of eggs back to the house, Mia looked across at Nerys, kneeling beside the graves of those who had died not so long ago. It had been too dangerous to take the dead to Sudcliff, so they had been buried at the edge of the wood, away from the stream. How could she leave them? How could she stay with them? If only she knew what to do for the best.

After nearly eighteen months of relative peace and quiet and no further incidents since Valerie and Ida had been murdered, the thing, which everyone thought had gone, had returned on its lethal path of destruction leaving four children without parents and the three young adults with little idea of how to continue.

~*~

The harvest was gathered in eventually, wood cut for heating, the animals tended and with emotional difficulty gradually slaughtered over the cold wet months of winter until, following a particularly bad and demanding February, they decided they would leave and try to find somewhere else.

On the day they set off under a bright blue hopeful sky, the two horses pulled the cart and the group followed on foot taking it in turns to drive. They hadn't heard any news over the Military radio since Christmas after the transmitter had been blown up by revolutionists fighting further south against the Military's control of the country.

The cart rumbled north towards Norleigh and west past Summerton. They picked up thirteen year old Paul Unwin outside Westwater having found him by the side of the road playing with a toad. After his father Martin's murder, he had been taken in by Melvin Trott owner of the hardware store not far from where Martin had worked in the travel agency. Mel was one of the last adults to die in his commune, but without him as protector, Paul had been bullied away from their farm a little over a week ago, ending up wandering about, not knowing what to do. Here he sat by the side of the road, covered in a duvet and raincoat, hoping someone would pass. He'd been there four days and they were the first people he'd seen. He'd run out of food and was about to try to go hunting for more when he'd heard the cart.

With his new friends as reinforcements, they made their way to his former home. The place was deserted. Nerys and Mia, with help from Craig and Stuart, stripped the house of what they could carry and use, filling the cart even higher. The bullying children were nowhere to be seen; evidently the four of them, between twelve and fifteen years old, had also decided to chance life elsewhere.

As they drove onwards, trees grew unchecked in daffodil lined ragged hedgerows, the roads were broken and full of pot holes, power lines had come down over fields and the few houses they passed were deserted and often blackened shells. They managed to find the occasional small community and when Ross bravely walked down driveways and paths to speak to the occupiers, making sure they could see his rifle, he was always sent away.

At night they slept huddled under the cart in the sleeping bags they'd brought, letting the horses eat along the verge. At least one of them kept watch all the time. Night time was dangerous because of animals roaming wild with less fear of people. They hadn't come across as many packs of wild dogs as Ross expected, but they heard badgers and foxes. Wolves, bears and others escaped from wildlife parks and zoos had been breeding happily in the de-peopled countryside, living off deer, feral sheep, wild cattle and goats. Ross hadn't much ammunition and would prefer to use it for emergencies only, so driving off wild animals became the children's role and the use of catapults compulsory. Fire helped too and like travellers of old, they carried a can of smouldering coals with them ready to blow into a fire quickly.

After they travelled a wiggling path for a week they reached a small village about a hundred miles from Sudcliff. At first it looked remarkably intact, if shabby. Dubiously, Ross, cradling his rifle, walked slowly down one side of the main street while Nerys walked down the other, a cricket bat over her shoulder. The cart, reins held firmly by Craig, stayed next to the decaying *Welcome to Swithenhurst* sign.

Ross tensed on hearing a gate creak. Nerys heard it too but couldn't see anything. They continued. The gardens were overgrown and full of rubbish blown in from a nearby landfill site. Peering through windows, some of which were still intact, Nerys saw the houses had been stripped to the floorboards just as her own commune had done. Washing, probably done a couple of years before, still hung raggedly on the line behind one of the cottages. Street signs were overgrown with ivy and bindweed, nettles were beginning to show through cracks in the pavement, brambles encroached footpaths, hedges were rampant, trees devoid of leaves swayed in the wind, and birds sang and flitted everywhere.

Ross wasn't watching nature or admiring how rapidly it took control again once man had been removed. All his senses told him he and his sister were in danger, but he had a compulsion to carry on walking and meet whatever it was. A large shape ran across the road in front of him and before he could stop himself he fired at it, blasting the rat squealing five feet into the air before it landed twitching and dead in the middle of the road. He wiped the perspiration from his top lip and forehead, tightening his grip on his gun, and didn't look at Nerys.

Nerys rolled her eyes and smiled at her brother. Typical she thought just before the scythe swished through the air and cut her head clean from her shoulders. She fell to the ground in two, only the thud of her body making a sound. Ross looked across the road in horror, immobilised with wide-eyed shock. He raised the rifle eventually at the shape behind his sister's body but the weapon was dashed from his hands by a clubbed blow from behind and he died the instant the knife cut his throat, spraying arterial blood in an arc into the neighbouring garden.

Seeing what had happened to their friends, Craig tried to get the horses to turn the cart around, but he wasn't fast enough. An arrow thudded into his back and another into his thigh. Aware of the searing pain from these wounds, and the agonised screams pouring from his mouth, he was conscious of Stuart falling from the cart and landing on his back with a surprised look on his face, a bloody arrow protruded right through his neck.

Holly screamed and jumped from the cart, running for safety into the wild fields beyond the hedge. She took an old footpath and ran as fast as she could, trying not to scream again. Frank, Mia and Paul left on the cart, were soon surrounded by five boys aged between twelve and fifteen, all dirty, in ragged clothes looking half starved. They each had a bow drawn back ready to fire. Not bows children might make from bits of birch twig with string and a flimsy arrow with a couple of goose feathers stuck on for flights, these were sporting goods crossbows, the sort marksmen used. A taller girl of about eighteen wielding a blood stained scythe joined them.

'Off the cart,' she snapped, flicking the scythe from them to the ground. They jumped down without protest, avoiding Stuart while trying to help Craig. He managed to stand while holding onto the cart.

'He's hurt,' said Mia forcefully through her terrified chattering teeth. 'Let me help him.'

Without blinking the girl swung the scythe straight across Craig's neck and cut his head off. 'He's OK now. Move!' she barked.

Completely stunned, the three of them moved into the road away from the cart which contained everything they owned which might keep them alive, and watched helplessly as Craig's body was tossed aside by one of the boys who then stirred the horses into action, taking the cart on to the village. They stood mute and immobile for a couple of minutes before they realised what had happened.

'Where's Holly?' asked Paul dully.

'She went down here,' said Mia in a monotone, leading Paul and Frank down the footpath Holly had taken. 'She was really frightened; she might have gone a long way.'

'Unless one of them got her,' said Paul without thinking.

Frank kicked the back of his leg. 'She's my sister!' he snapped.

'Quiet you two. If anyone's in these woods, we don't want to draw attention to ourselves.' They jogged on avoiding brambles and traps as they went. More than one rabbit had not been so lucky and a few had not made it to the pot either, having been stolen by foxes, just leaving the bloody heads behind pinned in the jaws of the trap, covered in flies and maggots.

Holly had run down the path for about ten minutes until the stitch in her side had become too painful and she had dived for cover in a hazel coppice to catch her breath. Breathing hard, she tearfully watched the path. Two boys had followed her through the woods, but had given up after a few minutes and the sound of the cart rumbling had called them back to their village. She jumped out of cover when she saw Mia and heard Paul and Frank arguing softly.

Having embraced them and been told the terrible news, she pulled them into her hiding place and asked what they were going to do now.

'We've lost the cart,' complained Paul.

'No.' said Frank emphatically, 'the cart was stolen. That's our stuff and we have to get it back.'

'How? There're more of them than us and they know the village, we don't,' said Paul.

'Wait for nightfall,' suggested Mia.

Paul was flabbergasted. 'Are you mad? You're not seriously thinking of going in there and getting the cart back are you?'

'They killed Nerys, Ross, Craig and Stuart without blinking an eye. They've just left the bodies to rot or be eaten by animals,' said Mia forcefully. 'Are you going to just lie here and let them get away with that? We weren't doing them any harm.'

'Not that that has anything to do with it,' said Frank in agreement with Mia.

'Are you wanting me to fight?' asked Holly, eyes wide, lip trembling.

'You can look after the horses, but you might have to defend them if one of that lot tries to hurt them,' offered Frank thumbing over his shoulder at the village.

'You're mad!' was all Paul could manage. 'We don't know how many of them there are.'

'You want to sit by the roadside until someone else passes and offers you a lift, a home, food and company - be my guest,' said Frank getting to his feet and pushing through the bushes. 'Let's recce the village and work out what we're going to do to get our stuff back,' he said, leading the way through the wood, back to the village. Mia and Holly scrambled along behind. Paul, reluctantly and grumbling quietly, followed.

As it grew darker, they put their plans into action. Paul, who had been talked round by Mia, ran behind the cottages closest to the wood and furthest from the former filling station and garage where the cart had been taken, and waited.

Frank moved across to the other side of the road, hiding in a front garden but where he could see Paul and also Mia further down the road. Holly had made her way round the back of the garage and using a screwdriver, broke into the backdoor. The garage looked more like a barn being devoid of vehicles but with benches covered in tackle and harnesses, and a stock of hay and straw. The horses seemed pleased to see her and with a practiced hand, she manoeuvred them between the shafts and began to open the front garage doors softly.

One of the village boys spotted the door opening and was about to raise the alarm when he was hit on the temple by a stone shot from Paul's catapult. Unfortunately he fell onto the flaming torch next to his sentry post which set light to the dry scrubby material in the garden at the end of the row of cottages, catching the broken picket fence and continuing on to the yard next door.

Seeing the increasing flames from the vantage point of a guard post outside the house the village children lived in, another young sentry yelled 'FIRE!' and ran towards it only to be felled by a stone as his fellow had been. The other three boys, hearing the alarm and seeing the flames, ran out carrying buckets to fill with water from the borehole well in the centre of the village. They tangled and quarrelled with each other, tripping and spilling much of the water but didn't manage to stop the spread. Inevitably, the end cottage with its neglected wooden door and window frames, soon caught alight. As they turned to refill their buckets, all three were caught by stones from Paul and Frank's catapults.

The girl however had not gone to the fire but had realised this might not be an accident. Instead she went towards the garage, getting there in time to see Holly driving the horses from it. 'No you don't missy!' she yelled, whirling her scythe and slashing it towards Holly in the driver's seat. Holly ducked and the scythe wedged into the wooden board. Holly tried to get the horses moving but they weren't keen on travelling in the pitch dark.

The girl wrestled the scythe free as she walked along beside the cart and the frightened Holly. A stone whistled passed her, narrowly missing Holly. 'Pick on someone your own size,' said Mia, wielding a scythe of her own over her shoulder, another stone ready to throw in the other hand.

The girl smiled and took a step from the cart while Holly continued to urge the horses slowly away from the fighting. Paul and Frank arrived having made sure the boys were either dead or seriously unconscious. They couldn't help Mia with the catapults as the older girls were circling each other and occasionally making tentative slashes with the scythes. Holly had moved the cart out onto the main road and now stood the horses so she could turn to watch, conscious of the bloodstain on the tarpaulin next to her where Craig had died.

Mia swung, the girl blocked, the scythes locked for a few seconds, the two young women testing each others strength like stags. Free once more, they circled again, leering at each other. The girl offered taunts; 'that young man yours was he? Your brother's in the cart were they?' Then she struck again, unable to get through Mia's guard. Still circling she continued. 'Ever killed anyone before love? Know how much force you need to cut someone's head off do you?' Riled, Mia flashed wildly, missing her target but receiving a cut on her right shoulder. They continued to circle, and Paul was about to get a shot in with his catapult but realised Holly was in the line of fire if he missed. The two boys made their way round the combatants to the cart.

'Got any idea what we're going to do to those young things when I've finished with you?' the girl taunted.

'Who's *we*?' yelled Frank, annoyed that Mia hadn't finished the girl off. 'We've sorted out your little band of boy scouts and set your village on fire.'

The girl looked over her shoulder at him for a second and Mia was able to take advantage of the distraction. She lunged and hit the girl's leg with a downward slash. The girl hissed and retaliated instantly with a sweep which only just missed, cutting the front of Mia's jacket. The girl looked down the village street at the orange crackling glow which lit the scene and the five bodies lying in the road. Maddened, she slashed furiously, whirling the scythe and carving so fast Mia could do nothing to block her swings. Jumping up as the scythe swung under her feet, she narrowly missed losing both her legs.

Both girls were angry and went on the attack, swinging ferociously and causing many minor injuries. The thought that a few months ago Mia wouldn't have had the strength to fight for this long crossed her mind as she glared fiercely at the girl. However, bleeding from leg, chest and arm wounds, Mia began to tire, but so did her adversary. With one last almighty effort, the girl hefted the scythe and brought it crashing onto Mia, splitting her head open. Her moment of victory lasted only a microsecond as her momentum carried her onto Mia's upturned scythe which embedded itself in her stomach. Blood poured from her mouth as she fell on top of Mia's body; both were dead by the time she reached the ground.

The three children stared in horror as they watched Mia die. Holly screamed and Paul caught her to prevent her from running towards the enmeshed bodies. Frank flicked the reins on the horses' backs and the cart lumbered away from the fire ravaged village, leaving the five boys and two girls dead in the roadway.

The horses carried on walking until daybreak several hours after the terrible scenes in the village. Holly had fallen asleep and Paul and Frank took turns to keep watch while driving the cart. They stopped by a gate and watched the sun rise over open farmland on a cold bright morning. 'You any idea where we are?' asked Paul. Frank shrugged. 'Do you suppose we'll find anyone else alive?' Frank shrugged again.

Holly woke, stretched and rubbed her eyes. 'Where are we?' she asked.

'We don't know,' said Paul. 'Let's have some breakfast.' Turning back the tarpaulin – he had turned it round so the bloodstain was at the far end of the cart - he rummaged for a tin of dried biscuits and a jar of preserve. With a dirty knife, he spread jam onto two crackers each and passed them to his friends.

'We'd best collect some water,' said Frank as he jumped from the cart and taking a red plastic bucket, he disappeared behind the hedge. He knew water would most likely be at the bottom of the hill and near the greenest vegetation. They were in northern England somewhere and if there was one thing England had plenty of, it was water. He regretted they hadn't been able to restock their water supply from the borehole in the village of death, but he had no desire to return to it once he'd thought of the idea – he'd rather die of thirst.

Paul and Holly remained at the cart, checking the supplies and equipment and tidying things which had shifted. Fortunately the village boys hadn't bothered to unload their treasure once they'd taken the food they wanted for their supper.

Frank was surprised he didn't find water straight away and became conscious he was getting further from the cart as he wandered down the wooded hillside in his search. He stopped to listen for a stream, but could hear nothing except a jay distressed by his presence and a green woodpecker laughing. He continued a little further as the ground became boggier and more promising. He stumbled and fell, rolling down the slippery slope, letting go of the bucket in his tumble. Eventually coming to a halt in an ignominious heap, he slowly got to his feet feeling groggy. The bucket had come to rest slightly higher up the slope and he could now hear water running below him.

He looked up for the bucket but he'd knocked his head and his vision was blurred. Shaking his head to clear it, he got the impression something was moving towards the bucket from above. Struggling to his feet he lunged for the bucket, missing it but grabbing a mouldy branch. He tried to get to his feet again; still unable to focus on whatever it was after his bucket. He swung the branch and it connected with something. The something gave a startled yelp and backed away. Satisfied, Frank yelled at the thing to go and leave him alone.

He picked up his bucket and started to move down towards the sound of water. He still couldn't see properly, missed his footing and slipped on the thick layer of wet leaves, this time sliding on his bottom until he came to rest against a small twiggy hazel bush. He lay stunned for a few moments but sensing that the something hadn't gone far, he tried to get up again. Now his leg hurt, he couldn't see properly and he was scared. He swung the branch again but this time whatever it connected with was solid and the branch disintegrated. The something roared loudly and slashed at him with its long sharp claws. It caught him on the side of his head making him fall over. Frank gave a startled scream as the animal got close enough to come into focus. At first he was aware of the white strip of fur around its neck, and the contrast this made with the blackness of the rest of it. Its small dark eyes stared at him angrily as it swung again with its claws, cutting his face, splitting his nose and mouth. The screams of agony from Frank only seemed to make it more aggressive and it continued to slash until Frank was silenced by a cut across his throat which severed his jugular vein. Once he was silent, the black bear calmed and having sniffed the body, lumbered off towards the stream.

Holly and Paul were aware Frank was taking a long time and decided they should go and find him. Risky as it was to leave the cart and horses unguarded, Paul couldn't leave Holly alone with it, nor send her into the woods to find Frank. Having followed the same path as Frank, they came to the spot where he had fallen, the skid marks and broken bracken showing where he had gone down the bank. Carefully climbing down, they found the bucket, and then Holly screamed as she found Frank's mangled body torn and bloodied next to the hazel bush. Paul, instantly on his guard, collected the bucket, swiftly made his way to the stream to fill it and left the site immediately dragging the wailing Holly with him.

'How could you just leave him like that?' asked Holly through her tears. 'He's my brother. Can't we at least cover him over so the … foxes can't get at him?'

Paul, who wanted to jump on the cart and ride away as quickly as possible, said he would go back and cover the body. He made her promise to lie low under the tarpaulin and not make a sound. 'He was killed by an animal,' he said. 'It might still be around and I don't want anything to happen to you.'

Bravely, he returned to Frank's corpse, covered it pointlessly with some browned bracken leaves, collected Frank's catapult, compass, penknife, box of matches, and trainers then climbed back to the cart.

Paul and Holly travelled together for another few days seeing no other humans but plenty of signs that their battle against the group of village children was not an isolated incident. Decayed bodies lay by the roadside, in ditches, on pavements. Most had weapons of some description with them; all had signs of violence be they knife wounds, or protruding arrows. A few had bullet wounds but all had been chewed by animals or pecked by birds to some extent and the smell of decay marked where they lay long before they saw them.

They had tried to avoid larger settlements, but the road they travelled widened into a main road and eventually led to a city. Taking what was once the ring road, with the overgrown sponsored roundabouts full of weeds and rubbish, Paul encouraged the horses to move as fast as possible knowing the buildings they passed could house any number of ambushers or snipers on look out. As it grew darker, Paul decided they would have to stop for the night and pulled up amongst an avenue of trees which lined a park.

He unhitched the horses and left them to feed on the meadow which would once have been cut lawns. Owls hooted and bats flew overhead. He decided not to light the fire as it was a relatively mild night and he didn't want to draw attention. They ate dry biscuits and cold pottage of vegetables. Holly, although she was eleven years old, needed a story before she could sleep and Paul recounted tales from his brief life of fishing with his father, kite flying on the beach with his grandfather, and country walks with his grandmother. He made some up too, trying to give them all a happy ending.

Tonight he was telling her a story about three baby giraffes which had escaped from a zoo when he heard a roar. The sound wasn't loud especially, but it resonated in his stomach. Holly froze with fear instantly and almost stopped breathing. Paul threw the tarpaulin over her and bravely withdrew his large hunting knife recently extracted from the corpse of a boy in a ditch five miles outside the city.

The roar came again but it was much closer this time. Too late, Paul realised the horses hadn't been tethered but he had just left them to find suitable food. He lurched for the reins of one, but his own movement shied the other away from him, and she wouldn't come back when he called. Ears pricked, she trotted nervously away from him. Out of nowhere a large tawny brown shape appeared in the air and landed on the back of the startled horse. She bucked and kicked but her attacker had a firm grip and its sharp claws dug deep into her side and a second shape had grabbed her by the throat, trying to pull her down. The horse managed to stagger away from the cart with the two lionesses on her, but she soon succumbed to their combined efforts and died with a loud groan. Two more lionesses appeared out of the gloom to join their sisters and before long the sound of contented rumbling, the ripping of flesh and the smell of warm blood filled the air.

Paul meanwhile hitched the remaining horse to the cart and steered him away from the lions' feast and they moved away as fast as one horse could manage. Holly cried a lot after Paul told her what had happened. As he could do nothing to console her, he let her cry herself to sleep as they kept moving slowly.

By dawn they were away from the city and back onto an open main road. They hadn't seen another living human for a fortnight and Paul was despairing of them ever seeing anyone else. The horse was struggling with the cart on his own. He would either have to find another horse or a smaller cart.

Having used a pair of binoculars to check first, they followed a promising track which led them to a deserted farm. The barn door creaked alarmingly as Paul pulled it open but when no famished dog or other wild thing jumped out at him, he used the precious torch to see if there was anything they could use. Tucked away at the back was a small cart for two people with space behind for luggage. He spent a while clearing away all the stuff around it and hauled it out into the bright daylight. The wheels and axel were intact and the shafts would fit the horse.

They spent the next hour or so taking everything off the big cart, deciding what they needed and placing these things in the smaller cart. Holly investigated the house for food, bringing tinned goods, some matches, torch batteries and another duvet each. They would need these as they had to sit at the front all day, even if the weather was dry. Paul found a two-man tent and having had a go to see how easy it was to put up, secured it over the rest of their possessions.

Setting off again in the afternoon, they were caught in a heavy downpour and were glad of the Barbour jackets they had taken, even if they were too big. Supper of oatcakes, cheese and a rare treat of sausages helped down with a couple of bottles of beer meant they slept well for the first night in a while.

When they woke next morning, Paul wasn't feeling well and had a temperature. He drank a lot of water and Holly had to walk about a mile to find a stream to refill their water bottles. When she got back Paul was much worse and had a fever. Having no idea what to do, she lit a fire and wrapped him in the duvets, trying to stop him shivering.

'I think I've cut myself … when I was getting the cart … out of the stable,' he managed to stammer. 'My leg hurts,' he explained, trying to move it so Holly could look at it.

She undid his boot and took off his sock. Rolling up his trouser leg, he called out in pain as she reached the spot where the torn trouser covered a bloody deep gash about twenty centimetres long, a vivid red with an unhealthy looking green tinge and unpleasant smell. Holly cleaned it as best she could with water and the cleanest cloths she could find, dabbed it with antiseptic cream which made Paul cry in pain, and then bandaged it with stuff from the first aid kit.

Holly could do nothing else but sit by and watch Paul fight the infection now spreading through his body. Although he was young, he had lived on a meagre diet for the past few months and was not as strong as a boy of his age should be.

Holly tethered the horse allowing him to eat as much grass from the verge as he liked and went in search of whatever wild food she could find, returning with a small collection of berries, by which time Paul was delirious with sweat pouring from him. Attempting to change the dressing, Holly was appalled at the state of the leg wound which was now black and smelled dreadful. Mopping his brow with a damp cloth, she cried to herself, praying he would recover soon.

As she was frightened by the animal noises on all sides she had trouble sleeping. She struggled but was determined to put up the pop-up tent and drag Paul into it, but he was unconscious and oblivious to anything she did. He didn't cry out when she had to pull the bandage from the septic wound on his leg as it oozed greenish puss. Once again, she sat next to him, rocking backwards and forwards, fearful tears rolling down her cheeks as she watched him in the dark.

She awoke next morning to the sound of blackbirds welcoming the new day. It sounded so pleasant and reminded her of better times she almost forgot where she was. She screamed when she saw Paul's open eyed inert body next to her, being familiar enough with death to recognise it when she saw it. She scrabbled from the tent and wailed, forlorn and bereft. Throwing herself on the ground near the horse, she cried for some time.

Coming to herself after a while, reality dawned and she knew she would have to deal with Paul's body and move on. Dragging him clear, rolling him into the ditch and covering him with bracken leaves she cut with Frank's penknife, she apologised for having to leave him and prayed his soul was in a better place. She hitched the horse to the little cart having stowed everything in it, and set off again, with no idea where she was or where she was going.

Numb and chilled by another rain shower, she let the horse decide the pace and path. She stared hollow-eyed in front of her not registering any sights, sounds or smells. The horse stopped outside a cottage and chewed on fresh leaf buds of a bush by the gate. Holly stirred herself and decided to investigate the place. If it was empty, she would like to stay in a house for a change and sleep in a real bed.

The garden had gone wild with the path barely discernible and the front door was open, which was a bad sign. Armed with a machete, Holly pushed it open wider and went inside. The cottage, while covered in dust and debris blown in from the garden, was remarkably intact and tidy. Nct curtains covered the grubby windows, flanked by chintz curtains matching the sofa and two armchairs. The fireplace was full of soot and old nests, but the dusty pile of logs next to it had been neatly cut and stacked.

Holly tentatively walked up the stairs, machete at the ready, wary of animals which may have taken up residence. Only a grey squirrel darted out through a broken bedroom window. The three bedrooms, like downstairs were all tidy and well looked after except for leaves. Whatever had happened to the owner, the house hadn't been disturbed since they had left. Relaxing all the time, Holly went down to the kitchen with it's neat table and chairs in the middle and tidy work surfaces except for a thick layer of dust, and looked through the cupboards. Breakfast cereals, tins of fruit and tomatoes, packets of flour and pasta; all years out of date but no one worried about things like that anymore.

The best thing was the Aga. Once she wiped the dust off it, the chrome shone brightly. Smiling she contemplated cooking herself something and wondered if there might be wood or coal somewhere other than by the fire. Noticing a hand water pump poking above the brambles in the back garden, she decided to draw some water for the horse, get the Aga going and make herself a pot of tea.

Walking into the scullery she came to an abrupt halt. Lying on the floor was the dust covered dried out corpse of a woman, dressed in a flowery housecoat and fluffy slippers covering her feet, she was stretched full length resting on her extended right arm. Holly swallowed and backed away, closing the door again.

A mixture of emotions overcame the girl; shock, fear, grief and yet the desire to fulfil her dream of a hot cup of tea and sleep in a bed tonight. Going through the front door, she collected the red bucket from the cart and carefully slashed her way to the hand pump with her machete. Reluctantly, gratingly, it began to work and after a few minutes of heavy pumping, gushed a supply of cold fresh water. Taking a bucket full to the horse which had moved on to eating other delights in the garden, Holly secured him lightly to the gate post.

Starting a fire in the Aga with kindling from the wood shed and the box of matches from the cart, she heated a copper kettle of water and explored the bedrooms again. The wardrobe in one was full of the old lady's dresses of flowery cotton and smelt of stale lavender scent. A row of brown and black sensible shoes were at the bottom and a large hat box on the top shelf. Holly amused herself by trying on the clothes and hat, laughing at herself in the grimy full length mirror hanging behind the door.

The kettle began to sing and she went down again to make herself some tea. She turned her nose up at some mouldy biscuits she found but ate her way through a mixture of cartons of sultanas, currants and almonds whilst exploring further.

The books on the self in the living room didn't appeal being about historic houses, autobiographies of politicians, and gardening. She flicked through some to see the pictures, but got bored quickly. To her delight, she found an old wind-up gramophone. Having seen one once in an old black and white film, she knew you turned the handle to get the turntable to revolve, and having chosen a Mozart piano concerto, for the first time in months, she heard music, however scratchy, played to her from modern technology.

Relaxed now, she checked the horse was all right, unhitched him and brought him into the garden where he could roam happily all night un-tethered. Holly opened a tin of tomato soup and warmed it on the Aga, had another cup of tea and followed this with a tin of peaches. Having chosen which bed she was going to sleep in, she cleaned the grate and lit a fire before curling up on the sofa, watching the flames flickering, content and comfortable for a change.

She contemplated staying here for a while, but the supplies in the house and those she had brought wouldn't last her for long, so she would have to find out where the nearest settlement was before committing herself. She sat bolt upright, having had a brilliant idea. This old lady must have had some post, something which would have her address on. If she could find out where she was, she could find out where the nearest settlement was.

She jumped up and began looking around for somewhere the lady might have kept papers. Nowhere in the living room looked obvious so she hunted in the kitchen. Drawers had instructions for various pieces of equipment, but nothing with an address. Upstairs she was more fortunate. A bureau in the largest bedroom was where she kept her bank statements and letters. Mrs G Finchley, Lobelia Cottage, Smithy Lane, Oakridge, Dovedale. She had an address, now to find a road atlas or map book. The map book she found was ten years old, but that didn't matter. It showed her Dovedale was in Derbyshire and Oakridge was a small village about ten miles further south. Pleased with herself, she went back to enjoying the fire.

The night was chilly in the damp house so she banked up the logs to heat the room and light it with a warm amber glow. Watching the shapes of shadows shifting across the ceiling, Holly fell asleep, dreaming of a warm comfortable bed, her mother baking on the Aga and Frank playing football in the garden with the horse.

Smoke gradually filled the room since the chimney hadn't been swept for many years and several nests had fallen down it. The fire caught one and it burned inside the chimney. One of the logs rolled off the grate and began to smoulder on the woven hearth rug until it too caught light. Holly slept on oblivious, as slowly the fire spread until it engulfed the room. Holly was overcome by the smoke and fumes long before the fire reached her. Within half an hour the cottage was aflame, the chintz burning merrily, flames crackling along the ceiling to the kitchen, up the wooden open stairs and the upper rooms. Had there been anyone to see it, the fire at Lobelia Cottage could be seen for miles around, lighting the cold March night and fanning sparks into the air. The horse was long gone by this time, frightened off by the first crackling and sparking as the furniture burned.

Holly never woke from her dream.

Epilogue

Fifty planetary orbits of the star later

The explosion was heard for miles around. Those close to it were blown off their feet. The closest were incinerated and blasted to dust. Humans may have been gone for over fifty years, but their persistent presence was felt by the rest of life left behind.

Tons of radioactive material billowed from the decommissioned nuclear power station. Uranium, plutonium, strontium, caesium caused shortness of breath, inflammation around the mouth, hair and fur loss, haemorrhages and other symptoms of radiation sickness, maiming or killing anything downwind of the plant. Chernobyl-like accidents continued to happen despite the half-hearted attempts to shut the power plants down in the last days of mankind's reign. As usual, lack of care, understanding, time and money prevented the job being done properly. Any area close to a nuclear power station was at risk.

The earthquake shifted the vault holding back the buried vitrified radioactive waste exposing it to underground springs which carried the slowly decaying atoms away, warming rocks in its path to the surface to destroy life at some future far off date.

In Norleigh, a peregrine flew across the crumbling skyline to its nest in a tower block filled with trees. Thousands of pigeons and black-headed gulls were its neighbours ... and lunch. As roofs collapsed, rosebay willow herb, buddleia, elder and ash grew in living rooms, in gutters, in cracks in stonework. Leaves, soil, dust and dirt blew in through windows smashed by vandals, storms, bird-strikes or wear and tear. Bears and wolves lived in kitchens, bathrooms, bedrooms.

In the ruins of coastal cities, crabs scuttled amongst the debris left by submerging tsunami, storm surges and flattening flooding. Earthquakes and fires demolished eroding apartments and hotel tower blocks. Seaweed wafted as waves rolled over battered breeze blocks and rusting reinforced concrete. Lobsters floated amongst ruined piers, weather-beaten harbours and derelict boats. Marram grass and red fescue grew out of broken buildings buried with sand.

The graveyards choked with burials, their headstones vanishing beneath layers of mosses, lichens and ivy, were quartered by a pair tawny owls calling their familiar duet, and the ghosts of barn owls in search of rats, mice and voles proliferating unhindered by pesticides and checked only by taloned predators.

Bees droned over plants taking over shattered greenhouses pummelled by wind and hail in weed-filled gardens, dandelions and thistles, ground elder and bindweed, brambles and nettles ruled. Thirsty tomatoes and lettuce disappeared as polytunnels contracted and cracked. Paints and dyes pealed, bleached in the sun, the wood and metal beneath exposed to rot and corrosion. Mice built nests amongst the framework, harvesting seeds and fruits peacefully.

European summers turned pink along railways, rivers and waterways lined with unchecked Himalayan balsam. Soiled water no longer reached rivers or the sea from cracked and clogged sewage pipes and storm drains. Water spilled where it would, covering roads and pavements, winter frosts shattering levelled surfaces. Roots of dandelion and thistle disrupted tarmac and concrete alike. Edges blurred with grass and daisies, straight lines merged with verges, voles scurried unhindered across motorway carriageways, only to be picked off by kestrels.

A pack of five wolves plunged into the swollen river below as they fell from the Severn Bridge as it collapsed. Suspension bridges, engineered to allow metal to expand and contract with the seasons failed catastrophically once the necessary high maintenance was gone and the joints rusted, the paint cracked and pealed and rain got in. As the Forth, the Humber and many more bridges went the same way, swimming across or walking around were the only options for getting across wide rivers and estuaries.

Bats hung from the bare rafters of Canterbury Cathedral. Swallows nested high in the walls of Carnarvon Castle. Blenheim Palace, even the rooms once closed to the public, was home to foxes, wild cats, and long-eared owls. Spring Farm house – last home of Mia, Nerys, Ross and the others – survived, providing shelter to sparrows, starlings and rats, much as ancient monuments from earlier civilisations had done thousands of years before; the Aztec temples, the Egyptians pyramids, the Greek Acropolis, the Chinese Great Wall, becoming gradually swamped and buried in time. Ancient dry stone walls continued to divide the landscape, covered in moss, lichen, bracken and ivy, until the stone flaked and crumbled, and the holes knocked through by animals turned them into rows of gap-toothed smiles across the countryside.

By the reservoir, the only warning the small herd of fallow deer got before the dam burst was the low frequency rumble just audible to their sensitive hearing. They bolted away from the lush grass growing by the side of the trickling stream issuing from the bottom of the wall of concrete and steel. Clambering up the steep valley sides in alarm, they were the only witnesses as the dam finally burst. Unable to withstand the pressure of the silt which had built up for decades, millions of tons of rushing riotous water forced the debris of its imprisoning walls crashing along the valley bottom, sweeping away any trace of human habitation and returning the river to its natural course once more.

The blue flame of the methane burning from the landfill site was fanned by stiffening winds on the hot summer's day as it leaked, sending foul smoke across the valleys and woods surrounding it. Foxes and herring gulls no longer haunted these sites as even they could no longer find sustenance from the rancid, rotted and decayed matter. Nothing drank from the contaminated pools of water collecting at the bottom of the artificial mounds. Lining materials, chiefly high density polyethylene stretched beyond their tensile strength proved unresisting to punctures from stones beneath or broken glass within the refuse dumped on top of them.

Years before the end of humankind, whole tyres had been stopped from entering landfill sites because they were seventy five per cent void space which trapped methane gas, causing them to become buoyant and bubble to the surface. Bubbling tyres damaged landfill liners installed to help keep contaminants from polluting local surface and groundwater. Shredding tyres on site was a cost-effective solution, providing a lightweight backfill in gas venting systems, leachate collection systems, and operational liners. It got rid of the tyres and meant other construction materials were not needed to cap, close, or daily cover landfill sites.

However, with maintenance crews gone, the plastic or rubber coverings was long since dried and cracked by the sun, blown away by the wind or disturbed by rats, foxes and other scavengers drawn by the smell of decay. Rubbish floated around the planet only breaking down gradually, littering everywhere as if people had never left.

A buzzard soared over an immense man-made quarry, looking amongst the abandoned rusting monster machines for signs of life as rabbits chewed on straggling bits of grass and weeds. Weasels and stoats leapt about with their usual carnivorous enthusiasm in search of mice and voles hiding around the discarded boulders and tyres. The frost shattered floor captured soil and dust allowing moss and lichens to build up enough soil for shrubs and trees to take hold. Rain fell and collected to fill ponds and pools created by the diggers and dynamite for tadpoles to swim, their parents having crawled into the undergrowth of rush, veronica and St John's Wort growing around the edges. Trousered rooks called rawkishly to each other from their twiggy nests in sections of ash and sycamore woodland which had once covered the whole area before excavation began. Lifting off, they flew away to find open ground to search for insects, grubs and leatherjackets, their favourite food.

Wildlife gradually recolonised the best of these brownfield sites naturally, slowly developing grassland, heathland, wetland, scrub and woodland. Particularly important for butterflies and moths though, were areas of sparse vegetation. Caterpillars found attractive violets, meadowsweet, cranesbill and raspberry as food plants, whereas adults looked for nectar sources in notifiable weeds; thistles, docks, nettles, ragwort. As no one was around to pull them up, more food was available. Bare patches with shelter provided the right conditions for warmth-loving species like slow-worms and lizards.

Butterflies benefitted by the haphazard approach to hedge and verge trimming of browsing deer, cattle, antelope and elephants. Sunny patches of nettles left egg laying sites for tortoiseshell. Rides created in woodland by buffeting elephants, nibbling deer and winter gales left warm basking sites for brimstone and holly blue. Crazy grazing left a mixture of lengths of grass suitable for brown argus and marbled white, and beetle banks in amongst the fallen trees where the former gardener's friends, the ground beetles, hoverflies and ladybirds sucked and chewed their way through aphids just as they had done in gardens.

Wolves, bears and bats were always attracted to caves, but stumbling across abandoned mines full of tunnels could prove fatal. Ancient roof supports collapsed at a breath; wet and weakened ceilings caved in. The entrance to an old mine, always dangerous, may have weathered earth and rock surrounding it, land ready to slide at the slightest vibration, sealing the way in and out. With over half a million abandoned mines in the United States alone, anything wandering in to explore found out how dangerous they could be. Deadly gases or simply the lack of oxygen in the air could asphyxiate. Seepages of standing infiltrating water hid deep pits or trapped gases below the surface making drowning ever more likely.

The mass of loose shale and rocky scree slid under its feet as the curious bear cub slithered down the side of a giant artificial mountain. It scrabbled back to its anxiously calling mother, away from the mine tailings. With ninety nine per cent waste for one per cent of ore, these edifices were left where forests full of nuts and berries should have been. Toxic slurry accumulated in ponds dammed in valleys. One or two failed each year, spewing million of tons of waste into local rivers and water courses. Trout, perch, roach, frogs, newts, dragonfly nymphs, crayfish, to say nothing of the plants of water-milfoil, alder and willow trees along the bank perished as the landscape turned vivid oranges and livid greens by heavy metals, and contaminants such as lead, iron, copper, mercury and arsenic, killed everything downstream.

Daisies, clover and grasses would one day reclaim the polluted riverbanks which had become deserts until sufficient rain washed the poisons away and floodwaters rose high enough to dilute the nastiest. Acid and acrid soils eventually became covered with enough dust, windblown soil and leaf debris to bury them, allowing pioneering grasses and heathers to spread and colonise once more, adapting to the chemical and physical conditions they found.

Beside the abandoned chemical plant, a red deer stag, his antlers proclaiming him to be a healthy male of ten rutting seasons kept a watchful eye over his harem of seven hinds and ruminated quietly, having spent the night grazing on grass and lichens on the waste tips. He nibbled the grass, unaware of the periodic leaks of the contents of bunded reservoirs and settling tanks, spilling uranium, arsenic, alumina, lead, benzene and pesticides into his local river and plenty of others around the world. Eventually the seemingly innocuous spillages stopped; slurry, milk whey, or orange juice into the waters of the Rhine or Danube, altering the chemistry, acidity and visibility for anything happening to live in or depend on them for a drink. One day riverine life would thrive again.

Feral and wild goats clambered around Spanish and Portuguese hillsides having learned to avoid the mined valley floors left by human combatants in the final war raging across Europe before the end came. Decades before, less fortunate sheep unwittingly cleared many of the hidden deathtraps. Barbed and razor wire continued to ensnare and bring an early demise to many millions of creatures, great and small, providing meals for vultures, crows, foxes, jackals and other scavengers. Years after all war had ceased the death toll of innocents hadn't diminished.

The black-footed albatross disgorged another crop full of food for its chick suspended high above the crashing waves on a thin ledge. The chick wasn't growing properly despite the ample amounts of fish its parents brought it. In amongst the wholesome proteins and oils were the worst legacy bequeathed by man and it would never go away but remain lethal and persistent; only reducing in size. Plastic tossed overboard, dumped in landfill sites then blown or washed out to sea, circled the globe, rubbing to and fro, gradually reducing to miniature fragments, washed up on beaches as tiny coloured particles mixed with the sand.

Huge rotating whirlpools – gyres - collected plastic debris in the North Pacific Ocean attracting pollutants such as PCB's, DDT, insecticides and other toxins to them and poisoning the ocean and anything trying to live in it. Nurdles, tiny disc-like feed-stock for the plastics industry lost overboard through spillages, formed a large part of the problem.

On shore, tube worms, mussels and cockles lived amongst this debris, ingesting it. Parent gulls fished bits out of the oceans thinking as it floated it must be food, feeding it unwittingly to their helpless chicks and eating it themselves until they all starved to death with their bellies filled with indigestible rubbish. Turtles became enmeshed in six pack carriers or invisible netting. Left in the water, man's last plastic coated gift to nature became food for larvae, plankton, fishes, jellyfish, birds and mammals, contaminating the marine food chain for eons, causing suffering, starvation and death.

Along the mighty Amazon River, monkeys called and swung through rainforest of teak, mahogany and rosewood reclaimed from the coffee, tea and cocoa plantations no one was around to drink anymore. Ironically, just before the end, people began to realise the benefits of rainforests not only as sources of raw materials such as wood and medicines, but for the fundamental ecosystem services provided – supplying oxygen and removing carbon dioxide. After various attempts at re-forestation and a-forestation, it was discovered the best place to grow lots of trees quickly was in the tropics – where all the rainforests had been growing before they were destroyed.

Trees laced with lianas, orchids, birds of paradise, parrots and monkeys replaced sugar cane, once the largest tonnage of any crop grown, but no longer needed to satisfy man's sweet tooth or cravings for rum and bio-fuel.

Evolution rebalanced once the interfering people were removed from the equation. Trees and shrubs spread their seeds downstream from refuge nature reserves and parks, carried by rivers and flood-waters covering planes previously cleared for cattle, timber, palm oil and other fast cash crops, reverting to forests once more. Cockroach and crickets scurried under the leaf litter. Tapir, peccaries and agoutis fed on nuts and fruits. Vultures and opossums scavenged on the dead. Leaf cutter ants and termites lived on the trees and anteaters lived on them. The flooded rainforest spread once more, removing foresters' roads and swathes cut by chainsaws, expanding territory for caiman, egrets and cormorants fishing amongst the giant water-lilies with parakeets squawking overhead. Families of giant otters caught piranha amongst the shimmer of brightly coloured aquarium fish.

Coconut and date palms covered islands as sterile bananas died off. Bighorn sheep, pronghorn antelope and chipmunk returned to the desert along with the Joshua trees, barrel cactus and desert lily as California's irrigated orange groves succumbed to drought and the lack of a human to care.

Eucalyptus was one introduction which got out of hand being dangerous to rival trees by releasing a chemical into the soil which killed native competitors. Essential oils in its leaves contain compounds that are powerful natural disinfectants, toxic in large quantities, while its flowers produce nectar, providing food for many insects, birds and bats. Its wood once made fine pulp for high quality paper and many natural dyes as well as disinfectants and cough sweets.

In seasonally dry climates oaks were often fire-resistant, particularly in open grasslands where a fire would be unable to ignite scattered trees. But because of its highly flammable, explosive oil, which when warmed, forms a vapour rising above the trees in a blue haze, fires in eucalyptus forests travelled easily across the tree crowns and the flammable bark and fallen branches. The trees were well adapted to periodic fires and obtained long-term fire survivability from adapted buds, tubers and fruits.

Eucalyptus drew vast amounts of water from the soil and were planted to lower the water table, reduce soil salination and, by draining swamp habitats they helped prevent malaria by reducing mosquito larvae, but destroyed ecologically productive areas at the same time. In South Africa they were considered invasive as their water-sucking capabilities threatened water supplies.

In the similar climatic conditions to their native Australia in Portugal, Spain and California, pulpwood eucalyptus plantations often replaced oak woodlands resulting in monocultures and a loss of diversity. With no oaks there were no acorns for animals and birds to feed on, no hollows for birds to nest in or small mammals to shelter in or bee colonies to live in. In plantations no deadwood was left for fungi or insects to live on. Several species became invasive reducing local ecosystems by removing wildlife corridors. Much of Madagascar's original native forest was replaced with eucalyptus, threatening biodiversity by isolating remaining areas into parks and reserves.

British gardens became filled with invading plants like periwinkle along with other spreading plants; lily of the valley, celandine, common bugle, golden rod. Dandelions and other mass seed producing plants joined them; willow herb, thistles, teasels or aliens like rhododendron, killing rivals by shading them out, and Japanese knotweed, Virginia creeper, Russian vine which had no natural native enemies. Plantains, nettles, ground elder, cleavers, forget-me-nots, ash and brambles broke through and covered every artificial surface used to pave driveways, patios and yards.

The cultivated desirable forms of tender orchids, bougainvillea and others raided from places with warmer climates, were left to fend for themselves in crumbled greenhouses and decayed conservatories perishing in frosty winters and hot dry summers. Sterile hybrids of trillium, ornamental lily, banana and watermelon died off without people to propagate them.

Grasses, nettles, thistles and brambles quickly choked wheat and crop fields. With a third of the planet previously taken up with growing food for people, once they were all gone, things could meld back to a life before agriculture developed. No chemical sprays protected them; no fertilizers fed them so the selectively bred and modified crops only survived a couple of years at best. As some crops could not regenerate from their own fallen seeds - thanks to greedy seed producers - after grasses gobbled up the fertilizer, leaving soils leaner and hungrier, dormant seeds from poppies, daisies, cornflower and other meadow plants, germinated and thrived turning the countryside red, white and blue once more.

Hawthorn and blackthorn scrub encroached from field edges creating thickets. Elder and birch grew in amongst them until finally oak balanced the soil and allowed beech trees and others to grow.

The ringing sounds of reed warblers, calling corncrakes, booming bitterns and crying harriers, buzzards and osprey hung around misted marshland. Willow scrub and alder carr developed quickly once pumping and draining ceased. Irrigation systems became swamped, sluices broke and ditches blocked, as fields flooded, water-logging lowlands enough for water weed and reeds to grow leading, over the next few hundred years to woodland creating a green and brown patchwork landscape once more.

Owls, swallows and martins took over decayed factory farm buildings which had fallen into ruin in many Western nations as they became impractical to manage after the over-bred caged pig and chicken breeds died off. Stinking chicken sheds rotted where birds once pecked each other to death and confining pig cages which not only deprived young animals of their mothers but also the ability to move around were abandoned and left derelict for the more active birds to make better homes in and raise young to a life of freedom.

Watercourses poisoned by algal blooms caused by the excess of phosphates and nitrate fertilizers for many years, reduced quickly as the nutrients were flushed away and dissipated. Having deprived everything else of oxygen throughout the summer, only to exacerbate the problem through their death and subsequent decay using even more oxygen, the former eutrophic waters of lakes, rivers and estuaries became clearer slate blue again instead of cloudy green or red.

Rabbits nibbled, keeping close cropped heathland grass in check, with the help of feral sheep and horses. Only sandy or chalky sites remained where thin poor nutrient soils were unable to sustain anything other than grasses or herbs and small shrubs like gorse and broom. Even if they managed to get a roothold, no tall trees could grow without being blown down quickly in gales.

Wallaby, chimpanzee, lynx, hippopotamus, meerkat, giraffe, Siberian tiger. Captives from wildlife parks and zoos were disgorged onto unsuspecting and unprepared native species. As a translocation or re-introduction programme it would have been interesting to observe the results. Native northern hemisphere species thrived; boars, bears, beavers and bison spread out filling nooks in the naturalising landscape with leopards, cheetahs, crocodiles and wolves feeding off any surviving domesticated animals. These, having been bred to be fat, large, docile and slow, didn't last long.

Packs of jackals and hyenas competed with prides of lions for the large herds of deer roaming the European countryside as it became marsh or forest once again. Zebras, various gazelles and antelopes were also on the menu, but they found cold northern winters harsh and deadly with little grass growing. As prey numbers were checked, so predator populations reduced. New migration patterns developed.

Herds of elephants used their long remembered tree felling skills to keep some grassland open by clearing young trees to get at the succulent leaves on top. These meadow areas were kept open for a while with herds of wildebeest, but regenerated to woodland slowly with native species of birch, ash, beech and oak.

A hedgehog blundered across a narrow country lane, short-sightedly sniffing his way to his supper. He, and the rabbits, blackbirds, badgers and other former victims of road-kill survived. The relentless, destructive process stopped before the last human died allowing small birds and mammals to live in safety from the unremitting onslaught. Barrier fences rotted and hedgerows went wild and flourished, becoming wooded.

The small roach, quietly searching out mosquito larvae for his lunch and in no danger of being hooked by an enthusiastic angler, didn't spot the small pack of perch coming at it from out of the shadowy depths. The aqueous drama was one of many played out in rivers, streams, lakes and lochs all around the world except for the different cast. For although pesticides and herbicides lingered long after the people who valued them had vanished, their deleterious effect on fish numbers reduced leaving waters cleaner and clearer. More mosquito and other insect larvae survived providing food for the chain from roach to perch to pike to heron.

Packs of mongrel dogs - crosses of Jack Russells and Alsatians, greyhounds and retrievers - scavenged and fed, competing with old and new wild animals, who introduced unfamiliar diseases as they spread. Pet cats - moggies not highly bred pedigrees - having never really lost their wildness and ability to survive, fared better, even those who had been pampered and cared for by well-trained owners soon put their survival skills to good use. Taken everywhere to eradicate the rats and mice which always hitched lifts, they killed everything else they could too, this time for food, not simply for fun.

A hen-sized dull blue heron-like bird, the kagu, had its nest raided on New Caledonia in the western Pacific by rats carried there unwittingly by a film crew interested in indigenous island species. After its mate died, it was left alone to forage for insects and small prey, never performing a courtship display revealing its barred wings, and never again threatening a rival. The last flightless cormorant died on the Galapagos Islands after an accident at sea left it injured. Its family had gradually dwindled as nests were destroyed by pigs and eggs eaten by rats, hedgehogs and other birds. Without human intervention to remove small mammal predators like rats, mice and mongoose which should never have been there, island species of flightless and ground nesting birds vanished quickly. Their niches were filled eventually by other birds blown in on storms, just as their ancestors had been, but these retained the ability to fly and nest in trees, if they were available, or cliffs if not.

New Zealand's native plants, devastated by possums and rabbits as well as deer and goats, fared little better than native flightless birds which fell prey to the introduced mammals; cats, dogs, ferrets, stoats and weasels, with hedgehogs and rats eating eggs and pigs squashing nests. Being adaptable and usually having a varied omnivorous diet, they continued to thrive where they had no enemies and plenty of food. Without generations of people to keep these enemies in check with expensive and lengthy eradication programmes, only a few individuals of the precious endemic species survived. In a few million years, these introduced species would evolve through isolation into species native to New Zealand and would be as unique as the ones they had displaced.

Blackcaps, Cetti's warblers, garden warblers, robins, blackbirds, skylarks, and song thrushes, the much appreciated British songbirds whether migrants or residents increased in numbers as habitats were reclaimed from farmland or housing estates, even allowing for those lost to cats and sparrowhawks. Trees, shrubs and scrub flourished, providing nest sites, shelter from the elements and protection from predators as well as food. With no people shooting them for fun on migration routes, or netting them for food at over wintering sites, nightingales, turtle doves, swallows, and many species of waterfowl like garganey and pintail, benefitted from the absence of humans in a big way.

The large elegant mute swan, accidently brushed the tips of his two metre wing-span against the strands of the steel reinforced aluminium power line, but unlike many hundreds of his predecessors, all he got was grazed feathers. With no current being carried his touching them didn't complete the circuit and he didn't get electrocuted. Even flying into the lines became less likely as many lines corroded away from their towering pylons of artificial trees, falling to the ground to be rapidly buried by brambles and ivy.

The River Thames, swelled by seasonal flooding, regained its natural course, bursting through constraining canalised banks, bunds and levees. Houses built on the beautiful fertile flood plane were undermined and collapsed, with carpets and furniture decomposing under layers of muddy, slimy mould.

The Colorado River reached the Gulf of California once more, with the delta flooding to the marshland it had been in the 1930's. Once the twenty reservoir-creating dams along its course were gone, it began to erode the Grand Canyon ever deeper again. Its waters were no longer channelled to produce unneeded power, nor for irrigating unwanted crops, watering non-existent cattle or oranges. Again it provided a home for trout and a drink for buffalo, coyote, and prairie dog.

Canal banks crumbled flooding roadways and fields around them as they burst through lack of maintenance and undermining by moles and voles. Beaver dams spanned forest streams creating natural wetlands behind, leading to the familiar succession of brambles, hawthorn, holly, hazel, and finally oak, elm and beech.

The baleen whales - blue, right, and sperm - much persecuted by hunters, increased in numbers as oceans pulsated to the sound of whale song. No over-exploitative fishing meant more food for their cousins, the toothed whales - dolphin, orca and porpoise - as well as sea-lions, elephant, fur and grey seals, and sea birds like terns, guillemots, kittiwake and puffins, and other bigger fish - marlin, tuna and the sharks. Fish could die of old age, if they hadn't been eaten by a predator before hand.

More baby fish and young plants made more plankton to absorb more carbon dioxide from the atmosphere, helping to stabilise it. No dolphins were caught as by-catch. No albatross drowned having been snared by thoughtless long-line fishing. No salmon farms polluted coastal waters with fish faeces, antibiotics or hormones. No submarines disrupted whale song. No turtles' eggs were dug up by islanders to sell them to the Japanese.

Wrinkled brains, cabbages, table tops, antlers, wire strands and pillars. Coral reefs, among the richest and most diverse ecosystems, flourished surrounded by nutrient-poor tropical ocean waters. Growing best in warm, shallow, clear, sunny and agitated waters, these conditions were under threat for decades from climate change, leading to sea temperature rise, sea level rise and ocean acidification. Other threats existed, be they overfishing from blast fishing and cyanide fishing for aquariums, disease, coral mining, digging of canals and access into islands and bays, harmful land-use practices including urban and agricultural runoff and water pollution which encouraged excess algae growth. Once humans had gone these threats diminished and finally disappeared.

Coral reefs support over a quarter of all marine species while they cover less than one tenth of one percent of the surface of the world's oceans. They often depend on surrounding habitats, such as seagrass meadows and mangrove forests, for nutrients supplying dead plants and animals rich in nitrogen and in turn provided grazing areas for fish and animals from the reef. Reefs protected the shoreline by absorbing wave energy and produced sediment for the mangroves and seagrass to root in. Many small islands would not exist without them.

A form of limestone, corals were able to take advantage of some of mankind's waste and grew on many substrate materials like dumped vehicle tyres, scuttled ships, and concrete piers. They also grew unaided on abandoned oil rigs and other marine structures.

As time passed, the atmosphere gradually lost much of its excess carbon dioxide as more trees grew and more plankton was able to absorb it from seawater which gradually cooled. Polar bears and seals were saved just in time as the Northern Polar icecaps refroze.

Hurricanes, born in tropical waters of 27°C or more, still curved their way across the Atlantic and west Pacific, shifting heat north, but less frequently and with less ferocity. Tornados, those supercell thunderstorms of rapidly spiralling air, dust and debris much appreciated by chasers but feared by house owners, still devastated the former south eastern United States, passing unwitnessed except by animals sensible enough to get out of their path. El Nino stopped being so fierce in its weather reversal, flooding deserts and halting monsoons.

Volcanoes still blew sulphur and carbon dioxide into the atmosphere and oozed lava as earthquakes moved the mobile plates around the planet's surface, and meteorites large and small still hit the Earth's surface. The time of humans would eventually only be a thin black line in the rock strata, one of many telling of a particular period of time when a form of life came to dominate and suppress all others, much as extinct dinosaurs had once done millions of years before.

But, in one of the remoter parts of the African Rift Valley on the flat rock overlooking the dry dusty orange plane, the naked man rested on his haunches, his throwing stick held against his shoulder. He waited. He had waited since dawn and the sun rose high in the sky, burning down on his dark brown skin. His black eyes pealed the valley below watching for the antelope he knew must come to the shrinking waterhole.

His patience was rewarded. A family group of gazelles approached the waterhole warily, on the lookout for lions or even cheetahs. Big cats were more common in recent years, since the others had all gone.

With a barely noticeable hand gesture, the man signalled to his friends hidden in the long dried grass below. They crawled forwards as low as possible towards their quarry. Timing was everything as to strike too early would make the gazelles scatter and soon be out of range, whereas if they got too close, they might get kicked.

The three short, firmly built people each with long wiry black hair, crept forwards again until with hardly a movement, the man on the rock told them which animal he had singled out; a young buck with a dark strip down his back. The three closed in and at another signal, all stood and threw their sticks at the animal. Hit on his flank, neck and back, he collapsed from the shock. His family scattered, leaping high and kicking out in their flight as the people ran towards him, finishing him off with a skull shattering blow to the back of his head.

These four, part of an extended family group, were the only survivors from the human catastrophe. Isolated, shy, withdrawn, they had avoided contact with other human races. Their DNA was pure. They hadn't distilled their blood with chemical medicines, unhealthy foods, or inaction. They moved softly through the country, unnoticed, undisturbed, following the herds of animals in search of grass and water.

Joining in the struggle for life on Earth, they never felt apart or superior. Dealing with respect and appreciation for the creatures they lived along side and relied upon, living as one with the wind in the trees, the water running in the stream, coloured by the sun in the sky.

In peace.

###

About the author

Jenni was born at Port Stanley in the Falkland Islands but lived most of her life in Lincolnshire, working as a bank clerk, an administrator for a nursing home and after an extended visit to New Zealand, works for the RSPB at Leighton Moss nature reserve in Lancashire. She gained a BSc Honours degree in Natural Science through the Open University and while in New Zealand, earned a Post Graduate Diploma in Resource Studies at Lincoln University near Christchurch.

She took up creative writing in September 2008; sure she had a novel in her. With the help of an excellent tutor, Collette Lawlor and support from the marvellous group of fellow beginners, who have formed the writing group, the Jelly Friskers, *The Streets Fall Silent* is her fourth novel, and the first with an environmental basis.

Three novels in the Matt Stevens series; *The Sails Turn, Trust in Matt* and *Matt's Inspirations* are available on Amazon Kindle.

Lightning Source UK Ltd.
Milton Keynes UK
UKOW040019021012

199918UK00002B/111/P

9 781781 764954